STACY McANULTY

MY *Life* ACCORDING TO BARBIE

A NOVEL

My Life
According
To Barbie

Stacy McAnulty

ISBN-13: 978-1460954270
ISBN-10: 1460954270

LCCN:

Cover Design by Kate Wojogbe

To Brett

Blonde is more than a hair color, it's a way of life.

Chapter 1

My fifteen-year old daughter solicits patrons outside Crosstown Mall as I video record from our car. Homework has changed dramatically in the nineteen years since I was a sophomore. We used encyclopedias and the microfiche to do research. We didn't do sociology experiments around town.

Through a hidden mike, I hear her talking to a fiftyish man.

"Excuse me," Erika says. "Can I borrow your cell phone? I need to call my mom for a ride home." She's dressed in an oversized Jets jersey, baggy jeans, and a dark knit cap that's more appropriate for an Albany winter than a seventy degree, September day.

"Sorry. I don't have a phone." The man doesn't stop walking.

The experiment is simple. First, Erika dressed as a preppy teen—khaki skirt, a lavender sweater, hair held back neatly with barrettes—and asked twenty people if she could borrow a phone. Nineteen people handed them over willingly. The only no came from a woman who forgot to charge her battery. Then Erika changed into her urban attire and started asking the question to another twenty individuals. People have been less willing to depart with their phones.

After the final person is accosted, Erika joins me in the car.

"That was amazing." She takes the video recorder from me. "Mr. Barber is going to love this. He was so right about people." I'm old-school, preferring hard sciences like physics, biology, and chemistry. My experiments need test tubes, eye protection, dead fetal pigs.

I start the Passat. It's already after seven, we haven't had dinner, and Erika has other homework to do. She doesn't have a set bedtime, but I'd like lights out by eleven. Tomorrow is interval training for soccer and she needs to be in the school weight room by 6:30 a.m.

"Based on my clothes," Erika says, "people made immediate conclusions about me."

"This is shocking to you?" I try not to think what conclusions people would make about me. Paige O'Neal-Russell, a thirty-four-year old woman dressed in faded men's jeans and a plaid camp shirt. Brown hair in need of highlights and held back in a ponytail. I did apply makeup this morning but it has since faded.

"Mr. Barber showed us results of a similar experiment done in 1989 by college students. They asked for money instead of a phone, but they had the same kind of numbers." She gets her own phone out and thumbs a text.

"Who are you texting?"

"Mr. Barber. I have to tell him the results. We made a bet."

"A bet?"

"Yeah, a bet. I said people were different today than in the eighties. More open and accepting."

"What did you bet?"

"A cup of coffee."

"I don't like you drinking coffee. I especially don't like you having coffee with your teacher." I've made it a point to meet most of Erika's teachers at St. Mary's, but Mr. Barber is new.

I pull the car in front of Wanna Wrap and hand Erika a twenty.

"I'll take tuna on a whole grain pita."

"You're not going in?" Erika looks around. "Oh."

A pack of little, furry monsters—some may call them squirrels—are enjoying their dinner on the sidewalk. Two women on a bench throw them bits of their tortilla wraps.

There are three things in life I absolutely avoid.

One, animals—any nonhuman, breathing entity scares me. From tigers to goldfish, I have panic attacks if not separated from them by glass.

Two, avocados. I get a rash just touching the skins.

Three, dancing in public.

Erika returns to the car with our dinner. I'm starved. I've only eaten half a bag of pretzels and a Mounds bar all day. I remove the foil from my pita and dig in. Obviously, a picnic is out of the question.

"Mom, I need to talk to you about something," Erika says, her wrap remains unopened in the bag.

I swallow hard. "You're not pregnant are you?" I try to joke, but I was nineteen when I had Erika. Maybe it runs the family.

"No. I'm not going out for basketball this season."

"What? Why?"

"I'm trying out for cheerleading instead."

"No. You've been playing basketball since you were six. You were on varsity as a freshman. Don't be ridiculous." I take another bite giving her a chance to respond with a useless rebuttal.

"I was on varsity last year because our team sucked. We didn't win a game."

"It was a rebuilding year."

"And I've quit the choir." She glances over at me, probably waiting for an explosive reaction. I've been working with a priest-slash-therapist for months on curbing my explosive reactions. You stab your husband with a paring knife when he says he's leaving you and suddenly everyone thinks you're unstable.

"You can't quit. You're an O'Neal. We don't quit. I've never quit anything."

"You've also never had to work."

"I work. I may not get a paycheck, but I work." Her comment feels like a slap in the face. I've devoted much of my life to her. Volunteering at the school. Raising money for that winless basketball team. Making certain she has every opportunity to succeed. Who proofreads her essays? Who corrects her precalc homework? Who has installed spyware on her PC? Me. Being Erika's mother is a full-time job.

"Well…Uncle Ryan quits things all the time. College.

Jobs."

"I doubt he's really an O'Neal."

"He's your twin brother."

"Erika, what's going on? Am I putting too much pressure on you? I can make an appointment with Father Nolan for us. Maybe some family counseling?"

I've been waiting for Erika to crash. I've read about it in magazines and seen it on *Dr. Phil.* She's a straight-A student, plays varsity level soccer and basketball. She'll be making her confirmation at St. Mary's church in the spring. She's in their youth choir. She's the treasurer of the student government and a member of S.A.D.D, the yearbook committee, and Key Club. The only qualification her resume lacks is community service. She did organize a team for the heart walk last year, but she really needs something on a regular basis.

"You're not pressuring me any more than Mrs. Holmgren pressures Nicole. I just want to try something different."

"Like cheerleading?"

"Yes, cheerleading."

"Please tell me why you want to cheer for the boys' basketball team when you could be playing basketball yourself? Let the boys cheer for you." Not to mention the outfits are outrageously small, tight, and provocative.

"Because it's what Barbie would do," Erika replies, as if her answer makes complete sense.

"Barbie who?" I thought I knew all of Erika's friends.

"Barbie, Barbie. You know the doll. She's about this tall." Erika holds her hands up for emphasis.

"I never let you have a Barbie doll."

"I know. See...we've been studying role models in Social Science Class. Most of the class thinks Barbie is a horrible role model for girls. I think they're wrong. Mr. Barber has challenged me to prove it."

"Is this another coffee bet?" In the back of my mind I'm penciling in a parent-teacher conference.

"No. Better. I can do this experiment instead of taking the final exam."

"What experiment?"

"For the next twelve weeks I'm going to live my life according to Barbie."

"How is that an experiment? Where is the control group? What is the measurable data?" Whatever happened to adding vinegar to baking soda? Now, *that* was an experiment.

"Okay, you got me. It's more of a social commentary. Like when a supermodel puts on a fat suit and discovers what it's like to not be pretty. Or when a guy dresses like a woman or a white man pretends to be black."

"You're not going to jeopardize your high school resume to live like an anorexic bimbo. You've worked too—"

"She's not a bimbo and she's not anorexic."

"Watever. The answer is no."

"I never asked a question."

I shove my pita wrap into a drink holder and put the car in reverse. Anger has replaced my hunger. Erika and I do not fight often. When we do it is epic. She's as stubborn as... well, me. We both know she's going to go through with this experiment unless I find a bargaining chip, even if it means she has to walk five miles to cheerleading practice.

We don't speak for the remainder of the evening. I'm left watching reality television alone with a bottle of Shiraz for company. A heavy-chested blonde wearing too much lipstick and not enough bikini sits in a hot tub with three guys. She tells them she only does two things really well, and one thing is shopping. Then she challenges the guy to the right to discover the other talent for himself.

I bet she grew up surrounded by Barbie dolls.

The next morning, I find Erika eating a bowl of corn flakes at the counter. Her dirty-blonde curls are pulled into a ponytail. She's wearing workout clothes—a white cool-weave T-shirt and a pair of navy shorts with *score* written across the butt. I hate those shorts.

"Did you get all your homework done?" I ask and start the coffee maker.

She grunts an affirmative. Even when we are getting along, Erika is a girl of few words in the morning.

"Do you need me to check anything?"

"No, Mom." She drops her bowl into the sink. It takes all my restraint not to nag her about her attitude.

"Listen," I lean on the counter next to her. "I'd really like you to meet me at Father Nolan's office today."

"Mom..."

"I want to talk some more about you quitting basketball and choir and this Barbie nonsense. I think we'd do better with a mediator. Don't you?" I'd stayed up half the night trying to make a convincing argument against the great Barbie experiment. "Because I said so" was the best I had come up with.

"When?"

"How about eleven-thirty?" I already have a standing Thursday appointment.

"Fine. That's the middle of precalculus." Not her favorite class.

I scribble a note for Erika's teacher excusing her for our appointment. "Here." I hand it over. "And try not to become anorexic between now and eleven-thirty."

It's not about having stuff,
it's about accessorizing your life.

Chapter 2

Thursday. 11 a.m.

I'm in the same place I've been on Thursdays at 11 a.m. since Max left me five months ago.

"Good morning, Paige," Father Nolan's secretary says. "How are you?"

"Tired. I stayed up all night eating dark chocolate and doing Sudoku puzzles." That's a bit of a lie. I wasn't eating dark chocolate, I was drinking chocolate liquor and the only puzzle I worked on was figuring out Erika's strange behavior.

"Have a seat." The secretary gives me a closed-lip smile. She knows my past, so maybe she doesn't want to do anything to set me off. Though I've been incident-free for months.

The three mismatched wooden chairs in the waiting area make the pews in the church look like first-class seating. The only reading material on the coffee table is a church newsletter from last March and a hymnal.

"Is he running late?" I take a seat.

Before she can answer, a man rushes in. He goes right for Father Nolan's door. The secretary leaps up and steps in his way. Who knew the little woman could move so fast.

"Hey, Betty. Is Father Nolan in?"

"He's busy and Mrs. Russell has the next appointment. Perhaps you should try making an appointment, Isaac." I don't correct her mistake. It's *Mrs. O'Neal-Russell*.

"Come on. This isn't a dentist office," the man says.

Betty stands firm.

The man retreats and takes a seat next to me. From his attire—faded jeans, wrinkled T-shirt—I wouldn't have expected him to smell so good. What is that? A combination of Irish Spring and peppermint. I keep my eyes averted trying to mind my own business, but I can still gauge his age. Mid-thirties. He's fit with a tangle of blond hair that needs to be trimmed.

"Excuse me," he says to me. "I realize you have an appointment, which is vitally important around here." He glares at the secretary. "But could I jump in line and speak with Father Nolan for a few minutes?"

I look up and meet his blue eyes. "How many minutes?"

"Five, ten. Forty-five tops. Just kidding." He smiles. It's been awhile, but I'm fairly certain he's flirting with me. "No more than ten minutes." He crosses his heart with his index finger.

The secretary snorts and returns to her desk.

"It's very important," he says.

So is my business. "What's so urgent you practically

ran over little Betty?"

"Doubts. I'm entering seminary in a few weeks and I'm starting to have second thoughts. I need to pray with Father before I lose my way."

"You're going to be a priest?" I hate to make a snap judgment, but I'd never pick him as a man of the cloth. Maybe it's the eagle tattoo on his forearm.

"You don't believe me?"

"No. Sorry."

He shrugs. "How can I prove it?"

"What seminary are you going to?"

"St. Paul the Apostle in Connecticut. It has an excellent rating by the Vatican review board and a helluva crew team."

"How long will you attend?"

"The standard four years. While I am gifted, I don't think you can test out of classes."

"Say the Apostle's Creed."

He recites the prayer without hesitation. I still don't believe him.

"Fine. You can have ten minutes."

"Thank you. God is smiling on you, my child." He pats my knee.

I turn my attention back to the hymnal while we both wait for Father Nolan. I try to find the Christmas songs. Maybe I can learn the next verse to *O Holy Night*.

"Good reading?" the man asks.

I shrug.

"What's your business with Father Nolan?" His knees jiggle up and down. He can't stay still or sit quietly. His elementary school teachers must have loved him.

"I'm not sharing that with you."

"Come on. I shared my doubts about the priesthood with you. I didn't even tell my mother about my second thoughts."

I roll my eyes. "You could say that Father Nolan is my parole officer. Can we leave it at that?"

There's a deep sigh.

I look up to see Father Nolan standing in the doorway to his office. He looks disappointed. It's a good look for him. Not that I've ever seen him look bad—chiseled features, broad chest, full head of chestnut hair, perfect teeth under a symmetrical smile. The first time I met Nolan I fell in love—as did every woman parishioner at Saint Mary's. He's a priest like none I've ever met—always calm, charming, pulled together with a theatrical-like flare. If he wasn't delivering homilies for a living, I could see him as a cruise director.

"Paige, stop telling people I'm your parole officer. I'm your spiritual leader and court *suggested* counselor." The charges were dropped, but the judge strongly suggested I get help.

The man stands up. "Can I talk to you?"

Father Nolan looks to me.

"I can wait."

The men go into the office and close the door. I give up on looking for Christmas songs and read the old newsletter.

Five minutes have passed.

I rid my handbag of old receipts, expired coupons, and a leaky pen.

Ten minutes have passed.

I delete the seldom used numbers out of my cell phone.

Fifteen minutes have passed.

I shift uncomfortably in my chair. Curse under my breath. Chew on my thumb nail.

Twenty minutes have passed.

That's it. I get up and knock on the office door. It opens and the men walk out.

"Sorry," the man says.

"Is your faith restored?" I ask.

"Absolutely." He shakes Father Nolan's hand. "Thanks for your input. I'll see you at tryouts."

"You're not going into the seminary, are you?"

"No. Did you believe that story?"

"No. I did believe you'd only be ten minutes." I push past him and take a seat in one of the leather winged back chair across from Father Nolan's desk.

"He's all yours." The man waves goodbye.

"Who was that?"

Father Nolan closes the door. "Isaac Barber. I personally recruited him from Bishop McGuiness to coach boys' varsity basketball. The year he took over they were four and eighteen. Last season they went undefeated until sectionals."

"Barber?" Why do I know that name? "Does he teach the social science class?"

"Yes. It is the only class he teaches. We have a policy at St. Mary's; our coaches must be employed by the school."

"Is he certified to teach social science?"

"Sure. Please don't stress. I have something for you." He walks to his antique desk, pulls out a small Macy's bag from a drawer and hands it to me. Father Nolan plays many roles in my life. He's my priest, shrink, and self-appointed fashion therapist.

After the *incident* in April, my mother recommended Father Nolan Malone. I was raised in a house where psychiatrists are for the weak though confiding in a priest was acceptable. At our first meeting I knew Father Nolan was just what the judge ordered. He's helped me with my anger, my insecurities, and even my gardening.

"Thanks." I open the bag. It's a pink and lime striped silk scarf.

"I knew you'd be in all black and black is really more my color. Now if I could just get you to update your hairstyle. Are you actually wearing a scrunchie?" His head shakes with disapproval.

I touch my dark hair that's pulled into a loose ponytail. My hairdryer has been on extended vacation and my curling iron may have run away from home. It's been awhile since we've spent any time together.

Father Nolan is a Diocesan Priest and therefore did not take a vow of poverty. He receives a salary and can own a car, investments, and possessions. He is encouraged to live a frugal, simple life. Instead of buying items for himself, he buys for his flock. Food for the hungry. Clothes for the poor. Accessories for me.

I tie the scarf around my neck—I don't want to have the same fight we had a few months ago over that stupid ladybug brooch—and let Father Nolan begin our session with a prayer.

"Amen," I mumble as he concludes.

"We missed you at mass on Sunday," he says, leaning

back in his chair. "I saw your mother. I saw your father. I saw your daughter."

"Don't worry. I still paid my membership."

"It's called an offering. Paige. Or a tithe." St. Mary's has gone high tech. I can pay with a credit card online. It saves me the trouble of writing a check or remembering what time mass starts.

"Right." I love giving Father Nolan a hard time. He's come to expect it.

"It's not going to hurt you to attend mass. Put on your Sunday best. Perhaps a pair of shoes that a podiatrist wouldn't recommend."

I tuck my feet under my chair trying to hide my black clogs with arch supports.

"And Erika is going to be making her confirmation this year. She's a very bright, caring young lady."

If he only knew. "I'm afraid she's veering off the right path."

"How so?" Father Nolan tilts his head slightly.

I check my watch "You'll see. She'll be here in a few minutes."

"She's a good kid."

I shrug. "What did she say in confession last week? I know her confirmation class comes on the first Wednesday of the month. Did you hear her confession? Is she sexually active?" For a moment, I think I have an *in* on my teenage daughter's life.

"You know confessions are private matters."

"I thought that was just in a court of law."

He shakes his head and his hair flops unto his forehead. I'm used to my priests having receding hairlines and ear hair. Father Nolan is thirty-eight and genetically blessed with thick hair. He's thirty years younger than the other two priests at Saint Mary's—and four years older than me. He was brought in by the diocese from somewhere in New Jersey because attendance had been slipping for years. Families were moving away from the stained glass of Saint Mary's to the new mega-churches that have T.G.I.S signs on their lawn and electric guitars in their praise bands.

"How are you feeling about tomorrow?" he asks, not giving me even a hint of Erika's confessed sins.

"What's tomorrow?" I fiddle with my wedding ring.

"I believe you will be signing your divorce papers." He raises an eyebrow. "Have you even looked at them?"

"I've got a lawyer." I pause. "And Max may not go through with it. I've changed. Maybe we can still work things out."

"Paige…"

"Well, I believe in miracles." My nine year marriage needs a miracle. While I'm praying for divine intervention, Max has his hand on the life support plug.

"Sweetheart, Max won't be changing his mind." Not every priest can get away with calling his parishioners Doll, Sweetheart, or Dawg, but it works for Father Nolan.

"Do we have to talk about this?" I pull at the pink and lime striped noose around my neck. "And whose side are you on? The Catholic Church doesn't condone divorce."

"No, we could talk about the surrogacy issue."

"Ugghhh." I bang the back of my head dramatically on the chair. "I know you don't approve." I'd agreed to be my best-friends' surrogate months ago, but I have yet to undergo any procedures. Trisha and Manny are exhausting every option before turning their embryos over to my uterus. I try not to take it as an insult that I'm their last resort.

"I've been doing some research. Did you know most surrogate agencies require their surrogates to be married? They also want you to be done having your own children. You need health insurance. Not dependent on alcohol. Never convicted of a crime." He hands me a print-out from a website.

"Trisha and Manny don't have the same requirements. And I do have insurance—"

"Until the divorce is final."

"And I'm not dependent on alcohol."

"But you do enjoy it."

"And I've never been convicted."

"Only because the charges were dropped."

There's a knock on the door—Thank, God—and Betty opens it a crack.

"May I send Erika in?" she asks.

"Please."

"Hey Father," Erika takes the seat next to me. She drops her messenger bag that looks to weigh thirty pounds and adjusts her parochial skirt. When I went to Catholic school the uniform was considered boring. Now there is this naughty, sexual fantasy associated with it. Damn that Britney Spears.

"So who would like to start?" Father Nolan asks.

"She hasn't been pleading her case for the last hour?" Erika asks.

"I haven't told him a thing."

Father Nolan confirms my statement with a head nod.

Erika states her case to our impartial judge. When she explains the project is for Mr. Barber's class, Father Nolan sits up straighter. And I realize I may lose. Both of them are enthralled by Isaac Barber.

"I've never really thought about Barbie's positive traits," Father Nolan says. "Paige, what would you like to add?"

"I want to know what she's really trying to accomplish with this Barbie experiment." I air quote 'Barbie experiment.'

She lets out a long sigh. "I told you. I'm going to prove she's a good role model."

"How exactly? Other than becoming a cheerleader and quitting choir."

"You really want to know?" Erika asks.

"Enlighten me."

She unzips her bag and shuffles through the binders and notebooks. She pulls out a yellow legal pad. "Ready for this?"

I nod.

Erika pushes her blond curls behind her ears and begins. "My plan has fifteen requirements for enjoying the Barbie lifestyle."

"Is anorexic one of them?" I ask.

"Lay off the anorexia."

"Bulimia?"

"Paige, let her speak," Father Nolan says.

"There are the physical requirements like physique, hair, clothing, and shoes. Then there are the internal and personal requirements. Career—"

"You're in high school. You don't get a career." I say.

"Okay, a career path. Then there are hobbies, goals, and relationships. Do you want me to go into more detail?" She looks up from her notes.

"I'd like to hear," Father Nolan says.

"Okay. Let's look at relationships. There is Barbie's boyfriend Ken—"

God, this is getting worse. She'll be on the prowl for a boyfriend. For years I've been teaching her defense—no, means no—and here she goes on the offense.

"—who is first, and foremost, a friend. Ken is also Barbie's ultimate accessory. She doesn't need him in order to be accomplished. Ken wasn't necessary for Barbie to buy the dream house or a car and she's had a zillion careers without him."

Guess that seems positive.

"And Barbie has had over forty friends with her best-friend being Midge. They have a great relationship—no jealousy or rivalry. Look around, that's hard to find in high school."

"What about family?" I ask. "Barbie doesn't have a mother, does she?"

"Not in doll form," Erika says. "But parents have appeared in her books."

"You've done a lot of research," Father Nolan says. "Maybe I could learn something from our little blonde friend."

Erika smiles.

"Hang on. I still need some clarification before King Sal makes his decision."

"Who?" Father Nolan asks.

"King Sal. The guy in the Old Testament who suggested chopping the baby in half."

"King Solomon," Erika says.

"Whatever. Tell me this. Are you doing this strictly as a class project? It's not some desperate cry for help because your parents are getting divorced?"

"My mother is getting a divorce from my step-father," she says. Max is not Erika's biological father. He's not even her adoptive father. But he's the only father she's ever known.

"So this Barbie-as-a-role-model idea is strictly a class project?"

"Yes." She dramatically slaps the legal pad in her lap.

"Great," I say. "Then let me be your subject."

"What?" She crinkles her nose.

"I'll take on your experiment. I'll follow your Barbie rules. Wear pink clothes and curl my eyelashes."

Father Nolan chuckles. "Sorry. Thought you were joking."

"Seriously?" She sighs.

"If you promise to stick with basketball and not quit choir or anything else. I'll be the subject of your experiment." What else do I have going on? No job. No husband. I can devote my time to sculpting my body, tweezing hairs, and acting bubbly.

"You're the anti-Barbie," she laughs. "You'd be out to prove she's the source of everything wrong with our society from the lack of women in Congress to skimpy clothes."

"And you started this thinking she was the ultimate woman. You're diving head first into an experiment assuming you know the outcome. Your objectivity is compromised."

"Is not," she says, sounding fifteen.

"Erika, if this is really just some kind of sociology experiment, then please, let's play with my life." There isn't much left to it anyway. "If you really feel the need to transform your appearance and your personality into... well, into something like a Barbie doll, let's talk about this."

"Mom, it's just an experiment." She rolls her eyes at my concern.

"Erika," Father Nolan clasps his hands together. "Why don't you come up with a list of things you want your mother—"

"She won't go through with it." Erika says.

"I'll do anything." I pause for a moment. "I mean...I'll do anything that can be easily undone at the end of.... How long is this project?"

"Twelve weeks."

"Anything that can be undone at the end of twelve weeks. No buying a yacht or moving to Paris."

"So no breast augmentation surgery?" Erika asks.

"No, sorry. You'll have to limit your experiment to padded, push-up bras."

"I guess. Let me ask Mr. Barber what he thinks." Erika chews her bottom lip and I know she's actually considering my proposal.

"This is going to be fun." Father Nolan says. "I want to be there for the make-over portion of the program."

Neither friends nor shoes are a dime a dozen.
But at least friends won't go out of style or cause blisters.

Chapter 3

To commiserate the eve of my divorce settlement I bring home a large pepperoni pizza and a six-pack of beer. I'm a wine girl, except when eating pizza. Unintentionally, I set the hot, greasy pizza box on top of Erika's instructions for the Barbie experiment. (At least I will claim it was unintentional if ever directly questioned.)

"What are you hiding under there?" Trisha points to the pizza. We've been best friends since high school. While I've been able to talk my way out of a speeding ticket, convince my mother I was virgin until the night Erika was conceived, and lie to my doctor that I only drink alcohol occasionally, I've never been able to pull anything on Trisha.

"I think it's the list from Erika I was telling you about." I pull the sheet out. Rings of grease have formed on the typed page. Somewhere between all her classes, soccer practice, and a student government meeting, Erika was able to compose the beginnings of her social experiment. The project is due in twelve weeks. I was hoping she'd burn a week or two brainstorming.

I read the instructions before giving it over to Trisha.

Subject Requirements.
1. Complete makeup. (Daily) You are not to leave the house without appropriate makeup. Blistex and eyeliner are not considered a makeup application. An initial beauty consultation at a Clinique counter is suggested.
2. Hair maintenance. (Daily) Your hair should be clean and styled. A ponytail and/or headband are for workouts only. All other hair should be waxed or shaved on a regular basis, not just during swimsuit season.
3. Exercise. (4/week) Suggesting thirty minutes of cardio and fifteen minutes of strength training during each work out.
4. Feminine Attire. (Always) Clothes need to be clean, ironed, and fit well. Styles should be feminine ranging from sweet to sexy, never slutty. Whenever possible high heels should be worn.
5. Good manners. (Always) Remember the magic words whether speaking with friends, waiters, or your daughter.
6. Positive Attitude. (Always) Wake up expecting to win the lottery, expecting to

meet your own Ken, expecting great things. It can happen.

7. Find your own Ken. (Continuous) Look for a man who is a good friend and maybe more. (Marriage, or the prospect of, is not necessary.)

8. Pursuit of a fulfilling career. (Continuous) Barbie has had over forty careers. Do not settle for something that makes you miserable. Go after something exciting and new.

9. Be there for Midge. (Continuous) Midge has been in Barbie's life almost as long as Ken. Put friends first and count on them when necessary.

10. Try a new sport. (At least once) Such as gymnastics, hiking, doubles tennis, skiing, skating, or horseback riding.

11. Be a fashion model. (At least once) Try modeling—print, television or runway. Showcase Agency (518-555-8357) hires people of all ages and sizes.

12. Get a pet. (Soon as possible) Not all things furry are rabid. Barbie has adopted dogs, cats, horses, and even a giraffe.

13. No drinking alcohol. (Always) Barbie does not need a vice.

14. Read *The Barbie Files: An Unauthorized Biography*. (As soon as possible)

Become familiar with her history, traits, and characteristics.
15. WWBD? (Always) Ask yourself "What would Barbie Do?"
16. Complete the assessment survey. (Nightly) To track your progress, you are required to answer a simple five question survey at the end of each day.

"And you agreed to this?" Trisha asks after reading the list.

"Yes, but I may have to request a few adjustments." Like numbers 3, 4, 7, and 11 through 13. I open two bottles of beer and hand one to Trisha.

"No, thanks. I'm hoping..." She pats her stomach. "Plus, I'm on call." She puts the beer down. Dr. Trisha Stevens is one of the most sought after veterinarians in the Capital District. She went to veterinary school in California and interned at the San Diego zoo—which is the vet equivalent of a political science major interning at the White House. Now she shares a practice with two other doctors. Their office is in Delmar. They also offer house calls for an astronomical fee.

While I call Erika down for dinner, Trisha sets out three paper plates and napkins.

"Maybe you should be the subject of Erika's experiment," I suggest. "You have most of the requirements covered. Love animals. Great job. Great friends. Great Ken, though you married him."

"Aren't I the fool? You're overlooking one huge problem."

"Yeah?"

"I'm a short, curvy, *black* woman."

"The words Caucasian and blonde are not once mentioned here." I hold up the list.

"Yes, they are. Several times in code." She spells it out for me. "B-A-R-B-I-E"

Trisha's beautiful, just not in a Barbie way. She cuts her own hair using an electric razor with the guard set at a level two. The two must stand for two centimeters. The look works because she has a beautiful face—huge eyes, accentuated cheek bones, high arched eye brows and flawless skin. She could have advertised acne cream when we were teens and wrinkle serums now that we're in our thirties.

"Hey, Trisha," Erika joins us in the kitchen. She grabs a slice of pizza and takes a bite before sitting down. Between a teenager's metabolism and two soccer workouts daily, Erika could consume three thousand calories and not gain an ounce.

I put my beer on the table and get out two cans of Diet Coke for Trisha and Erika.

"What's that?" Erika points to my beer. "Didn't you read your requirements for the experiment?"

I take a last long swallow. "Yes, I read it. I don't think giving up alcohol is going to make any difference." Not to mention I went to Montreal last weekend and have two hundred dollars of duty free I'm not about to let go to waste.

"Barbie doesn't drink." Erika says.

"Your mom sure does," Trisha says. That's not really fair; Trisha bought three hundred dollars at duty free.

"Barbie's sixteen. Of course, she doesn't drink. Maybe that's one part of the experiment you could put into practice, say until you're thirty. That and abstinence."

"There's no way Barbie practices abstinence," Trisha says.

I shoot her a look. Abstinence is a way of life in this house for daughter and—unfortunately—for mother.

"Barbie's not sixteen. The youngest reference has Barbie as seventeen. But she's been a presidential candidate, which would make her a minimum of thirty-five. Officially she was *born* in 1959." Erika has been doing her research.

"How can a girl that has a million cocktail dresses not drink cocktails?" I get up for the open beer I'd offered Trisha earlier.

"Mom," Erika sighs. "You said you'd try."

The guilt makes my chest tighten. "Tomorrow," I say. "I need a day to digest all this. Okay? Can I start tomorrow?"

"Sure. You can still fill out the assessment tonight."

I agree. After Erika polishes off three slices she excuses herself to her room under the guise of having to finish homework. I know she'll spend just as much time chatting with her friends online as reading for American History. When I initially set up her laptop I installed spyware. Every keystroke is recorded and logged in a phantom file nightly. I've yet to read any of her chats. I only monitor what websites she visits. Really, it's no worse than knowing where your daughter keeps her diary and the diary's key. It's insurance. There if I ever need it.

Trisha throws away our dinner ware and I open

another—and I swear my last—bottle of beer.

"What are you going to do about getting a pet?" Trisha asks. "You panic at the sight of an empty dog dish, not to mention an actual dog."

"That's because an empty dish means a hungry dog nearby. Actually, the pet requirement is easy. I'm going to get a horse."

"A horse?" Trisha laughs.

"Obviously I can't keep a horse here, so he'll have to stay at a stable. So I'll buy a horse, rent a stall at a barn, pay for his room and board for twelve weeks then sell him at the end. Simple." Sometimes I amaze myself. "Just one question. Are horses like cars or houses?"

"Excuse me?"

"Will my stallion appreciate or depreciate in twelve weeks?"

Trisha rolls her eyes. I guess owning a horse won't be a money-making opportunity.

I take my beer, and Trisha and I move into the living room. It's seven o'clock.

"*Wheel of Fortune* or *Entertainment Tonight*?" I ask Trisha.

"Really? This is how you want to spend your evening? Tomorrow you're getting divorced *and* you're devoting your life to Barbie." She makes it sound like I'm joining a convent or going to jail. "Let's do something."

"You're right. Let's go."

Thirty minutes later we're strapping on rented shoes at Leisure Lanes.

"This is not what I had in mind," Trisha says. "I thought we'd go to a club. Dance, burn some energy."

We both know I don't dance in public. "I haven't bowled in years. Not since you were allowed to smoke in here." The stale smell of cigarettes still lingers. I select a nine-pound ball that's royal blue. I'd prefer a ten pounder, but the only one I saw was cotton candy pink. I'm not doing pink tonight. The royal blue suits my attire of dark jeans and a grey, scoop neck T-shirt with *Paige* embroidered on it. A little outdated? Yes. Appropriate for a bowling alley? Also yes.

Before we throw our first ball I order a pitcher of beer and some fries. So I guess that means I drink beer only with pizza and at places that offer "Wine: red, white, or pink - $3." Even though Trisha still isn't drinking, I ask the waitress for two glasses, because I'm afraid what it would look like if I asked for only one.

"Care to make a wager?" I ask Trisha.

"Whatcha got?"

"If I win the first frame, you buy the next round. If you win the first frame, I buy the next round." Trisha is the better bowler. Hell, she's better at everything.

"Why not?" Trisha steps to the line and throw her first ball. Wham! The screen above the lane shows animated pins running for their lives. Strike.

My turn. The first ball gets three pins. The second ball taps another. It doesn't fall down.

"I'm a mediocre bowler, but you make me look professional." Trisha says.

We continue to bet and at the end of the game I owe Trisha a box of Thin Mints, an hour of cleaning, a scratch-off lottery ticket, one of Mom's apple strudels and five dollars—after the fifth frame my creativity dried up and we started betting a dollar a frame.

"I'm going to go get you that round of drinks I owe you." I don't think the waitress will be back around now that league bowling is in full swing.

"You drank all that? Maybe you should slow down."

"I spilled some." I show her the quarter sized spot on my jeans then head for the bar near the front entrance. There are swinging saloon doors separating the bar from the bowling alley. The lighting inside is dull and seems to come mostly from overhead televisions tuned to baseball games. A couple of guys are watching at the far end.

I order another pitcher of beer. Before the bartender gives me my change the swinging doors creak, a man walks in who makes my jaw drop and my plans for the evening switch course. Imagine taking Bon Jovi sex appeal mixed with Brad Pitt sex appeal. That's a lot of sex appeal.

It's optimistic of me to think Mr. Sex Appeal will show me any interest. But over thirty fluid ounces of courage makes me see life as full of possibilities.

Mr. Sex Appeal takes a seat at the end of the bar. He sits alone.

What the hell? Instead of grabbing the pitcher, I take a seat two away from Mr. Sex Appeal. The bartender sets down my change then takes the man's order. Mr. Sex Appeal doesn't bother to give me a second look. I wait until his beer arrives before I speak.

"I'd offer to buy you another, but I don't believe you're twenty-one."

He laughs at my horrible line and flashes a mouth full

of perfect, straight, glowing-white teeth. Some women like a tight ass, some prefer six-pack abs, and some are into eyes. I love a smile with gorgeous healthy teeth.

"Here." He pulls out his wallet and hands me his driver's license.

September sixth—same birthday as my mom. Four years majoring in mathematics hasn't failed me. He's twenty-three. "Guess you pass."

"Now that you know my name—"

Shit! I didn't even look at his name.

"—what's yours?"

I point to the embroidery on my shirt. Maybe he can't read, either. "It's Paige O'Neal-Russell." I offer a hand. "I mean Paige O'Neal. Well, it's still O'Neal-Russell."

"Nice to meet you, Paige O'Neal-Russell, O'Neal." He slides over to the empty seat separating us. With barely a raise of an eyebrow he has the bartender bring us over two shots of tequila. He hands me the glass. "To new friends." We toast and swallow.

Mr. Sex Appeal is charming and smooth—like old scotch. Or is it whisky? Damned if I know. He starts by touching my arm. Shoulder. Thigh. Whispering in my ear.

"You've got to meet my friend," I say. Who knew I could pick up a hot twenty-three year old? I need Trisha as a witness. Then a thought suddenly hits me. Maybe Mr. Sex Appeal could be my Ken. He's cute enough and we have a lot in common—such as we both like tequila.

"I'd love to meet your friend," he says with a wink. Is he thinking of a Ken, Midge, and Barbie sandwich?

"Relax, she's married. Happily, if not annoyingly so."

I drag Mr. S.A. back to lane seventeen, drinks in tow.

Trisha is untying her rented shoes. I wasn't gone that long.

"Hey, aren't we going to play another game?" I ask.

Trisha looks up. Her focus is on Mr. S. A.

"I found us a third bowler." As if two wasn't enough.

"Sorry, Paige, we have to go. I just got called in. Seems a Chihuahua of an unnamed channel thirteen news anchor had a run in with a curious three-year old and a clothes dryer." She points to my bowling shoes. "Let's have 'em. You can say good bye while I exchange our shoes."

Without loosening the laces or sitting down, I pry the red, white, and blue shoes off—only knocking into a table once—and hand them over to Trisha. I check my watch, it is eight-thirty. At least I'll be home in time to watch a *Law and Order* or a *CSI*.

"Well, it was nice to meet you." I offer Mr. Sex Appeal my hand.

He turns my hand over and kisses my palm. I'm too worried about what my hand might smell like to find this very erotic.

"You seem tense." He circles behind me and rubs my shoulders. "Relax."

And I do, because I'm not worried what my shoulders smell like. Now this is nice. I slump into a chair and close my eyes. A moan escapes me.

"I could take you home," Mr. Sex Appeal says.

"No!" Trisha's voice snaps me to attention. "Paige, I have to leave now for the animal hospital. I've called Father Nolan. He's on his way. Promise me you'll wait for him."

"I promise." I hold up three fingers and cross my heart.

Trisha gives me a hug. "I'll call you later." Then she turns her attention to Mr. Sex Appeal. "And you, let me see some ID."

He fishes out his wallet for a second time this evening. Maybe this is a new and accepted part of the dating culture.

Trisha looks at it. "Okay Mr. Timothy Bordon, if anything should happen to my friend I will track you down. Got it?"

He nods.

Either Timothy is more of a gentleman than I gave Mr. Sex Appeal credit for, or he is genuinely scared of Trisha. He helps me get my shoes on. Out of nowhere bending over makes me very light headed and queasy. He waits for me as I use the ladies room. Then he sits with me outside as I wait for my ride.

When a St. Mary's Church van pulls to the curb and the window unrolls, Timothy is visibly relieved.

"How's my favorite soon-to-be divorcee?" Father Nolan asks.

"Are priests allowed to have favorite divorcees?" I ask. Timothy has to help me to my feet, then makes his escape. Never even got his number.

"No worries. We'll get an annulment when it is final," Father Nolan says. "Get in."

"I'm warning you, I may get sick." I open the passenger side door and notice we're not alone. Seven red-hat ladies are riding in the back. I wave hello.

"We were at the Italian Community Center. Thursday is bingo night." Father Nolan says.

"You made us leave early," says one of the gals.

"Sorry."

"Gert, I promise to make it up to you. We can hit the Moose Lodge tomorrow night. Hear they have a progressive jackpot that's near nine hundred dollars." Father Nolan pulls the van into traffic.

The scents coming from the back of the van is nauseating. It's a cross between flowery drug store perfume and Ben-Gay. I crack a window.

"I brought you something. I'd planned to drop it off after bingo. Look under the seat."

I reach down and find a Barnes and Noble bag. Father Nolan is a publisher's dream. He spends hundreds a year on books. I asked him once if he'd ever heard of a library. He thinks the idea of a library is repulsive. "Like borrowing someone's underwear, only more intimate."

The bag contains a used Barbie doll and three books. Two trade backs and one coffee table picture book. They're all about Barbie. One is a collection of essays. One is the unofficial biography I'm required to read. And the big book is about her fashions through the decades.

"I figured if you were going to live your life according to Barb you should know something about her. Like her measurements. 40-18-32 in real woman sizes. I read a few pages."

"What's he talking about?" Gert asks.

"Nothing." I clutch the books to my chest. "Where did you get the doll?"

"Lost and found. Poor thing has been in there for about a year. Probably some six-year old was so moved by my homily she forgot all about her doll."

The Barbie doll has pale blonde hair—with layers and no bangs—that comes to the middle of her back. She has blue eyes, natural-looking makeup except for carnation pink lips. Her feet are arched. Her breasts are—of course—nipple-free. "Where are her clothes?"

"Don't look at me. Found her that way." When we pull up to a stop light Father Nolan turns to me. "Are you going to give this a sincere effort?"

"Do you think I should?"

"Colossians 3:17. *And whatever you do, whether in word or deed, do it all in the name of the Lord Jesus, giving thanks to God the Father through him.*"

"Huh?"

"If you do this—and we both know you will because you've never let Erika down—you need to give it one hundred percent."

"I'll read the books."

"Wonderful. I want a full update on Monday. I want to see a plan."

"There's a list," I say. "Erika has created the playbook for this game."

Father Nolan drops me off at home with my naked doll and new books. I sit outside for a few minutes trying to sober up on fresh air. A fine example I am for my daughter.

I go inside and follow the muffled music from the foyer up the stairs to Erika's room. We have a house rule; she won't lock her bedroom door if I knock before coming in.

"It's open," Erika yells.

I pop my head in, not wanting to get close enough for Erika to smell my breath. "Just letting you know I'm home."

"Okay." Erika says.

"Think I'm going to bed."

"Don't forget to fill in your daily assessment," she says. "I left it in your room."

I groan.

"Come on, Mom. It's five questions."

I find the survey on my nightstand, and to insure my participation Erika has even left me a pen.

Daily Self-Assessment   *Thursday, September 9*
Rate the degree to which you agree with the statement.

    5–completely agree 1–completely disagree

1. I accomplished something today.
2. I felt connected with my friends and family today.
3. I was interested in sex today.
4. I laughed today.
5. I am looking forward to tomorrow.

Notes:

I fill in Erika's survey with all fives, except for the sex question. That gets a one. If I were being honest, they'd all be threes, except the part about looking forward to tomorrow. That would be a negative seven on the satisfaction scale.

Instead of worrying about the divorce settlement I dress for bed. I get a bottle of water from the mini-fridge in the wet bar and a handful of Tylenol. I chuck the naked Barbie into my nightstand drawer. Then I start reading one of the Barbie books Father Nolan gave me—*The Barbie Files: An Unauthorized Biography*.

I'm not interested in her age (created in 1959) or her sales number (two sold every second) or her full name

(Barbie Millicent Roberts). I just need to know if the gal ever took a drink. Wine, beer, Jell-O shots, I don't care. Sobriety isn't something I want to start on the day Max divorces me.

*There's more than one Ken in this world, even if
you only have one in your doll house.*

Chapter 4

I can smell the fresh-brewed coffee before I get to the
bottom of the stairs. *Bless that child.* My head is in no
condition to calculate scoop-to-water ratio this morning.
Yet my stomach is craving strong coffee with cream and
Splenda.

"You look rough," Erika says. Then she hands me a
narrow sheet of paper, like something I'd write a grocery
list on.

"What's this?" I can't even think of reading it until I
drain a cup of coffee.

"Another copy of your instructions—the condensed
version. Thought you might want to carry it in your
handbag."

I pour my coffee, grab a store-bought brownie and sit
at the counter. I take a look at the list. There are no
changes, as I can remember. Still no alcohol—which right
now, I think is a great idea.

1. Complete makeup. (Daily)
2. Hair maintenance. (Daily)
3. Exercise. (4/week)
4. Feminine attire. (Always)
5. Good manners. (Always)
6. Positive attitude. (Always)
7. Find your own Ken. (Continuous)
8. Pursuit of a fulfilling career. (Continuous)
9. Be there for Midge. (Continuous)
10. Try a new sport. (At least once)
11. Be a fashion model. (At least once)
12. Get a pet. (Soon as possible)
13. No drinking alcohol. (Always)
14. Read *The Barbie Files: An Unauthorized Biography.* (ASAP)
15. Complete the assessment survey. (Nightly)

"And Mom, I don't think you were being completely honest on last night's survey." Erika leans in and gives me the form. "I'd like you to take it over."

"Fine." I cross off my fives and change them to threes. I leave my interest in sex as a one.

"Thanks," Erika kisses my cheek. "Good luck today. With everything." And she's out the front door. I think I like it better when she's grouchy in the morning.

Three cups of coffee and a hot shower transform me, not into a bubbly Barbie doll, but into a functioning woman. True to the list, I wash and style my hair. (I also shave my under arms, but stopped there because bending down builds up so much pressure in my skull I think my eyes are going to pop out.) I apply makeup, though I'm out of mascara, foundation, eye shadow, and lip liner. And I dress in a black skirt with a gray oxford shirt, and my only pair of high heeled shoes—black leather pumps. This new beauty routine is a ridiculous waste of ninety minutes.

"You look nice," Mom says when she picks me up. She insists on driving me to the meeting that'll end my marriage. "Wish we were going somewhere nice instead of…" She can't seem to say the words.

"Me, too."

The O'Neal family is of proud Irish descent. We celebrate St. Paddy's day like most families would celebrate Fourth of July or Thanksgiving—big party, plenty to eat and drink, music, games, at least one incident that requires a first-aid kit. We like U2—at least Ryan and all our cousins do. The parents prefer the Chieftains. We decorate our homes with Celtic crosses. We serve potatoes *and* a starch at every dinner. We're Catholic. We gather most Sundays for a meal. We like beer.

And as with any big family having strong bonds, certain things are expected. Whenever possible, you keep things in the family. If you need a car, see Uncle Pat and Aunt Shirley who own Reliable Used Cars on First Street in Hudson. If you have a leaky roof you call your second cousin Mitch—he works at a transmission repair shop and is good at fixing anything. And if you're getting divorced you use your first cousin Joe, a graduate of an unheard of law school who passed the bar on only his third try. Test anxiety—reportedly.

"Have you talked to Joseph? Is everything in order?" Mom asks as we creep along the Northway.

"I think so." Our divorce is considered uncontested.

We've agreed to work it out on our own terms and submit them to a judge. There shouldn't be any need to go to court.

"What is Max saying is the reason for the divorce?"

"The reason is … he doesn't want to be married to me anymore." For almost five months I've tried to understand why my husband left. He'd said I put him last. When? When I was folding his underwear? When I was cooking his dinners? When I was scheduling everything from his doctor appointments to tee times?

"Could there have been someone else?" Mom whispers.

"No."

"Are you certain?"

"Now I'm not." Of course, the thought had crossed my mind. The humiliation and hurt of an affair would be unbearable. Avoidance with a shot of denial seemed like the best course of action.

When we pull up to the law offices of Rogers, Rigby, and Roy, I give a nervous laugh as I imagine Scooby Doo working as their receptionist. *R-ello. Tanks for ralling Rogers, Rigby, and Roy.*

Relax, Paige. I take a breath and follow Mom inside.

"You act like we're going to a funeral," Mom says. "At least take off the dark sunglasses." Mom has always had her own sense of style—a cross between mobster-wife and June Cleaver. Today she wears her faux-platinum hair somewhat contemporary—sleek with the ends flipped out. Her makeup hasn't changed in decades—clumpy mascara, red-as-hell lipstick, and pink blush. She finds eye shadow trashy. Her brown slacks and blue sweater set are set off nicely by a strand of pearls.

Joe's already waiting in the lobby when we arrive. His eyes are closed and he's rocking back and forth mouthing something. Maybe a speech. His wrinkled navy suit with a carnation yellow shirt probably fit when Joe was two hundred pounds—that was fifty pounds ago.

"Good afternoon, Joseph," Mom interrupts his monologue.

"Hey, Aunt Nancy." He stands and gives her a hug. "My first divorce case. This is exciting." He gives her a double-thumbs up. "Sorry, Paige."

The receptionist says they'll be ready for us in a few minutes.

I nod and we all take seats on the paisley couch. The room ranges somewhere between extravagant and gaudy. Dark, cherry tables. Detailed sculptures with an oriental flare. Brass fixtures and a chandelier. Persian rug. Everything looks like it was bought at a garage sale from the Taj Mahal Casino.

"Paige," Joe interrupts me as I flip through a magazine with the words *Break Ups* written on the cover. "I was reviewing divorce law this morning and—"

"This morning?" I ask. "This isn't the first time you've looked into it?"

"Last month I went to a conference in Atlantic City and they had a whole workshop on divorce law in New Jersey."

"How will that help us in New York?" I'm tempted to walk out. Can't divorce me if you can't find me.

"They're similar."

"Ms. O'Neal-Russell. They're ready for you," the receptionist says before I have a chance to strangle Joe.

I pull on Joe's coat sleeve. "Just make sure I get custody of Erika."

Mom stays on the sofa as Joe and I head toward the conference room. We'd agreed she'd wait for me in the lobby. But when she gives me her sad, I-labored-sixteen-hours-for-you eyes, I break.

"Fine. You can come in. Just don't say a word."

As we enter the room, Max and his lawyer stand up. It would be considered chivalrous if this wasn't the slaughtering of my marriage. I take a long look at Max. He's changed since the last time I saw him in April. He's making an effort. His hair is darker. His skin is tan. The bit of belly he had is gone. Dammit! He looks good.

"Hi, Nancy." Max walks around the table and gives my mom a hug.

"Good to see you, Max." Joe shakes his hand.

I want to scream, "This is not a damn family reunion."

"Paige," Max gives me a slight nod of the head. No hug. No handshake. "You look…"

"Please, have a seat," Max's lawyer says. "I'm Phillip Rogers." He offers me his hand across the table. I freeze. Could it be him? He's taller and his hair is shorter, but he still has the same cleft and gray eyes.

"Joseph O'Neal." Joe takes Phillip's extended hand. "Paige, you okay?"

"Yeah." I take a seat not believing Phillip doesn't recognize me. I swear the guy was in love with me for a whole semester in college. We'd met at a party, went to a few basketball games together, saw a Bare Naked Ladies concert and marched on the state capital over tuition hikes.

Mom sits to my right and squeezes my shoulder almost

lovingly. I know she's waiting for her moment to scream "I object!"

"Let's begin." Phillip opens a large folder. "Mr. Russell is hoping to get this on the court calendar for next week. As an uncontested divorce we simply submit all the papers to the judge for review. There will be no hearing."

Joe has substantially less paperwork than Phillip. He pulls a spiral bound memo pad out of his suit coat pocket. "Anyone got an extra pen?"

Phillip offers Joe his pen and continues. "Assuming there are no objections, we should be able to get through this today." Phillip slides a folder across the table to Joe.

"Why don't I take that?" I move the folder in front of me and open the thick file. "You just take notes."

"In this case, Mr. Russell is the Plaintiff and Ms. O'Neal-Russell is the Defendant." Phillip explains.

"Defendant," Joe says as he jots it down.

We all wait until he's done.

"And, as I mentioned earlier, the divorce is uncontested so long as both parties agree to the terms herein."

"Can we get straight to the terms?" I ask.

"My client is demanding sole custody of her daughter, Erika. We will not settle for anything else." Joe pounds his fist on the table in an unnecessary gesture that causes him to rub his hand.

"Mr. Russell is not the child's biological or adoptive father. He is not seeking any legal rights to the child. He does hope Ms. O'Neal-Russell will allow occasional visits with the minor."

"Great." Joe slaps me on the back. "You got what you

wanted."

"Shhh." I snap. "What about the assets?"

"In the Affidavit of the Plaintiff, section five, Mr. Russell has graciously agreed to equitable distribution of marital property."

"Wahoo!" Joe gives me a nudge. "This is easy. You're getting half of everything, Paigey."

"Please be quiet." I shuffle through the one-inch stack looking for the affidavit. "Can I order him to not speak?" I ask Phillip.

Phillip finally gives me a smile. "Equitable distribution does not mean fifty-fifty, equal split. It means a fair split. For example, Ms. O'Neal-Russell will keep her Roth IRA account and Mr. Russell will keep his 401K account."

"He has four times as much money in his account."

"That's not true," Max says.

I don't know exactly how much either of us has. Max is the accountant. He kept track.

"The proceeds from the sale of the house will be split in half." Phillip continues.

"Sale of the house? The house isn't for sale."

"The house will be put on the market within ten days of the divorce settlement. And, at that time, you are asked to vacate the property so as to not impede with the selling."

Where am I going to live? What about Erika?

"You can move home." Mom says, reading my mind. "I converted your room into an exercise room, but we can still fit the roll-away in there. You just need to be up and out of the room Monday, Thursday, and Saturday by seven. That's when my Pilates instructor comes over." Erika has a room at my parents'. She doesn't stay over much since puberty hit, but the finished attic is set up for her in case she ever decides to run away from home. I get a roll-away in the exercise room.

I sink down in my chair. "Anything else?"

"The Passat." Phillip says, his voice is almost a whisper. "The car and the loan are in Mr. Russell's name. Either you can purchase the car from my client at fair market value or you need to turn the vehicle over."

"Are you serious?" I ask. It's only in *Mr. Russell's name* because I couldn't get down to the dealership to sign. I don't think Max has ever driven the car.

"Cheer up, Paigey," Joe says. "Maybe we can get you some alimony. What do you say Max? Give my cousin a few bucks a month. Just some spending money for lattes and lip waxings."

I cover my lip with one hand and point to the door with the other. "Joe. Wait outside."

"Paige, don't be rude," Mom says, but when I shoot her a look she shuts up. She doesn't want to join Joe in the lobby.

I shuffle the papers around mostly for show. "Where is the section on alimony?"

Phillip clears his throat. I have a feeling this is hard on him. He must pity me. I hate pity.

"Mr. Russell is not offering alimony or child support."

"What? This is bullshit." Erika's list of requirements nags at me, but I'm done being polite.

"Paige," Max says. "You have a degree in mathematics and an MBA."

"I don't have a job. I've never had a job."

"You no longer have a young child at home to care for

and with your education we can argue your earning potential is very promising." Phillip says. Then he dives into the details of bank accounts, credit card bills, mortgage payments, and health insurance.

I try to listen, but my head is ringing. A sharp pain has developed in the back of my neck and runs through my head to my temple. I may be sick.

"Do you have any questions so far?" Phillip asks.

"Do you expect me to sign this today?"

"You have twenty days to reply to the defendant summons. Like I said, Mr. Russell would like to wrap this matter up quickly. If we could settle any outstanding matters today..."

"Sorry, Max. I think I need some more time to look this over." I stand to leave.

"Wait." Mom grabs my arm. "I have a question." She looks across to my soon-to-be ex. "Max, you and Paige were so good together. You kept her grounded and you're great with Erika. Why do you want a divorce?"

"Let me answer that," Phillip says. "The grounds for dissolution of marriage are cruel and inhuman treatment."

"What?" I'm ready to leap across the table and strangle my bastard husband. "Are you saying I was cruel to you?"

"You did stab the man," Mom says. "Twice."

A bad day is an excuse to go to bed early
and catch up on your beauty sleep.

Chapter 5

The problem with the temporary insanity defense is the definition of temporary. A stoplight is a temporary delay in your commute. A nap is a temporary break in your day. The earth experienced a temporary ice age.

My temporary insanity lasted twelve hours.

Max told me he was moving out as I stood there in the kitchen preparing our anniversary dinner. He kissed my forehead. He insulted my cooking. He said we were over. I stabbed him in the ribs.

It wasn't premeditated. How could it have been? It was self-defense. Max was attacking my life. Beating it. Killing it.

The two inch paring knife blade went in easily, almost the whole way. Max was a little overweight, so the first inch must have been all skin and fat. It went in at an angle, which we later learned saved him from a punctured lung.

I don't think the stabbing hurt, initially. The look on

his face was more shock than pain. He was even able to speak. "Shit. What did you do that for?"

The knife remained sticking out of the side of his chest. I didn't pull it out. I didn't react at all. I'd seen enough medical dramas to know when you impaled yourself on a wrought iron fence or have an issue with a nail gun, you don't pull out the imbedded object because you could bleed to death.

Max never did watch the same shows I did, preferring the History Channel or CNBC. He pulled the knife out and blood started flowing fast. Then I reacted.

I put a dish cloth on the wound. Max yanked it away. The pain must have finally registered.

"Stop crying, Paige." Max yelled. His breathing sounded like an overweight, middle aged man who'd just run a mile. "And call an ambulance."

I dialed nine-one-one and the operator asked me what my emergency was.

"My husband needs an ambulance."

"I will send help. What is his medical problem?"

"He's bleeding."

"From where?"

"His chest. Just hurry."

"Is he injured?"

"Yes." Of course he's injured, or I wouldn't have called. Not wanting to say that I'd stabbed my husband I don't hang up. I put the phone on the counter.

The police arrived in under six minutes. It had felt like an hour, listening to Max, who sat at the kitchen table cursing and sucking breath between his front teeth.

They banged on the front door, ignoring the door bell,

their hands poised on their guns. I pointed them to the kitchen.

The younger officer immediately went to work on Max, laying him on the floor, applying pressure to the wound. I was told to sit in a kitchen chair. Moments later the paramedics crashed a gurney through my hallway, scraping the wallpaper and nicking paint.

The paramedics loaded Max while the police officers asked him questions about the *incident*. I couldn't hear everything over the crackle of radios and the additional conversations, but what I heard sounded ominous, with words like *assailant* and *assault*. Firemen arrived. More police. I felt like I should offer everyone coffee.

As they rolled Max out of the house I got up to follow, but the young officer grabbed my arm. Apparently, I was going to get my own ride. I didn't struggle.

A fireman, fulfilling his duty, turned off the oven and pulled out my burnt romantic dinner.

Max was taken to Albany Memorial hospital. I was taken to the police station. My first impression - this place is efficient. Or maybe it was just a slow crime day. I was interrogated and booked all within two hours. Under direct questioning, I broke down and confessed.

Officer 1: Did you stab your husband?

Me: Sort of.

Officer 2: Were you trying to kill your husband?

Me: No.

Officer 1: Why did you stab your husband?

Me: He said he was moving out. (Pause.) And he insulted my cooking. What's going to happen now?

What happened was, the next morning I was released.

All charges were dropped because during the night the police officers had interviewed Max and he said he would not testify and did not want to press charges. I was free.

Mom met me outside the police station. She said she couldn't find a parking spot. I think she didn't want to go inside. She offered to bring me home or out for breakfast or to her house. I wanted to go to Albany Memorial.

Max was in room 404. Our anniversary date was April fourth—how ironic. I stopped in the gift shop and bought some flowers before going up to his room.

He looked good sitting up in his hospital bed watching CNN. He'd showered and was rested. Unlike me, I was wearing my wrinkled wrap dress and I'd slept only a few hours in a chair. He said he felt fine and the doctors said no serious damage was done, though he needed stitches and a tetanus shot. He'd stayed the night because our insurance covered ninety percent of the cost on overnight stays but only fifty percent on emergency room visits.

I apologized and gave Max a hug. He patted my back with the kind of warm affection a houseguest gives an annoying, slobbering retriever.

"I'm really sorry," I said again and took a seat on the vinyl chair. "I didn't mean to hurt you. I love you."

Max used the remote attached to the bed to change from CNN to FOX News.

"When can you go home?" I perched on the side of his bed and laid a hand on his leg.

Max muted the television then removed my hand from his thigh. "I'm not going home. I'm moving out."

I stood up. "Why?"

"You know. We aren't good together any more. I need

a woman who can be there for me. Everyone and everything comes before me. Erika, the booster committee, your parents, Trisha."

I stumbled back a step. How could I forget he started this mess? I'd blocked the fact he really wanted to end our marriage. I grabbed the wheeled tray that held his lunch to steady myself.

"Hey," Max motioned to his untouched lunch. "Can you run out and get me a sandwich or something? Hospital food is almost as bad as Paige-food."

"You ass!" I grabbed the fork off the tray and slashed at his head wildly. The tines met the tip of his ear.

Max screamed.

Nurses rushed in.

I was promptly returned to the police station. And so ended my twelve hours of temporary insanity.

Size does matter. Don't settle for
less than eleven and a half inches.

Chapter 6

I'd sum up my divorce proceedings as quick and painful—
like a cheap bandage that leaves glue on your arm but takes
off the hair. It was quick because I gave up. I accepted all
of Max's terms and signed my part. And it was painful
because ... it just was. Max was so calm and cold. He
really wanted this divorce. To my credit I did maintain
some dignity because I never cried.

The only shining moment came when we were leaving.
As I shook Phillip Rogers' hand, he held it a little longer
than is customary and he said, "It was good to see you
again, Paige." Finally, he stopped calling me *Ms. O'Neal-
Russell*. And I'd swear he even gave me a slight smile.

Instead of worrying about my lack of housing,
transportation, and money, Mom and I go to La Casa Fiesta
Mexican Restaurant to celebrate my new *independence*.

To start, we order queso dip and Diet Cokes. Chips and
queso are so much better with a Margarita, but I resist.

"Paige," Mom sets her menu down and takes a deep breath. "There's something I've been meaning to tell you. Your father and I—"

"Are getting divorced? I can give you the name of a lawyer I wouldn't recommend."

"Please. O'Neals don't divorce."

I throw up my hands. "Excuse me."

She shrugs. "You know what I mean. Anyway, your father and I hired a private investigator to dig up some dirt on Max. We thought it would help with the divorce. You stabbed him, but perhaps if he had a cocaine addiction or a second wife—"

"Mom, why are you telling me this now? I just signed all the papers."

"Because we didn't find anything incriminating on Max." She pulls an envelope out of her purse. "He seems to be a descent upstanding citizen."

"That's great news." If the waiter was within earshot I would be ordering tequila right now.

"There's something you should know and I wanted you to hear it from family." She rests her hand on mine. "Max is seeing someone."

I feign surprise. "We're been separated for over five months." While this confirms my fears, I still have no way of knowing if he dated while we were married.

"It's Vanessa."

"Vanessa? Vanessa Davis? My Vanessa Davis?"

"Yes."

Vanessa Davis has been my hairdresser for five years. She's wonderful. Great color. Great cuts. Great *friend*? I've been telling her intimate details of my life for years. Only

Father Nolan and Trisha have more dirt on me.

I put my hand over my mouth to fight back the feeling growing in my stomach. Suddenly, I remember. I'd introduced them. This was my fault. Last winter I'd made Max an appointment with Vanessa. He'd never spent more than ten dollars on a haircut and I wanted him to get a decent cut before our family Christmas photo. The picture needed to be perfect.

Mom hands me the envelope. There's a black and white photo of Max helping Vanessa out of his car. The next he's holding her hand as they walk into a restaurant. The third, they're kissing just inside the doorway.

"Don't worry, dear. I've come up with a solution. I've already talked to Marge. She can work you in next week. I'm thinking highlights and a cut. Maybe something a little different." She reaches out for a strand that hasn't been touched by color or sheers since the day Max left.

"I'm not going to your hairdresser." Losing a hairstylist is the bigger catastrophe here according to my mother. "I'll be fine. Let's order."

I try to read over the menu, but my mind keeps returning to Vanessa. When did they start dating? Was Max having an affair? Is she why he left me? Hairdressers should have to take an oath, like lawyers and psychologists. Everything said should be held in confidence. I'd told Vanessa a lot of intimate details like how Max and I listened to Sinatra music during sex and how he loves the smell of baby powder. Maybe she used that information to seduce him. Covered herself in baby powder and played Sinatra as she trimmed his graying hair.

"Are you ready to order?" The waiter asks as he sets

down the sodas and dip.

"Yes, a double margarita on the rocks with salt." Barbie will have to let this one slide.

"Nothing to eat?"

"I don't have much of an appetite." I hand him my menu.

Mom orders pollo-something then launches into a series of questions. "Where are you going to live?"

"I'll get an apartment."

"What will you do for money?"

"I'll get a job."

"What about the car?"

"I'll buy a car."

"It doesn't sound like you've thought any of this through." She is obviously disappointed.

Finally, my double margarita arrives. The first swallows tastes delicious, and the last swallow improves my mood.

"I think I'm ready to date," I say. So what if Max is seeing Vanessa. I can date, too. That's what I'm going to do. Start dating. Maybe right now.

Mom looks surprised, yet happy. "That's wonderful." She picks up her Vera Bradley handbag and rifles through it. "I was talking about you to Barbara Alkins. Her son also just went through a divorce. He's a tad older than you…forty-nine I think… I bet you hit it off."

"No thanks. I can find my own dates."

She laughs. "Where?"

"Maybe right here." I scan the bar area for prey. The pickings are slim on a Friday afternoon. The only other patron is a hairy man in a wrinkled suit. He looks lonely nursing a beer at the bar. God, the man is more than hairy, he's practically furry. It's sprouting from everywhere. In his ears, on his neck and on his forehead—it's more than a monobrow. He doesn't have a beard. I have to assume he's shaved in the last ten minutes.

The wooly mammoth waves when he notices me staring. I quickly drop my head.

"Oh, Paige." I can feel sympathy oozing from Mom's smile. "It's not easy dating after a divorce. Especially in your thirties. Especially when you have a teenage daughter. That's a lot of baggage. But I'm sure there are some good men still out there."

The waiter drops off Mom's lunch and asks if I want another drink. Do I ever. But I decline, because I'm going to Erika's soccer game in a few hours.

"What about that Phillip?" Mom asks between bites.

"Max's lawyer. What about him?"

"He wasn't wearing a wedding ring."

"I don't think so."

Maybe Mom does have a sort of intuition. She doesn't know that Phillip and I were friendly in college. And if Max can date my hairdresser, why can't I date his lawyer?

You can do anything. You can be anything.
Poor G.I. Joe had to wait for leave to have any fun.

Chapter 7

Erika's soccer game has triple the usual crowd because it is
Friday night and St. Mary's doesn't have a football team.
Instead, the school rallies around soccer. The boys have
two Friday home games in September and in October. The
girls are given one each month and one in November. The
concession stand is serving popcorn, soda, and candy
bars—it doesn't have a grill. There are eight cheerleaders
making noise on the sideline. The girls soccer program is
only worthy of the JV cheerleaders and then, only on
Friday nights.

Mom and I sit on the third row bleachers and cheer
when we hear them announce Erika is returning to the
game. Don't know why the idiot coach took her out in the
first place. St. Mary's is only down by one and Erika has
had more shots on goal than anyone else on the team.

"It's about time the coach put seventeen back in," says
a man behind me.

I beam with motherly pride. As if her dribbling and kicking skills could be attributed to my parenting.

"That's my granddaughter," Mom says. While I beam inwardly, she prefers to share with the world.

"Erika O'Neal is your granddaughter?"

"Yes."

"Great girl. She's in my social science class."

I turn around and see the infamous Mr. Barber—part basketball coach, part faux-priest, part new teacher all the girls have a crush on. I'd rather Erika's male teachers dress in tweed and be older than my father. Mr. Barber is in his thirties and instead of a sensible blazer he's wearing jeans, a Dr. Pepper T-shirt, and a St. Mary's baseball cap with his blond hair sticking out underneath.

"I'm Nancy." Mom offers her hand.

"Nice to meet you. I'm Isaac."

I don't bother to introduce myself. I pretend to be interested in the action on the field—a time out.

"This is Erika's mother, Paige."

"We've met," I say.

"Yes, in Father Nolan's office." He gives me a wink like *Father Nolan's office* is code for a secluded motel on Route 44.

I turn my attention back to the game. A St. Mary's player heads the ball and Erika gets it. She dribbles past one defender—it looks like she's dancing with the ball, her feet move so smoothly. Then she passes the ball up to the other forward. This will be a beautiful assist. But the whistle blows. St. Mary's is called off-sides.

"That's crap!" I stand up. I want to yell *bullshit*, but we are a Catholic school. "What the hell is wrong with you?"

"Boooo! Bad call." Mr. Barber joins me. I think he's mocking me.

"Paige, sit down." Mom pulls on my arm.

And I do. "Where do they get these refs? Title IX may require schools to offer women sports, but I guess they can get any hack off the street to referee."

"I'm in the mood for some Junior Mints." Mom can't get away quick enough. It's the fourth game of the season. The other parents seem to sit farther and farther away each game. By the last game, they may be watching from a closed circuit television inside the school.

"That wasn't a very Barbie thing to do." Mr. Barber moves down a row and sits next to me.

"What?"

"Yelling obscenities at a soccer game. Isn't one of your Barbie rules having good manners or being polite?" He's smiling.

I shake my head. "You've seen the list?"

"I've approved the list. And if this experiment somehow has a happy ending I'll post the list in my blog. With Erika's permission, of course."

"You don't think it'll have a happy ending?"

"No. Not really. It's a lot of unrealistic pressure to face in one semester. Cool idea. Not very plausible."

"Do you give all your students this much encouragement?"

"You're not my student."

"Does Erika know you think her experiment will be a failure?" I'll poke him in his Caribbean blue eyes if he put one negative thought in her head.

"I'm one hundred percent behind her. And if she concludes Barbie is not the ultimate role model, that's not a failure. Maybe her subject was to blame."

"Well, Mr. Barber, I'm trying. She can't expect me to change overnight."

"You've started?" He tilts his head forward.

"Yes. I'm wearing a skirt and heels at a soccer game." Can't believe I have to point this out to him. "You know, the easiest thing would be for you to tell Erika this experiment is inappropriate for a sophomore level class and she should just take the final exam."

"Now, how is that encouraging my student one hundred percent?"

At this point, I'd be disappointed if Mr. Barber decided to call off the experiment. He is so smug. He's certain this isn't going to work. Maybe Erika is on to something. What's wrong with being independent, beautiful, and multitalented?

When the first half ends Mr. Barber stands up. "I have to go." He offers me a hand. "Good luck, Paige. I'm looking forward to the final report." I bet he is.

That night after the game—which ended in a tie—I find my second assessment on my nightstand. I fill out the survey a little bit more honestly this time.

Daily Self-Assessment   *Friday, September 10*
Rate the degree to which you agree with the statement.
      5–completely agree 1–completely disagree
1. I accomplished something today. *2*
2. I felt connected with my friends and family today. *2*
3. I was interested in sex today. *1*
4. I laughed today. *1*
5. I am looking forward to tomorrow. *5*
Notes: *I had one drink. Tomorrow I will have none. I promise! Tomorrow, I will make this work!*

*Always dress to impress, whether it's for your mother,
Your man, or the camera inside the ATM machine.*

Chapter 8

I wake up Saturday morning and get dressed in a lavender
yoga outfit I received for my birthday. I should be worried
about lack of housing, money, and car, but I want to focus
my attention on making this Barbie thing work—and
proving Mr. Barber wrong.

I pull my naked Barbie out of my night stand. "Where
should we start, Barb?" We examine Erika's list and decide
to stick with the simple stuff.

3. Exercise (4/week).

Max has a collection of exercise equipment in the
basement. Contraptions to help you do sit-ups without
hurting your neck. A strength resistance machine that uses
a series of large, colored rubber bands. A stationary bike
that powers a small television if you pedal fast enough. No
thanks.

Instead, I call Trisha and beg her to take me to Tri-city
Fitness. She's a member and can invite me as a guest for

free. She agrees so long as I promise we're going to exercise. Last time I went I didn't burn many calories because they'd just put new bulbs in their tanning beds.

Trisha and I have been friends for almost two decades. We'd met the summer we worked at the town park. I was a lifeguard at the pool where I was safely removed from every animal—except the occasional bird—by a ten-foot-high chain-link fence. Trisha was a lifeguard at the lake where squirrels darted in and out of the nearby trees and minnows tried to bite off your toes. I was a tall, white rail in my red bathing suit, like a Popsicle stick stained red after all the cherry flavored ice melted away. Trisha was short and curvy with coffee-and-cream colored skin.

For the first two weeks of that summer we didn't exchange a word, just tight lip smiles as we passed in the locker room. During our lunch breaks I'd eat Fritos and Diet Coke and read romance novels. Trisha bummed cigarettes from the old men fishing on the dock. It seemed we couldn't have been more opposite. Then one Friday she asked me for a ride home. It was raining and she had *borrowed* her dad's motorcycle, which she couldn't drive on wet roads.

We hopped into my Cavalier and a friendship—the best friendship—began. I found Trisha fascinating. She'd lived everywhere—Hungary, Ireland, Korea, Miami. She smoked, she swore, she drank. She was afraid of nothing. I think she found me interesting, too. She couldn't believe the bubble I lived in. No smoking. No swearing—other than the occasional *damn*. No drinking. And I was afraid of everything that breathed, literally. The only area where I had more experience was with boys because Trisha only dated men. But Trisha never pushed me into anything. She'd offer me a cigarette or a sip of beer and if I said no, she took it to mean no.

Trisha began at St. Mary's that fall, and from then on I always had a place to sit at lunch. We spent the next two years closer than sisters. We went to separate colleges and kept in touch through phone calls and letters. After college, we didn't see each other for years. Trisha's parents moved to Australia, so she had no reason to come back to New York.

Trisha finally returned to Albany for our ten year high school reunion. That's where she found true love. Not with one the boys from our graduating class, but with the bartender. That night she brought Manny back to her hotel room. What started as a one-night stand led to marriage.

On the way to Tri-city Fitness, I stop by the toy store to get my Barb some clothes. It feels strange carrying a naked Barbie doll around. Maybe clothes will help.

What does a girl wear to sit in a purse? I look for something I might wear like jeans and sweater. There's a pair of flared jeans with sequins, but no plain shirts. I settle for a wild looking peasant top. For a moment I debate a pair of platform sandals, but the jeans and top are already costing me over ten dollars.

Barb gets changed in the car. Then I throw away the pink packaging from her new clothes. All traces of my new lifestyle gone.

"Nice," I squeeze her little hand and tuck her in my purse. I'd cleaned out one compartment just for Barb so she wouldn't accidentally get a Tic-Tac stuck in her hair.

I wait for Trisha by the front door of the gym. When I

see her walking across the parking lot, I know something's wrong.

"Are you okay?" I ask before we go in.

She gives me a half-hearted smile. Her puffy eyes tell the real truth. "I got my period," she says. "It's kinda funny. I've spayed or neutered hundreds of animals, and it turns out I'm as infertile as they are." Trisha and Manny have been trying to get pregnant for a year and a half. At first they'd laugh it off and say maybe next month.

"I'm sorry. I'm ready, willing, and able to carry your offspring." I give her a hug. "Just say the word."

"This was only our first round of in vitro. I'd like to give it another go." She shrugs. "And don't you think you have enough going on?" Trisha seems to be having second thoughts about my suitability to be a surrogate. When I was married, she was ready to go forward. She spoke with her doctor. She called her lawyer (only to find out surrogacy contacts are void in New York). We were setting up appointments. Then I stabbed my husband and she has second thoughts.

"Maybe." I motion toward the gym. "We don't have to do this today."

"No you don't. You aren't going to use me as an excuse. Get your ass in there."

After signing in and unloading our gym bags in the locker room, Trisha and I climb onto elliptical trainers. It's my first day so I set the machine to level one, the course to beginner and the time to fifteen minutes. My legs easily move with the machine. Very nice. Very relaxing. I watch the time tick down. Fourteen minutes left. I look at the calories burned. One!

I thought you burn two calories a minute while sleeping. I'm only burning one per minute while exercising?

"What level are you on?" I ask Trisha.

"Eight, but I wouldn't…"

Seven it is. I stab the up arrow until I reach my goal. This is better. I'm burning a calorie about every ten seconds. Yep, this is better. I'll just lean on the sides a bit. A cramp develops under my ribcage. I hunch over for relief, my head inches away from the control panel. I have a death grip on the side rails.

"You okay?" Trisha reaches over and changes my level to four. "Let's start here."

When my fifteen minutes are up, I abandon my machine to a woman in a jogger bra and Everlast shorts. Trisha marches on so I pretend to stretch to the other side of her.

"This sudden interest in exercise is from the Barbie list, right?" Trisha asks.

"Yep."

"No offense, but fifteen minutes on a machine isn't going to get you a Barbie body. That only comes from a combination of anorexia and plastic surgery."

"She's not anorexic." Now I sound like Erika.

"Well, she's damn skinny with missile breasts."

"Actually there's a reason for her figure." I finished reading all three Barbie books late last night.

"Our oppressive male society?"

"More like the laws of physics. Barbie is roughly one-sixth the size of a human woman, so all her clothes have to be scaled down to one-sixth their size. However, you can't make silk or cotton or denim one-sixth of its thickness. Barbie needs to have big breasts, a tiny waist and narrow hips to accommodate the seams and hems of her clothing." I feel like a professor and suddenly wish for a chalkboard. "Imagine if you will, Barbie is wearing a skirt with elastic, a sweater, and perhaps a fitted jacket. If Barbie's waist was proportional to a thin human woman, those three layers of clothing, elastic, and stitching would cause her waist line to bulge out beyond her breasts. She'd look like she's wearing a pool float around her waist."

"You learn something new every day." Trisha says.

"Store mannequins have as little fat as Barbie and the dolls made since 2000 have larger waists and hips." I make my last point.

"Paige, I'm proud of you. This Barbie experiment is ridiculous, but you are once again in control. I haven't seen you motivated since Max walked out."

"Thanks." *I think.*

"I'm just glad you're focused again." Trisha steps off the machine. "And if I can help in any way. I will."

No doubt. Trisha is my Midge. But I don't need her help, I have to give her mine. I want to … I need to … carry her baby.

I waste the rest of the day shopping. Unlike Barbie, I hate shopping. I don't like salespeople offering to help me and I don't like the salespeople ignoring me either—like the girls in Sunglass Hut who prefer to assist the hot, twenty-something guy with the Maserati key ring. They have to know you can get the key ring without buying the car.

Every purchase is agonizing. I'm usually a responsible person. I don't have a job. I don't have alimony. And my savings won't get me through the month. Yet I still buy eighteen dollar mascara, hip hugging jeans in size six (when eights would actually snap closed), and two pairs of high heeled shoes.

When I'm safely in my car, I open my purse.

"I might not be able to pay the electric bill, but I have a new pair of kick-ass zebra print heels. I blame you."

Barb smiles back at me. She seems to know the master plan and this puts me at ease. This must be what it's like for Father Nolan when he talks about faith. Just on a much, much smaller scale.

Good posture is better than a
push-up bra and high heels.

Chapter 9

The happiest day of my life? My wedding day. Granted, if I knew then what I know now, maybe it would have put a damper on my delight. Luckily, I was blind. It was a sixty degree, partly cloudy, breezeless, April day. We were married in St. Mary's with 150 guests sharing our joy. Flowers were everywhere, birds sang and butterflies fluttered in the background. Six-year old Erika made a beautiful flower girl. Yet as wonderful and picturesque as it was, the smile plastered across my face for the entire day was due to anticipation for the future, not the Disney-like present. We were leaving the next morning for a week in Aruba. When we returned, we were going to start house hunting. I was finishing my MBA. Eventually—not immediately, maybe in a few years—we were going to have children of our own—hopefully a boy first, Max junior, then a girl, Amy. I didn't expect things to always be rosy. I knew grandparents would pass away, roofs would leak, stocks would dip, and Max and I would steer through the rough times together—happy and secure in our love.

Now Max is gone, and I have no copilot, just one passenger depending on me. And I don't know what to expect from the future. Only a few things are certain, I need to move out, get a job, and find transportation. Will I ever meet someone? Do I want to? Should I bother? I'm thirty-four, so if I meet a guy I like this year (which seems unlikely because I hope to be pregnant by Christmas), we date for two years, are engaged for one, I'll be thirty-seven or thirty-eight on my wedding day. Erika would be in college. Then we'd need a year to ourselves to enjoy each other's company before we can consider having another child. Now, I'm thirty-nine. And if we want a second child two years after that, I'm forty-something, and the alarm on my biological clock will have been buzzing for years.

None of that matters right now. Basic needs first—shelter, money, and transportation.

I had taken a vacation from worrying to focus on my Barbie. I promised myself that today, Sunday, I'd buckle down and begin tackling the real issues. I choose Sunday because everything I need—employment, apartment, and auto—are easily found in the fat Sunday *Gazette*.

When I wake up at seven, I'm tempted to run to the corner convenience store for the paper and a cup of coffee, but Erika's rules nag me.

1. Complete makeup. (Daily)
2. Hair maintenance. (Daily)
4. Feminine Attire. (Always)

So instead of heading out in sweats, I take a shower and almost run out of hot water by the time I wash, shampoo, and use a five-minute conditioning rinse. Barb watches from the towel rack, smiling approval.

As of two days ago, I was a lip gloss and eyeliner girl. Not any more. Now, I take the time to use foundation (new), blush, lip liner (borrowed from Erika), eyelash curler, tweezers, brow pencil, mascara (eighteen dollars—new), and perfume. It's still subtle and natural. My lifeless brown hair takes the most time to tame. Each section of hair needs to be moussed, blown under and sprayed in place. As I pull at a front section, I realize I really need a trim, and I also need a new hairdresser. Do they still make that hair cutting tool you hook to a vacuum?

Finally, I'm ready to dress—clingy beige sweater, brown wool pants, and my new heeled boots that'll hurt my feet before I make it to the front door. I throw on my leather coat, because September in New York can mean sunny and seventy or forty with fog.

Taking a look in the full-length mirror I think, *Not bad.* Taking a look at the clock, nine-fifteen, I think, *Very bad.* I'm going to have to shave some time off my new beauty routine—or shave my head.

Erika is still sleeping so I make the trip alone. Instead of going to the convenience store a few blocks from my home, I decide to reward myself with a sun-dried tomato bagel with low-fat, veggie cream cheese and a skinny latte. I throw Barb into my faux-leather tote and head out to the chain bakery-coffee-bar.

The parking lot is crowded with luxury cars—Lexus, BMW, Mercedes—and few high-end American cars—the kind of crowd that can afford five-dollar chocolate drizzled croissants and four-dollar cups of coffee. I park between a

Z3 and a Hummer then walk to the newspaper box on the corner. I put in my six quarters.

When I look up, I see a Channel Ten news van has pulled into the parking lot and is setting up. Maybe someone choked to death on a mini-Bundt cake or perhaps a celebrity is here signing autographs and raising awareness about carbohydrate intake. Being generally nosy, I walk closer to the van in hopes of some answers.

The well-manicured newswoman—I wonder how long it took *her* to get ready this morning—is interviewing a gray-haired man. I can't hear what they're talking about and decide it's time for that latte because I'm going into caffeine withdrawal.

Before I hit the front glass door, I realize the "Excuse me, Ma'am" is directed at me. I turn around to face the newswoman and her cameraman. She introduces herself and asks if I will answer a few questions on camera about our mayor. Instinctively, I want to say no.

What would Barbie do?

We girls can do anything. I imagine Barb saying from the depths of my handbag. It's her slogan from the nineties.

I pat my bag for reassurance and agree to the interview, and for a brief moment I see it all leading toward a new glamorous career in acting or news casting. I could be discovered. Barbie has done it! All it took was nearly two hours of prep time. This was too easy. Mr. Isaac Barker is going to eat his words.

A little background. Our Mayor, Jonas Whiting, was sentenced to a two-year jail term last week for statutory rape. Turns out he'd been sleeping with his housekeeper's seventeen-year old daughter for the past year. On top of that, the housekeeper and her family are illegal immigrants. On top of that, Mayor Whiting is a married man of some thirty years. On top of that, his twenty-five-year old son is now engaged to the same housekeeper's daughter. Mayor Whiting plans to serve out his political term and his jail term at the same time. I know the story inside and out because it's steamy and my hairdresser Vanessa—or should I say ex-hairdresser—also does Mrs. Whiting.

Before the camera lights come on, I give the woman my name, town of residence and occupation—I say I'm a freelance artist because there's no way to prove I'm not. A few people gather around to watch.

"We're rolling," the camera man says.

My heart beat goes from a steady-joggers pace to a sprint-for-your-life speed. You'd think I was being chased by a kitten.

"Do you think Mayor Whiting's sentence is fair?" she asks.

I take a breath before answering. "As a mother of a teenage daughter I find his actions intolerable. Not being in the courtroom, I can only have faith in our judicial process. From what the media has reported, it seems he had a fair trial with good legal representation."

How did that sound? Wish I could have thought of a better phrase than *good legal representation.*

The woman goes on to ask me more questions, which I answer in the same yes-but-no-but-maybe kind of way. I can see she is disappointed in my responses, probably hoping for something like "Burn the bastard at the stake." I need to open up a little more.

"Would you vote for Mayor Whiting if he were to run

for another term?"

"No. Any man who cannot understand the sanctity of marriage and the importance of a vow cannot be trusted to take out the trash, let alone run our city."

When camera is lowered, one woman claps at my response. The newswoman tells me I did great, and it'll be on tonight's five o'clock. I feel like I actually did do a good job. I also feel like crying.

Why did Max break our vow? Why did he leave me for Vanessa? What am I going to do now?

I make my order a to-go. Coffee and bagel for me and a bear claw for Erika. On the drive home I debate going to mass, but I just spent seven dollars on breakfast. That would be a waste.

Erika joins me at the kitchen table. She takes the sport section turning to the last page looking for the girls soccer standings. I start searching for housing.

"I think we may need to get an apartment. I'm not in a position to buy a house. It'll just be for a few months."

"Okay."

I scan the classifieds for two-bathroom apartments in a safe area. Two places have definite possibilities, and three more are maybes. The advertised rent is more than Max and I pay in mortgage on this house, but I wouldn't have property taxes. I circle each of the ads and promise myself to call first thing tomorrow.

With a few viable housing prospects, I now need a way to pay for them. Reluctantly, I look for Employment which is not a section on its own but the last few pages of the classifieds. First, I waste more time and window-shop. I'm not really looking for anything—guess I need a car, but that can wait. Treadmills, farm equipment, furniture, pedigreed puppies, nothing very interesting. Until I run across 'HORSE FOR SALE—3yr-old Palomino, healthy, must sell, $2000 or BO.'

My heart leaps.

12. Get a pet. (Soon as possible)

And I love horses—at least in pictures. I've never ridden one, touched one or even been close enough to smell one. Every August I go to the Off Track Betting Tele-theater to bet on the ponies. They're beautiful creatures. And Barbie has had horses—a Palomino named Dallas and even an Arabian called Blinking Beauty. I've never had a pet, though Erika once won a goldfish at the fair, and I slept in the car that night. Luckily the fish disappeared the next day. If I had the money...

Money, dammit! Focus, Paige!

I scour the help-wanted ads, from C.F.O. to school custodian. I give serious consideration to each before, inevitably, dismissing them. Bank Manager—don't have the years of experience. Truck Driver—don't have the right class license. Hooter's Waitress—don't have the boobs. And there's no listing for a thirty-four-year old model who is out of shape (Requirement 11 will have to wait).

After all my searching, I'm only qualified for one job—Computer Help Desk Technician. Need a four-year degree, able to work flexible hours, start immediately, and experience helpful though not required. The job doesn't sound interesting—Barbie would never be a computer help desk technician—and I don't think I'd be very good at it. I can't write programs or scripts. I can't network a series of printers. I can't even get the spam off my own laptop.

"Here's a job," I say. "Think I could get a job working at a computer help desk?"

"That's your idea of a fulfilling career?" Erika raises her eyebrows.

"It's my idea of a paycheck."

"Angelina Jolie has her dream job and she brings home a good paycheck."

"Well, it doesn't hurt to have a resume." I grab Barb from my purse.

Erika rolls her eyes at the doll.

"She's my inspiration. And don't give me that look. You started this."

"I've created a monster."

Barb and I go into our home office, boot up the computer, and start my word-processing program. After entering my name, address, and education, I still have half a page to fill. I up the font size, increase the margins, and still have half a blank life. Since my potential employer probably isn't interested in knowing I worked at Dairy Queen fifteen years ago, I'm forced to embellish my nonprofessional accomplishments.

Published in Times Union: Truth—had a letter printed on the subject of noisy street sweepers.

Volunteered in homeless shelter: Truth—they *fired* me for forgetting to wear my hairnet.

Successfully ran home-based business: Truth—by successfully I mean I was a Pampered Chef consultant for about a week. I only wanted the discount to buy some stoneware.

After adding a few more glorified details my resume doesn't look half bad. I spell check and reread, satisfied with the end product. I decide not to apply for the help desk job.

"I don't want this job," I say to Barb. I'd be disappointment if I didn't get the job and depressed if I did. *Something better will come along.*

Instead, I waste time taking career assessment tests online. Turns out my ideal jobs are movie producer or U.N. ambassador. Neither job is something I'm likely to see advertised in the Sunday paper.

The phone rings later that evening while I'm on eBay showing Barb how much a pair of her vintage shoes is worth to collectors.

"Hello."

"Paige, you look great! I could hardly believe it was you. And you sounded so put together. I'd hate to give Barbie credit... I'm proud of you girl!" Trisha says.

"Thanks. What are you talking about?"

"You were just on the news, Channel 10. That was you, wasn't it?"

I'd forgotten about the time. "Did I really do okay?"

"You were better than okay. You were intelligent, beautiful, and confident."

"You didn't happen to TiVo it?"

"No, sorry. My machine is full. I'm addicted to a new series on Animal Planet."

I let Trisha run on for a few minutes telling me how wonderful I am. That never gets old. I only end our conversation when call waiting beeps. This time it's Father Nolan, who also saw the interview, and who also thinks I looked like a new, improved woman. He didn't tape the news, either. I cut him off when another call comes in. This time from Mom. Am I the only one who missed the news? When call waiting beeps during Mom's gushing I don't click over. I'm enjoying her rare praise too much.

"Will you be home later?" Mom asks.

"Yes, why?"

"I need to drop something off."

We say our goodbyes and end the call. I immediately check my voicemail message.

"Paige, it's Max."

I don't breathe.

"Just saw you on the news."

My heart stops.

"So I thought I'd give you a quick call."

My knees quake.

"Just wondering when I can pick up the Passat."

Fists clench.

"I think I have a buyer interested."

Lips purse.

"How about Wednesday?"

Blood pressure skyrockets. I'd call him back and give him hell if it wasn't dinner time. Low blood sugar might make me say something I'll regret.

Barb sits not-so-discreetly next to the toaster while Erika and I make dinner. Barb's angelic face smiles at our healthy mother-daughter relationship. Barbie has never had children, but she's been a model big sister to Skipper.

"You know, she doesn't count as your new pet." Erika says as she strains the spaghetti.

"Huh?" I stir the sauce that's been heated in the microwave.

"You need a real pet. Not a pet rock. Not a doll."

"She's not a pet." I move Barb from the counter to the table, next to my water glass.

"She's eating with us?"

"Don't be silly. She doesn't eat people food."

"People food?"

"You know what I mean."

We take our seats. As we fill our bowls with spaghetti, the doorbell rings. Before I can get to the front door it rings again. I know it has to be Mom. If we don't get to the door within ten seconds she assumes we're lying unconscious on the floor.

"I don't see why you just won't give me a key," she says when I open the door.

"Hey, Mom." She follows me into the kitchen.

"You're eating spaghetti with jar sauce for Sunday dinner?" Mom asks. "Why didn't you come over? We had a nice ham."

"I need to carb-load, Gram," Erika says. "Big workout tomorrow."

Mom sighs. "I just wanted to bring you this. Your father and I have been talking and decided...well...you'll see. Open it after I leave." She hands me a blue envelope.

"You're not staying?"

"No, I have ironing to do." She kisses Erika on the head. "Love you." And she's gone.

Mom's notorious for buying cards. Not just Valentine's Day, Christmas or birthdays, but also congratulations-on-buying-a-new-car or thinking-of-you type greetings. I knew a divorce-sympathy card would be on the way. I was hoping it would be accompanied by a delivery of cookies or a cheesecake. I open the envelope expecting to find a sympathetic gospel-like message, which there is. I didn't expect the gift that flutters to the floor. A check for five thousand dollars. The memo line reads, "To get you back on your feet."

Much better than cheesecake.

Make the most of every moment. You never know when you'll be put back in the toy box.

Chapter 10

I don't have a scheduled appointment to meet with Father Nolan on Monday, so I phone ahead. He says he has a few minutes between morning mass and yoga class. Assuming nothing comes up...

When I pull into St. Mary's parking lot, I notice a man getting out of his car. It's Mr. Isaac Barber. He's not getting ahead of me again.

Quickly, I park the car in an unmarked spot and jump out. At a speed walker pace, I head to the front door. Not this time. I can hear footsteps approaching. I glace behind. He's running.

"No. No. No." I start to jog. My shoes put me at a disadvantage. My heel continually slips causing me to shuffle.

I'm halfway up the sidewalk when he passes me. I try to grab his T-shirt, but can't get a grip. *Damn tight fitting clothes.* I purposely stumble playing the role of damsel in distress. My fall is half-hearted because I can't afford to put holes in my pants.

"Errgg." I grab at my ankle.

Mr. Barber halts at the door. He looks back at me. "I'm not buying it." He goes inside.

"Jerk!" I dust myself off and follow him in. The game is not lost, yet. I charge into the church office and find the man going through Father Nolan's door.

"Hey."

He waves goodbye and disappears.

I bang on Father Nolan's door because it's locked.

"Here," the secretary holds up a key.

"Thanks."

The door opens before I slip the key in. Father Nolan is standing there with a big smile.

"I was really hoping you'd try to break it down," he says. "Perhaps get out some of your aggression."

"I need to talk to you."

"Take a number," Mr. Barber says.

"It'll only take ten minutes." I try to mimic his voice.

"No way."

"Father Nolan?" I look for him to take my side. "I will go to mass this week."

"So will I," Mr. Barber says. He probably doesn't even have anything important to talk about. This is just a game.

"I will go to confession," I say.

We all wait for Mr. Barber to up the bet. He says nothing. His sins must be really juicy.

"Ladies first," Father Nolan says. "Isaac, can you please wait in the lobby? We'll only be a moment." He puts an arm on Isaac's shoulder and leads him out the door.

I must be a bad person because I take a lot of satisfaction in seeing Isaac beaten. I give him a smile that makes him glare. I know he understands.

When we're alone I show Father Nolan Erika's Barbie rules.

"Wonderful. This is good for you." He gives me back my list. "And I like your new attire."

I stand and give a twirl showing off my usual black pants. I've paired them with a yellow top I borrowed from Erika and my new high heel zebra print shoes. They match nothing so they go with everything.

"Now, we know you have all appearance issues under control with your new take on wardrobe and once you get your eyebrows waxed—"

"Hey."

"I'm only trying to help."

I touch my eyebrows. "I can't get 'em waxed. Vanessa used to do my eyebrows and I think Max is dating her." I show Father Nolan the pictures from Mom's private investigator. "Do you think she's the reason he left me?" I need to know when they started seeing each other.

"A marriage doesn't end for a singular reason."

"Even if that singular reason is an evil blonde with a good memory and attentive attitude?" Vanessa always had a way of making me feel like her most important—and interesting—client. I see how the male species could interpret her attentiveness.

"If Max had an extramarital relationship, he was in the wrong. But I doubt he left solely for this Vanessa woman."

"You're blaming me. You think I was a bad wife." Maybe if Max had written his needs in a note, like he did when he need more deodorant and foot fungal lotion.

Paige,
1. *Please stroke my ego.*
2. *Show appreciation for all I do.*
3. *Hang on my every word.*
Thanks,
Max

"This is all in the past and we don't have much time to talk. Let's set it aside and discuss what's next for you and your role model."

"So stalking Max and Vanessa shouldn't be a top priority?"

He shakes his head.

"Well…I need a job. And a car. And a place to live." I explain to Father Nolan the terms of my divorce.

"You have no job prospects?" Father Nolan asks.

"Nada."

"I know of a job that may interest you." He leans back in his chair. "It probably won't utilize your degree in mathematics."

"What is it? As long as I don't need good grammar or have to use a plunger I'll consider it."

Father Nolan scribbles a phone number on a sticky note and hands it to me. "Her name is Lisa Fields. She's looking to expand her business."

"Is she member of St. Mary's?" Maybe I know her.

"No, she's Episcopalian." He whispers this. "Her mother owes me. The job is yours if you want it."

Seems too easy. "What kind of job is it?"

"You'd be a consultant…"

Good.

"...for the dating service company Prrfect Connection."

Huh? What do I know about dating? I went from pregnant eighteen-year old to single-mom college student to wife.

My session ends with Father Nolan after he calls Lisa Fields to set up an interview for tomorrow afternoon.

"If the job is mine, why do I need an interview?" I'd asked. He assured me it was just a technicality. I don't know if there has even been a Cupid Barbie, but this job seems like something she'd try. Helping others find love is so Barbie. I don't admit it to Father Nolan, but this could be a fun job.

Barb and I are in the car heading to Fountain View Apartments, when the Passat seems to turn itself onto the wrong exit.

Where are we going? Barb asks from the passenger seat. I don't make her ride in my purse when we're alone.

"I don't know."

The car takes a few more turns on its own and I realize we're heading to Max's office.

This is a bad idea.

The car loses its magical self-driving power when I'm forced to parallel park two blocks from his building. Six tries and I'm in. Now what?

We can barely see the front door to the building, but I think we'd notice Max leaving. However, we cannot see the back or side doors. There are several ways he could exit. And I don't know if he's even here.

"I'm going to go check his parking spot," I tell Barb. "Just see if he's at the office."

Barb is dubious.

I put her in my purse. "It'll only take a minute. Then we're apartment hunting. I promise."

It had taken five years for Max to finally get a coveted, reserved parking spot behind his building. We celebrated the night of the parking pass by taking Erika to Olive Garden. Later, Max drove us downtown to show off the curbstone with his name painted on it. He admired it the way an architect would look at a vacant lot he'd one day fill with his masterpiece. Erika and I feigned excitement.

I walk up the tree-lined block trying to be inconspicuous. What would I say if I bumped into Max? I have no reason to be downtown. I round the building and head into the parking lot. I can't remember exactly where his spot is. I know it's in the third or fourth row, close to the south wall of the neighboring federal building—the night he brought us down here he'd kept bragging about the afternoon shade and how cool the car would stay in the summer.

"Bingo." Max's Cadillac sits quietly between a Beemer and a Honda Hybrid. I touch the hood. It's cool. I never liked the long, silver land yacht, but Max's family has driven Cadillacs for three generations. Whenever his family came over we had to hide the Passat at a neighbor's.

I walk around the car and look inside. Neat and tidy like I expected. The only thing that's in the car that wouldn't be there if it were in the showroom is a sports jacket thrown across the back seat.

That's weird. He always uses a hanger and the hook in

the back seat. He'd never haphazardly throw down his jacket. Unless…

Then I see it. The mauve handles of a shopping bag. Not any shopping bag, but a bag from Desdemona's—a small, custom jeweler. Henrich, the owner, made our wedding bands and every anniversary present Max ever gave me.

I pull Barb out of my purse and hold her against the window. "Do you see that?"

She's silent.

I try all the doors. They're locked but no alarm sounds. Something takes over in me—a little temporary insanity relapse. I still have a spare key. For a moment I wonder if I have a split personality and I will definitely ask Father Nolan for his opinion Thursday. Without any more thought to motive or consequences I let myself in.

What am I doing?

Well, I'm sneaking into my ex-husbands car and stealing the bag from Desdemona's. Then, like an expert criminal, I wipe the door handles clean. I leave the car unlocked hoping Max will think he forgot to lock it. Any thief could have noticed an unlocked car and stolen his valuables.

What's done is done.

I open my purse. "Move over." I tell Barb and stuff the small mauve bag next to my disapproving role model.

When it comes to careers, think buffet, not single serving.

Chapter 11

Daily Self-Assessment   *Monday, September 13*
Rate the degree to which you agree with the statement.
    5–completely agree 1–completely disagree
1. I accomplished something today. *2*
2. I felt connected with my friends and family today. *2*
3. I was interested in sex today. *1*
4. I laughed today. *1*
5. I am looking forward to tomorrow. *5*
Notes: *Did all the following: Complete makeup. Hair maintenance. Feminine attire. Positive attitude. Pursuit of a fulfilling career (maybe). No drinking alcohol. Complete the assessment survey.*

***

My interview is set for one on Tuesday. I pull into Prrfect Connections with two minutes to spare and use the time to double-check my makeup in the rearview mirror. I'm wearing the outfit Father Nolan helped me pick out last night over the phone—gray tailored pants, a light pink rayon shirt neatly tucked in, my leather boots, and a pair of gold hoop earrings, which are accentuated by my upswept hair.

"Wish me luck," I say to Barb before stuffing her into the glove box. "Sorry, you have to understand. I'm going in alone." It'd be too hard to explain if I opened my attaché case to grab my resume and out she pops.

Good luck and remember good manners and a positive attitude.

The Prrfect Connection office is located on the first floor of the old brick post office in downtown Albany. I open a door with a corny logo etched in glass of two silhouetted cats with entwined tails. I'm immediately assaulted by the not-so-stale smell of cigarettes, which is strange considering all buildings in New York State are non-smoking. When I meet the forty year old proprietor of the establishment, I understand the lack of compunction about the law.

"Lisa Fields," she says when we meet in the lobby. She offers me a hand manicured with two-inch, acrylic nails. A lit cigarette and cup of coffee are in the other.

"Hi, I'm Paige O'Neal. Nice to meet you." Though the divorce is not final, I've decided to use just my maiden name.

"Come."

I follow her into a stylish office that's smells like a rundown casino. Everything from the stapler to the trashcan to the picture frames is color-coordinated—all blood red. I wave my hand in front of my face, trying to clear some air, then realize that might not be the right way to start off.

"Sorry," she says and turns on a noisy yet efficient air filter. The haze lifts almost immediately.

"I love your office. It has a very modern feel."

"Target." She motions for me to sit down across from her desk.

"Thank you so much for meeting with me. I really appreciate this."

"Resume?"

"Yes, it's right here." I hand it to her. I'm beginning to wonder if the woman can speak in full sentences.

"Okay," she says. "Good." A moment later. "Nice." Then another, "Nice." She tilts back in her chair. "Paige, what makes you interested in the dating service business?"

Fortunately, this is one of the questions I anticipated. "Well, I've always felt that there's too much luck involved in meeting a mate. Who wants to constantly evaluate every man—or woman—they meet. You go to the dry cleaner, is the guy behind you a possible date? Is the woman who works in Accounting eligible? It's tiring."

"Father Nolan said you were desperate for a job."

I try to laugh it off. "That's true, too."

"Let me tell you a little about Prrfect Connection." Lisa lets the *r* roll off her tongue, almost like a—

Uh-oh.

"Pumpkin! Giggles!" She looks around her office. "Where are my little darlings?"

Most of the blood seems to drain from my body. I want to run but am unable to move. I'd like to think that's because I know how important this interview is, and I'm willing to set aside my fears for the greater good. But it's more like a nightmare where you can't move or scream, and you're going to die an awful death at the hands of some hideous monster.

A beautiful white monster jumps into Lisa's lap, and she uses her lethal nails to scratch behind its ears. "Are you okay? You don't have a problem with cats?"

I sense this is the most important question of the interview. Not, have you ever been to jail? Or, did you graduate from high school?

"Yeah. No. I just thought you were conjuring up spirits." I add more uneasy laughter. "Pumpkin. Giggles." I wave my hands over an invisible crystal ball.

Suddenly an orange cat leaps onto the desk out of nowhere. He struts across the desk and stares intently at me. His claws click-clack on the wood as he walks. They sound sharp. I'm certain they could rip open my jugular vein.

"That's Pumpkin. Go ahead, he's friendly." Lisa says.

"Oh, I would, but—"

"You aren't allergic?" The second most important question.

"No, I probably smell like dog. My lab—Rover. Don't want to scare the poor kitty."

This satisfies Lisa for the time being. Thank God, she shuffles the beasts out of the office and she proceeds to tell me about Prrfect Connection, a company she started six years ago, inspired by her two *lovelies*. At first she worked out of her home, but she wasn't comfortable with *some of these losers* knowing where she lived. She moved to this location last year. While most of her competitors use the

Internet, Prrfect Connection is a personally tailored dating service. She interviews every client and matches them based on her evaluation and intuition, not some computer matrix. She calls it homemade matchmaking, back to basics.

Currently the company has two employees—Lisa and the receptionist, Penelope. Lisa is looking to hire another matchmaker to lighten her load because she's starting another business.

"I'm opening an acrylic nail salon in the West End Plaza next to Walmart." She examines my hands. "You should really consider getting yours done."

I nod, and she continues to tell me the details of the job. The salary barely covers my monthly bills, but I'll get a commission for every new client I bring in. The hours are nine to six, Tuesday through Friday, half days on Saturday and a few evenings throughout the month. I tell her no problem.

"Also," Lisa says, "because we are a small business there's no medical."

Guess I can't get sick.

"No dental."

I'll have to floss after every meal.

"And no maternity leave."

"That won't be a problem," I say. When the time comes for me to be Trisha's surrogate I won't need a traditional maternity leave. Maybe a week off to recover. I won't be home with a newborn who needs constant care and refuses to sleep through the night.

"You don't want any children?"

"No. I have a daughter and—"

"I noticed you aren't wearing your wedding ring." Lisa holds up hers for emphasis.

"Oh, I'm not married."

Lisa bites her lower lip. I've blown it.

"Let me explain the nature of this business. People come here to find love and commitment. I don't even like the term dating service." She gives me a set of air-quotes. "We are matching souls. Someone looking for a one night stand or a free dinner will go to a bar. Am I right?"

"Yes," I say, though I don't completely agree.

"So, when you go to get your hair done, you don't want the girl with the blue spiked hair cutting your new French coif."

I nod.

"You don't want your eye doctor to squint. You don't want your cleaning lady to be a slob."

"And you don't want your butcher to be a vegetarian," I add to illustrate my comprehension.

"Exactly. So when someone comes here, they don't want—well, you know." Lisa starts to stand. "Maybe this isn't the kind of work you're best suited for."

"No, no. I'm suited. I am—was—am in a long-term relationship."

"Am or was?"

The required answer is obvious. "Am. I am."

"And how long?"

"Long. Ancient. Long."

"Are you living together?"

"No."

"I still don't think this is going to work."

"We're engaged."

"Great." Lisa sits back down. I still have a fighting chance. "Where's the rock?"

"I told him to save the money. We're looking to buy a house. And, and—it's a very short engagement. He only asked me last Friday, and the ceremony's this weekend. In Jamaica."

"And this will be your second marriage?"

I hesitate. "Yes."

"That's great. Nearly thirty percent of our customers are 'bounders—rebounding from a divorce. You'll be their icon for second chances. Can you start after you get back from Jamaica?"

"Definitely."

After going through a few more details, Lisa walks me back to the waiting area. "You'll really like working here. It's a great feeling to help people find their soul mates."

"I'm looking forward to the opportunity. I'm curious, and I hope you don't mind my asking, did you meet your husband through a dating service?"

"No, I met the ass at a poetry reading. He mumbled something about the naked truth of a blade of grass. I was twenty-two. Thought he was deep. Turned out he was stoned. I've been supporting Nate ever since. How did you meet...?"

"We met at a bar." First thought that enters my head.

"Guess that has to work every once in awhile. What's his name?"

I want to say Max but a heavy feeling deep in my stomach stops me. No other male name seems to exist. I look around the room for help, and I think of Barbie. "Ken," I say. "Kenneth."

"I better let you go. A bride, no matter how small the wedding, always has things to do. We'll see you in a few weeks." She offers her hand and a yellowing smile. "And don't forget to bring us pictures."

I wave goodbye to Penelope and dance all the way to my car. "Hi ho, Hi ho, It's off to work I go." I finally understand why those Dwarfs were so happy. I open the door to the Passat and pull out Barb.

"I got it."

I swear she gives a deep sigh of relief.

"I have to call someone." I pull out my cell phone and try Father Nolan. No luck so I dial Trisha.

"I've got great news," I say after we're connected. "I got a job!"

A dog howls in the background. "What's the job?"

"I'm working for a dating service. I'll be the number two woman in the company." Sounds impressive—even to me.

Trisha knows me. "Two. Out of how many? Two?"

"No, three."

"What's the pay like?"

"Not great."

"And the benefits."

"There aren't any tangible benefits *per se*."

"Then tell me again why this is so great. Is it a Barbie thing? Because I don't ever remember there being a Matchmaker Barbie."

"No, not a Barbie thing. Father Nolan set me up with the interview, and at first I went only out of desperation, after giving it some thought, it's a pretty noble calling—trying to help someone find love."

"Ranks up there with feeding the homeless. So are you going to pillage the files and pluck a man for yourself?"

"No. I can't because I'm marrying Kenneth this weekend in Jamaica. Gotta go. Bye." All I hear before hanging up is a cat screech.

The phone rings a few seconds later.

"Don't ask," I say.

"Your little joke just caused me to insert a thermometer a little too far into a cat."

"Oohh, did you hurt its throat?"

"Funny," she says.

"Sorry, it's not a joke. My new boss wanted to hire a married woman."

"That's discrimination."

"I know, but she made some good points. And I'm desperate. And I want *this* job."

"Does Barbie like this idea?" Trisha asks.

"Lying to get a job? No." Barb is still smiling at me. My lie is already forgiven in her blue eyes.

"No, you stole her lover's name to be your imaginary husband. Could add some tension to your relationship."

"She's flattered. And Ken isn't her lover. He's her boyfriend."

"Even if he isn't anatomically correct, my Barbie and Ken got it on in a shoebox every chance they got. Listen, I have to run. Are you free Saturday night?"

"I guess."

"Janet Ellis is in town. She's coming over for dinner. Why don't you join us? And feel free to bring someone."

I tell her I'll be there even though Janet is not one of my favorite people. We all went to high school together and Janet was the materialistic girl who built herself up by putting others—namely me—down. She idolized Trisha and tagged along with us whenever she could. She was also in love with my twin brother Ryan.

After a celebratory lunch of drive-thru fries and a chocolate shake, I go to Mom's house to tell her the good news. Before I get out of the car, Mom is outside. My heart sinks. Something must be wrong.

"What's going on?" I ask.

"Don't be mad, Mom says. "The Fountain View Apartment people called."

"Yeah?" I'd put Mom and Dad down as reference on the apartment application yesterday and Mom also agreed to be a co-signer if need be.

"Your father talked to them…"

"Come on, Mom. Say it."

"Your application has been denied. Your father decided it wasn't a good idea for you to be on your own. 'Too many crazies out there,' he said. So he wouldn't provide a reference."

"What?" I ball my hands into fists. When one thing works out, something else goes wrong. Like when you plan to spend your tax rebate check on a vacation to Ireland, the hot water heater will need to be replaced.

"I'll just find someplace else," I say.

"Won't you even consider moving home?" Mom asks. "I'll move my exercise equipment and you can have your old room back." There's a hint of enthusiasm in her eyes. She misses having children to care for. Sure she waits on

Dad, but he doesn't need words of wisdom and chocolate chip cookies.

"I'll think about it." I get back in the car. I no longer feel like visiting my parents because I'll probably be living here by next weekend.

Most Barbies sleep in a shoebox at least once.

Chapter 12

What I had:

A four-bedroom, 2600-sq-ft, colonial on a half-acre lot. The lower level had a gourmet kitchen—complete with walk-in pantry, double oven, and Jenn Air range—dining room, living room, family room, and guest room. The basement was finished and had an office, laundry room, and mini-gym. The second floor had the other three bedrooms including the master suite.

What I have:

My childhood bedroom with floral wallpaper, a minuscule closet, and an air mattress. Erika gets the finished attic which is three times the size of my room

By Tuesday evening, I'd decided moving home was a good idea—economically speaking. The rest of the week was a race to the big move on Saturday. Packing and paperwork. When I was too tired to wrap another dish in newspaper and put it into the box marked *kitchen*, I filled out change of address forms. Somewhere in my heritage I must have gypsy blood because few others could uproot their entire life in four days.

The actual move went quickly. When you have a family with twenty-seven first cousins, most of whom live within a three-block radius of their childhood home, it's easy to round up volunteer movers. All it cost me was a couple of cases of beer and Mom threw in two pans of lasagna.

Most of the boxes and furniture went to self-storage. Sure, I don't have to pay rent at Chez O'Neal, but a storage unit is costing me seventy-nine dollars a month.

The crowd cleared out in the early afternoon leaving Erika, Mom, and I to unpack. Downsizing my living area by ninety percent was like giving birth. It doesn't seem possible to pass something the size of a bowling ball through a marble-sized-hole.

"So what do you think?" I ask Erika about her new room. She hasn't lived in the renovated attic bedroom since she was five.

"It's fine." She sets up her computer as we chat. Wait until she learns they only have dial-up.

Mom follows me back down to the second floor and my bedroom. Maybe Erika wouldn't object to me putting a baby monitor in her room. She seems so far away.

"Isn't this better than some tiny apartment?" Mom asks.

"The price is right."

I start putting my cotton underwear and sensible bras into my old dresser. Not very sexy. Not very Barbie—but I think she goes commando most of the time.

"Does Erika still play with dolls?" Mom pulls Barb out of a kitchen container. I'd thought it was a good hiding place and I'd left the top loose so she could breathe.

"Mom, that's not hers." I grab my role model.

"Why are you keeping a Barbie doll in Tupperware?" She puts her hands on her hips. It's the same posture she'd use when I was in high school and she'd ask questions like, "Why did you cut the neck off your sweatshirt?"

"Never mind."

"Mom's the subject of my experiment," Erika says from the hallway. "Here." She hands Mom the list.

"Why are you giving her the list of requirements?" I ask.

"To help keep you in line," Erika says.

"I don't know about this." Mom presses her lips together. "Did you discuss it with Father Nolan?"

"He's on board," Erika says. "Don't worry, Gram. It's only for twelve weeks. Though, it should be noted, I never asked her to start carrying the doll around."

"That was Father Nolan's idea," I say.

"Well, then..." Mom's not about to go against the priest.

I spend the rest of the afternoon trying to calm Mom's fears as we unpack. I'm not joining a cult. I'm still Catholic—the kind that goes to mass three times a year. I'm not a lesbian. She will never find pictures of me on an Internet site of kinky wanna-be Barbies.

As I unpack another box, I see the bag I stole from Max's car. I should just throw it away.

"Ohh, Desdemona's." Mom recognizes the bag. "Who's that from?"

"It's a gift. A divorce gift."

"From who?" Mom tries to take the bag off my finger.

"Max...Max's lawyer." Why would I pick him? I have no imagination when it comes to lying.

"Phillip? Why would he give you a gift? Is he sweet on you?"

"No one says *sweet on you*. It's more like a thank-you-for-making-my-job-so-easy present."

"Well, what is it?" This time she does grab the bag. She fumbles with the paper and for a flash I panic. I never opened it. I have no idea what it contains. What if it's an engagement ring? What if it's a man's watch worth thousands? I've just made my mom an accessory to my insanity.

Mom carefully pulls the small, velvet-covered box from the bag. It's more engagement ring size than watch.

Oh, God.

She flips open the top.

"They're lovely," she holds up a dainty pair of sapphire earrings. "If I ever need a lawyer I'll be sure to use Phillip."

I know the earrings must have been for Vanessa, but if she can steal my husband I can steal her damn earrings. I still feel guilty over my theft, but maybe a little less so.

The most important things in your dream house are your Skippers, Midges and Kens.

Chapter 13

When Trisha invited me over for dinner and said *"feel free to bring someone"* she was probably implying a date. A romantic date. Instead I'm bringing the three most important people in my life—Erika, Barbie, and Father Nolan. I probably should put my mother in the top three, but after she hyperventilated about my new Barbie lifestyle and recommended I give over custody of Erika to her or *any other semi-sane person in upstate New York,* she's been bumped.

Father Nolan, being the gentleman he is, picks us up Saturday evening from my parents' house. Erika has on a tight maroon shirt and low-rise jeans that show off her flat teenage tummy. I suggested she change into something that doesn't reveal her underwear when she bends over. She couldn't be persuaded. I have on my size six Levis and a pink cashmere sweater. The top was a gift from Max three Christmases ago. It never seemed to be Paige. It does seem to be Barbie. The jeans will help limit my caloric intake.

"Are you carrying?" Father Nolan asks as we walk to his Rav4.

I flash open my purse revealing Barb. *Don't leave home without her* is my new motto.

Father Nolan nods his approval.

Trisha only lives twenty minutes away. Just enough time for Father Nolan to fill us in on his new charitable cause—Bikes and Bibles, and his latest diet—no sugars on odd days, no fats on evens.

We pull onto the long, gravel driveway. The house is hidden from the main road by trees. It's a farmhouse with a wraparound front porch, complete with swing, rocking chairs, and dog dishes—the water dish is bigger than the bowl I use to make a double batch of Toll House. I could probably soak my size-9 feet in it. We're in the middle of the suburbs, but it feels like Norman Rockwell country.

When we get to the front door Trisha greets us with hugs. (The dogs have been sentenced to the fenced backyard for the evening.) Father Nolan brought a bottle of wine. I should have brought a dessert, but I forgot to think of it until this very moment. Instead I carry a concealed Barbie doll. Trisha compliments Erika's sense of style and Father Nolan beams when Trisha notices the bottle of wine he brought is from her hometown. He has a knack for buying perfectly personalized gifts. He says it only takes the Internet and a little creativity.

"Come into the kitchen." Trisha takes our jackets, hangs them up.

Manny stops chopping vegetables. "Hey, good to see you again." He shakes Father Nolan's hand and then gives

Erika and me hugs. Manny has, literally, perfect features. I've never met a person more symmetrical. His eyes are dark, clear, and aligned. His nose is straight. His smile, set against stubble-free peach skin, is wide with perfect white teeth lined up in a row. Most people, even if they have straight teeth, have a lopsided smile. A lip curls up higher on one end or draws back farther on another. His doesn't.

"Dinner will be in about thirty minutes," Manny says. "Make yourselves comfortable."

"I'll help you," Father Nolan says.

Trisha walks Erika and me to the guest room she's recently redecorated. It's an Asian theme done in teal. The birds on the throw pillows perfectly coordinate with the flowers in the valance. The queen sized bed looks plush. The furniture, antique.

"It's beautiful. I should've moved in here and not with parents," I say.

"Any night you need a break, come on over," Trisha says. She seems to have her life so together. Great house. Great husband. Great career. Hopefully, they'll have a family soon.

We make our way back to the living room when the doorbell rings. Trisha excuses herself to answer it.

Janet's happy shrieking makes the muscles in my shoulders tighten and my jaw clench.

"What wrong?" Erika asks when she notices my eye roll.

"Nothing."

Trisha escorts Janet into the living room. Damn, she looks good in a high dollar way. Donna Karan clothes. Sexy shoes I saw at Macy's for one hundred and fifteen bucks. Trendy haircut with flawless blonde highlights. I can almost smell the essential oils that make her hair glow.

"Paige," she throws down her Dior handbag. "Give me a hug."

I oblige and try not to crush Janet's bony frame.

"Janet, this is my daughter Erika."

"The last time I saw your mom she was out to here." Janet clasps her fingers and reaches her arms far in front. "She was huge."

I really wasn't. I only put on twenty-two pounds. From the back I didn't even look pregnant. Or so my mom reassured me.

"Nice to meet you," Erika says.

"I'll introduce you to the men in a minute. They're finishing up dinner." Trisha says. "What can I get everyone to drink? I was going to open a red." Trisha holds up a Pinot Noir that had been sitting on the corner bar.

"Sounds good," Janet takes a seat.

I look to Erika with pleading eyes. She holds up a finger giving me permission to have one drink.

"I'll have a glass."

"I thought you weren't allowed to drink." Trisha says.

"Are you pregnant *again*?" Janet asks.

Again? I haven't been pregnant in fifteen years. She makes it sound like I'm an old fashion Catholic on her eighth child.

"No."

"On a diet?" Janet whispers.

"No!" I instinctively suck in my belly.

"Alcoholic?"

"She's doing an experiment for me." Erika says.

Janet tilts her head. "What kind of—"

"Never mind." I say.

Trisha hands out the wine to Janet and me and gives Erika a Diet Coke. We try to catch up on sixteen years in a half hour. Of course, Janet's accomplished so much more than me. We both went to college stateside. While I worked as a waitress in the summers and raised a baby, Janet went on archeological digs, worked with sick children in Africa, and was a volunteer for a Republican presidential candidate. While I married and became a working mom, Janet started her own greeting card business. She finally married last year to a man she claims is a distant relative of Prince Charles.

Manny and Father Nolan announce dinner is served before she finishes telling her love story. Trisha takes care of introductions and we all sit down. The table is set for six with beautiful Toile china and crystal glasses. In the center, there are bowls and platters of food.

"Chicken stew with apricots, warm spinach and sausage salad, asparagus au gratin, corn flap jacks, and honey-wheat rolls," Father Nolan announces. "Isn't it glorious?"

Glorious is Father Nolan's highest form of praise.

"Wow!" I say. Manny worked as a bartender when he met Trisha. Now he's a chef. Not the kind who cooks nightly at a restaurant. He's hired by establishments to set up their menus and teach the full-time staff how to prepare the dishes. As a consultant chef, he's worked all across the United States and parts of Europe.

Father Nolan says a blessing over the meal, and then Trisha gives a toast to old friendships. I blink rapidly to keep tears from forming. No wonder she was chosen as our speaker on graduation day.

Manny, Janet, and I drink the red Father Nolan brought. *This is my last glass.* Father Nolan has only a taste. He knows I'd flip out if he had a couple of glasses. He's my designated driver. More importantly, he's my daughter's designated driver.

"Janet, you didn't finish telling me how you met your husband." Erika says and serves herself the warm salad.

Janet flips her hair over her shoulder "Well, I was in London promoting my new line of cards—Forgiveness. Got the idea when my sister went to AA. For four-ninety-nine you can be forgiven for past grievances like breaking your Mom's Faberge egg when you were five.

"Anyway, I sold my new cards to a distributor and went back to my hotel to celebrate. When I returned to my room, it was flooded. The man upstairs had started the tub and then fallen asleep. The hotel was very efficient and moved me to another room. The man—Prince Charles' cousin's stepson—still felt terrible and insisted on taking me to dinner. And that was the start."

"Does he have a name?" I ask.

"Harold." Janet takes a sip of wine. "What about you, Paige? Trisha tells me you are recently divorced."

"Yes. So recent it's not even final yet."

"And no job?"

"I'm starting a new career next Monday."

"And dating a priest?" She laughs and pokes Father Nolan in the side.

"We're not dating."

"That's so Paige. Always wanting the unavailable."

"What's that mean?" Erika asks.

"Janet and your mother had similar taste in men," Trisha says. "In high school, they dated in the same circles."

"Sounds like there's a story there," Manny says.

"Oh, there is. I even made a greeting card for it in the Forgiveness line."

"So what's the story?" Father Nolan asks.

"Let's not go into details," Trisha says.

Salads are done and we move onto the second course. Stew and sides and a third bottle of wine. I feel the warmth of the drinks and refuse another glass. I also vow to re-start sobriety tomorrow.

"What brings you back to New York?" Father Nolan asks Janet.

"Work." Janet says. "I'd usually send an employee for such a small market, but I wanted to meet up with old friends." Janet reaches out and squeezes Trisha's arm. I get no squeeze.

"I've seen Meg Wilcock. She's gotten fat. Lynn Walsh. She's gotten fatter. Scott Felding. He looks good. And I tried to pay a visit to the Swansons. Seems they moved."

Erika's head pops up at hearing that name. Michael Swanson was my brother's best friend, the school's star point guard, and Erika's biological father.

"They moved thirteen years ago. After the accident," Trisha says.

Michael and Janet dated for two years, on again, off again. They were *off* over Thanksgiving break when I got pregnant. Erika met Michael when she was a baby. She doesn't remember. He died in a car accident when she was only eighteen months old.

"Your mom doesn't know this, I actually saw you when you were a baby. Michael and I were dating when you were living with the Swansons." Janet takes another drink. "They always dressed you head-to-toe in pink and lace. You reminded me of a frilly bedroom pillow. I bought you a denim jacket and hat from the Gap because all that pink was nauseating."

Janet bought *that* hat. Erika wore it all the time. At her first birthday. In pictures. I never knew. I would have burned it.

"When did we live with the Swansons?" Erika asks.

"It was a long time ago." I concentrate on my dinner.

"You're mother didn't live with the Swansons. Bet she wanted to." Janet says.

Father Nolan coughs. "Please. Water. I'm having a reaction to this roll. It could be the fennel."

"Yes, water." Trisha says. "Janet, go get the water."

No one moves.

Something seems to click for Erika. "It was just me who lived with the Swansons?"

"What?" I try to make the idea sound ludicrous.

Father Nolan pulls at his collar. "Water. Someone, please."

"Mom, you didn't want me?" Erika's voice shakes.

"Erika. It wasn't like that." It's all I can say.

"Oh no, what did I do?" Janet says. "You never told her about the adoption."

We all suddenly go from warm-tipsy to freezing-sober.

"You gave me up for adoption?"

"No. Not technically."

"Technically?"

"Technically, I surrendered you, but I changed my mind. I got you back."

"How long was I without a mother?"

"It's not like I put you in a basket on the Nile like Noah."

"That was Moses, Paige." Father Nolan says.

"Thanks. Let's hold off on the Bible lesson," I snap. "Erika, it was forty-five days. And I left you with grandparents who loved you."

"What made you change your mind?"

"Because I love you."

"No. Why, after forty-five days, did you want me back?"

"Because, it was my last chance. After forty-five days I could no longer have you back." In New York State, the birth parents have forty-five days to change their minds after surrendering a child. After that, an adoption is possible and it is irreversible.

"God, Mom. Did you wait until midnight, too?"

"Can we talk about this later? You're flipping out."

"Of course I'm flipping out. You! Abandoned! Me!"

Erika roughly pushes herself away from the table rattling the wine glasses. She walks into the living room, screams, and disappears down the hall. A door closes and a lock clicks.

I put my elbow on the table and catch my head in my hands. What just happened? Did an old *friend* rat me out to my teenager? Who am I mad at? Who should I be mad at?

Someone needs to be at fault. Please don't let it be me. Everything already seems to be my fault.

Trisha and Manny apologize in unison. Father Nolan joins the chorus. Janet only shakes her head.

Erika stays in the bathroom. Father Nolan talks me into giving her twenty minutes of alone time. I agree because I need time to find the right words. So after the table's cleared, dessert refused and nineteen minutes ticked off the clock, I knock on the door.

"Erika, let's go home and talk about this," I say to the door.

There's no response.

"Erika?" I start to think she's gone out the window. Then the door opens. Thank God.

"Come on. Let's go home," I say.

"I've called Dad. He's going to pick me up."

"Dad?"

"Max." In the nine years I was married to Max, Erika called him Dad three or four times and then only when she wanted something. The tactic always worked. Not because he was buttered-up, he was embarrassed and wanted her to stop.

Erika brushes past me and goes out to the front porch. Father Nolan and Trisha watch helplessly. Like me, helpless.

I scurry after my daughter. "Please, Erika, just come home. We'll work this out."

"No."

Headlights illuminate the tree lined driveway. Did Max really agree to pick Erika up? He has no legal rights. He's not her father, not her stepfather anymore, not even an emergency contact on her soccer registration form. The car stops in front of us. It's a sporty, red, two-door thing, which seems small enough to fit under the belly of a semi. Not Max's Caddy. But it's Max who steps out of the red mid-life-crisis-mobile.

"Hi, Paige," he says. "You ready, Erika?" He holds the driver's seat forward so she can climb in the back. There's a woman in the front seat. Probably Vanessa but I can't see her face.

"She's not going with you."

"Yes, I am." Erika climbs in the back seat.

"Erika Marie O'Neal, get out of that car."

No one moves.

"One. Two. Three." Counting to three used to work—when she was three.

"Max, if you take her I'll call the police. This is kidnapping."

Max sighs, perhaps taking me seriously for the first time. He closes the door and walks up onto the porch. A parental sidebar, just as if he were a real parent.

"Listen," he says, "she needs some cooling off time. She's overwhelmed by this revelation. She'll be fine with me. We'll bring her to your mother's in the morning."

"Bring her home tonight."

"I promised her that I wouldn't. It was either that or she threatened to call her boyfriend."

"She doesn't have a boyfriend." At least not one I've met.

"It doesn't matter. She's safe with me." Max reached out for my hand and stops, probably thinking better of it.

I cave. "Bring her to Mom's tomorrow by noon, unless

she wants to come home sooner. I'll pick her up whenever she wants. Midnight. Three a.m."

"She'll be fine." Max walks back to his car. They drive off. Everyone's deserting me. They can't get away fast enough.

I sit down on the steps and ask Father Nolan to bring me my purse—and Barb. Part of me—a very small part—is relieved my secret is out. Now my problem switches from hiding my past from Erika to mending my future relationship with her.

That night in my childhood bedroom there is no nightly survey waiting for me. So I grab a sheet of notebook paper and write my own.

Daily Self-Assessment   Saturday, September 18
1. Accomplishments. 1 (Sure, I moved today, but back into my parents' house.)
2. Friends and family today. 1 (An old friend caused a rift with my daughter.)
3. Sex. 1 (Waiting for marriage. —ha-ha)
4. Laughed. 1 (Only at my answer to number 3.)
5. How I feel about tomorrow. 1 (I'd like to do today over.)
Notes: Had a few drinks.

What I don't write is I'm about to raid Mom's liquor cabinet for another.

Confidence is the foundation in the makeup bag of life.

Chapter 14

For twenty hours, I haven't slept or eaten. I'd spent most of the time willing the phone to ring. That didn't work, so I actually went to early mass. After the service, Father Nolan called my attendance a *miracle*. Max had dropped off Erika while we were at church and she was now refusing to leave her attic bedroom. I'd hoped she'd come around by dinner. Optimism is very Barbie-like

Mom's Sunday dinner hasn't changed in thirty years. There's always a roast, potatoes, veggies, and a homemade dessert. And even when it's only Mom and Dad at home, there will be enough food to feed at least six.

When the pork loin is done, Mom, Dad, and I sit to eat. So much for optimism, Erika is still in her room. There isn't much conversation, which isn't unusual. It comes from growing up in a house with Ryan. He was always an athlete and could eat a whole chicken by himself. If you wanted more than Ryan's scraps, you had to eat quickly.

He'd take the food right off your fork.

While Mom excused herself to the kitchen to get the German Chocolate cake, I made Erika a to-go plate. Maybe she'd eat it in her room later.

"I've got some good news," Dad says while he waits for his slice. "I've found you a date."

"Isn't that wonderful?" Mom hands Dad a double helping of cake and gives me a sliver.

I shake my head. "I'm not in the market for a blind date. I'm in the market for a car or a house."

"I'm only talking a single date, not an arranged marriage. He's a young-up-and-comer in the office. He has potential. I hired him myself." My dad is pimping me out. I wonder if a date with the spinster-daughter was part of the hiring package.

"Please, Paige," Mom says. "Go on one date. For me. I worry about you ending up alone."

"I've only been alone for five months. And do you worry about Ryan ending up alone? When's the last time you set him up on a blind date."

Mom shakes her head. "It's not the same, dear."

No, it's a double standard. No one is worried about Ryan. He's single and homeless. And last I heard his double-A baseball team didn't make the playoffs so he's soon to be jobless too.

"You're getting your mother upset," Dad says. "Just go on the date. What's it going to take?" Dad, always the negotiator.

"Fine. I'll do it for another slice of cake."

"I don't know if that's a good idea. There's a lot of fat and calories in the slice you've already had." Mom's weight has never fluctuated by more than two pounds. She's been able to wear a size six since Ryan and I were a few months old. She worries about me because I could require a six, eight, or ten all in the same month.

"Nancy, give her the damn piece of cake."

After Erika leaves for school Monday morning—she's still not talking to me—I decide to work a few tasks off my list. I take a Pilates class with Mom. For a sixty-two year old, she's very flexible. I do my hair and makeup. I put on a denim skirt, embellished top, and my zebra print heels.
I'm all dressed-up with no place to go.

There are two items on the list that need to be done only once. Try a new sport. Be a fashion model. My attire isn't really suitable for mountain climbing or even bocce ball. So modeling it is.

Half hour later I'm walking into Showcase Modeling Agency. The waiting area is very modern. Everything is black and white including the poster-sized pictures of attractive people on the wall—curly-haired toddlers, flat-bellied teens, perfectly coifed thirty-somethings and elegant seniors.

"May I help you?" asks the receptionist.

"Yes," I try to muster courage and confidence. Of course, Barb is in my handbag to back me up. "I'm...um...looking for work."

"Certainly." She hands me a clipboard. "For yourself or a child?"

"Just me." I take the clipboard and fill in my name, address, age, and answer a few simple questions. Then I take a seat and look through a photo album of their clients' work. Looks like mostly print ads for local companies.

"Paige," a woman in jeans and a company T-shirt calls for me. "Hi, I'm Susan. Let's talk in my office."

I follow Susan into the back. The trendy, modern feel is gone. This is more like a dated doctor's office with a balance scale, worn carpet, and mismatched furniture.

"Please, have a seat." She motions to a mauve-colored chair and sits next to me. "What kind of modeling work are you looking for?"

"I'm flexible. Whatever you have so long as I can keep my clothes on?"

She fakes a laugh. "Of course." She turns to the laptop on her desk. I can't see the entire screen, but I think she entered me as *middle-aged* and my looks as *average*. Or maybe I'm overly paranoid. I've never applied for a job where my weight and complexion matter.

"Do you have any experience on a runway?" Susan asks. "Because there is a bridal show this weekend and we have a need for thin, mother-of-the-bride models."

I give her ten-points for calling me thin, but I'd like to give her a slap for suggesting me as a mother-of-the-bride.

"No, and I've only recently learned to walk in heels."

"Understand." She clicks and scrolls through some more options on the computer. She keeps shaking her head.

"No luck?" I ask.

"Not in print. Will you excuse me for a second? I'd like to check one more thing." Susan gets up from her swivel chair and disappears behind a screen used for photographs.

While she's out, I can't help but look at her pc. She

didn't close the laptop so she probably wouldn't mind. I stand up to get a better angle.

I'm not qualified for much. Most jobs are looking for twenty to twenty-five year olds. Everyone wants *fit* which must be the politically correct term for skinny. Just as Susan returns I notice a familiar name on the screen. Isaac Barber.

Susan immediately closes the screen before I can see what Mr. Barber is doing in a modeling agencies database. Sure he's attractive in that bad-boy kinda way. But a model, I don't think so.

"Paige, we may have something that interests you," Susan says. "It's a brochure for a minivan. Our soccer mom just had to cancel. I think if we had your hair bobbed, you'd be perfect. What do you say?"

"Maybe." The curiosity is killing me. "Why is Isaac Barber in your computer?"

"You really shouldn't be—"

"Sorry, it's just that I know the man. He's my daughter's teacher and I had no idea he was in the modeling world."

With a sigh Susan opens her laptop. "Isaac Barber isn't a model. He's a client. He's looking for a model."

"What? What kind of model?" My mother-brain immediately classifies Mr. Barber as a pervert wanting to take pictures of young girls in his basement studio.

"He's looking for a twenty-five to thirty year old, fit, Caucasian, preferably blonde for a book cover design."

I was right. Pervert.

"I want that job."

"Paige, we take great pride in meeting our clients'

expectations."

I stand up. "Set up the meeting with Mr. Barber for this evening. I will meet him at his house. And do not tell him my name or that I requested this appointment." I lean over Susan, click the mouse and get his home address. "If I'm not exactly what he's looking for, you can find him someone else." With that I leave the agency.

Susan calls my cell that afternoon confirming my appointment with Isaac Barber for six o'clock. She wishes me the best of luck and says the minivan job is still available if this doesn't work out.

I arrive at the Barber residence ten minutes late. The ranch is well maintained with a neat lawn, a few boxwood bushes and a young maple tree. There are no flowers or garden statues which lead me to believe Mr. Barber must be single.

When Mr. Barber opens the door he doesn't look surprised. Did Susan give me away? I'd really been looking forward to making his jaw drop.

"Paige O'Neal, come on in."

"I'm here for the modeling job." In case he thought I was here to discuss his class or Barbie.

"I know. My studio is down the hall on the right."

Not really much better than in the basement, still creepy. I make my way through the living room when I see it. A huge grey creature asleep on the leather coach.

"He won't hurt ya," Mr. Barber says. "Won't even move unless you have a brisket in your purse." He nudges me to move down the hall. The dog doesn't even lift his head.

The back bedroom has been converted to an artist studio. Mr. Barber has an easel and a desk which is covered with colored pencils, charcoal, and pastels. There are no cameras.

"What do you do here, Mr. Barber?"

"You have to call me Isaac."

"No I don't."

"Yes, you do. You're working for me." He takes a seat on a high stool and spins around. "I do cover art for books."

"I thought you were a sociology teacher and a basketball coach."

"I wear many hats." He puts a sheet of paper on his easel. "Now take off your clothes."

I knew it. He's pervert.

"I'm going to report this to—"

"Shut it, woman." He says with an I-gotcha-smile. "I need you to change into that." He points to a silver costume hung over the back of a chair.

"Really?"

"The book is a futuristic romance novel. *Moon Passion* or something like that. I only read like twenty pages. It's not my thing."

"The agency said you wanted a hot twenty-five year old." I'm starting to think I should have taken the minivan gig.

"I can pretend you're twenty-five and hot. I have a good imagination." He points to a door. "There's a bathroom through there."

I take the costume and go change. It's a skin tight, silver cat suit with a hot pink belt. There's a giant keyhole opening to show off cleavage and it's backless. Most definitely designed by a man.

"How long is this going to take?" I ask when I emerge from the bathroom. I keep my arms folded across my chest trying to look angry and trying to hide the cleavage.

"It'll take about twenty minutes to rough it in. Is that good enough?"

"You have fifteen."

"Think you are forgetting who the client is." He hands me a water gun.

"What's this?"

"Your laser gun."

"Looks like a water gun."

"Again. I'll let my imagination fill in the gaps. Now tousle your hair, get down on one knee, and aim your weapon at the window."

And with a heavy sigh, I do.

Isaac stares at me intently. It's kind of unnerving. Can't ever remember being studied like this. Using a pencil his hand moves rapidly on the paper. I can't see any of it. Probably a good thing.

"Hey, Paige, I don't mean any disrespect or anything, but do you mind sticking your chest out a little more."

"Use your imagination. And do you have a pillow or something, my knee is already throbbing."

He tosses me a flat pillow from his desk chair and gets back to work.

Slowly. Subtly. I arch my back millimeters at a time trying to stick my chest out. I don't want Isaac to catch me doing this. But I also don't want him to think I'm an A-cup when I'm really a B. Maybe a B-minus.

"How's the experiment going?" Isaac asks when he goes to erase something from his masterpiece.

"Excellent."

"Really? Erika was saying today she may call the whole thing off. Asked if it was too late to change her mind."

"She's just mad at me. It has nothing to do with the experiment. She's fifteen and emotional." As far as I know the experiment is on. She left me a daily self-assessment on my bed last night.

"I think you'd be emotional too, if you found out you were almost given up for adoption."

"She told you?" I get up off my knee.

"We talked after class for a few minutes. Relax. Sometimes a kid needs—"

I throw the water gun at his head.

"Hey."

"I don't relax. And I don't like the influence you have on Erika. There will be no more coffee bets, no more texting, and no more talks outside the classroom."

"What are you accusing me of?"

"I'm accusing you of interfering. Remember your place, Mr. Barber. You are her teacher. She may be impressed with you now, but in twelve weeks you won't matter."

"I think I got enough." He puts his pencil down.

I grab my purse and my clothes and walk out.

Barbie knows all the secrets of life,
but only little girls are listening.

Chapter 15

Daily Self-Assessment   *Tuesday, September 21*
Rate the degree to which you agree with the statement.
    5–completely agree 1–completely disagree
1. I accomplished something today. *5*
2. I felt connected with my friends and family today. *2*
3. I was interested in sex today. *1*
4. I laughed today. *5*
5. I am looking forward to tomorrow. *3*
Notes: *Modeled for a minivan ad. Got paid in free floor*
mats.

.

***

As a divorcee—or soon to be divorcee—the thing my loved
ones think I need most is a date. They offer to hook me up
with someone—usually another divorcee. Hell, if we have

failed marriages in common, we're bound to hit it off. What I really need is to start working, not start dating. The money Mom and Dad gave me is rapidly draining away. I still need a car and a pet. These things aren't cheap.

"Dating is supposed to be fun," Father Nolan says as we observe a group of preschool girls playing with Barbie dolls in the St. Mary's daycare. Instead of having our usual Thursday meeting at the church office, he'd suggested we do field research. Father Nolan even supplied the class with half a dozen new dolls.

I shift in my uncomfortable, child-sized plastic chair. "How would you know?"

"I've been on dates. I wasn't born wearing a collar." The thought of Father Nolan taking a woman out to dinner, paying her compliments, making her feel like she's the only one that matters isn't really all that foreign an idea. "Dating is not a form of torture, Paige. Go out. Meet someone new. Just keep your tailored, black trousers on. Please."

"Guess you're right. And if Max can be in a serious relationship then I can go out on a date."

"Ohh, revenge dating. That's a splendid idea." Then Father Nolan points to a pretty blonde child with a grape juice mustache. "Watch her. See how her Barbie is flying?"

The Barbie is wearing a baby doll bib for a cape along with a short red dress and boots. The child flies the doll around above the other children.

"You want me to fly?"

"I don't want you to be constrained by limits. Think in terms of *can* instead of *cannot*."

When a boy approaches the group of girls and their Barbies, Father Nolan gives a little clap of excitement.

"This is bound to be really interesting," Father Nolan whispers.

We observe without moving or making a sound.

The boy picks up a beach ready Barbie in a two piece bathing suit, a sarong, and sunglasses. The sunglasses come off immediately as he examines her. I guess the eyes *are* the window to the soul. Rather roughly, he bounces Barbie up and down on the carpet. When she withstands this test, he moves her arms and legs around, not to imitate motion, but to see if he can rip them off. No luck. He is also unable to decapitate her. Mattel does make a quality product. Instead, the boy undresses Barbie.

"This can't be good." I say.

"Shhhh. Watch."

The Barbie doll is naked. The boy isn't particularly interested in her anatomy. He examines her like he's looking for a secret button. When he doesn't find anything, he strikes the Barbie against the bookshelf. She withstands.

"Wow," Father Nolan says. "Did you see that?"

"Yeah. I'm pretty sure we have a future serial killer in front of us." I reach my hand into my purse feeling for Barb. She's safe.

"Paige...Look again."

The boy is now playing with the naked, abused Barbie doll. He has her towering over building blocks. Fighting dinosaurs. Riding in a speeding car.

"I see it," I say. "Even stripped down, she is still powerful."

"Yes. What else?"

"She prevails against giant adversity."

"Yes. And..."

"She is still Barbie no matter what life throws at her."

It's evening and blind date time. I force myself to give Will—the 'young-up-and-comer' from Dad's office—a chance.

Dad has assured me that Will is great. Will knows I have a daughter and stabbed my ex-husband and he had no qualms about the date. I wonder where he would draw the line. Ax murderer? Quaker mother of seven?

At six o'clock I'm dressed and ready to go—pencil straight denim skirt, a red, fitted knit top, and black leather heels. Barbie is safely stashed in my purse. For a moment I thought of leaving her in my bedroom, but it's my first real date in ten years and I need the backup.

"Do you mind staying here by yourself?" I ask Erika. Mom and Dad have gone to a free concert in the park.

"No," she says in a voice that's not hers. "You left me for forty-five days. What's one more night?" She walks off refusing any physical contact with me. Last night I snuck in her room and kissed the top of her head because this give-me-space episode is killing me.

Since it's a first date, I meet Will at a neutral rendezvous point—a NASCAR-inspired arcade in the mall. He chose the location. Initially, I think we'll just meet there and then go to a nearby restaurant or the movie theater that is also in the mall. Then Will, a good-enough looking guy, shows up still dressed neatly for the office with his own pair of driving gloves.

I try to be a good sport and drive a couple of laps in a Tide-sponsored car. It turns out Will is very competitive and, after kicking my ass a few times, wants more of a challenge. I give up my car to a thirteen year old, buy a Diet Coke from the snack bar and stand behind Will's vehicle. I try to cheer him on, making ohhh-and-ahhh noises for a good ten minutes before he tells me I'm distracting him. I back off and talk to another out-of-place patron, the mother of second grader who is also burning rubber. She seems to be a nice lady—a dental assistant, James Patterson fan, and a black belt in kickboxing. We exchange e-mails. I enjoy the hour we spend together.

When Will finally tires of driving, he asks me to join him for dinner in the food court. I think about ending the date immediately, but I'm starving and a taco doesn't sound half bad. After a combo meal—the phrases *combo meal* and *first date* do not go well together, but I've already given up on this one—I tell him I have to get going, that my dad needs me. And my dad does need me. He needs to hear hell from me. What the hell was he thinking?

"This has been cool." Will walks me to my car. "We should go out again?"

"Sure, maybe next time we could play mini-golf." I slip my left hand into my jacket pocket because Will keeps trying to grab it.

"What about Saturday?" Okay, sarcasm is not part of his repertoire.

We arrive at the Passat and I unintentionally fiddled in my purse for the keys.

"Saturday, huh? Let me see." Instead of pulling out a PDA or a date-book I pull out Barb. "Are we available Saturday night?"

Wills smile becomes wider, tighter like a creepy

funeral director. "What's going on?"

"I don't make any decisions without checking with her first." I hold Barb up to my ear. "She wants to know if you could bring her a date, too."

He steps back. "Actually, why don't I just call you? Sometime."

"Well, okay. How about a kiss good night?" I have Barb ask our date. I shove her an inch from his lips and throw in a few kissy noises.

Will walks off. "Have a good night, Paige. And you too, Barbie."

"You work better than mace," I say to Barb.

It's a gift.

Optimism, imagination and a good wardrobe
will take you farther than an MBA.

Chapter 16

Friday morning, I relax on the couch watching an episode of *Little House on the Prairie* on cable. The show reminds me of my childhood—of watching it with my family, not living in on a farm in the Midwest. Mom walks in shortly after Half-Pint runs away because Pa loves Mary more.

"Max is out front," she says. "Maybe you should go say hello."

"What?" I run to the large living room window. Max is trying to steal my car. He's fumbling with a key at the driver's side door. He doesn't know I snapped off my old key in the door last winter and never bothered to get it fixed. You have to get in through the passenger door or use the keyless remote. Which he doesn't have.

His feeble attempts give me a chance to rush to my Passat's rescue.

"What are you doing?" I'm freezing in my yoga pants, T-shirt, and bare feet. I'd worked out this morning and hadn't bothered to take a shower yet. If I'd been following the Barbie rules I'd be a scary, hot bitch who commanded attention, instead of a sweaty slob.

"Hello, Paige. I thought I'd take her off your hands."

"Step away from the vehicle."

"Max, is everything all right?" A female voice comes from inside Max's little red E.D. vehicle. It's Vanessa. She is Bonnie, he is Clyde, and my poor Passat is a helpless bank vault.

"It's all fine," Max shouts.

I walk over to him and ask, "Why is she here?" I do this with as much tact as a five-year old who has just been served sashimi.

"She had the morning off and offered to help me collect my belongings."

"How nice of her."

"Stop making those faces. It's not very attractive."

"How long have you been dating Vanessa?" Her name tastes like metal in my mouth.

"I'm not answering that. Let me take the car and I will leave."

"You said I could use it until I find alternate means of transportation." I put myself between Max and my helpless car and hold my keys in hand like a weapon.

He steps back. "Have you tried to find alternate means of transportation?"

"Sorry, Max. Car shopping hasn't ranked very high on my list. Been kinda busy trying to find a job, raising a kid and looking for a place to live and all. Not everyone has someone as sweet as Vanessa to help out." The muscles in my shoulder start to ache. I need to know. "Was Vanessa helping out while we still married?"

"You need to let it go. Maybe it's time for you to find someone and move on."

"Maybe if you didn't bring your girlfriend around to steal my car I could let it go... and... and maybe I am seeing someone." It's not the most coherent sentence I've ever mumbled, but how dare he assume, one, that I'm still interested in him and his life, and two, that I'm not madly in love.

"Are you seeing someone?"

Is that jealousy in his voice?

"I've dated." Somehow the floodgates to my imagination open. "Actually, I have a date with someone you know."

"Who?"

"Won't it be fun trying to find out?" I reach out to pat his arm. He flinches wildly and moves back a yard.

"Good for you. I hope it works out." Max walks back to his sports car.

He actually seems happy for me. *Damn him.*

"Oh, and good news. The divorce was filed with the county clerk yesterday. You are officially Paige O'Neal again." He waves. "I'll call you next week about the Passat."

After he's gone, I realize that talking about an imaginary date to your ex-husband isn't a very Barbie thing to do. To justify it, I think of my exaggeration as forecasting the future, not an out and out lie.

The following is the official Paige O'Neal boyfriend history. First, let's define boyfriend.

A Paige O'Neal Boyfriend — (boi-frend) Noun.

1. A guy with whom I have had at least four dates, with neither of us dating anyone else;

2. With whom I have shared a kiss and some additional form of intimacy; and

3. About whom I have talked extensively with friends.

Senior year high school—Ben Holiday (on and off, seven months)

Sophomore and junior year college—Bradley Dumermuth (on and off, twenty months)

Senior year college and on—Max Russell (twelve of the best years of my life, if not his)

In between my three serious men I dated a bit, but not enough for them to meet my boyfriend criteria. Including Michael Swanson, Erika's father.

One guy fell into that gray area between *boy friend* and potential *boyfriend*—Phillip Rogers. We never went on any official dates. We just hung out. When I summoned the nerve to make the first move, he had a girlfriend. When he seemed interested in me, I'd started dating Max. Barb agrees, Phillip has the most Ken-potential of the men in my life.

Once I'm sure Max isn't coming back to car-nap my Passat, I head to the basement. Barb watches from a shelf as I sort through stacks of boxes. There's only one plastic container marked *Paige*. I'd have sworn I'd left four or five. I should have written *Ryan* on the boxes if I wanted it to remain safe. Ryan's baseball trophies, even from when he was six, will have a place in this house until Mom and Dad are buried. My stuffed bunny was thrown to the curb minutes after I moved in with Max.

Luckily, the single remaining container is full of souvenirs from my college days. My university experience was different from most girls. After class I didn't return to the dorms, I went home to a toddler. No sororities. Few parties. I never even needed a fake i.d. The box contains mostly academic paraphernalia—grade reports, articles from the school newspaper, papers I wrote. At the bottom of the box I find a collection of pictures.

It's funny how the mind chooses to remember things. I recall Phillip as a strong, dark-haired guy with a cleft chin and chocolate eyes. In the picture taken outside the student union he looks tall but thin, with hair falling into his eyes and a stud earring. He looked better a few weeks ago in his tailored suit and his hair showing some gray. It doesn't matter. Ken didn't always looks his best either, like when a little girl would cut his hair or draw on his face. Besides, the earring resonates. In 1993, Barbie had Earring Magic Ken.

"What do you think?" I hold up Phillip's picture for Barbie.

He looks like someone very special.

I hope he is. "God, please help me find this man."

"Why don't you try the phonebook?" Mom says as she walks downstairs with a basket of laundry.

Very helpful. Instead of the phonebook, I go to Dad's den and boot up the computer. I look up Rogers using the online white pages hoping to find a home number. There are dozens in the Albany area but no Phillip. A Google search offers pictures of P. Rogers naked and free live chats with Phillip-Phor-Pleasure. I can't imagine it's the same

Phillip.

"Where are you, Phillip?" I ask.

You could always call him at work.

I bring up the yellow pages and get the number for his law office. Now, how to meet him again? I could stake out the restaurants near his office. Maybe tail his car, learn his habits, and bump into him at the health food store. Too time consuming. I'm starting my job soon.

Just call him. Be brief. Be direct. Be polite.

Then I call his office using Mom's phone. Hope they don't have caller ID. What am I going to say? I should have thought this through.

"Thank you for calling the Law Offices of Rogers, Rigby, and Roy. This is Rhonda. How may I help you?"

"Ummm."

"Hello?"

"Yes. Sorry." I clear my throat. "I need to make an appointment with Phillip Rogers. Please." An appointment is as good as a date, right?

"Are you a current client of Mr. Rogers's?"

"No. I have a referral."

"Excellent. Can you come in Friday, October eighth at four?"

"Sure."

"Your name and a number I can reach you at."

"You need my name?"

"Yes, ma'am."

"It's Trisha Stevens." Then I give her my cell phone number.

Barbie seems to shake her head. I've screwed up again.

"Okay, Ms. Stevens. I have you down for the eighth at

four." Rhonda confirms. "Will you be seeing Mr. Rogers about a separation, divorce, or prenuptial agreement?"

"Divorce, I guess."

"Thank you. We'll see you on Friday."

"Wait." I stop Rhonda before she can hang up. "I have one question. Can you tell me if Mr. Rogers is married?"

"No."

"He's not." My heart gives a little leap.

"No, I cannot tell you. May I inquire—"

I hang up the phone before she can inquire. I'll find out soon if he's married. When I show up at my ex's lawyer's office for an appointment in someone else's name. This isn't good.

"We need a plan," I say to Barb.

"Paige," Mom says from the hallway. "We're going to pick up Ryan from the airport. Do you want to come?"

Ryan is moving back home because baseball season is over. Every year he hopes to get called up to the majors and it has never happened. Mom and Dad encourage him to no end. They've always been follow-your-dreams kind of parents.

"No, can't. I've got stuff to do." Like convince my best friend to divorce her husband just so I can meet my Ken, so we can start to date and make my ex-husband jealous, all the while carrying on a fake relationship with an invisible husband named Kenneth. I vow from now on to have only one enormous lie in life at any given time.

Math class is hard, but the best things in life are.

Chapter 17

Having a twin makes it hard to feel like an individual. Every birthday, the start of a school year, any coed sports team, Ryan was by my side. Mom knew I sometimes felt like Ryan-and-Paige instead of just Paige, so on occasions she'd declare it *girls' day.* We'd go to the movies, dinner, spa and on one time, bowling. There was never any talk of schoolwork or attitude problems or Ryan. Mom and I were friends, not mother and daughter.

"Erika," I tap her shoulder still under the warm covers. "It's time to get up."

"It's Sunday. I don't have to." She sinks into the pillows.

"It's ten o'clock and I'm declaring today girls' day." I turn on the light. "Get dressed. We're going to brunch."

Forty minutes later Erika emerges from her room dressed in ripped jeans, a hoody and baseball cap. She's gone to great effort for our special day. Defiance is better than resistance.

"Are you going to say something about my clothes?" They certainly aren't Barbie-like but I don't bring that up. "Nope. They're perfect. We're going to the Waffle House. Before we go, I need to ask you to do me a favor."

"What?"

"No iPod. No cell phone"

She takes the iPod out of her pocket and lays it on the couch. "I'm not giving up my phone?"

"Vibrate?"

"Agreed."

We head out for the Waffle House. I try some small talk, wanting to keep the deep stuff for the breakfast table where I can stare into her eyes and gauge her reaction. Every question I throw out there gets one word answers. No matter how open ended the question is.

Me: How are you?

Erika: Tired.

Me: How are soccer playoffs looking?

Erika: Fine.

Me: What are the first three sentences to the preamble?

Erika: Mommmmmmmmm.

I know she knows the whole preamble. She worked on it two weeks ago for U.S. history. Two weeks ago when things were, in fact, fine.

We order identical breakfasts. Short stack. Link sausage. Coffee. When the drinks arrive I launch into my own preamble.

"Erika, it's time we talked. I know you have questions, but if you could save them for the question and answer portion of the program, I'd appreciate it."

I smile, but don't get one in return.
"Okay."

Even before I needed maternity clothes I felt the effects of pregnancy. My breasts were massive. Now a college guy might not notice if his English professor shaved her head and grew a beard, but he'd notice a change in bust size. Every guy in my dorm watched me go from a B to a large-end D. My hair and nails grew like beanstalks while my bladder shrunk to the size of a shot glass.

Trisha and I were both home from college for spring break. We'd gone to McDonald's on my request—chalk it up to craving a minty Shamrock Shake. When we got back to her house I was already regretting my large shake and hit the bathroom looking for bladder relief. When I pulled down my panties there was blood. Not just a little streak, a crimson spot the size of a half dollar. I could feel more warm wetness between my legs. I screamed and cried. I was sure my baby was in serious trouble.

Trisha called my parents. They called an ambulance. I rode to the hospital alone. My blood pressure was dangerously high, probably more from fear than the pregnancy. The medics were watching my vitals, giving me oxygen and an I.V. No one was worried about the baby. There was nothing they could do for it.

I was rushed to Albany Memorial. Mom and Dad met me there. My blood pressure returned to normal. It seemed like an eternity before an ob-gyn came to check on the baby. She brought an ultrasound machine. I was only sixteen weeks along. My scheduled sonogram was still three weeks away.

She coated my tummy with jelly and moved the wand around. "There's the heart beat," the doctor said, and I cried with relief. She moved the wand around some more.

"Can you tell if it's a boy or a girl?" Dad asked.

"Paige, do you want to know the sex?" the doctor asked.

"Ummm...no."

The doctor told us we should schedule an appointment with my regular ob-gyn. But everything looked fine. Just a little spotting. I was relieved—and scared.

From that day forward I gave up everything—college, friends, all my interests. I wanted nothing to do with my old life. I lay around the house refusing to see anyone. Ryan was even forced to not have friends over. No one was allowed in the house.

Self-imposed house arrest gave me a lot of time to read, watch TV, and think. What was I going to do? The first few weeks after the hospital I was certain I'd give it up for adoption. I'd even talked to an agency. They told me an adoption would go smoother if the father consented. Since I hadn't told the father, I put that option off.

Around week eighteen, I felt my baby kicking for the first time. I knew then I wanted to keep it. My baby. I loved him. My baby. I couldn't let it go. My baby. My raging hormones and fear about everything from finances to my ability to put on a diaper had me changing my mind again.

I decided to leave the answer up to fate.

I went in for my next ultrasound. Doctor visits were my only vacations away from my double bed. The medical reason for the second trimester ultrasound is to check the baby's size and development. Most parents look forward to finding out the baby's sex. After I peed in the cup and had my blood pressure and weight checked, Mom and I sat in an exam room with plastic vaginas on the desk and diagrams of breasts on the walls.

I told Mom that if the baby was girl, I'd raise her. If it was a boy, I'd give it up for adoption. Mom shrugged and suggested I give the decision some more thought.

When the doctor arrived and started asking about swelling, I wanted to strangle him with his stethoscope. I'd made a decision about my baby's future and needed to know the answer immediately. The ultrasound finally got under way. The doctor kept saying, "good" as he took measurements and pictures.

"Do you want to know the sex?"

"Yes," Mom and I said.

The doctor searched with the ultrasound wand. He hesitated like a presenter at the Oscars opening the Best Picture Envelope. "Sorry, I can't tell for certain," he finally said. At least everything else appeared in good order on his little screen.

I told my parents and Ryan—the only people I was talking to at the time—that I planned on giving the baby up for adoption, though I made no arrangements. Ryan didn't seem to care. He just wanted the baby named Ryan Junior if it was a boy. I told him that implied he was the father.

"That's sick, Paige," he said. "So who is the father? Some frat guy?"

I hadn't told anyone who the father was. I'd told Ben, my unsteady boyfriend of five months, that he wasn't the father. But he knew that. We'd never had sex. Of course my parents had asked and I didn't want to talk about it. Luckily they were the don't-push-her-she'll-talk-when-she's-ready type. Trisha had asked. I avoided the question by faking severe morning sickness.

"Michael Swanson." I said the name for the first time to anyone.

"What?" Ryan's voice cracked like we were thirteen again. "Mike knocked up my baby sister?"

Ryan's only seven minutes older than me, but he loved playing the role of big brother. Ryan didn't give me time to explain. He bolted from the house. I could hardly give chase.

That night Ryan was escorted home by a police officer. He'd met Mike in the parking lot and they'd tried to settle things like only eighteen-year old guys can. The next day the O'Neal family and the Swanson family had a sit-down in our living room. It was one of the most uncomfortable conversations of my life.

"Are you sure Michael is the father?" Mrs. Swanson asked again and again.

"What are you insinuating?" Mom asked. "Paige doesn't sleep around."

"I'm saying, without a blood test, we can't know for certain."

Drama ensues. In the midst of it, Mike shrugged and smiled at me. Even with a black eye and swollen lip he was cute. I knew we'd have an adorable child.

The conversation grew uglier as Mrs. Swanson was certain I was trying to ruin Mike's life. He was on a full scholarship to play basketball and couldn't be expected to give that up for me—or a baby.

"Paige doesn't even know that she wants to keep the baby." Dad said as a way to defuse the situation.

"Are you talking abortion?" Mrs. Swanson whispered.

It was far too late for that. When I first discovered I was pregnant I debated abortion for about five seconds. I would never be able to go through with it. "No. We're talking adoption." I said.

That's when Mrs. Swanson flipped from you're-ruining-Michael's-life to Michael-has-rights. "This is Michael's child, too. He should have a say."

"I should?" Mike asked.

More drama. I was certain the neighbors could hear. I longed for the isolation of my bedroom. My heart raced and my stomach grew tight. Almost painfully so. Mom noticed me grabbing my belly.

"Paige, are you okay?"

I wanted to lie down. My stomach tensed again. It was a contraction. And I was rushed off to the hospital, again. No ambulance. Dad drove. The Swansons followed.

In the maternity ward, they monitored me and the baby. Everything was fine, again. My body was just reacting to stress—an anxiety attack that caused the minor contractions. As I lay in the bed waiting to be discharged, Mom, Dad and Ryan were with me, watching *Wheel of Fortune.* The Swansons waited outside. The thought of everyone talking again made me feel nauseous, but if we needed to talk it was better to do it here where security guards and pain pills were never far off.

I had the Swansons invited in and this time, I did the talking.

"I'm not keeping the baby. I'll probably regret it every

day of my life, but I can't take care of him. Even with my parents help." I turn to Mike. "We need to find him full-time parents. We need to give him up for adoption."

"Him? It's a boy?" Mike asked.

"Did they tell you that?" Mr. Swanson asked.

"No. I just have a feeling."

Mrs. Swanson cried. She'd gained and lost a grandchild all in the same day.

A week to the day after my hospital run Mrs. Swanson came over to our house. She said that they'd given the situation a lot of thought and Mr. and Mrs. Swanson wanted adopt my son. They started calling him Jack. ("Or Jill," Mr. Swanson would joke because we weren't certain of the gender.)

I wanted to be relieved that the Swansons were adopting Jack. It seemed like fate. They already loved the baby that wasn't due for another three months. They came around all the time with gifts for the baby—blankets, onesies, booties—and gifts for me—chocolate covered pretzels, magazines, stretch mark cream. I accepted the arrangement and tried not to second guess it.

Erika was born July twenty-first—a month early. Mrs. Swanson was in the delivery room with me and mom. She was so happy holding my precious newborn. I was so tired. I could tell my mom wanted to run over and snatch my daughter out of Mrs. Swanson's arms. We both just watched. The baby would have a good home. The baby would be loved.

They named her Chelsea.

My hospital stay was shorter than Erika's. After two nights, I was discharged. Erika was still in the NICU, doing well, under observation. Before I left the hospital I went to see her. I held my four and a half pound baby while she slept. She was so small. I thought of stashing her in my overnight bag and taking her home. I left without her. That was the worst day of my life.

I cried constantly for the next few weeks. My parents sent me back to the doctor who promised I'd feel better once my hormone levels stopped fluctuating. It wasn't hormone levels. I wanted my baby back.

Mom arranged for us to visit the baby they called Chelsea one afternoon. The visit with the Swansons was awkward. Erika was sleeping. They didn't want to wake her up and let me hold her. They seemed to think if I just touched her I would love her and want to take her away from them.

I kept telling myself to just get through the first forty-five days. Then it'll get easier. Up until forty-five days I had the right to terminate the surrender agreement and get Erika back. I thought that was my problem. Once the choice was gone, my feelings would be gone too. The night before the forty-fifth day I knew the rest of my life would be a mistake if I didn't get Erika back.

In the morning we called a lawyer and had Erika home by supper time. I had her name changed to Erika, as if that would make her time as Chelsea disappear. The Swansons did try to gain joint custody of Erika on Michael's behalf. As the father, he could petition for visitation and other rights. While the issue was in family court, the Swansons were allowed to visit Erika at my parents' house. Michael even stopped by a few times with gifts like a small, pink basketball and a jersey with his number seventeen on it.

Michael died before a final decision was ever ruled. We tried to keep in touch but the Swansons pulled away from us. When Erika was about five, I heard Mrs. Swanson died of cancer and I think Mr. Swanson moved to Virginia to be near his remaining family.

Erika listens intently to my story. She doesn't question or interrupt. Her expression never changes.

"I'm sorry I didn't tell you. I didn't know how. Or when." I open my purse and pull out a picture. I hand her the photo of an overjoyed woman holding a tiny baby girl, swaddled in pink.

"This is me?"

I point to the writing on the back. "Chelsea Swanson."

Erika stares intently. She's lost that pissed-off expression scorned teenagers seem to have mastered. "Can I ask a question now?"

"Sure." Let it be an easy one.

"I want to meet Mr. Swanson."

"That's not a question."

She shrugs and we both know she did not intend on asking.

In an election year, run for President.
In an Olympic year, try the pole vault.

Chapter 18

It's my first day of work, I have a new purse, office accessories, almost-new shoes borrowed from Trisha, a new outfit—with the tags neatly tucked in, in case I get fired before lunch. I use the top drawer of my desk to make Barb a nest. I line it with a pink towel and throw in a change of clothes—for her. Don't know why.

I place her on the fuzzy towel. "I'll leave the drawer cracked so you can hear all the juicy office gossip."

You'll do great. Just remember the rules.

Subject Requirements
1. Complete makeup. (Daily)
2. Hair maintenance. (Daily)
3. Exercise. (4/week)
4. Feminine attire. (Always)
5. Good manners. (Always)
6. Positive attitude. (Always)

7. Find your own Ken. (Continuous)
8. Pursuit of a fulfilling career. (Continuous)
9. Be there for Midge. (Continuous)
10. Try a new sport. (At least once)
11. Be a fashion model. (At least once)
12. Get a pet. (Soon as possible)
13. No drinking alcohol. (Always)
14. Read *The Barbie Files: An Unauthorized Biography.* (ASAP)
15. Complete the assessment survey. (Nightly)

I'm busy arranging my desk with matching clock, pen holder, frame and coffee cup when Lisa knocks on the door and pops her head in.

"Welcome aboard," she says and waves a doughnut. "May I come in?"

"Sure."

She enters, leaving the door open. I pray the cats don't follow.

She bites into the doughnut I had presumed was for me. "How's everything coming?"

"Great. This office is huge."

"Still smaller than mine."

I force a laugh.

Lisa grabs the picture frame off my desk. It's a photo of my mom, dad and Erika, taken last year in the Magic Kingdom. It was the only five-by-seven photo I could find that didn't have Max in it.

"Pretty girl. Your parents?" Lisa asks.

I nod.

"I want to see pictures of the blushing bride in

Jamaica."

"We didn't really take any. Small wedding."

"None?"

"Well, a few."

"Then let me see."

I shrug. "They haven't been printed yet."

She wrinkles her lips in a show of disappointment. "Well, when they are, bring them in. I want to see what Ken—"

"Kenneth."

"I want to see what Kenneth looks like."

"He's ordinary. Very common looking. He stands in police line-ups all the time as a decoy."

"Where's his family from?"

"Here and there. They're not that close. They didn't even come to the wedding." I hope we're through with this line of questioning.

"Well, I look forward to meeting him."

"He's really busy. Maybe he'll stop by sometime." I need to get Lisa off the Kenneth kick. "Do you want to show me your filing system now or this afternoon?"

"That can wait." She finishes her doughnut and follows it up with a gulp of coffee. "You are bringing Kenneth next Thursday night, right?"

I blink hard. "Thursday?"

"You probably haven't had a chance to read your e-mails yet. We host a Monthly Mingle on the second Thursday of every month. All our clients are invited to come and socialize. We usually have forty or fifty people. It's at the Hyatt. I want you and Kenneth there."

"I don't know if he'll feel comfortable. He's more of

a—"

"Tell him your job depends on it."

I can't tell if she's offering me a suggestion or issuing a threat. I open my still-empty calendar and pretend to check our schedule for the second Thursday in October. "We'll be there."

"Good." Lisa stands and walks to the door. "I have a new client coming in at eleven. Why don't you watch my interview and see how it's done."

"Sure."

I sit in on Lisa's appointment which seems to consist mostly of friendly chatter and leaves me feeling I can do this job. Then I have lunch, read dozens of files, organize my office and file all the necessary federal and state paperwork without ever taking my mind off Kenneth. Sometime in the next ten days I need to find a husband or another job.

When I leave work at six. I call Mom and tell them to have dinner without me. I'm going to be late.

"We need to see Trisha," I tell Barb who's peeking out of my bag. I couldn't stuff her inside after she's been in a drawer most of the day.

I bang on her front door. Trisha's retrievers immediately answer by barking and banging their heads against the glass. "Trisha, it's me. Put the dogs in the garage. I'm coming in."

She calls the dogs, and they quickly bound away. I let myself in and make my way to the dining room. Manny's been at it again. Looks like they just sat down for a dinner of chicken with a creamy sauce, asparagus and red potatoes.

"Sorry to interrupt your dinner, but it's an emergency." Manny stands and gives me a quick peck on the cheek. "You're always welcome."

"What's wrong?" Trisha asks as she walks in from the kitchen.

I take a seat at the table. "Lisa, my new boss, wants to meet Kenneth next Thursday." I pluck a potato from Trisha's plate. "What am I going to do?"

"Your Jamaican husband?" Manny asks. I've learned whatever secrets I divulge to Trisha, I'm also divulging to Manny. Luckily, the trail ends there, so I've accepted it.

Trisha sits down and moves her plate out of reach before I can snag anything else. "Manny, can you get Paige a plate?"

"And if you have any more of that wine we had on Friday..." I add without considering the consequences.

"It's in the cabinet over the fridge," Trisha says.

Manny goes into the kitchen. "Anything else, ladies?" he asks with a British accent.

"Carry on, Jeeves." Trisha turns her attention to me. "Now, start over."

"There's this party-thing next Thursday night where clients come to mingle. And Lisa insists that my damn husband attends. My damn imaginary husband. Soon, I won't have a job, and I have all these bills to pay, and my daughter will starve, and I need a car. And I don't know what to do."

Manny sets a huge glass of red wine in front of me along with a plate of food.

"Thanks." I take a bite of chicken—it's wonderful—and chase it with a long swallow of wine. "What am I going to do about Lisa? About Kenneth?"

"Tell her he can't make it."

"She's not going to buy that excuse. Besides, if I get out of it this month, what will I do next month?" My appetite falls by the wayside, but not my thirst. I finish off my glass of wine.

"Maybe Father Nolan can stand in?" Trisha asks. "He'd make a great husband. You already know each other."

"That would have been a great idea if the idiot hadn't stopped by today." And I can't imagine anyone believing Father Nolan as a husband.

"Why'd he stop by?" Manny asks.

"To bring me a plant and buy a dozen gift certificates."

"What an ass," Trisha says.

"He's already introduced himself to Lisa. He's out." I bury my head in my hands. The situation is hopeless.

"You could hire a husband," Trisha suggests.

"An escort? How much would that cost?" It's not exactly something I was budgeting for right now. I imagine an *affordable* escort is a cross between a Pee-Wee Herman type and a Jeffery Dahmer type.

"I have no idea the cost. We'll have to make some calls. Relax." Trisha pats my hand.

"I'll do it for fifty," Manny says.

"She's our friend," Trisha says. "You can't charge her money."

"How 'bout twenty? Twenty dollars for an evening with Manny. It's a bargain." He flashes his perfect smile. Manny could fetch hundreds as an escort.

"It really is. When I spend an evening with him, it

usually costs me my sanity." Trisha gives him a wink. "You still can't take money from her."

"I'm not taking a second wife without some kind of dowry."

"Would you really do it?" I'm hopeful to have found a solution so easily.

"First, two questions. What's involved? And, what's it worth to you?" Manny tries out a mobster's accent.

"You'd only have to stand next to me, smile and shake peoples' hands. And, in return, I'll get you a bootleg copy of that vampire video game from Ryan."

"That's what you said last week when I helped you rearrange furniture."

"You broke the handle on my dresser."

"You didn't tell me the thing weighed three tons."

"You guys sound like you're already married." Trisha says. "I think this will work."

Relief! This will work. I get up and give both of them hugs. "There's only one other little thing. Wedding pictures."

An hour later, dinner is done as is the bottle of wine. I'm barefoot and wearing a cream color sundress Trisha found in the back of her closet, and Manny has on khakis, a Bermuda shirt and sandals. He looks too good. There is nothing plain and ordinary about Manny. He's gorgeous and anything but forgettable.

"This needs to look tropical," I remind them. "We're supposed to be in Jamaica."

"We're in Albany, in September." Trisha says. "It's eight o'clock at night and fifty degrees outside."

"Let's turn on all the lights." I suggest. "And we need

to make the pictures blurry, so no one will question them."

"What do you need me to do?" Manny ask.

"We need to be moving. Action shots." I move around with the grace of a sumo-sized belly dancer.

"Or... I can move the camera as I take the pictures." Trisha says.

"Better idea. No wonder you're my favorite wife." He gives her a quick kiss. Even during the good times, Max and I were never like Trisha and Manny. If I wanted to share good news, bad days or worries, I talked with Mom, Trisha, or Erika. A spouse is supposed to be your best friend. Max and I never reached that level.

"Excuse me, guys," I break up their kiss. "Let's get these pictures done. And Trisha, try not to get his face straight on. I don't want Manny to be recognizable. Okay?"

Trisha takes twenty shots. She takes pictures of us embracing, standing at the altar—a shot of us from the back, being married by a plastic house plant, our hands interlocked, some of me alone and a half dozen of the floor, the lights and other oops shots. For fun, we do one with Barb as a flower girl.

When the wedding-photo shoot is over, Trisha and I sit on the couch with jumbo cups of coffee. Manny, having enough Barbie and dress-up for one day, leaves to take the dogs for their nightly walk.

"Have you thought any more about letting me be your surrogate? I don't get medical insurance through work, but I've found an affordable plan online."

"You really want to do this?"

"If I can?" I still need to go through a medical review with Trisha's fertility specialist. Make sure I'm STD-free and pass a drug test.

"If this round of in-vitro doesn't work we'll talk. Until then…" She pauses. I can tell she doesn't want to discuss it anymore. "What's happening with the Barbie experiment?"

"Don't laugh." I help Barb sit next to a candle on the coffee table.

She rolls her eyes. "No promises."

"I've been thinking about it, and I think I've found my Ken." I cringe, waiting for her comeback.

"The eleven-inch version or the six-foot version?"

"The living, breathing thing. The way I figure, Barbie and Ken have been friends forever. He's always been there. So, instead of looking for a new man, I've decided to look to my past."

"So you're looking for a guy who wasn't good enough the first time."

"Maybe the timing wasn't right. Or maybe I didn't give him a chance the first go around. People can change a lot in twelve years."

"Twelve years? How far back are you going?"

"College. An old friend—Phillip Rogers." I sit up and tell her about the Phillip I know from college. I don't tell her that I used her name to set up an appointment for a divorce. It seems a little much to divulge after I just pretended to marry her husband.

"He sounds almost perfect," she sips her coffee.

"Wait. I haven't told you the best part. In college, he used to live in KEN-more Apartments."

"Well, good luck." We touch mugs.

***

The next day I get the pictures printed on my lunch break. I take the clearest pictures out of the envelope and throw them in the trash. Back at work, I go straight to Lisa's office.

"Got a second?" I ask. There's no sign of Pumpkin or Giggles. Thank God.

"Come on in." She's busy touching up her nails and smoking a cigarette, which I think is only slightly safer than throwing a firecracker into a paper factory.

"They're here." I hold up the envelope of pictures.

"Let me see. Let me see."

"Okay, don't get anything on them."

"I promise." She screws the top back on the bottle of lime-green nail polish and puts out her cigarette.

I hand over my beloved pictures.

Lisa flips threw them, turning the pictures this way and that. "Paige, these are awful."

"Please. These are all I have to commemorate the most special day of my life." I try not to sound sarcastic.

"I'm sorry. They're great."

I leave her office smiling. Barbie may not have started this lie, but she's proud of my resourcefulness.

A man on your arm is no more necessary
than a coat on your cat.
Both may be cute, but each is only there for show.

Chapter 19

Daily Self-Assessment   *Friday, October 1*
Rate the degree to which you agree with the statement.
   5–completely agree 1–completely disagree
1. I accomplished something today. *5*
2. I felt connected with my friends and family today. *4*
3. I was interested in sex today. *1*
4. I laughed today. *5*
5. I am looking forward to tomorrow. *5*
Notes: *Made my first match at work. They're going out tonight. No drinking. (Four days in a row!)*

***

Daily Self-Assessment   *Tuesday, October 5*
Rate the degree to which you agree with the statement.
5–completely agree 1–completely disagree
1. I accomplished something today. *3*
2. I felt connected with my friends and family today. *2*
3. I was interested in sex today. *1*
4. I laughed today. *5*
5. I am looking forward to tomorrow. *5*
Notes: *My match was failure. The woman tried to strangle the man with his own necktie. (He probably deserved it.) Over a week without a drink.*
Ran-walked two miles, celebrated by buying new, sexy underwear.

***

Thursday night, I ordered Chinese food for the family. Mom shouldn't have to cook every night. Erika talked about her day, only once accusing me of abandonment. After, we broke open our fortune cookies. Mine said, "Your luck can always change if you choose it." And my luck has changed. I'm employed. I have a roof over my head. My kid doesn't hate me as much as she did last week. Maybe my problems are solvable.

I chose a light blue, knee-length dress for tonight's Monthly Mingle. If I hold in my tummy and stand perfectly straight it doesn't look bad. Now, if I can only settle on shoes. My black pumps are scuffed, so back in the closet they go. I'm sick of my zebra-print heels—I wear them every other day.

"Are silver sling backs too flashy for a company

event?" I ask Barb. I have ten minutes before I need to leave to pick up Manny.

My cell rings before I can make my decision.

"Don't panic," Trisha says on the other end.

"Saying *'Don't panic'* makes me panic." And I really panic—my chest hurts, I start to sweat, my grip tightens on the phone.

"Manny's stuck in Chicago. He won't be back until tomorrow morning."

"What?"

"Honey, I'm sorry. There's good news. I found you a substitute."

"Thank God. Who?"

"Dante Calkins. My lab tech. He's a tall, delicious African-American specimen."

"He's black?" I snap.

"So am I. And since when has race mattered to you?"

"Since I have photos of me and a white groom. Remember?" The room starts to spin. I sit down on the bed and put my head between my knees. Picking out shoes suddenly becomes the least of my worries.

"The pictures are blurry. Who's going to notice?"

"Anyone not color-blind." There's no time to argue the racial makeup of my pretend husband. "Thanks anyway, Trisha. I'll figure something out."

"What are you going to do?"

"I may go stag. I may step in front of a bus. I may have a brilliant idea in the next—oh, my God—ten minutes. I really have to go. I'll call you later."

"I'm really sorry," she says.

I do have an idea. It's far from brilliant. It's more like

risky and stupid, but with the time constraint, I can't sit around and wait for a miracle. I slip on the silver shoes and walk down the hall to Ryan's room.

I haven't seen Ryan yet today. He'd told Mom he was sick. He's infamous for thinking he has the flu when it's usually a hangover. His bedroom door is closed. I knock and walk in without waiting for a reply.

"Get up. I need your help." I hover over a semiconscious Ryan.

"Go away. I'm dying." He pulls the faded sports-motif comforter over his head. Ryan's room is, and always will be, a shrine to Mom and Dad's little slugger. There are shelves of trophies and silver-framed photos. Newspaper articles are pinned to a corkboard. Ryan will never have an opportunity to forget the glory days.

"Are you naked?"

"What? No!"

"Good," I say and rip the blankets off his bed. "You're just hung over. Now, please, get up. We have to get going."

"Where?" He puts on a *Rolling Stones* T-shirt that was crumpled next to the bed to complete the boxer-and-T-shirt look that's popular in dorm rooms.

I rummage through his closet looking for something suitable for him to wear. "Don't you own any shirts without pictures or bumper-sticker-sayings on them?"

"Leave me alone, Paige." His voice is muffled under the pillow. He curls up into a fetal position and shows no intention of getting up.

There's nothing even remotely passable in Ryan's closet, so I head to Dad's. I select a blue button-down, a burgundy tie, and khaki pants. I'm not even sure Ryan and

Dad are the same size, but this ensemble, even off-size, will look better than sweatpants and a baseball jersey.

"You're still not up," I complain as I reenter Ryan's room and lay Dad's clothes on the back of a chair. "Please. I'm going to lose my job. I need you to go with me to this party."

"A party?" Ryan sits up in bed. He's so easy.

"Yes. See, I told my boss that I'd bring my husband and—"

"You aren't married anymore. Wait." He must realize what I'm suggesting. "Oh, no. That's disgusting." And like that, he's back under his pillow.

"We shared a womb for nine months. We can pretend to be married for one night. Please."

"No!"

If he's going to be this way, I'll play the you-owe-me-big-time card. "Who cosigned your car loan two years ago? I did. Who lied to her doctor to get you prescription medicine for athlete's foot when you didn't have medical insurance? I did. Who went to all your baseball games—high school, college and double-A—that were within a three-hour drive? Not Mom. Not Dad. Me!"

"You should give without expecting to receive. Didn't you pay attention in Catechism class?"

It's hopeless. I slump down in the chair and start to cry.

"Fake tears don't work on me. I've know you too long."

I stop the sobbing and get down to business. "How much?"

"What?"

"I'll pay you. How much will it take?" I pull the checkbook from my purse. If I write him anything over fourteen dollars, the check will bounce.

"Five-hundred."

His audacious suggestion catches me off guard. "What?"

"Take it or leave it."

"Fifty dollars and I won't tell Mom what happened to her crystal gravy boat. You can't cash the check until next week."

"I'll have to think about it." He scratches his head in deep thought.

"Let me help." I grab his ear and twist it. "So what do you say? Do we have a deal?"

"Deal. Deal. Now let go." He swats my hand away. "I need five minutes to shower."

"You have two."

Ryan cleans up nicely, even if he's wearing enough men's body spray to camouflage a week-old cadaver. We walk to the car and he pulls my hair once—on accident—and punches me once in the arm when a VW Beetle drives by. It's like we're twelve all over again.

"That's your one punch-buggy of the night. Get it?" I get into the driver's seat of the Passat and start the car. "Damn it."

"What's wrong?"

"I forgot someone." I run back inside and grab Barb. She's too big to fit into my evening bag, but I feel better knowing she's in the car.

"Aren't you going to ask me about Barbie?" I ask Ryan.

He looks at her. "Figure you're smuggling coke in her stomach cavity."

"Ha ha. Mom told you, didn't she?"

"Yep. Thinks you're going nuts."

Ryan's I.Q. is only two points lower than mine, but through school, I was always the smart one and he was always the athlete. Studying and memorization never came easily to him. So in the car on the way to the party, I try to keep the *facts*—a.k.a. lies—to an absolute minimum.

"There are a few things you need to know before we get there," I tell him.

"Is this going to be *Three's Company*-complicated where Jack pretends to be Chrissie's husband but Janet's lover until Mr. Roper finds out Janet is dating—"

"No." I stop him before he gets us both confused. "Nothing like that. Just a few simple details. First, your name is Kenneth."

"Cool." He flips down the visor and looks at himself in the mirror. "Hello, Kenny."

"It's Kenneth. Second, we got married almost two weeks ago in Jamaica." I pull the Passat into a parking spot outside the Hyatt. I open the ashtray and pull out a wedding ring I'd bought earlier for seventeen dollars at a pawn shop. "Here." I hand it to Ryan. It's a little big, but it'll do. "And the wedding pictures didn't really come out too well."

"Why not?"

I bang my head against the steering wheel. "What do you mean *why not*? Because we didn't really go to Jamaica. Because there was no wedding. Because you're my brother."

"Calm down. I've done this before."

"Done what before?"

"Lied my ass off for a woman." Ryan gets out of the car.

I follow after, checking my lipstick one last time in the rearview mirror and winking goodbye to Barb who's lounging in the back seat. I walk over to Ryan and give him some last-minute advice. "Just smile. Be polite. And, please, don't talk much."

"Yes, ma'am." He offers me his arm, and we head in.

A few of the hotel staff are putting together the finishing touches out for the party. The ballroom is nice, but the atmosphere is cheap—silver paper tablecloths, fake flowers, plastic silverware, and music from a stereo—not a band or even a DJ.

Lisa's changing a CD when she notices us and comes over. "Paige, I was beginning to worry." Her gold, low cut dress matches her long gold nails and toenails perfectly. She looks like a showroom model just past her prime.

"Sorry. Took me longer than I thought to find the place." I step aside and offer up Ryan. "Lisa, I'd like you to meet my husband, Kenneth. Kenneth, this is my boss, Lisa Fields."

"Nice to meet you," Ryan kisses her perfectly manicured hand.

"Same to you." Then she leans toward me and whispers, "Nicely done. I bet I can guess why you were really late."

I fight back a feeling of nausea. "So, what would you like me to do?"

"Over here." Lisa leads us to a check-in table covered with rows of nametags. "I thought you could help people sign in. It'll give you a chance to meet our unattached clients."

Ryan, already looking bored, says, "I'm going to hit the bar. Do you ladies want anything?"

"No," I say. If twins are supposed to have telepathic abilities, Ryan and I were gypped. In my head, I tell him to stay with me. The message is never received—either that or it went straight to voicemail.

"I could use a drink. I'll join you," Lisa says. "Paige, go ahead and get situated. Yell if you need anything."

A half-hour later, I check off the names of two more guests and give them their nametags. The night is young, and already twenty-eight people are here, looking for love. Ryan finally returns with a rosy, alcohol-induced glow.

"Where have you been?" I ask.

"I was mingling." He waves to a woman near the stereo. "There are a lot of good-looking women here."

"You can't mingle. You're married," I remind him.

"Oh, yes. Right you are." He fishes his wedding ring out of his pocket. "Don't worry. Lisa didn't see me take it off. Between you and me, she's more on the prowl than any of 'em."

"No. She's married."

"I know. That's her husband at the bar." He points to the thin man with a gray ponytail mesmerized by a glass of beer. He doesn't drink it. He only stares at it.

While Ryan rambles on about Lisa's lingering hands and suggestive language, a light-haired man enters through the far door.

"Move out of the way," I say to Ryan. "You're blocking the table."

The man has his back to us. He's heading toward the bar.

I get up from my seat and give chase. "Excuse me. Excuse me." I tap his shoulder.

He stops and turns around.

"Isaac?" I let out a deep breath. Before he even speaks I know he's going to make this difficult.

"Hello, Paige. Do you mind if I get a drink before you drill me about my job, car, and future ambitions?"

"Excuse me?"

"Isn't that what women do at these things? Corner a guy and assess his earning and marriage potential."

"Don't know. I'm not a client. I work for Prrfect Connections. I just need you to sign in." I walk Isaac back to my table. "And here's a little hint, you'll have much better luck if you give the woman a chance to finish a sentence."

"Noted."

I shove Ryan from my seat and scan my guest registry. "You're not on the list. Did you RSVP?"

"No."

I grab a note pad. "Let me just get a little information. How long have you been a client?"

"When did I walk through the door? Two minutes ago? I've been a client for two minutes." He gives me a crooked smile that's not as charming as he intends it to be.

"So you haven't signed a contract at our office?"

Instead of answering verbally, Isaac pulls a wrinkled gift certificate out of his back pocket and slides it across the table. Then he grabs a blank nametag and fills it in—

Isaac, 37, Renaissance Man

Income $17,000 give or take $100,000
Hates: Thai Food and Board Games
Loves: Pizza, Reality TV, and College Football

"That should do it," he says. "Now point me toward the... interesting... women." He does a set of air quotes when he says the word *interesting*.

"That brunette over by the stereo, in the green dress, she's hot, speaks three languages and runs her own business," Ryan offers.

"That's a start," Isaac says. He peels the backing off the nametag and sticks it to his shirt. Most of the men in the room look respectable, like they have come from work at the office. Isaac, in dark jeans, sneakers and a *Led Zeppelin* T-shirt, prefers the I-just-got-off-the-couch look.

Ryan points to the information on the nametag. "Have you seen the new show where they follow the strippers around Vegas?"

Isaac nods. "I love Jessica, the girl who's sick of not being taken seriously."

"Good luck with that political career."

"Honey, enough!" I smack Ryan in the chest.

"You're with her?" Isaac points to me.

"Married almost two weeks," I pull Ryan by the sleeve closer to me.

"You're married? I thought—"

"Yes. I *am* married."

Isaac shrugs. "I never would have guessed."

"Me neither, she wouldn't take no for an answer. She was practically begging." Ryan smiles. He's never going to be able to keep our arrangement a secret.

"Isaac Barber." He offers his hand to Ryan.

"Kenneth," he hesitates.

Shit! I never gave him a last name. Just don't say O'Neal.

"Succotash." Ryan smiles. "Kenneth Succotash."

What?

"Interesting name. I take it your wife kept her maiden name."

"Purely for professional reasons." I slip my arm around Ryan's waist. To his credit, he doesn't flinch or say gross. "Mr. Barber doesn't want to hear any of this."

"No. I find it intriguing. Your step-daughter is in my Social Sciences class." Isaac gives me an amused look.

He's onto us.

"I know," Ryan says. "She loves your class. It's the first book she cracks when she gets home from school." Ryan *is* good at this lying business.

"Kenneth, what do you do for a living?" Isaac keeps digging for information.

"Archeologist."

My eyes bulge. He probably thing archeologist is a kind of foot doctor.

"Really?"

"No. I run my own business—Guy's Night. I arrange strictly adult entertainment. Babes in cakes. Wet T-shirt contests. Strippers." Ryan pats his pockets. "I don't think I have a card on me."

"That's fine," I add. "This isn't the time to promote yourself. Besides, Mr. Barber isn't staying. Sorry, we can't let you in without running a background check and getting some information."

"Then give me the money back for the gift certificate."

"I can't do that either." I point to the fine print. "No refunds, exchanges, or transfers."

"It took me forty-five minutes to get here. It cost me ten-dollars to park and another twelve for beers in the hotel bar." He turns to Ryan. "Wanted to see the end of the Ohio State game."

"At least you didn't waste any money on your attire," I say under my breath.

"She dresses you, doesn't she?" Isaac asks Ryan.

"Against my better judgment."

"Kenneth, look." I point to the woman in the green dress. "Looks like her drink is getting low. Why don't you take care of it?"

Ryan salutes and is off to fulfill his duty.

Isaac seems determined to enter. "Either let me in, or I want one-hundred and fifty dollars for this gift certificate."

"Again, I'm sorry, I can't. Just come in to our office tomorrow, and we'll get you set up." I stare into his blue eyes as if my glare could will him to back down.

"I want to speak to the manager." He's smiling and I don't know if he's at all serious.

"Certainly." I stand and go find Lisa, I'm glad to let someone else handle Isaac Barber. Lisa is entertaining three people with a story about her cats and a mishap with a self-cleaning litter box. I wait until she finishes before telling her about the rude, unregistered customer at the check-in table.

At least, he was at the check-in table. Where did he go? He's joined Ryan and green-dress at the bar. Lisa and I walk over.

"Can I help you?" she asks. "I'm Lisa Fields, the

owner."

"A friend gave me this gift certificate, hoping to add that one missing something to my life. I was skeptical at first. Maybe even a little scared. I decided to give it a try. I drove all the way here from Saratoga hoping to meet a nice woman. Someone I can just talk to. I didn't know there would be all this paperwork and all these regulations."

When did he start talking like a commercial?

"Your assistant—"

"Assistant?"

"Your assistant says I need a background check, like I'm a criminal. I don't know if I'm ready for this kind of interrogation."

Of all the nerve!

"Please. You're a serial liar." I turn to Lisa. "The first time I met him he was pretending to be a priest. And he doesn't live in Saratoga. He lives in Burnt Hills."

Lisa steps in. "Normally we do require an initial interview, but we can make an exception, this once. Right, Paige?"

"What about our promise to our other clients?" I ask through clenched teeth.

"Paige, can I speak to you privately?" Lisa hooks her arm around mine like we're two best gal-pals heading to the restroom to check our lipstick and enjoy a little gossip.

When we're out of earshot, I start. "We promise these women we have conducted background checks on all the men here. We need to at least make sure Isaac is his real name and that he's not a criminal." I doubt he's using an alias or has been to jail. Mostly I just want him kicked out.

"Look around." She points. "Nerd. Loser. Nerd. Nerd.

Loser."

I have to admit the men here look more chess club than football team.

"That guy there." Lisa points to a skinny, thirty-something with bad posture, a twitching eye, and an outdated haircut. "He could be a serial killer or a stalker. Not Isaac. I'm not going to turn a good-looking guy away. It's bad for business."

Lisa returns to Isaac without giving me a chance for a rebuttal. It probably would have gone something like "*He's not that good looking.*"

I follow along, defeated. I wish for Barb. She's in the car. I'd like to join her.

"Isaac, may I see your driver's license?" Lisa asks.

"Sure." He takes his wallet out, removes his ID and hands it to Lisa. She glances at it, and then passes it to me.

"I'm satisfied," Lisa says. "Now, promise me you'll come down to the office next week, and we'll get you properly registered."

I give Isaac back his license. I hate him and his flattering picture. He actually looks like he's laughing at me.

"Can I show you around?" Lisa asks.

"Thank you," Isaac says. They start to walk away. I can still hear their conversation. "I hope your clients are warmer than your employees."

"She's new," Lisa wraps her arm around Isaac's hips, letting her fingers slide lower along his butt.

"I do like her husband, though."

Lisa laughs. "Me, too."

I walk back to the check-in table, steaming inside. I

paste a permanent smile on my face and pretend to enjoy myself. I feel like Barbie—a plastic face that never moves. The next two hours crawl by. Everyone seems to be having a good time. Lisa moves from man to man flirting obnoxiously. Ryan and Isaac laugh over beers and occasionally talk with the women ordering drinks at the bar. Green-dress seems to have found a soul mate in the guy Lisa proposed for the role of serial killer. They hold hands and giggle at one of the small cocktail tables until they leave together. I have to remind myself that my Ken is out there somewhere. Hopefully at the law offices of Rogers, Rigby, and Roy.

And if all goes well, my storybook romance will begin tomorrow.

*Buying a wedding dress every year doesn't
make you desperate, it makes you a collector.*

Chapter 20

According to my college film study class, most romantic comedies have a meet-cute. (I took a few cinema courses my first year. I wasn't sure if I wanted to be a mathematics or drama major.) The meet-cute is the first time the man and woman have an encounter and, usually, it's sweet. I've never had a meet-cute. Maybe that's why my relationships don't work out. So, after a lot of thought, I've arranged the beginning of my own romantic comedy, and Trisha—though she doesn't know it yet—is going to help.

Father Nolan and I pull up outside the vet's office. There's no way I'm getting out of the car, and Trisha would never expect me to. My blood pressure rises just watching a girl walk her terrier. Father Nolan, the brave soul, goes in to retrieve Trisha.

"You're safe. You're safe," I tell myself over and over with Barb in hand. I leave the car running, anyway, in case I need to make a quick getaway.

My fear of animals doesn't have a specific triggering incident. Even before a chipmunk got in my tent at Girl Scout camp and terrorized me. Even before a bird tried to pull the ribbon out of my pigtail on the pier in San Francisco. Even before the neighbor's dog knocked me off my tricycle. I've always been afraid. When Ryan and I were born, Mom and Dad had a Scottish terrier. Mom says I screamed every time the dog came into the room. Within a few weeks they gave the dog to Grandpa. They claimed I was allergic.

"Should I have worn a skirt?" I ask Barb. I don't feel very feminine in camel-colored slacks and a lavender oxford.

No, but you're too buttoned.

I undo the top two to show off some skin. Sexy, not slutty. I'd used a diffuser on my hair so it had a touch of curl. My makeup looked natural, though it was anything but—liquid concealer followed by foundation, then powder, then blush, along with lipstick, lip-liner, eye shadow, mascara, and a brow pencil.

It's five minutes before Father Nolan's back with Trisha. She's wearing jeans and a fitted brown top that hugs. She looks good and ten times more confident than I feel. Maybe I need to lose another button. I put Barb away in my attaché before Trisha climbs into the front seat. Father Nolan settles into the back.

"So, where are we going?" Trisha asks.

"Hi, nice to see you, too."

"Sorry. Hi. Now, what's on the agenda? I haven't taken an afternoon off in months. I'm excited. Where are we going?"

It's my second week of work and I'm already taking an afternoon off. I'll make up the time this weekend reviewing the files of our eligible clients.

"Yeah, where are we going?" Father Nolan asks. "I'm on pins and needles with anticipation." He lets loose an honest laugh.

I pull out of the parking lot and get the car up to thirty miles an hour before I answer the question. I don't want them jumping out.

"Well?" Trisha's growing impatient.

"One-o-five Wolf Road"

"What's there?" she asks.

"Ohhh. Is it the new wine bar slash book store?" Father Nolan asks. "I read about it in *The Gazette*. Forget lattes. You can check out new titles while sipping a chardonnay."

We're now cruising at fifty-five. No one will be jumping out. "We're going to see a lawyer. Remember— Phillip." Both Father Nolan and Trisha know different bits about my Phillip.

"This is her idea, isn't it? Where is she?" Trisha opens the glove compartment and sorts through it.

"Who?" I ask.

"You know who." She takes my purse and dumps it on her lap. "Nope."

"You better put that all back."

"Try in here." Father Nolan hands her my attaché case from the back seat.

"I know she's here somewhere." Trisha opens the case. "Ah-ha. You evil blonde bitch. What did you do to my friend? She used to be sane—no imaginary husband, no chasing down men she knew twelve years ago. She used to be boring."

"Stop. Barbie has transformed me. Sure, before her I didn't have Kenneth. I also didn't have a job, a place to live or much of a future."

"Father Nolan got you the job and your parents gave you a place to live. And a car."

"I wouldn't have accepted this job without Barbie's approval. I'd have done something boring. Now, stop complaining. And don't forget, you owe me one."

"For what?" She uses Barbie as a puppet to ask the question.

"For Manny standing me up last night."

"That wasn't my fault. Besides, things worked out well with your brother. That was very Freudian, choosing your brother. Don't you think, Father Nolan?"

"Last night alone has guaranteed me several more months with Paige. I could drop all my other responsibilities to solely focus on her and still be pressed for time."

I ignore Father Nolan's plight to make me his life's work. "You think last night worked out? I'm married to a man named Kenneth Succotash, who runs wet T-shirt contests for a living and probably deals in porn on the side."

"Your fault," Trisha whispers to Barbie.

"You cannot blame Barbie for Paige's mistakes," Father Nolan pulls Barb out of Trisha's hands. "Barbie has a standard of values and ideals that Paige needs to aspire to. Respectability. Of course, she's going to stumble a little."

Trisha grabs Barb back. "Barbie is a betrayal. No one

woman can be all that you claim Barbie is."

"My dear Trisha. Barbie represents perfection and of course that is not attainable. Especially for Paige."

"Hey, I'm right here."

"Barbie also represents possibilities." Father Nolan snatches Barb again.

"Don't hurt her." I say trying to focus on the road.

"Strive for perfection. Anything is possible if you go at it with the right attitude."

"Including failure." Trisha says. "Don't get me wrong. I don't hate the girl. But what has she done that has you so impressed, Father?"

Father Nolan has read all my Barbie books to help me through this sojourn. "She's accomplished so much. From doctor to tennis star she—"

"Those are just costumes. She plays dress up." Trisha says.

I can almost hear Trisha rolling her eyes.

"Perhaps to the unimaginative they are just costumes," he says. "In the hands of little girls the clothes represent possibilities."

"And this all goes beyond careers," I say. "Barbie is her own woman. She's not someone's wife. You have to admit, she's a better role model for girls than any of the Disney princesses. Cinderella, Snow White, Jasmine. Their life's purpose is finding a husband. And have you looked at Jasmine's body? Her waist is the size of her neck."

"Mulan kinda kicks butt," Father Nolan says.

"Enough," Trisha puts Barbie back into the case. "How's the list going?" She holds up my abbreviated version.

Subject Requirements
1. Complete makeup. (Daily)
2. Hair maintenance. (Daily)
3. Exercise. (4/week)
4. Feminine attire. (Always)
5. Good manners. (Always)
6. Positive attitude. (Always)
7. Find your own Ken. (Continuous)
8. Pursuit of a fulfilling career. (Continuous)
9. Be there for Midge. (Continuous)
10. Try a new sport. (At least once)
11. Be a fashion model. (At least once)
12. Get a pet. (Soon as possible)
13. No drinking alcohol. (Always)
14. Read *The Barbie Files: An Unauthorized Biography*. (ASAP)
15. Complete the assessment survey. (Nightly)

"Did you get a pet yet?" she asks. "Number twelve."

"No."

"I think I can help you out with that one," Trisha says. "I have this dog and—"

"A dog? I don't think so."

"Trust me. This dog is different and you can give him back at the end of the experiment. He just needs a foster home." Trisha says.

"We'll see."

Trisha puts the list away. "Enough Barbie-talk, it's killing my brain cells. Tell me about the party last night."

"It was wonderful," I say sarcastically. "Thanks to Father Nolan's friend."

"Isaac's not that bad." Father Nolan leans forward between the seats. I already complained to him about Isaac on the drive to the vet. "Promise me you'll set him up with someone. He has a lot to give."

"Who's Isaac?" Trisha asks.

"Erika's teacher and a complete pain in the ass." I describe Isaac, portraying him accurately in an unfavorable light. He ruined my evening. He complained about me to my boss. He insulted me in front of my *husband*. He ignored my instructions. And I think he knows Ryan wasn't my husband.

"My boss only let him stay because she thought he was good looking," I say.

"I know lots of women who find him attractive," Father Nolan says.

"If you're into tall, blond, and horrible. His hair is too shaggy for my taste. His smile is crooked and a little evil."

When I finish complaining, I notice I'm doing eighty-five, so I slow down. Then I notice the dashboard clock. It's nearly three. I speed back up and do ninety.

"Woo! What's the hurry?" Trisha grabs the armrest.

"Our appointment is in ten minutes."

"What appointment? I thought we were just going to be stalking Phillip. We're actually meeting him?" Trisha asks.

"Yes. Actually, you're meeting him. I made an appointment for Trisha Stevens. Father Nolan and I are only along for moral support. Don't worry, I have a plan."

"Famous last words," she says.

"You're interested in hiring him. But when we meet Phillip, there will be a conflict of interest and you cannot retain his services. Then he'll ask me for coffee, then, who knows."

"What conflict of interest?" Trisha asks.

I shrug.

"That's your plan?" Trisha asks. "I've seen recipes for ice water that are more complicated."

"Don't worry."

"Why do I want to hire him in the first place?"

"It doesn't matter. It won't get that far. We'll be too busy reminiscing about frat parties and basketball games."

"You've never been to a frat party," Father Nolan says.

"So."

We arrive in the lobby of Rogers, Rigby, and Roy with no time to spare. Trisha gives the receptionist her name and we're asked to take a seat. We plop down on the ornate sofa. Trisha picks up a *Time* magazine. Father Nolan selects *US Weekly*. I work on my breathing, trying to relax.

"You okay?" Father Nolan asks.

"Fine."

"Then stop with the jittery leg. I'm getting seasick over here." Trisha never looks up from her magazine.

Father Nolan folds down his magazine and flashes me Barb. He's smuggled her in from the car. "She's here if you need her."

I try to remain calm and practice deep breathing. I fish a mirror out of my purse and check my makeup. Everything is in place.

"Here, read this." Trisha hands me her magazine. She picks a business card out of the brass holder on the table and examines it. "Paige, what kind of lawyer did you say Phil was?"

"I didn't."

"He's a divorce lawyer."

"It doesn't matter," I reassure her. "It won't get that far."

"Was he your divorce lawyer?"

"No," Father Nolan says. "He was Max's lawyer."

"Paige!"

The receptionist interrupts us. "Ms. Stevens. Please come with me."

We all follow her to the large conference room where my marriage ended four weeks ago. It's lined with bookcases and an oval table that seats at least fifteen. All the wood is dark and shiny enough to check makeup in. I run my hand along the back of one of the black leather chairs. It's soft like a suede jacket. The receptionist leaves the room after assuring us someone will be right in. We take seats on the far side of the room near the windows. Father Nolan keeps Barb in his lap. Not a minute later, the double doors open, and a young man—maybe twenty—walks in with a manila folder.

"How long do you think this will take?" Trisha slumps into a chair.

"He'll be here in a few. I'm sure."

"No, I mean all together—the reacquainted, the flirting, and the falling in love. How long? Will we get back before dinner time?"

"Actually, for your help in this matter, I have a little surprise for you both. I wasn't going to tell you until later, but what the heck. I made us reservations at Olive's."

Olive's is a new sushi restaurant in Albany that's overpriced, yet still packed every weekend with white-collar types who consider themselves too good for regular bars. While Trisha isn't that type, she does love sushi and swears it's the best in town. Father Nolan is a regular.

"Excellent. What time?" Trisha asks.

"Five-thirty. It's all they had."

"Then let's meet your man and get back home." She starts to get up as the doors swing open and Phillip appears.

It's like a movie. The room falls silent except for the soft jazz music wafting in from the lobby. Time slows down, and every step he takes seems to last a minute. As he approaches, his face comes out of the shadows. His skin is smooth and tan. His hair is brown, graying at the temples and neatly combed. His eyes are dark. His nose is perfectly straight. His chin is strong with a cleft. His smile shows off perfect teeth. He isn't male-model pretty, more TV-anchorman respectable in a two-thousand-dollar dark-blue suit and shiny loafers.

Phillip gives me a hard stare. "This is a surprise. Ms. O'Neal-Rus...I mean...Ms. O'Neal. I wasn't expecting to see you, again. How are you?"

"Good. Very good," I realize that I'm slouching. I quickly suck in my stomach and pull my shoulders back.

Phillip introduces himself to Father Nolan and Trisha. "How can I be of assistance?" He asks as he takes a seat.

"My friend, Trisha, is looking for a lawyer." I say. "A good lawyer. But that would probably be a conflict of interest. Right?"

"No. There is no conflict of interest. Your divorce is settled and there is no client-attorney confidentiality breach if your friend hires me." He flashes me a smile. "And, Ms. O'Neal, thank you for the referral. I appreciate it."

"Please, call me Paige."

"Shall we begin?" Phillip shuffles the papers in the file.

"Actually...um...while we were waiting, I believe Father Nolan talked Trisha out of the idea of a divorce. Right?"

Both Trisha and Father Nolan stare at me. I really can't expect a priest to lie on my behalf, but Trisha could at least nod.

"Catholics are anti-divorce." I say. "It's in the ten commandments."

"No, it's not." Now Father Nolan speaks up.

"Regardless. Trisha isn't ready to dump her husband." I look to her for help.

"We're not going to divorce. We're trying to have a baby instead."

"So no one needs a divorce attorney?" Phillip seems confused and maybe a bit pissed off.

"Guess not. Sorry." I say. Please ask me out. Please ask me out. I plead with my eyes, my mouth, my whole body—everything except my voice.

Trisha taps her fingers on the table, making me very aware of the awkward pause in the conversation.

"People are allowed to change their minds. Ms. Stevens, I hope you and your husband have many happy years." Phillip gathers his papers and stands up.

Oh, no.

"Phillip," I stand up, too. "Do you want to get a drink or something?" Did I just ask him out?

He hesitates and I want to shrink to eleven inches tall.

"It would be nice to catch up." He finally says. "There

is a pub two blocks down. Joe's. Can you give me twenty minutes?"

"Sure."

"Great. I'll meet you there." He offers a hand to Trisha, then to Father Nolan. "It was nice to meet you. Take care." Phillip escorts us to the door. My stomach flips when he puts his hand on my lower back.

I float to the car. That couldn't have gone better. It was a meet-cute all the way.

"What did you think?" I ask the moment we get in the car.

Trisha shrugs.

"He seems respectful," Father Nolan says. "I have a feeling he's Methodist."

"We all have flaws. And why don't you like him?" I ask Trisha.

"I'm not ready to make a judgment yet. He didn't score any points by not inviting Father Nolan and me along for drinks, too. What are we supposed to do while you have drinks?"

"Well, I don't know. Just come along with me. He won't mind. I won't mind." And I really wouldn't or at least shouldn't. Trisha and Manny never make me feel like a third wheel and Father Nolan's been my platonic date for everything from soccer games to family picnics.

"No, this is your chance." Trisha says. "Let's see you work your Barbie magic. We'll make ourselves scarce."

"Thanks."

"We just better not be late for dinner." Father Nolan says.

"I promise."

*A lull in the conversation is an opportunity
to show off your smile.*

Chapter 21

I check my watch. I have only twenty minutes to reunite
with Phillip, and form a fast friendship-slash-romance
before taking my best friends out to dinner. I take the last
sip of my diet soda and pretend to be intently watching the
Yankee game on the flat television hanging over the bar. I
wonder what I look like to the other patrons—a single
woman, sitting alone in a bar on a Friday afternoon,
watching baseball and checking her watch every ten
seconds.

I also wonder what they must think of Trisha and
Father Nolan. A nonromantic couple sitting at a dimly lit
table near the restroom, sharing a bottle of Merlot. They'd
promised to sit quietly in the corner if I allowed them to
rummage through my attaché case. I think they're reading
the files from Prrfect Connections that I brought home to
review. I've been working there two weeks and haven't
made a successful match yet—plenty of first dates that

don't result in second dates.

A hand touches my shoulder, and I turn around to see a more casual Phillip. The suit jacket is gone, the tie is loosened. If possible, he's even more attractive than he was half an hour ago.

"Hello, again." He gives me a kiss on the cheek and sits on the stool to my right. "So…what have you been up to?"

"Since college or since you helped my ex-husband get everything?" I mean it as a joke. I hope he takes it as a joke.

He smiles. "College."

"Well, as you know, I'm recently divorced. I live in Schenectady. My daughter is—"

"Erika."

"Yes. She's fifteen. I work for a customer service company." No need to say it's a dating service. "Guess my life is fairly boring. Thirty-something typical."

"You do look great," he says, and I feel my face redden. "You haven't changed much."

"Yes I have. I no longer have The Rachel haircut."

"This suits you." He plays with a lock of hair and I hold my breath.

"What about you?" I feel uncomfortable talking about myself.

"As you know, I'm a lawyer. I live in Delmar. I like to play golf. And don't laugh, I'm an actor in the Albany Little Theater."

"That's great. You finally got over being rejected for the part of Mercutio."

"My therapist recommended it. Am I revealing too

much information? I'm not nuts. Promise."

"I don't think you're nuts." I don't add that my therapist is a priest and my role model is a Barbie doll, both of whom travel with me.

"Anyway, we just finished doing *Oliver* and we've started rehearsals for *Death of a Salesman*."

"I'll have to come check it out."

"Will you be bringing a date?" He asks. He stares intently waiting for my answer. Do they teach lawyers to stare like that in school? It's unnerving.

"Doubtful, unless I bring Trisha or Father Nolan or my brother."

"How's Ryan doing? Did he ever break out of the Minors?" The stare vanishes.

"Good memory. No. Now he runs an imaginary wet T-shirt company." I let out a small sigh, thinking about last night, Ryan—I mean Kenneth Succotash. "Never mind. What about you?"

"What about me?" he asks.

"Are you seeing anyone?" I have to be blunt. I check my watch and see that if I want to make our dinner reservation I need to leave in fifteen minutes.

"No."

The baseball game breaks for a commercial, and the bartender takes the opportunity to clear away my empty glass. "Want another soda?"

"Please."

"And what can I get ya?" he asks Phillip.

"Sam Adams." He turns his attention back to me. "Do you want to order some food? I skipped lunch."

T-minus fourteen minutes. Can we order and eat in

fourteen minutes? Phillip is already looking at a menu. "You go ahead. I have dinner plans."

Phillip orders a bacon cheeseburger with no mayo or pickles. And that's exactly what I would have ordered if I wasn't going to be eating raw fish in an hour.

"Phillip, please excuse me. I'm going to the ladies' room."

I head for the restroom, brushing Trisha's shoulder discreetly as I walk by. Both Father Nolan and Trisha get up and follow.

"Are we ready to go?" she asks when we're inside the single-stall bathroom.

I check myself in the mirror and realize I could use more lipstick. "It's going really well. Thanks for asking. I haven't been this excited about a guy since ever. And I haven't been this excited about anything at all since...before I started needing eye cream."

"Remember," Father Nolan says. "What would Barbie do? Be friendly, open, honest, confident, beautiful, and intelligent, worthy of—"

"I got it."

"Good, then let's get out of here. Leave on a high note." Trisha suggests. "Keep him wanting more."

"We can't go. He's ordering lunch."

Trisha looks disappointed. "We have reservations. The waiter gives me the creeps. And something furry ran over my foot." She's just trying to scare me with thought of wild animals running around; at any minute they could jump up and bite me.

"Fifteen more minutes. That's all. This is going too well. And we'll still go to dinner. We can do eighty the whole way there, and if we're ten minutes late, they'll still hold our reservations."

Trisha doesn't respond.

"Just fifteen minutes."

Trisha seems to be debating the offer, then she pulls Barbie out of the back of her jeans. She's smooth, like a gangster with a glock. "You can have ten minutes. Any longer, the doll gets it." She points to the toilet.

Father Nolan shakes his head. "That's not right."

"She's my little insurance ticket."

"It's not about *that doll*," I say. "I can always get another." I try to blow off her threat.

"Nine-and-a-half minutes. Do you want to stay here and debate, or do you want to go win over Phil?"

I walk out of the bathroom and back to Phillip without saying another word. It's only a doll, I remind myself. Only a doll. There's like two sold somewhere in the world every second. I can get another.

"I took the liberty of ordering you some fries. I can remember you always like to steal my fries."

"And onion rings." I notice Trisha and Father Nolan slinking back to their table in the corner. She doesn't look happy. He's as comfortable as a hostage.

"So, before my infamous divorce, when was the last time we really spoke?" I try to get the conversation flowing again. "I can't really remember."

He cracks a sweet, knowing smile "I tried to kiss you at the Nirvana concert. You turned your head and told me you were dating an older someone. "

"Max," I say. "I don't think that's the last time we saw each other."

"No, but it makes a good story. You dump me for another man and many years later I am the lawyer who facilitates the divorce."

"It would make a good story if it had a happy ending." I say, as my phone rings. "Excuse me." I grab it out of my purse and press the talk button. "Hello."

"You have six minutes to say your goodbyes or—" I end the phone call before she can finish.

"Wrong number?" Phillip asks.

My phone rings again. "I'll just turn it off."

"Do you golf?" he asks. "I'm a member at Oak Crest."

My heart leaps. Is he suggesting a date?

He continues. "We play a mixed scramble every spring. It's a lot of fun."

The spring? That's half a year away. He's not asking for a date, he's making polite small talk. "I've only played the miniature version. I really should learn. Maybe I could get lessons."

Maybe golf could count toward the list—try a new sport. I imagine Phillips arms wrapped around me and guiding my club.

Phillip is suggesting different golf pros when a tiny-waisted, big-busted waitress interrupts.

"Excuse me, miss. I think this belongs to you." The waitress discreetly opens her clenched hand. It's a tiny plastic high heel. Is that teeth marks?

I moan.

"What's wrong?" Phillip asks, standing up. He didn't see.

"Nothing, it's just the back of my earring. Sit down." I pretend to slip it back on, then casually put the shoe in my pants pocket. "How often do you golf?" I ask.

"League play just ended. I was playing Mondays and Thursdays. I still play on weekends when the weather is nice."

I'm really trying to listen to Phillip talk about his golf game, but my attention lies with the heavy-chested waitress. She's walking back to Trisha. The waitress nods and holds out her hand.

What's it going to be this time?

"Sorry to bother you again." The waitress says this time with a Jersey accent. "I think they mean business." She slips the second mutilated shoe into my palm.

"What's going on?" Phillip eyes the waitress.

"Change. I must have dumped my purse." I grab the waitress' arm and pull her close. I whisper to her, "I'll give you twenty dollars to make it stop."

The waitress smiles and points over her shoulder. "That lady is paying me more." And she walks away.

I turn back to Phillip as the bartender delivers our plates. A thick cheeseburger for Phillip and thousand calories worth of soggy fries for me. Phillip cuts his sandwich in half and offers me a portion.

I shake my head. I don't have much of an appetite, but I eat a limp French fry anyway. "Can I get some ketchup?" I ask the bartender.

The waitress is back before I get my Heinz 57. "I'm sorry, sweetie," she places something under a napkin on the stool to my left.

What the—?

I lift the napkin and let out a whimper. Barb's severed head smiles up at me. I know she's not in any pain, but she doesn't deserve this. I grab the tiny head before Phillip sees it. He's too busy devouring his meal.

"I gotta run. Sorry." I'm up.

"What's wrong?"

"I have an appointment I forgot about." I scribble my number down on a napkin. "Please give me a call sometime." I don't wait for a response or any kind of long goodbye. I head for the door, hoping I seem more mysterious than strange.

"Paige, wait," Phillip chases after me. "In case I don't see you for another twelve years." And Phillip gives me a kiss that I will remember for the next twenty years.

*Fear and anxiety are terrible for your mind,
but great for your metabolism.*

Chapter 22

My Aunt Sheila and Uncle Edmond look like a couple who belong together. He's a few inches taller, both are equally round in the waist, his hair is brown and cut short, her hair is also brown and always in a ponytail. Every time I see them, they are wearing jeans and some top with a sports team logo on it.

Now, my parents' neighbors are a couple who could be poster children for opposites attract. She's a thin, sophisticated, supermom who's always wearing Ann Taylor. Their three kids are involved in sports, music, and their church, and she's their coach, concert director, and youth group leader. Not to mention, she works full time in pharmaceutical sales. Meanwhile, her husband has long, graying hair and a beard, a pierced ear, and he wears his black leather jacket in summer and winter. He does odd jobs fixing motorcycles or landscaping. It doesn't make sense to me. Both my aunt and uncle and my parents' neighbors have been married for countless years and seem very happy. So what makes a relationship work?

In my first weeks as a Relationship Consultant with Prrfect Match, I set up a dozen different couples. All ended in disaster—one literally ended with the woman's car upside down in a pond. I tried to pair up all of them based on their likes, dislikes, and hobbies. If they both liked tennis or Indian food or vacationing, I figured they'd like each other. Embarrassed over my failures, I turned to Lisa for some advice. She told me to get to know the clients. She sometimes talks to them for two or three hours during an interview. From there, it's all instinct. I worry that maybe I don't have *that instinct* but decide to give it a try.

On Tuesday, I met four new clients. I spent a few hours with each of them, learning not only about their likes and dislikes, careers, and hobbies but also about their goals, dreams, funny stories, childhoods, and deep thoughts.

One client revealed that he'd really like to leave his successful job as a financial consultant and go to cooking school. A woman divulged that she often wakes at two in the morning with an urge to do something drastic like drive to the beach to watch the sunrise. Another guy likes to go to the park and watch people, and then he follows them home. I called the police on that guy.

The point is, I didn't get to know my clients by asking them, "What type of music do you listen to?" I got to know them by just letting them ramble.

On Wednesday morning as I type up my notes from yesterdays meetings, there's a knock on my office door, and the receptionist pops her head in. "Your eleven o'clock is here."

I tell her to send in my new client—Thelma Walker.

A second later, in walks a twenty-something, black-haired, Elvira type with a tight leather miniskirt, matching tank and three-inch heels. All my other clients have been typical, white-collar people. Thelma will officially be my first character.

I shake her hand, ask her to take a seat, and offer her a drink. She wants guava juice but settles for orange. I use the office camera to take a picture. We don't give out the photographs. They are for staff's eyes only. It helps us remember clients.

We start the interview with the basic, boring exchange. I tell her about our fees and policy, and she tells me her name, age (twenty-eight), address, and phone number. I half expect her to be like a punk kid who's been dragged by her father to a college entrance interview at his alma mater, but she's surprisingly polite and open.

I put my pencil down, turn on my tape recorder—with her consent—and begin the fun part of the interview. "Thelma, what do you do for a living?"

"A bit of everything. I read Tarot cards. I do calligraphy, ya know, for wedding invites and stuff. I pet sit and house sit. I write an online astrology guide. And for awhile, I was a taste tester for a pet food company."

"That is a bit of everything." I try not to imagine the taste of veal in gravy kibble. "What kind of job do you see in your future?"

"Paranormal research."

"What is that exactly?"

"Using scientific methods and modern technology to prove the spooky stuff people always claim see. Crop circles, ghosts in the attic, big foot, aliens. I haven't finished my degree yet. I'm working on my BS."

Is that bullshit or Bachelor of Science? "You can get a degree in paranormal research?"

"No, physics. I'll graduate in December." She gives me a look that I can only interpret as So-*there*.

I move the conversation to the next topic—hobbies. Thelma is into everything from cross-stitching to training seeing eye dogs to scuba diving in the Hudson River (apparently there have been numerous shipwrecks). There is no way to categorize this woman. She's in a league of her own.

Thelma picks up on my loss for words and talks some more about her life passions. From there, we cover what love is, the meaning of life, what men really want, low carb diets, the American fuel crisis, and everything in between.

I don't know whether Thelma is someone to be admired (she did backpack across Europe by herself) or is she someone to be scared of (she knows seven ways to kill a man without using a weapon). After filling my digital recorder with our conversation, Thelma and I say our goodbyes. I'm drained and decide to go home an hour early.

On the drive, Barb sits in the passenger seat. Her head firmly reattached. No signs of her recent decapitation.

I love a good workout, I hear Barbs say.

I throw a napkin over her.

Erika's list wants me working out four times a week. This week I have yet to strap on sneakers.

"Fine," I say. "A quick jog around the block when we get home and maybe a couple sit-ups." That's all I have time for. I need to be at Erika's soccer game at six-thirty.

As I turn onto my street, I notice the blue Mercedes behind me does, too. It's the same Mercedes that was behind me on the exit ramp. I check out the driver. I can't see his face.

God, I wish I carried mace. But no, I carry a doll. I remove the napkin, not wanting to face the man in the Mercedes alone.

I pull into my parents' driveway—I probably should go to a safe public place like Price Chopper or the police station. The Mercedes pulls behind me and stops. He blocks me so I can't back out.

I grab a lipstick from my purse and place it in my palm as if it were mace. Should I get out of the car and run inside? Should I call the police? Do kidnappers usually drive high-end sedans?

Before I can decide, the driver gets out and walks toward me. He keeps his sunglasses on. He doesn't look like a serial killer in his khaki pants and sports coat.

"Stay calm," I tell Barb.

The man taps on my window. He looks familiar. "Paige O'Neal. Don't—"

"I have a gun," I shout, holding up my concealed lipstick. "Back off."

He doesn't look concerned. "That's a gun?"

"I mean mace. Now, get back in your car."

"Ms. O'Neal. I'm John Rigby, Junior. From the law offices of Rogers, Rigby, and—"

"I know. Why are you following me?" My heart leaps. Maybe Phillip sent John. I've never been asked on a date via a messenger before.

"I'm here for the car."

"I'm not giving you my car." I say, remaining inside. "Max said I can keep it until I find another vehicle."

"According to the settlement, you have rights to the vehicle until you find employment. And it has come to our attention that you've been employed now for almost three weeks."

Before I can respond, Max pulls behind the Mercedes. This is an ambush.

"How can you take my car? I have a child that needs rides to the doctor's office." I'm groveling as Max walks over. I don't want to plead in front of him. I'm not looking for sympathy—not from Max.

"Paige," Max says with a nod. "Step out of the car."

"You are not taking my car."

"My car." He holds up a wrinkled piece of paper, which, for all I know, could be a dry-cleaning receipt.

"I'll stay in here all night."

"Then we'll tow you in the vehicle," Max says and points to the tow truck that's just now pulling up.

"How am I supposed to get to and from work?"

"I'm sorry," John says.

I don't want to, I really don't. It just happens. Tears well in my eyes. My throat grows tight, so much so I'm afraid to talk. I hate that I can't control my crying. I cannot cry on cue like an actress, and I cannot stop myself from bursting into a fit of tears even though I want to. Mom always tells me not to cry in public, and to this day, I've never seen her so much as blot her eyes outside the house or a funeral home. Guess I didn't inherit that gene.

"Don't do this, Paige," I say to myself. I suck up my

tears and swing the door open and smash into Max's knee.

"Shit!" He grabs his leg. "You did that on purpose."

"Did not!" I'm standing next to Max. It would be so easy to push him to the ground or pull his hair. Beating up my ex-husband counts as a workout, right?

"Please," John says. "Ms. O'Neal. Mr. Russell. Remain calm."

A few deep breaths and all violent thoughts leave my body. Max brings out the best in me. "I'm okay. Just let me get my stuff out of the car."

"I'll take care of it," John says, probably not wanting to risk my locking myself in the car again. He moves to the Passat.

"I do have some good news," Max says.

"Really?"

"I've had an offer made on the house. The closing is at the end of the month." Max looks to me like I should be thrilled.

"Here you are, Ms. O'Neal." John hands me my purse, Barb, and my belongings—all except the car key he's trying to finagle off the ring.

"I'll call you and let you know the date and time. We need you to sign a few papers."

"You accepted the offer without consulting me?"

"I didn't think you'd mind."

"Is that legal? Can he do that?" I ask John who is still struggling with the key ring. "Give me that." I grab it from him and remove the key in a few seconds. I hand it to the tow truck driver.

"You really need to consult your own attorney, but I believe it is legal for him to accept the offer on good faith."

Max pats my shoulder. "It's done with. Just sign the papers at the end of the month Paige and you'll be thirty-thousand dollars richer. You can get yourself a new car,"

Having had enough of Max, all I want is to head inside. Plus—a tiny woman is walking her pony-sized dog down the street towards us. She's still a hundred yards away approaching fast. I want to be indoors before they reach us. I say a quick goodbye and start up the steps. Before I get to the door, Max yells to me. I turn around. The dog is less than fifty yards out.

"Paige, wait. Are you still dating a friend of mine?" He hides a snide little smile.

"I never said friend. It's just someone you know." I say and take another step.

"Why is it a secret?"

The dog has stopped to relieve himself, which buys me a few more seconds of safety.

"Why didn't you tell me about Vanessa?"

"I didn't want to hurt you."

"That's the difference between you and me. I'm not telling you because I do want to hurt you." I go inside.

I want to run away. I want to win the lottery. I want to smack the grin off of Max's face. I want a double chocolate mochatini or something equally sinful with caffeine, sugar, and booze but without a car I can have none of these things. I toss my stuff on the bench in the foyer and go into the kitchen. Then I do what any self-sufficient, grown woman would do in this situation—complain to Mom.

I tell her about my day, and she laughs and tells me things aren't as bad as I make them out to be. I do have my health and the health of my child to be thankful for. After trying for twenty minutes to get some sympathy I give in, and she gives up. She gives up her *spare* car. I can have the Accord for as long as necessary, so long as I promise to use only premium gasoline and get it washed once a week. I tell her I'll try.

It's safe to assume Barbie never had to borrow her mom's car indefinitely, but I'm desperate and don't have the luxury of driving a twenty-dollar pink convertible.

"I'm going to lie down before the game." I tell Mom. I grab my stuff—including Barb—and go to my room.

Barb has other ideas for the use of my time.

There are plenty of things to keep you busy. Doing sit-ups. Dusting. Going over client files. Reading Grapes of Wrath.

One of my new year's resolutions was to read a classic every month. It's October, so I'm only a tad behind.

Learning Spanish. Cleaning out your drawers. Backing up computer files. Making a hurricane ready kit. Practicing the clarinet.

"I haven't played since ninth grade."

My cell phone rings—thank God—and I dive on it, "Hello."

"He still hasn't called," Trisha says on the other end.

"Five days and no call. How did you know?"

"You practically answered the phone before I had a chance to finish dialing."

"I'm even desperate over the phone."

"Let's practice patience. I'm going to hang up and call you back. Don't pick up until the fourth ring."

"That's silly," I say. Trisha has already hung up.

The phone rings once. Twice. I pick up.

"I'm not doing this." I say.

"I'm being turned down for a date before I've even asked. That's a first."

"Phillip?"

"Yes. How are you, Paige?"

Shocked. Thrilled. Amazed. "Good."   Call-waiting beeps and I ignore it.

"I know it's short notice. I'd like to take you to dinner tomorrow evening."

I should play hard to get. I should say I already have plans. I need to seem aloof, unavailable and mysterious. I look to Barb.

"That would be nice."

My day has unexpectedly hit a high note!

Daily Self-Assessment   *Wednesday, October 13*
Rate the degree to which you agree with the statement.

    5–completely agree   1–completely disagree
1. I accomplished something today. *4*
2. I felt connected with my friends and family today. *2*
3. I was interested in sex today. *1*
4. I laughed today. *1*
5. I am looking forward to tomorrow. *5+++*
Notes: *Ken is on the radar!*

I'll never admit to Erika my hormones are in overdrive.

A first date is about conversation, not consummation.

Chapter 23

I'd been married long enough to have forgotten some of the great perks of being single, like coming home after a *wonderful* date, crawling into bed and dreaming—while still awake—about the *wonderful* man and all the *wonderful* times we'll have together in the future. If a drug manufacturer could bottle all those *wonderful* feelings she'd be a millionaire—and I'd be an addict.

As Phillip and I sit in his car, parked outside my parents', I'm looking forward to doing just that. I'm going to relive the entire evening in my mind—the half-dozen white roses he brought to my door, the fancy, five-course Italian dinner, and the goodnight kiss I'm expecting as soon as Phillip finishes telling this story I'm only half listening to.

"It was a priceless moment," he says.

"And then what did you do?" I ask.

"I said to the guy, 'Hey, I'm sorry. This is your wife's

coat.'" Phillip laughs with a big, open smile.

"I forgot how much fun we use to have," I say.

"I didn't." Phillip leans over the console and gives me a kiss. At first, it's slow, nice, gentle. I give him a little encouragement and he moves one hand to the back of my neck, pulling me closer to him. He moves his lip to my ear.

"It's late," I say, embarrassingly breathless.

"Not that late." He focuses his kissing on my neck. And I momentarily lose all focus.

"I'm sorry. I need to go." I'd promised myself not to sleep with Phillip. Not that it is even an option. I live with my parents, twin brother, and teenage daughter. There are only two bathrooms. It would be war in the morning.

"I'm not going to get invited in, am I?" He settles back in his seat.

"No."

"I respect that." He takes my hand and kisses my palm. I sigh. "Please, go."

He laughs. A good-looking lawyer probably isn't used to getting shot down.

"I had a nice time. We should do this again."

"We should."

I open the car door and go for broke. "Is there any chance you could teach me to golf this weekend?"

"Golf isn't something you learn in a weekend."

Was that a no?

"But I'd love to give you your first lesson."

"Great." We make plans to meet on Saturday morning at a public course in Schenectady. I get out of the car quickly to avoid another kiss. I'm only so strong. One more and I'd be braless in his backseat.

Phillip watches from the car as I go up the front steps. I give a final wave before going in.

"How was your date?" Erika asks. She's lying in the living room watching *The Daily Show*.

"Nice. We're going out again." I sit on the arm of the couch. "Hey, I've been thinking."

She pauses the television.

"If you still want to join the cheerleading team, I'm okay with it."

"What?" Her voice cracks.

"You were blessed with both beauty and brains. Why shouldn't you use your gifts? Be proud of what you have." I pat a silent Erika on the leg. "I know you work hard for your A's. Always studying. Doing your homework. But even with your dedication, some of it comes down to your IQ. So if you want to take advantage of your looks and work on your splits and peppy voice, I support you."

Erika studies me like she's looking for my horns. "I think I'll stick with basketball."

"That's fine, too." I kiss her on the forehead.

When I get to my room, I fill out the nightly survey. As always I score a one to the comment *I was interested in sex today*. If I was being honest I'm pushing a seven.

On Friday morning, I call Trisha from my office and give her all the details. She's not impressed by the swanky restaurant, the flowers, or the end-of-date kiss. For some reason, she's guarded when it comes to Phillip.

"Are you going to see him again?" she asks.

"Yes. We're hitting the links tomorrow morning."

"Links?"

"Isn't that what they call a golf course?"

"Whatever." Then Trisha starts telling me about her evening—something about installing a ceiling fan and Manny almost losing his head, literally—when my office door bursts open without so much as a knock.

Standing in the doorway is the ever-present Isaac-pain-in-the-ass-Barber. He lets out a loud sigh. "Isn't there someone else I can talk to?" He asks the receptionist, who's standing behind him.

Penelope looks to me, "Sorry, Paige. He insisted on seeing someone immediately."

"Trisha, I gotta go. I'll see you later." I hang up the phone and ask the receptionist, "Where's Lisa?"

"She took the day off." The phone rings in the lobby, and she heads back to her desk.

"Shouldn't you be teaching a class?" Isaac is lucky I'm still on a post-date high, or I would have kicked him out immediately.

"I teach one class. Eighth period. My school day doesn't begin until one-thirty."

"How can I help you?"

"I need a date for next weekend." He steps in, closes the door and makes himself comfortable in the chair across from me. And comfortable is how I'd describe his attire. More denim and a plain white T-shirt. He might look good in white if he wasn't such a jerk.

"We are not an escort service. We don't offer *dates*. We match people of similar values, ideas and personalities."

"Give it up. You make money off of people's belief in

romantic love. When in fact, romantic love—as we know it—wasn't invented until the Middle Ages. And people have been getting together for thousands of years prior to that without the help of flowers, love notes, and playing footsies under the table."

"I don't know if I believe that. The origins of romantic love cannot be proven, just argued." And arguing seems to be something Isaac rather enjoys.

"Why do people get married?"

I shrug. "What do you mean?"

"Why did you marry Kenneth?" He seems annoyed that I'm not diving head first into his set-up question.

"I love him." Of course I love him—like a brother.

"In our society that would be the number one reason people give for getting married. I love him. I love her. Before the 1800's, love may not have even been in the top five reasons for marrying someone." He sits back in his chair, somehow satisfied.

"What would be the top five reasons?"

"I don't know. Because my parents said so. Because I need someone to mend socks and she needs someone to plow fields. Because we want to make babies. Because we are British royalty and we need an ally in France to defeat the Spanish."

I nod my head slowly. "That last one probably happened a lot."

"Do you believe in romantic love?" He asks.

"Yes." And there is no way he's going to convince me otherwise. "I take it you don't."

"No, I do. And yes, I've even felt it. I just don't think it's a modern—relatively speaking—concept. It's something our society has been taught through literature, myths and lore, by our parents, and in Sandra Bullock movies." He folds his arms across his chest. I could interpret that as a defensive position. "Oh, and romantic love doesn't last."

"That's why today's divorce rate keeps climbing. The romantic love fades and so does the marriage. Centuries ago, husbands and wives grew to love each other over the years. They climbed the mountain. They didn't start on its euphoric peak like today's couples."

"Exactly." He claps his hands and leans forward.

"Noooo." I try to burst his bubble. "We have more divorce because we have more options. More lawyers. More independence. More acceptance of the single lifestyle. Especially for women."

"You're insane," he says. "Can you get me a date or not?"

"Did you meet anyone special at the party last week? Maybe love at first sight?" I ask, knowing my questions are driving him nuts.

"No. That's why I'm back."

"I'm not going to get a lecture on love at first sight?"

"I could. But everybody knows love at first sight only applies to cars."

"Have you started a file yet?"

"No."

I pull a new client folder from my drawer. For some unexplainable reason, I'm looking forward to interviewing Isaac. I imagine it more like a brutal interrogation than a fun conversation. If only I had a bright light, a wooden chair, and a water torture device.

I snap a picture for his file and it's gorgeous. I delete it and take another. His eyes are half shut and his jaw is slack. Perfect. Then I start the questions. We only get through name, date of birth, and address before Isaac looks like I am using a torture device on him.

"Is this going to take long?" He looks at his wrist as if he were wearing a watch.

"Yes. I have sixty-two questions for you."

"Sixty-two? After occupation and favorite book, what else is there?"

"Well, there's number forty-seven—What role does religion play in your life? And number eighteen—What were the traditional female roles in your adolescent household? Thirty—What are your retirement goals, financial and leisure?"

Isaac leans back and puts his hands behind his head. "And people really sit here and answer all these questions?"

"Yes. Most people like to talk about themselves."

He laughs. "That's because most people think they're more interesting than they really are. I've met maybe three truly interesting people in my entire life."

"Are you an interesting person?" I ask.

"You should read my memoir." He grins.

"You've written a memoir?"

"Written, yes. Published, no. I promised my mom I wouldn't publish it until she's playing bridge in the great hereafter."

"Then how would I read it?"

"I'll get you a copy. After you read it, you'll have more than enough information to go on. I think you'll enjoy it. There's a scene when I was fifteen—"

"I don't have time to read your memoir. I'm in the middle of *Grapes of Wrath*."

He smiles. Can he tell I'm lying?

"I mean I'm just beginning the *Grapes of Wrath*."

He laughs. "Because I like you, Paige O'Neal. I'll answer three questions. That's it."

"Gee, thanks." I flip through my list looking for the perfect ones—the ones that'll most aggravate Isaac. I want to see steam bellowing from his ears. I decide to make up my own.

"Which do you prefer, oregano or basil?"

"Basil," he says without missing a beat or questioning the relevance.

"Name one adjective that best describes your ideal mate?"

"Adaptable."

I think about his answer. Is it offensive, realistic, or original? Then I ask my final question, "How are you similar to Oprah Winfrey?"

"I'm well-read. I'm a good listener. And I, too, am very unlikely to ever take a husband. So, will you help me?"

"Based on our two meetings I think I have someone in mind. Let me call her, tell her a bit about Isaac Barber, and she'll contact you if she's interested." I can't hide a smile imagining Thelma—my Elvira client—with Isaac. Two people who each believe they have the most brilliant, original thoughts and, beyond that, love to share them. Maybe they'll actually hit it off!

"Tell her I need a date next weekend, so no waiting

weeks to call. This window is only open for a limited time." Isaac stands and taps his wrist for emphasis.

"Goodbye, Mr. Barber."

He shakes my hand and walks out of my office.

I suppress a smile and open Barbie's drawer. "Did you catch any of that?"

"Hey, Father," Isaac says from just outside my office. "You're not here looking for a date, are you?"

"No, Isaac. I'm spoken for," Father Nolan says.

Father Nolan walks into my office and sits in a chair across from my desk. This feels strange. For months he's been the one sitting behind the desk.

"Where do you want to go to lunch?" Father Nolan asks.

I ignore his question. "I can't believe you're friends with Isaac Barber. Then again you like everyone. But Isaac's so rude."

"He does have an odd sense of humor."

"He's crass."

"He speaks his mind."

"He never *stops* speaking his mind."

"He's not perfect. She without sin shall cast the first stone."

"Ugghhh." I pull Barb out of her drawer-apartment and put her in my purse. "Let's go eat."

Father Nolan stands. "Paige, you are going to try and find Isaac a suitable mate, aren't you? He deserves someone to spend his time with."

"He refused to fill out a personality profile. Can you make any recommendations of the type of woman that he'd mesh with?"

"Witty. Strong. Challenging. Attractive. A touch crazy. I guess someone like you, but I think he'd prefer a redhead. Now let's go get some lunch. I'm in the mood for curry."

What the hell did that mean?

*Don't let your pedestal be at the same
height as everyone's chair.*

Chapter 24

Subject Requirements
1. Complete makeup. (Daily)
2. Hair maintenance. (Daily)
3. Exercise. (4/week)
4. Feminine attire. (Always)
5. Good manners. (Always)
6. Positive attitude. (Always)
7. Find your own Ken. (Continuous)
8. Pursuit of a fulfilling career. (Continuous)
9. Be there for Midge. (Continuous)
10. Try a new sport. (At least once)
11. Be a fashion model. (At least once)
12. Get a pet. (Soon as possible)
13. No drinking alcohol. (Always)
14. Read *The Barbie Files: An Unauthorized Biography.* (ASAP)
15. Complete the assessment survey. (Nightly)

Playing golf with Phillip on Saturday morning fulfills a majority of my Barbie requirements. I've got the look. Khaki pants, long-sleeve peach shirt with a matching visor. My hair in a French braid and full makeup application. Golf counts as exercise. Phillip is my Ken. I won't be drinking at 10 a.m. I promise to remember my please's and thank you's. And every time I hit the ball I'll be thinking *Condor*. (That's four strokes under par. I did my golf research online last night.)

I borrow Mom's golf clubs and drive her Accord to the Schenectady Municipal Course. Golf bags are as versatile as cargo pants so I'm able to bring Barb along for the trip.

Dad had recommended that I arrive early and hit some balls. So I fork over twelve dollars at the pro shop for a giant bucket before Phillip arrives. This seems like a really good deal because a three pack of Nike golf balls costs seven dollars in the same pro shop. I just got about fifty. Who cares if they have an ugly orange stripe? I toss a handful in Mom's golf bag for future use.

I have been to a driving range before. I'm not a complete novice. It's been years, but I'd accompanied Max on occasional Sunday afternoons. Once I find a spot a few yards away from other golfers I tee up a ball. I select the biggest club from Mom's assortment. It's a wood—I think—with a head the size of half a grapefruit. No need to take a practice swing when I have over four dozen balls to practice with.

I line up. Slowly bring the club back. Think to myself, *whatever you do, don't miss the ball completely*. Then let it rip. The ball sails well over the one hundred and fifty yard marker and rolls all the way to the two hundred yard flag. I give an excited fist pump—that's what Tiger would do. It was a perfect ball. Straight and long.

And it was the last one of the morning.

My next shot never gets airborne and though there is no marker under fifty yards, I'd estimate it at twelve feet. I bobble a few more. I shank one—is that the correct term?—and it hits the leg of a plaid-pants golfer next to me. Most sail a few yards left or a few yards right. I'm pretty sure if I picked up one of the balls I could throw it farther.

"Warming up?" Phillip says as I break to change to a smaller, hopefully more manageable club.

"How much of that did you see?" I ask.

"Enough to estimate it would take us six hours to play nine holes."

"Ouch."

"Why don't we skip the course today and I can give you a lesson right here?" Phillip rests his bag against the fence. As always, he looks put together. A long sleeve white shirt tucked into wrinkle-free black pants. Everything fits perfectly, not tight, but snug enough to reveal a fit body.

"Sounds good." A day at the driving range with an instructor constitutes *Try a new sport* and it will get crossed off the list.

"Let's start with a nine iron." Phillip walks over and grabs the club out of my bag. "A nice easy swing and you should be able to get ninety yards." He tees up another ball for me. Such the gentlemen.

I step up to the ball.

"Keep your knees bent."

I pull the club back.

"Head down."

My eye is on the ball.

"Your left arm should be straight."

I start my down stroke.

"Pivot your hips!"

I pull up on the club trying to stop my swing. It still makes contact with the ball sending it rolling a few feet.

"What's wrong?" Phillip asks.

"You're a bit intense."

"Sorry. We can take it slower." He pulls a club from his own bag. "Let's start with the grip. It should feel like holding a baby bird."

Like I've ever held a baby bird.

"You need to be delicate and firm. You don't want the bird to fly out of your hands." Phillip places his fingers on the club. He points out the positions of his thumbs and the overlapping of his pinky and index finger.

I copy his example. This is so not natural.

"Good," he says. "Now take a practice swing."

And I do.

"Almost. You need to pivot more." Phillip drops his club and walks behind me. Dreams do come true. He puts his hands on my hips. "Try again." He guides me through a swing.

"Better?" I ask trembling a little.

"Yes. Let's try it with a ball."

I put a ball up on the tee, very conscious of Phillip's view from behind me. He doesn't guide my hips this time, which makes this much less exciting. I delicately swing and knock the ball about seventy-five yards. Damn, better than I thought. I figured anything under fifty would get me another lesson in hip motions.

"Good," Phillip says. Then he wraps his arms around me from behind grabbing my arms. "I think if you turn your wrists over after you make contact you'll get another ten yards." He demonstrates this action a few times. I close my eyes trying to store all this in my muscle memory.

Phillip helps me through my entire bucket. His lesson takes nearly an hour. Smelling his cologne. Feeling his grip. Brushing against his arms. This has been the best twelve dollars I've spent in a long time. After, I spend another thirty dollars on thank-you sandwiches in the clubhouse.

"Don't think I'm ready for the PGA tour, but this has been fun." I pick at the last few potato chips on my plate.

Phillip takes a drink of his ice water. "Next time we'll work on putting."

God, I hope there is a next time though I could care less if it's near a golf course.

"Most golfers don't spend enough time working on their short game," I say. Another fact I learned on the Internet.

"If I'm going to continue as your private golf instructor I'm going to need something in return."

"Name it."

"I need a date for a wedding next Saturday. I know the groom—a law school buddy. I won't know anyone else. Could be terribly uncomfortable chatting with drunken uncles, might even be sitting at the children's table. Interested?"

"What an appealing offer. How could I refuse?"

Phillip says he'll call me during the week with details.

I pay the bill and we walk to the Accord.

I wonder if he's aware that Max *stole* my Passat.

"Well, thanks again." I linger at the car door waiting for...

Boom! He kisses me. It's slight and quick. Guess a golf course parking lot is no place for passion. Even a peck of a kiss is better than a handshake.

The Dream House is anywhere outside of
your parents' home where
you have at least an underwear drawer,
a coffee mug, and a toothbrush.

Chapter 25

House hunting seems like a glamorous adventure until you actually go through it. Max and I bought our first house a year after we were married. I spent hours in Starbucks perfecting my must-have list and my would-like list. I flipped through realty magazines, circling all the possibilities. Then we started working with a realtor—a woman named Sandy with big hair and makeup like an Avon saleswoman from the sixties. Even with my lists, Sandy continued showing us houses that were not acceptable.

Must-have: Basement
Sandy interprets: Shed
Must-have: At least 2 bathrooms
Sandy interprets: 1.5 baths but also a large utility sink in garage
Would-like: Hardwood floors

Sandy interprets: Floors

Would-like: 1-acre lot

Sandy Interprets: 1-acre lot but shared by three houses

Eventually she did find our house, but only after I was too tired to protest any further.

Barbie, in the past, has been an apartment dweller, but she's known for her dream house. With the cash from the sale of my old house for a down payment, and if Mom and Dad cosign, I can get a traditional loan.

Sunday morning, I let Erika sleep in and keep busy by scouring the home ads. We don't leave the house until noon. We grab fast food for lunch and drive around the suburbs looking for open house signs. The first arrow-shaped sign leads us to another, then another, then another until, I swear, I've left New York. Finally, a small cottage appears. I don't know the age exactly, but judging by the *Martin Van Buren Slept Here* plaque, it wasn't built in the last century. No need to stop.

The arrows that led me to the Presidential Palace now elude me. I drive and drive but don't recognize a thing. I'm about to pull out the cell phone and call for help when I see a street name that could be fate speaking to me. I still have no idea where I am, but I'm compelled to check it out.

"Look at the street name."

"Malibu Lane," Erika says. "Probably one of the most famous Barbie doll lines."

I turn left and a few hundred yards down the road, the trees open up to a secluded neighborhood of new, large brick homes. Beautiful! Definitely dream house material. The third house on the left is for sale—a white-brick ranch with only a single-car garage. How much could it be?

"Now that's a nice house." Erika grabs Barb out of the cup holder for her to see. "What do you think?" Erika loves to mock me.

I pull Mom's Accord into the driveway and call the number listed on the sign. My call is transferred to the Realtor's cell phone.

"Missy Woods," a cheerful voice answers.

"Hi. I'm sitting outside 59 Malibu Lane. Can you tell me a little about the house?"

"You're there now?" she asks.

"Yes."

"I'll do better than that, I'll show you. Be there in ten minutes."

She doesn't let me get in another word, so I'm forced—by good-girl conscience—to wait. Exactly twelve minutes later, a white Lexus pulls in behind me.

Missy, wearing a pantsuit the color of pink cotton candy, with shoes and purse in the exact same shade, walks toward my car still chatting with someone on her cell phone. Her curled hair—a perfect helmet of platinum blond—doesn't move in the breeze.

I step out of my car and try to smile as wide as Missy. I have to tone it down for fear of splitting my lip open.

With extended hand—her nails are pink, of course—she says, "Hi. Missy Woods." She has a southern accent that belongs in Civil War movies.

"Paige O'Neal. This is my daughter, Erika."

"Paige, I know you're going to love this house. It just came on the market and it's a gem." She leads me to the front porch, all the while talking about the peaceful neighborhood, fabulous schools and nearby conveniences.

The woman never takes a breath.

While she works the lock to the front door, she goes on and on about the builder—his reputation, his attention to detail, his fair pricing, and his generous warranty.

"What's the asking price?" I ask when she stops for a second.

"Ta-da!" She swings open the heavy maple door. "Paige, check out this foyer. All wood flooring, nine-foot ceilings, crown molding."

"Wow! It's beautiful. How much did you say?"

"To the left is your dining room. You've got inlaid hardwoods and floor-to-ceiling, energy-efficient windows. How big is your dining room table, Paige?"

"Like in inches?" I try to remember my dining room set that has been sequestered in a storage unit.

"No, sweetie, how many does it seat?"

"Six."

"No, no. That won't do. This room is fifteen by eighteen. You could get a table big enough for ten or twelve. Imagine that, Paige. Christmas dinner, here, at your brand new estate."

"Estate?"

"It is all brick, located on almost three-quarters of an acre. Paige, do you want to see the kitchen? Even someone like me who'd rather order take-out could learn to love cooking in this kitchen, Paige."

I feel like every time she says my name I'm underestimating the price of the house by fifty thousand dollars.

"Six-burner, flat-top stove, two in-wall convection ovens, a state-of-the-art fridge, trash compactor, warming drawer, energy-efficient dishwasher with ten different cycles, granite countertops, stainless-steel farmhouse sink, walk-in pantry, and my favorite, a wine fridge."

"This is amazing. How much for just the kitchen?" Really, I could live just in this kitchen. The sink is large enough to bathe in. The warming drawer could be my bed.

Erika checks herself out in the reflection of the restaurant-quality fridge. Looking directly at her I don't see it, but in the reflection she's a woman. She's effortlessly beautiful. Barbie pales in comparison.

Missy continues the tour with the great room, the den, the office, the four bedrooms, the laundry room, all three baths and the bonus room over the garage. And in each room, I ask how much, to which she only replies with more details about tile, lighting, and dual-zone heating.

"When do you think your husband can come take a look?" she asks when we return to the foyer.

"She's not married," Erika says. "Max divorced her after she stabbed him."

She stares at my ring, and her face falls a few stories.

"It's for work." I slip it off and put it in my pocket. "So, what did you say the price was?"

Two days later, Father Nolan and I are with my new Realtor, Don—a Jeep-driving, khaki-wearing, slow-talking, retired school teacher. He shows me an old Cape Cod in need of TLC. The neighborhood is quiet, except for the nearby railroad tracks, the taxes are modest by New York standards, and there's a convenience store only two miles away—but you've got to go the back way, which is seven miles longer, because the bridge on Route 44 is under construction. Dan assures me it's only temporary. "Should be complete in a year or two."

Still, something about the house appeals to me. It's 1800-sq-ft with three bedrooms, a full basement, a wide front porch, and original hardwood floors.

"Potential. Lots of potential." Father Nolan holds his hands out like a director shooting a scene.

"Don, what's the asking price?" I ask after the tour.

"One-seventy, I think they'll take a little less."

"Can you give me a minute?" I ask and both men excuse themselves to the front porch. I take out my cell phone and pretend to make a call. I'm really talking to Barb. I open the flap on my purse. "What do you think? It needs a lot of work."

Hard work is nothing to be afraid of.

I close the cell phone—and the purse—and join Don and Father Nolan on the front porch. "Let's put in an offer."

"Congratulations, Paige," Father Nolan gives me a hug and spins me around the creaking porch. "Your very own dream house. I'm so proud of you."

"I'll get the paperwork started," Don heads toward his Jeep.

Low-carb or low-fat? When in doubt grab a Diet Coke and your best friend and go shopping.

Chapter 26

I remember learning in psychology class that when you ask someone for advice, you already know the answer she's going to give, and that you're really only looking for affirmation. So when deciding whether to buy the dream house I didn't go to anyone, except Barb, of course. Father Nolan saw potential in the house. He sees the good in everything. Even though Mom already had agreed to cosign the loan, she would not have approved of 1502 Chesterfield Road.

The whole process has been a whirlwind. Realtor Don helped me with the offer letter. An hour later it was accepted, and by the end of the second day we had a purchase agreement. I close in a few weeks. Since the house is practically a done deal, I feel I can now tell Trisha the big news.

"Guess what I'm buying on November fifth?" I yell to Trisha over the dressing room wall as I try on a floral, knee-length dress.

"A pink convertible?"

I emerge into the waiting area to find Trisha patiently flipping through a catalogue. "Do I look like a Mary Kay saleswoman?"

"No, you look like patio furniture. Next."

I don't disagree with the assessment and step back inside. Barb is on the lavender colored bench. She too shakes her head at the dress.

"I made an offer on a house." I yell out.

"The dream house? Does it have a balcony and a real working elevator?"

"I don't think it even has working faucets. It's what those in the industry call a *fixer-upper*."

"Now Barbie is a plumber?" Trisha asks.

"If she, I mean I—I mean if she wants to be. In this case we'll be doing it all. Plumber, carpenter, decorator, everything." I take off the shower curtain and try a short flapper-like dress. Barb doesn't seem impressed by the little number.

"Good for you."

"Really?" I model number two for Trisha. "I thought you'd say I've made a mistake. Or jumped in too quick. Or didn't think it through."

"Let's just say it's not the worst decision you've ever made."

"What is the worst decision I've ever made? Wait, don't answer that."

She points to the dress. "What else have you got?"

I quickly change into my third selection. A brown tank dress with matching jacket, very simple and practical. I

233

could even wear it to work.

"Nope," she says. "Too receptionist-like. You're trying to impress Phillip, not apply for a job."

"This is hopeless."

"That's because you're not following your own advice. What would Barbie do?"

"That's not fair. She looks good in everything."

Trisha shakes her head. "Wait here."

She returns a few moments later with three dresses. She holds up each one of them in turn. First, an off-the-shoulder black cocktail dress. Next, a short, blue, spaghetti-strap dress. Finally a long, pale-pink dress covered in some type of shimmery material. "Which would make her proud?"

"Give me the black one."

"Bullshit." Trisha throws the pink gown at me.

"Fine. I'll try the prom dress."

"Attagirl!"

One final time into the dressing room. I take off the receptionist costume and catch myself in the mirror. My white cotton underwear—wouldn't even call them panties—and a beige, well-worn bra look too practical. I can't feel sexy in such supportive undergarments.

"Hey Trisha, remember the obnoxious guy from the party I told you about—Erika's teacher?"

"Isaac? What made you think of him?"

"Because I'm standing here looking at myself half-naked and feeling disgusted. He brings out a similar feeling whenever he's around." I do feel strange thinking about him when I'm in my underwear so I pull on the pink dress. I have to squeeze my butt and suck in my gut. The tag says four. I'm a six on a good day—like after I've had the stomach flu. "Anyway, he came into the office again. Refused to answer any of the questions and demanded a date."

"Looking for a date at a dating service? Some nerve. What did you do?"

"Set Isaac up with a paranormal scientist who reads tarot cards. He wanted someone interesting. It may work." I fiddle with the zipper and walk out to Trisha without looking in the mirror. This could be comical.

"Wow!"

"Really?" I walk to the three-panel mirror at the end of the room. Right away I can see we have a winner. I just can't eat anything for the next twenty-four hours and sitting down is out of the question.

"Hate to admit it, the doll did good," Trisha says, coming up to stand behind me. "Get it and let's go. I'm hungry."

"Okay. Let's get some dinner for you and a Diet Coke for me." I check the tag. "Damn! I'm gonna need a pay raise. Lisa says she'll pay me a commission on any new clients I bring in. Know anyone looking for love?"

"Sorry, no. I'll keep my eyes open. And if one of your clients accidentally gets knocked up, let me know. Manny and I are looking to adopt."

I can only stare at her. This is their decision—surrogacy or adoption—but the rejection makes my chest ache.

"Another month, another box of tampons. I'm never going to get pregnant." Trisha shrugs it off.

"What about other options?" I feel like a selfish cow

even asking.

"We could try another round of in vitro. Why bother? The doctors are giving us single-digit odds. Manny and I've been talking about this. We'd love to adopt a baby. Give him or her a loving home."

I give her a tight hug. "You'll be great parents."

"Great parents? Maybe. Ideal adoption candidates? No. Mom works full time. Dad travels a lot. It may take years."

"And why won't you let me be your surrogate?"

"You have enough going on with Barbie and the divorce. You don't need to be saddled with a fetus. You'd have to give up drinking and dating—which you just started. Not to mention you're almost thirty-five. It wouldn't be fair to ask you to put your life on hold."

"But you were fine with the idea when I was married to Max."

"You were in a more stable situation. Listen, don't take this personally. Manny and I just don't want to screw up your life."

"No, that's my job."

Saturday, I'm wearing a new lacy bra—very sexy—and control-top panties—very functional. I put the finishing touches of makeup on. My $300 pink dress is hanging on the back of the bedroom door. I'm not putting it on until the last second. Phillip is due to pick me up in fifteen minutes. I'll head downstairs in ten and wait outside. I don't want to introduce him to my parents.

I borrowed a small pearl clutch from Mom. It's only big enough to hold a few credit cards, identification, a tube of lipstick and a cell-phone. There's no way to squeeze an eleven inch doll into my five inch bag.

"I can sneak you under my dress," I suggest to Barb who's sitting on my dresser.

You'll be great and I'll be there in spirit.

I can't remember the last time I went it alone. Barb has always been, at the very least, in the car. I pick her up and touch her to neck and wrists like perfume, trying to absorb some of her confidence, charm, and appeal. I can feel it working.

As I check my teeth one last time for poppy seeds or spinach, there's a knock on my bedroom door.

"Come in," I say after I slip into my dress.

"Hey, Mom." Erika walks in. "You look good."

"You sound surprised."

She takes a seat on my bed, a spiral notebook in hand. "My mom looks sexy. Takes some getting used to."

"You two started this." I point to Barb and Erika.

"I never asked you to carry a doll. And I know I didn't tell you to talk to her."

I laugh. "I don't talk to her. Not really."

"Whatever. We're six weeks into the experiment. You ready to admit that Barbie is a good role model?" She jots something down in her notebook.

"No," I pause. "She's a great role model. Am I going on record here?"

She nods.

"She represents the American dream."

"How so?" Erika plays the role of newspaper reporter and puts the pen to her lips.

"In every way. From home ownership to higher

education to employment mobility." I pause and look to Barb. "And she's got a lot of stuff."

"But what about her obsession with looks?"

"That's the American way. Good hygiene and a nice wardrobe are necessary if you want to be successful. Like it or not. Just look at your experiment at the mall. You were treated better when you looked nice. That's our society."

"What about Ken? You think Phillip is your man?"

"Potentially." I just pray he's more anatomically correct than Ken. A bump—that's what Mattel calls Ken genitalia—just wouldn't be much fun.

"And what are your plans to fill the pet requirement?"

"Don't know." I take a seat on the edge of the bed. Something has been on my mind since yesterday. "Erika, I want to ask you a question and I need an honest answer. So throw out the first thoughts that come to you. Don't overthink. Don't look for the right words. Just go with your gut and remember—"

"Is there really a question?"

"Do you think I'd be a good surrogate for Trisha and Manny?" I spit out the words as fast as I can.

"Yeah. It would be another baby for you to give up."

"Erika." I'm stunned. I thought we were moving past this.

She picks up my pillow and hits me with it. "Kidding, Mom."

"Hey. Watch the hair." I recheck everything in the full-length mirror on the back of the door. "It's just Trisha doesn't seem confident that I can handle it."

"I didn't think you could handle this experiment and you're proving me wrong. You look the part. You act the part…well, most of the time."

We're interrupted by the doorbell.

"Shoot. I gotta run, Sweetie. Before your grandmother invites Phillip in for a drink and an interrogation." I kiss Erika on the cheek. "Love you."

Phillip is introducing himself when I get downstairs.

"Shall we?" I say with relative calm.

Outside we walk arm and arm to his little sports car. He opens my door, and I slide in. For a moment my dress feels cheap. Phillip's suit probably cost ten times as much and he doesn't need to suck in anything.

"We shouldn't let the groom see you until after the ceremony," he says from outside the door.

"Excuse me?"

"He may have second thoughts." He closes my car door. Two points for him.

The forty-minute ride is nearly perfect. We talk about everything—food, politics, movies, football, our favorite fabric softeners—and we agree on almost all topics. Our biggest disconnect comes over chicken piccata. He thinks the chicken breast should be breaded and I don't.

I'd like to drive all night and skip the wedding.

We pull into the parking lot of the Chatham House, a restored historic mansion on Lake George. Phillip, being the gentleman, opens my door and offers me his arm.

The wedding takes place in the garden with lake and the fall foliage as the backdrop. They have twelve bridesmaids, six groomsmen, three flower girls and a ring bearer. The two-hundred-plus guests sit in white folding chairs adorned with bows. The whole ordeal is beautiful and traditional, like it was torn from the pages of a bride magazine.

After the receiving line, we go inside to the reception hall. Phillip grabs two flutes of champagne. I drink mine with ease. Champagne is my potent potable of choice. I remind myself to keep the sips to a polite minimum. We help ourselves to hors d'oeuvres and chat with the bride's grandmother who keeps calling me Cindy-Sue. I have one more glass of champagne to toast the bride and groom's first appearance as man and wife. We watch their rehearsed first dance from the edge of the dance floor. Halfway through, the band leader asks all the guests to join the happy couple, and Phillip and I oblige. Normally, I never dance in public, but the crowd is so thick there's only room to rock back and forth. Unfortunately, I keep brushing up against bridesmaids when I want to be brushing up against Phillip.

"Want to find a more private place?" I suggest.

"Definitely." Phillip grabs two more glasses of champagne, and we walk outside to a small courtyard. We sit on a stone bench that, despite the nearby portable heater, is cold. Luckily, after few swallows of champagne, I am warmed up.

"They seem like a nice couple," Phillip says.

"Yeah, I really think they'll make it."

"Really? What makes you think that?"

I was only trying to be funny. Now I feel stupid. I'm suddenly aware that I'm more than a few sips ahead of my date. Time to slow down.

"Just a feeling. Woman's intuition."

He grabs my hand and kisses the back of it. "What does your intuition say about us?"

"Good things." I moan. "Positive things."

There's silence for the first time all evening. It's his accompanying intense staring that means only one thing.

"I'm glad you joined me tonight," he says and moves closer for a kiss—more like a collection of small rapid-fire kisses that are appropriate for a park bench.

I lean back and smile my approval. Phillip receives the message and goes for a lingering, back row, dark-movie-theater-type kiss. His hands pull me closer.

Phillip kisses my ear. Then my neck. His hand moves to my thigh.

I let out a sigh. "I wish there was someplace we could."

"Your place?" He kisses my lips.

Moments pass before I break free. "I live with my parents. Remember? What about your place? I've got a few hours before curfew."

"Can't." He kisses behind my ear. "My wife is home."

The spot behind my ear—that part of neck that curves in below the skull—that's my magic *on* button and Phillip has found this secret control. It isn't until his lips move that I realize what he said.

"You're married?"

"You knew I was married." Phillip defends like any sleazy lawyer.

"You said you *had been* married and it didn't work out."

"And you assumed divorce?" He asks turning the problem on me.

"Legally, you are still married?"

"Yes."

I'm suddenly stone cold sober and standing. I'm glad there's not a paring knife around or I'd stab him. At the same time I wish I could throw a decent punch. A black eye would be perfect right about now.

"We're about to be legally separated. By the end of the month. I promise. There are a few sticking points in the separation agreement. That's all. If I leave before we have an agreement it could be considered abandonment."

"You still live in the same house?"

"I sleep on the couch in my office," Phillip explains.

"Goodbye, Phillip." I say and head toward the main house.

"How are you going to get home?" Phillip yells. "A taxi from here will cost you two-hundred dollars."

Damn, he's right. I turn back and get in face. "Give me your keys."

"No."

"Ugghh." I stamp off toward the house.

"Paige," Phillip calls. "Let me drive you home. Give me a chance to explain."

I weigh my options. I can't call Father Nolan for a ride. He'd just be wrapping up Saturday evening mass. Trisha and Manny have gone to Vermont for a romantic weekend. There's always Mom.

I decide to take my chances with Phillip.

"You will drive me home," I say when he catches up to me just outside the main house. "There will be no explaining. As far as I'm concerned you are still married. I don't want to be your Vanessa."

"Who is Vanessa?"

"Just shut up."

We ride in silence for the forty minute drive. I don't even look in his direction, afraid he'd think I've changed my mind. We pull into my parents' driveway at eight thirty. My date lasted less than three hours.

"Paige..."

I open the car door. "I don't want your entire marital history, just answer me one question. Why are you getting a divorce?"

He groans. "It's complicated."

"Of course it is. Good night, Phillip."

Daily Self-Assessment   *Saturday, October 23*
Rate the degree to which you agree with the statement.

    5–completely agree   1–completely disagree

1. I accomplished something today. *1*
2. I felt connected with my friends and family today. *1*
3. I was interested in sex today. *Negative 7!*
4. I laughed today. 4
5. I am looking forward to tomorrow. 1

Notes: *Need a new Ken!*

We've all had our embarrassing moments. Just ask
Growing Up Skipper and Earring Magic Ken.

Chapter 27

The allure of The Mall has always eluded me. Even in
middle school when all my classmates would hang out by
the food court on Friday nights, I'd rather go to dinner with
friends and gossip over fries and ice cream sundaes.
Nothing about a slew of small stores appeals to me.
They're full of identical merchandise, sixty-year old mall
walkers in their wind suits, young teens making out by the
fountain, and pairs of moms pushing strollers, blocking the
corridor, ignoring their screaming children.

Yet here I am, with Trisha and Father Nolan, pushing
Prrfect Connections. I give Erika ten dollars to go find a
bargain pair of earrings or something.

I need to bring in six new clients a week if I'm going
to earn enough money to pay the mortgage on my dream
house. Trisha, a fellow mall loather, helps me hand out
fliers to everyone over eighteen not wearing a wedding
band. Father Nolan doesn't help. He probably wouldn't be

good for business anyway. Instead he gets a ten minute, ten dollar shoulder massage from a pretty Hispanic woman.

"I still can't believe he's married," Trisha says. "And he seemed like such a great guy." Sarcasm drips from her words like an ice cream cone on a hot day.

"Separated," I correct her. "And he had a good reason for still living with her. He's just building a good case."

She grabs another stack of red fliers from my pile. "Married. Still lives with the woman he vowed to love and cherish forever. Just because he chooses not to wear his ring doesn't mean he's separated."

"What am I going to do?"

"What are you going to do? Nothing." She bats me on the head with the fliers.

"I really like him. He's a lawyer and handsome and punctual."

"Paige. Paige. Paige." Father Nolan picks up his head. "Ask yourself, why did he keep his situation a secret?"

"We all have secrets."

"I don't know much about Barbie," Trisha says, "but I can guarantee she never pursues married men. Am I right? Have you ever seen Home Wrecker Barbie on the shelves?"

"Would she meet him for lunch just to give him a piece of her mind?"

"No," they say.

I hang my head for dramatic effect. "Well, there's one good thing that's come out of this. Since I seem to be done dating…" I turn to Trisha. "…I'm free to carry your baby. Wasn't that one of your reasons why I wasn't a good candidate?"

"Father Nolan, tell Paige how the Catholic Church

feels about surrogacy."

Father Nolan looks up. "The Catholic Church frowns upon *most* of Paige's extracurricular activities." After handing out all seventy-five fliers, Erika and I head back to the house. My cell phone has three voicemails. I retrieve the messages.

"Paige, it's Phillip. Please, I need—"

I press Delete.

"Hello, it's me again—"

Delete, again.

I'm amazed at my strength. Or is it weakness? Like when you're on a diet and you throw out the forty dollars of Girl Scout cookies you just bought. Is strength getting rid of them, or is strength living with the temptation?

"Paige, are you avoiding me?"

Yep. Delete.

Two of Mom's handwritten messages lie on the table. Both say Phillip called. I throw the notes away, then I pull Barb from my bag. I clasp her in praying hands.

"Should I call him?" I whisper.

Ughh, that doesn't even deserve a response.

I put Barb down and pick up the phone. "I'm just going to tell him how disappointed I am. He deceived me. He's getting off too easy."

Think before you call.

Too late, I'm dialing his home number. The phone rings once. Twice. I start running through what I'm going to say to his answering machine.

A woman answers.

"Um…sorry to bother you. I think I have the wrong—"

"Is this Paige?"

"Yeah." I know I should hang up.

"Hang on. Phil's been expecting your call."

The nerve, *expecting my call*. Father Nolan, Trisha, Barbie. Three out of four people would not have called. He's lucky.

"Paige?" Phillip asks when he gets to the line. "Thank you for calling back. I need to talk to you."

"Shhh. You don't need to talk. You need to listen. I hate that you kept your situation from me."

"I thought if I told you, you wouldn't have—"

"I wouldn't have. To be completely clear, I do not date married men. It goes against my principles. So please, do not call me again." I hesitate. "At least not until...you're single."

"Do you mean divorced or separated?" he asks.

"You're the lawyer. Make your case." And I hang up the phone.

Back at the office on Monday, I finally feel in control. Lisa's cats, after a morning of playing keep-Paige-locked-in-her-office, have taken the opportunity to sun themselves in the front window. I was minutes away from using my fichus plant as a port-a-potty. My files are all caught up, and I've made a list of seven possible schemes to drum up new business.

As I take a relaxing, well-deserved break, the intercom beeps. "Paige, your husband is here."

"Who?" I ask before I realize what I've said.

"Kenneth."

"Right. Send him in. I thought he was in New Jersey

on business. This is a pleasant surprise." Paige, stop talking!

Ryan enters wearing gym clothes and smelling like he's been working out.

"What are you doing here?" I get up and close the door behind him.

"A husband can't stop in to see his wife at work?" He plops down in the chair reserved for clients.

"No."

"Can I borrow some money?"

"I don't have any money." Some things never change.

"Can you find me a sugar-mama?"

Before I can respond, my office door swings open and knocks me into the wall.

"Hey," I yell.

Ryan laughs like only a brother can at a sister's humiliation. He stands up and greets the visitor while I pick myself off the wall. "Isaac, how you been, buddy?"

Of course. Whenever things go badly, who's there? Isaac. He's a plague.

"Hey," The men shake hands. "Where's your *so-called-wife*?"

"What do you mean *so-called*?" I ask, giving away my position as I close the door before Penelope can hear.

"I know you aren't married," Isaac says. "Why would *Find Your Own Ken* be on the list if you were?"

"Well, I'm glad that is over," Ryan says. "Now about that sugar-mama. Preferably someone blond, tall and no more than a hundred twenty pounds. I want to be able to pick her up with one arm." He flexes then moves to the far side of the desk and takes a seat in my chair. Without hesitation, he searches through the files on my desk. "Nope. Nope. Maybe." He moves one folder to the side.

"Ryan, get out of there. And our marriage is not over. My boss still thinks we're newlyweds." I twist the wedding ring on my left hand.

"This married-to-my-sister deal is really turning my stomach," Ryan says and helps himself to the rest of my bagel.

"Ryan," Isaac says. "That's a helluva a lot better than Kenneth."

I move so I'm facing Isaac. "Why are you here?"

"To complain. That date you set me up with...that woman...she stole my car."

"What happened?" I ask. Thelma was strange, but her background check revealed no criminal activity.

"I took her to dinner at Willow Ridge and—"

"Isn't Willow Ridge a nursing home?" I ask.

"Assisted living center," Isaac says. "Visitors can eat there for five dollars."

"What's the address?" Ryan asks.

"Aren't you busy looking for a free ride?" I say and toss Ryan a few more files from the corner pile. I turn back to Isaac. "You're kidding? Please tell me you're kidding." And I thought my food court date was bad.

"No, five bucks gets you a main course, salad, bread, a drink, and dessert."

"Ugghhh." I sit on the edge of my desk. "You're joking. You didn't really take her to an assisted living cafeteria."

"Yes, I did. To meet my grandmother. She may not have much more time and Grandma is convinced I'll never be happy until I meet someone special. I told Thelma all this before we went out and she had no problems with it. Even thought it would be fun. Something about the place being filled with spirits."

"At what point did she steal your car?"

"In the parking lot. We were walking back to the car and I told her I thought she may be A.D.D. and suggested a shrink. She grabbed my keys and took off. There was also some yelling. Now I'm thinking she may be bipolar, too."

"You diagnosed your date?" I shake my head.

"Don't criticize. You set me up with a crazy woman. Just help me get my car back."

I look up Thelma's number in my files and give her a call. She's at the library and Isaac's car is safely parked at her apartment. He can pick it up any time, but she doesn't want to lay eyes on him again. I have a very similar feeling toward the man.

"Here's her address." I give Isaac a slip of paper. "The keys are under the seat."

"Good. Let's go get my car," Isaac says.

"How did you get here?"

"A buddy dropped me off, and I don't have a ride. I need my car now." Isaac steps closer.

We're like an umpire and a baseball coach. I wish there was dirt to kick onto his shoes.

"Sorry. I'm working until six. Maybe Ryan can take you."

"I rode my motorcycle." Ryan holds up a file. "Where do you keep the good ones?" He pushes away the stack of folders.

Isaac laughs. "It's the method. The questions are all

wrong. If it were me I'd ask completely different questions. Like…what beer manufacturer makes the best pale ale? What's more important: a good offense or a good defense? What's the best movie franchise?"

"What? Those questions don't tell you anything about a person?"

"Try it." Isaac says. "What's the best pale ale?"

"Saranac's." I say. "But I prefer wine."

"Good offense or good defense?"

"Good coaching."

He rolls his eyes.

"Fine. Defense."

"Best movie franchise?"

"The Bourne movies. So what do my answers say about me? Let's hear it Doctor Barber." I can't wait for the analysis. No matter what he says I'm going to tell him he's wrong.

"You're cautious and rarely jump into anything without Googling it first. You have high expectations of yourself, but you are more willing to overlook flaws in others. You take a creative approach to problem solving. You're able to think quickly. And you're a bad liar. We should play poker sometime."

"You got all that from three questions?"

"For the most part." He shrugs.

"Well, you're wrong. That's not me at all."

"Hmmp," Ryan says. "He's pretty close. He didn't mention anything about being demanding and always right, other than that, pretty close."

"Okay. So what kind of man would you set me up with?" I ask. We'll see how smart he is.

"Don't know. You're the paid professional here. I guess Matt Damon." He smirks. "I got that from the movie question. Unfortunately for you, I think he's married."

There's a knock on the office door, and it opens.

"Wow, a full house in here," Lisa says. "May I come in?"

"Of course," I say. "Lisa, you remember my husband, Kenneth." I emphasize husband. "And, this is—"

"Isaac Barber. I never forget our best looking clients." She gives him a wink.

Isaac? He's far from being a troll, but best looking? She's just being flirty. Well, I guess he does have chiseled features, nothing fantastic. He's not leading-man material—more like unavailable best friend's husband. No, he's too sloppy to be married. He's always in jeans. He's in jeans now. So he's more sloppy-athlete type with unreal blue eyes. He must wear contacts. That color can't be natural. Fine, he's leading man-good-looking, in a romantic comedy kind of way, not in an action-thriller. Can't see him chasing terrorists on a jet ski, shirtless, with a pistol in one hand and gripping the throttle with the other. Maybe he would look good without a shirt. He does have wide shoulders.

"Paige?" Lisa asks. "Are you with us?"

"Sorry," I say. "Just thinking of something I've got to do."

"I wanted to go over these ideas you e-mailed me," Lisa says. "When you're done, come to my office."

"Right. I think these guys were about to leave." I less-than-gently nudge Ryan out of my seat.

"Actually, Paige and I aren't quite through," Isaac

says.

"Yes, we are."

"No, we're not."

"What's going on?" Lisa asks.

"Nothing," I say.

"Lisa," Isaac says, "don't Paige and Kenny make a cute couple?"

"It's Kenneth," I correct.

"I think so," Lisa says. "They're great role models for our clients."

"Have you ever noticed how similar they look? There's almost a resemblance? Kissing cousins, maybe?"

"Yes, maybe a little." Lisa stares at us and I look down at the desk trying to keep her from getting a good look.

"Certainly have the same oval face, almond-shaped eyes and even the mouth—"

"Isaac, don't you have to get going?"

"I'm waiting for my ride." He smirks.

"I could give you a lift," Lisa says taking his arm, ready and willing to give him a ride. And whatever else.

"No, I'll do it," I say. "Lisa, you're too busy."

"Nonsense."

"I need to go out anyway," I add. "I need to pick up dog food."

"Dog food?" Ryan asks.

"Yes, for our dog." I can't remember the name I told Lisa. Isaac is right, I am a horrible liar.

Ryan smiles. "Right. I forgot to do it last night."

"If you're going to the pet store, do you mind picking me up a few things?" Lisa takes a pad off my desk and starts scribbling a list. "Here."

I read. "Tuna treats. Clay cat litter. Organic catnip. No problem."

"Keep the receipt. I'll pay you when you get back."

"Right. Isaac, let's go. Kenneth, I'll see you at home."

Lisa leaves, followed by Isaac. I wait for Ryan. On his way out, he steals a sheet of paper from a file. I ignore the infraction for now. I need to get out of the office before I kill my husband, client, and boss—not necessarily in that order.

Outside the building, I turn to the right. Isaac follows without saying a word. With any luck, he'll maintain his silence. Ryan crosses the street to his motorcycle.

The ride to Thelma's apartment starts off well. Isaac busies himself by playing with my radio. He checks out each of my pre-selected radio stations, nodding his approval to five of the six stations. I don't need his approval. Don't want it. I hope Thelma changed all his channels to Gospel.

"Interesting radio—"

"Please, let's not talk. Every time you open your mouth my day goes to hell." No sooner are the words out of my mouth that I look down and see a dark stain on my skirt. Where did that come from?

Isaac leans back in the passenger seat, complying with my request. He turns his head and stares out the window. I glance over, knowing he won't notice, and see he's not wearing his belt.

"Can you put your seat belt on," I say.

He latches it. "You know what's interesting about you—"

"I said no talking." If my hands weren't on the steering

wheel I'd put my fingers in my ears and hum not-listening-not-listening-not-listening.

"You're the one who started it," he says.

"What are you, twelve? I just asked you to put on your seat belt. That's not making conversation." I wish he'd stop smiling. I feel like the butt of a joke.

"If you really wanted to ride in silence, you wouldn't have said anything. Besides, I can't imagine you're too concerned for my well being."

"I'm not. I don't want to stop short, have you bruise your perfectly formed face on my dash, then sue me for millions I don't have."

"You think I have a perfectly formed face?" He flips down the visor and checks himself out. "I guess you're right. This is quite a nice mug."

"Shut up. Or please just talk about something else other than yourself."

"Phillip?"

"How do you know about Phillip?"

"Erika gave me a progress report on the Barbie experiment. It said you're dating a lawyer named Phillip."

"We can't talk about him either. I'll kick you out of the car right here."

"Let's talk about you. You've devoted your life to your kid's school project. You pretend to be married to your brother. You're always talking to a priest. You're deathly afraid of cats. I think you're pretending to have a dog, too. And you think I'm behind all your problems."

"I'm not deathly afraid of cats. Why would you say that?" As we pull to a stop light I make eye contact.

"When we were walking out, you went twenty yards

out of the way to avoid *Fluffy*. Your fists were clenched. Little beads of sweat appeared on your forehead, and I think you were holding your breath."

"I was not."

"I take notice of people. Call it research."

"Well, you're wrong." I want him to be wrong. I need him to be wrong. "I'm not deathly afraid of cats."

"No?"

"I'm afraid of all animals. I don't discriminate."

"So, I'm right. There is no dog."

"Of course not."

"Are you afraid of bunnies?"

"Yes."

"Baby bunnies?"

"Yes."

"Newborn bunnies that can't even hop yet?"

"Yes. All animals. Basically, anything that's not a rock, mineral, or plant. Okay?"

"Aren't you going to adopt a pet for the experiment?"

"Maybe."

"And how are you going to get the crap on Lisa's list? Those mega-pet stores allow owners to bring their animals in. You could be licked by a miniature schnauzer around every turn."

"I'm not going into a pet store. I've never been. I'm not starting today. I'll just go to the grocery store."

"You can't get organic cat weed from a grocery store."

"I'll figure something out."

"I could run in for you."

"No thanks." The last thing I need is to owe Isaac any favors. "Let's go back to not talking."

He turns back to the window. I concentrate on the slow garbage truck in front of me. At this rate, I'll be stuck in the car with Isaac for three days. I pull to the left to pass.

"Shit!" I swerve back to avoid an oncoming SUV.

To Isaac's credit, he remains silent. Wonder what he's thinking? Does he think I'm crazy? Married to my brother. Afraid of chipmunks. He has grounds.

"I'm not dating Phillip. Not anymore. He's married." I say.

"We're talking again?"

"No, I just wanted to let you know I'm through with Phillip." Mostly.

"Okay."

"And…"

"And?"

"And, my life is completely under control. There's nothing to worry about, except you spilling the beans to my boss."

"I won't."

"Good." And I believe him.

"So, your life is completely under control?" he asks.

Before I can answer my cell phone rings. My purse is in the back seat and I fumble to reach it.

"I'll get it," Isaac says. "You're going to kill us." He reaches back and brings my leather bag onto his lap. He goes to open the top.

"No." I slam on the breaks and the purse rolls to the floor. "You never open a woman's purse. Moron." I ease the car to the side of the road.

"What's in there? The secret code to women? You'd rather die than give it up. And now who's twelve? Calling me a moron."

"Sorry." I reach across Isaac and grab the bag. The phone has since stopped ringing. I check the caller ID. It's Erika. I call the number back and learn schools being dismissed early because of a water pipe breaking and flooding part of the school. She wants to get a ride home with a friend. I'm not keen on my baby—fifteen she may be—riding with a newly licensed, text-aholic, sixteen year old.

"I'll pick you up."

She pleads her case for a few more minutes. When I don't change my mind she hangs up on me.

"I have to stop and get Erika," I say to Isaac after I hang up. "Do you mind?" We ease back into traffic and head to the high school before he even answers.

"Not a problem."

"Why aren't you at the school?"

"Took a personal day. Car trouble. Remember?"

The school is less than five minutes away. We pull into the lot and find Erika sitting on a brick planter with a couple of other kids. She gives me a halfhearted wave, then she leans over and kisses the boy to her right. What the hell was that?

"Did you see that?" I ask Isaac. "She kissed that boy."

"Calm down. It was a peck. No tongue."

"That's my little girl." My face is on fire.

"Hi," Erika says to Isaac as she gets in the back seat. "What are you doing here?"

I'm too shocked to speak to her. I've never seen my daughter kiss anyone before. How much more are they doing? Was that her boyfriend?

"Hey, Erika. I'm your mother's client."

That makes me sound like a prostitute.

"Mom, I'm hungry." Erika says.

"It's only ten o'clock in the morning." I make eye contact in my rear view mirror. "Did you eat breakfast?"

"I was too busy studying."

"McDonald's is still serving breakfast. I could go for pancakes." Isaac offers.

I pull into the next McDonald's I see. We go in and order three pancake breakfasts. Isaac offers to pay, but I end up picking up the bill. Maybe I can write it off as a business breakfast.

"Is there a Barbie doll in your purse?" Isaac peeks in as I put away my wallet.

"No." I snap my bag closed.

"Yes, there is." Isaac carries our tray to a booth near the play yard.

Erika takes a seat on the same side as her teacher. "It's my Barbie doll."

I could kiss her!

"My life is traumatic, with Mom's recent divorce and her giving me up for adoption. I've regressed to playing with my childhood toys."

I could slap her! "It's my friend's."

"Just for the record, I don't believe you," Isaac says. "Either of you."

"Mr. Barber, I can't believe you'd need a dating service to find romance," Erika changes the subject. "Plenty of women would find you interesting and attractive."

Is she flirting with him?

"A friend gave me a gift certificate." He takes a sip of coffee. "Paige, how long have you been in the dating service industry?"

"Why?"

"I'm just curious. 'Cause you're not very good at it."

Just when I think the guy isn't a one-hundred percent jerk, he insults me. "Maybe we should go back to no talking."

"The woman your mother set me up with was a ...." He bites his tongue. "I have a feeling she wanted the date to be a disaster."

"I thought you'd find her interesting."

"You set me up with that crackpot on purpose. I should report you to the dating authorities."

"Maybe some people are unmatchable." I raise an eyebrow.

"Unmatchable? Is that an industry term?" He picks up his bacon and chomps.

"I just can't imagine the average woman is ready for Isaac Barber." I sip my coffee. My pancakes sit untouched. My stomach has soured.

"Thanks. That really hurts coming from an expert. Again, do I need to remind you that you're pretending to be married to your brother? God hasn't made the man who can deal with your antics. Pity is your biggest asset."

"Ouch," Erika says.

My skin prickles and flames heat my face. I grip the plastic knife on the tray. The urge to stab him is strong, but I don't want to go back to court over Isaac Barber. "We're done here."

He doesn't move.

"Get in the car. I'll bring you to your car then I never want to see you in my office again. I'll personally refund your money." I pick up Erika's Styrofoam plate, even though she's only half done. "Let's go."

"Mom, it was only a joke. Relax."

Isaac nods. "I hope you know not to take me seriously. Plenty of men would enjoy the challenge of—"

"Just stop." Don't let him see you cry. Don't let him see you cry. *Paige, don't cry!*

We get in the car and I blast the radio. Isaac finally rides in silence.

Whatever you resolve to be, resolve never to be boring.

Chapter 28

I'm sitting in the living room watching *Jeopardy* with Mom and Dad, trying to remember what British king signed the Magna Carta, when the doorbell rings. I hear the front door open followed by mumbling.

"Who is King John?" I yell at the television.

"Mom," Erika says.

I turn to see Erika, Father Nolan, Trisha and a—I can't even say it—a dog. Not any dog. A German shepherd. The beast is on a slack leash escorted by Trisha.

"What's going on?" I stand on the couch.

"Did I miss it? Did I miss it?" Ryan comes bounding down the stairs.

The dog barks.

I jump off the couch. Run through the dining room and kitchen and into the downstairs bathroom. I slam the door and lock it. My chest is tight. I could be having a heart attack.

There's a knock on the door. "Paige, luv," says Father Nolan. "Please come out." He jiggles the locked door knob.

"Not while that dog is here."

"Oh Paige, please."

"Why did you bring a dog to my house?"

"It's not your house." Ryan says. Now he tries the knob. "And we're doing an intervention. Cool, right?"

"An intervention?"

"Yeah," Ryan says. "To get you over your fear of dogs."

"Well, your fear of all animals," Father Nolan says.

"And you decide to start me on a German shepherd. What, couldn't you find a cougar or a rabid hyena?"

"Trisha was in charge of the animal selection," Father Nolan says. "We figured she was the expert."

"Well, I'm not coming out. Not while it's here." I put the lid down to the toilet and sit.

"And we're not leaving," Ryan says. "Neither is the pup."

This may take awhile. When I was sixteen, I went to borrow the car. Mom said I could. While Dad said Ryan could have the car. We both sat in the Honda, in the driveway, overnight refusing to give in. He missed his hot date. I missed my SAT prep class.

Twenty minutes later there is another knock.

"Paige, are you ready to come out?" Trisha asks.

"I'm not ever talking to you. Bringing a dog to my house. That's like bringing a cow to a Hindu's home. Or a pig to a synagogue."

"No, it's not!"

"I said I'm not talking to you."

"Then just listen. Beau is a great dog. He came from the Capital District Shepherd Rescue. He's gentle and well trained."

"Why did his owner give him up?" I imagine he ate the family's toddler or chewed off grandma's ear while she slept.

"He's recently retired."

"From what?"

"He was a cadaver dog. He can detect the smell of decaying bodies."

"Yuck." I don't want a dog, especially a dog that's used to cuddling up to corpses.

"Listen, Paige. I know animals and I know you. Beau is harmless and sweet. Give him a chance."

"Never."

There's silence. And more silence. An hour passes. I've won. I'm too far from the front door to hear any comings or goings. I have to assume my friends and their mutt have left. Still I take no chances. I wait another two hours before opening the door a crack.

There are no lights on in the kitchen or dining room.

I listen. Nothing.

My plan is to run to my bedroom quickly and quietly. Then I will move the dresser in front of the door and get a good night's sleep. It's a simple plan. They're always the best.

Maybe it's too simple. These are the people that know me best in the world. They'll be expecting me to return to my bedroom in the middle of the night.

I'll show them.

I easily slip through the kitchen and dining room.

There's a soft, blue glow in the living room from the television. Dad is asleep in front of the eleven o'clock news. He's alone. I don't wake him and make my way up the stairs, careful to avoid steps four and seven. They creak. I know this not because I used to sneak out in high school, but because as a nineteen year old I had an infant daughter who was a light sleeper.

My bedroom door is open. Can't remember if that's how I left it. There are no lights on anywhere except under Ryan's bedroom door. Instead of going to my room I take the stairs up to the attic.

My eyes adjust to the light. There's no intervention. There's only Erika asleep in her double bed. The book she was reading still on her chest.

I close *My Antonia*, put it on her nightstand and give Erika a kiss on the cheek. I switch off the lamp and turn to leave. That's when I notice Beau.

"Mom! Mom! Stop screaming!" Erika is shaking me by the shoulders. This is the next thing I remember.

Then Mom, in her ankle-length white night gown, rushes in with a baseball bat. There are two grown men living in this house and my petite mother is the one ready to go to battle.

"What's wrong?" Mom says.

Beau sits at attention. His focus is on the crazy lady with the bat.

"Beau, kennel," Erika says.

He retreats to a metal dog kennel that's been set up in the corner. Erika slides the two latched closed. I still don't believe he's sufficiently constrained. From what I've read, Shepherds are smart dogs. He could probably work the hinges off.

"Gram, give Ryan his bat. Everything is okay," Erika says. "I'll take care of this."

"Good night." Mom retreats down the stairs.

"Erika, we cannot have a dog."

"You agreed to do everything on the list."

"Yes. And it says I need to get a pet." I'd been thinking something along the lines of a Venus flytrap.

"Beau is a pet. He can even sleep up here with me. All you need to do is live under the same roof as him."

"No." There are limits as to what I can endure, even for Erika.

"Are you even trying anymore?" she yells. "You promised to try, then you go and yell at my teacher. You're lying about being married. You're not dating. You still drink. When's the last time you worked out?"

"I ran three miles yesterday. And I don't like your tone, Missy. I'm still in charge. I can still ground you." My God, did I just call my daughter Missy?

She glares at me.

"I'm trying, Erika."

"Well, not enough."

"What do you want me to do?"

"Start by keeping the dog."

"Fine. Keep the damn dog. I don't see what difference it's going to make."

"It means you're not giving up."

Girls can do it all. Girls can have it all.
Girls do not have to want it all.

Chapter 29

Daily Self-Assessment   *Thursday, October 28*
Rate the degree to which you agree with the statement.
5–completely agree 1–completely disagree
1. I accomplished something today. *5*
2. I felt connected with my friends and family today. *5*
3. I was interested in sex today. *1*
4. I laughed today. *5*
5. I am looking forward to tomorrow. *5*
Notes: *Good day. Erika made varsity basketball (I'm so proud). And I found a site on the internet that sells doggy-sedatives.*

My first job was working at a Dairy Queen. We weren't even the full-service kind—no hot dogs or burgers—just ice cream. I made sundaes and served Dilly Bars six days a week all summer long. I didn't mind standing on my feet for eight hours at a time, and I didn't mind having hot fudge stuck in my arm hairs because every Friday I received a paycheck. Looking back on it, it wasn't much money. At the time, it seemed like millions. And it was mine, all mine. I had an agreement with my parents to put half in the bank for college. Then I was free to spend the other half in any way I wished. This turned out to be mostly on music, clothes and makeup—no big marketing surprise there. I wish someone had told me to really enjoy that brief time when I received a paycheck and had no bills to pay. I had more disposable income than at any other period in my life.

Friday morning, Penelope opens my office door and cheerily announces, "Payday." She waves my check before putting it on my desk.

"Thanks." After she leaves, I tear it open. My heart sinks, even though this is my fifth paycheck. My pay, which is a base amount plus commission on new clients, is comparable to my Dairy Queen check. That was sixteen years ago, and I wasn't a week away from owning a house.

I turn to my computer, click open a spreadsheet of my finances and enter the amount of my pay. I'm $200 in the red for the week. How much could I get for a kidney on eBay? If I hadn't bought that pink, shimmery number for the wedding with Phillip, I'd have enough money to put gas in the car. Men make me stupid.

"Did you hear me?" I open the top drawer to my desk. Barbie now has a couch in her special drawer and is able to rest more comfortably. "I'm done with men. Not until I'm settled into my independent life will I date again."

Good for you. She's still in her silky red pajamas—more of a nightie.

"Maybe we'll talk about this later." I'm not sure if I can take advice from a doll who's not even dressed at ten a.m.

As I contemplate selling off other body parts and my eggs, the intercom beeps.

"Yes?"

"There's a gentleman here to see you."

I glance at my appointment book. I'm not expecting anyone. "Who?"

"He said he'd rather not give his name."

"He's not a debt collector, is he?" Are there such things? People who show up at your office looking for late payments?

"I don't think so. Can I send him in?"

"Sure."

The door opens and a smiling Isaac walks in, looking sinister and more slovenly than ever in cargo pants with a Dr. Pepper T-shirt and a baseball cap.

"God, why couldn't you send me a debt collector? A Jehovah's Witness? A leper? Anyone but him." I fold my hands in prayer for dramatic affect.

"Calm down, Saint Paige. I come in peace." He takes a seat without an invitation and puts a tray of four drinks on my desk.

"I don't believe you."

"See," he motions to the cups. "I brought you coffee. What do you like? I have a mocha, a caramel macchiato, a decaf skim latte, and a green tea."

"Which one has the cyanide?"

"That would be the latte." He points to one of the cups.

"I'll take it." I grab it from the tray and pop open the

top and examine it. Looks like coffee, smells like coffee, tastes like coffee. If there's poison in it, I just hope I go quickly and painlessly.

"Are we suicidal today?" He takes the green tea.

"I'm not having one of my better months." Years. Decades. "What about you? Cyanide or non-cyanide?"

"I'm a writer. Everyday I'm on the brink of jumping into the Hudson. Especially after a review."

"I thought you just did cover art?"

"No, I write, too."

"Well, I wouldn't dive into the Hudson. Your corpse would be all bloated. I'm thinking cyanide results in a prettier corpse." I take a long swallow. Barbie would definitely pick cyanide.

"Unfortunately, I've a tolerance for the stuff. After every rejection letter or crappy review I take a shot or two. Now, I'd need a Big-Gulp-size dose to do me in."

"What type of stuff do you write?" I'd guess fantasy novels that feature scantily clad women with wild hair on the covers.

"Are you writing this in my file?"

"No, strictly off the record."

"Graphic novels."

I choke on my coffee. The steaming liquid burns my nasal cavity. I try to recover, but cough myself into a deep fit of laughter. "Comic books?"

He plays hurt. "No. Check out Amazon. I write under the pseudonym, M. J. Dawson."

"Next time I'm looking for a graphic novel… I will. So Isaac, why are you here? After our last meeting I thought I was pretty clear—"

"This is my way of apologizing. Don't give up on me yet." He shrugs. "And I want Ryan's phone number. Thought we'd get a few beers. Watch a Jets game."

I scribble down Ryan's cell phone number. "Here it is. Don't call before noon. You'll wake him and that's not a pretty scene."

"Thanks. Now, how about a date?"

"I...um...you're my daughter's teacher. Her favorite teacher. I don't think it would be—"

"Isn't that would you do here? Set people up?"

"Right." God, how embarrassing. I give him the information on another potential match. "Her name is Nicole. She's intelligent, beautiful, and an avid reader."

"Thanks. See you around." Then there's a wink and he leaves. Men make no sense.

A feeling settles in my shoulders, and at first I can't identify it. Maybe it's the weight of my debt. It has more to do with my coffee delivery man. I lay my head on the desk.

Barb leaves the safety of her drawer apartment and sits on the desk. The little plastic smile should reassure me. It doesn't.

"What's wrong with me?" I ask her. "He's a horrible man and I just swore off men like ten minutes ago."

Be strong.

"Ahhheeemmmm." Someone clears his throat. Isaac's back in my office.

Great. I shove Barb back into her drawer. "Forget something?"

"Were you talking to Barbie?" He's intrigued like a kid learning the secret of a magic trick.

"No." I snap.

"Yes you were." He grabs his ball cap. "You were talking to Barbie about me. Just when I think you're normal." He shrugs and is gone.

I put my head back on the desk resting my cheek on its cool surface. After a couple minutes, I turn and give the other side a chance to enjoy the ice-pack feel of the desk. I notice the cups of coffee Isaac left behind. I can't take my eyes off the beverages.

"I have to admit, it was nice talking to Isaac over coffee."

Over coffee is nice.

The figurative light bulb goes off over my head. "I know how we can expand the business."

Barb and I jot down a few details in a notebook.

"This can work," I say.

You know it can.

Once we finish, I jump out of my chair and run to Lisa's office. Without knocking, I let myself in. A cat is sitting on her desk, but he's asleep. Still, I catch my breath.

"Lisa, you have to come with me."

"What's wrong?"

"Please. Just come to my office. I need to tell you something." In a moment of unbelievable courage, I walk past the snoozing pussy and grab Lisa by the arm. I don't know which is braver—grabbing your boss and pulling her away or walking past a snoozing, probably hungry, cat.

Lisa follows without much resistance. Once back in my office, I close the door to avoid any further animal distractions—or animal disasters.

"Paige, you have a wild look in your eyes. What's going on?" Lisa doesn't sit. She looks uneasy, like me around goldfish.

"Sorry. Don't worry, nothing's wrong. I just had a great idea that will double—maybe, triple—our business."

"Go on." She takes a seat ignoring Barb on my desk.

"Currently, we interview our clients. Get to know them. Then we evaluate their needs and give them a phone number for a voice mailbox of someone we think might interest them. And boom, we're done. Our clients still have the hassle of arranging that first date. The awkwardness, the risks."

She nods.

"What if we took our job one step further? What if we offered them that first date? A place to meet? Somewhere safe and secure, yet also intimate and discrete."

"We have our parties."

"They're only once a month. I'm talking about someplace open daily. Like a coffee bar." I grab a cup off my desk. Talking about my idea out loud makes me even more excited. This is going to work. "We could call it *Over Coffee*. Our offices would be in the back, where we'd still offer custom matchmaking. We'd still do interviews. The only problem I see is that the cats may have to go. I don't think animals are allowed in places where food is prepared." Another plus!

"Paige, I appreciate your innovativeness and your adorable enthusiasm. I'm not looking into putting any more energy or money into this business. My future is in acrylic nail care. But I love your fliers." She points to one on my peg-board. "Keep it up. I'm sure it'll pay off."

Me, balloon—Lisa, pin. I deflate into my chair. The weight of all my problems comes crashing back down.

Lisa stands up. "Don't look so beat up. Why don't you take the afternoon off and go home and screw your husband like a couple of newlyweds oughta."

Just when I thought I couldn't feel worse.

She points to the cup still in the tray. "May I?"

"Sure." I say, hoping it is truly laced with something more than Splenda.

After work, I decide to finally get something done I'd been avoiding for months. A haircut. I show up at Sheer Desire ten minutes before closing without an appointment.

"I really just need a trim." I tell Barb as we head inside.

I'd prefer if we tried another salon.

"No. Vanessa has been doing my hair for years. Just because she stole my husband and wasn't woman enough to tell me. Just because she's a sneaky cow doesn't mean she isn't a talented and professional hairdresser."

Promise me you won't touch the scissors. It's the last thing Barb has a chance to say before I stuff her in my purse.

The bells on the door ring when I walk in. Vanessa is blow drying a middle-aged woman's hair. In the other chair is a teenage girl with highlight foil sticking out of her scalp.

Vanessa turns off the hairdryer. "Paige, I haven't seen you in ages. How are you doing? You look great."

"Thanks. I know I don't have an appointment. I was hoping you could squeeze me in. Just a little trim, you know."

"Actually, I don't have much—"

"Please, Vanessa. Do this favor for me? I've been a *loyal* customer for years."

"Sure. It'll be just a little while. Take a seat." Vanessa returns to blow drying. I'd say she looks nervous.

Do I really have the upper hand here?

While Vanessa finishes with her other clients, I flip through a magazine of cutting-edge styles. Hollywood's leading ladies seem to have gone short for the season. I like my hair to cover my ears, at least. Not that my ears are anything I need to hide. But when I was in first grade, my mom cut my hair really short, because I cried every morning when she tried to brush out the tangles. For the next few months, everyone kept mistaking me for Ryan. That is very traumatic for a little girl.

"I'm ready for you." Vanessa holds up a cape for me to slip into.

We don't chat while she washes and conditions my hair. This is unusual. I'd normally tell her intimate details of my dull life. She'd listen intently and even remember the minor events I had shared on previous appointments. Like did I ever find a comforter with the right shade of sage? Or did I have a nice time at our annual block party?

Is she feeling guilty?

I move to the chair and she towel dries my locks.

"Just a trim?" she asks.

"Yes. I'm eager to get rid of the dead weight."

Vanessa starts combing me out. She doesn't make eye contact in the mirror. She's concentrating on my hair like it's a ticking bomb.

"So...how have you been?" I ask.

"Fine. How about you?"

"You know. Busy getting divorced."

"Paige. I don't think we should talk about...that. One of us will end up getting hurt."

"How is Max anyway? Can he still do that thing with his tongue? Does he still like for you to squeeze his—"

"Paige!"

"Come on. We're both adults. You're sleeping with my husband—ex-husband. Can't we compare notes? I could give you tips."

"I'm so sorry."

Finally, an apology.

I look up at Vanessa in the mirror and scream. She's holding an eight inch section of my hair and it's no longer attached to my head. She wasn't apologizing about screwing Max she was apologizing about screwing up my hair.

"No. No. No."

"I can fix this," she says. "Honestly, you've needed to update your style for a couple of years."

"How?"

"Trust me."

I hold off on calling her a cheating snake for fear she'll take a razor to my scalp. So I watch helplessly as she removes chunks of my brown hair. Large sections of hair slide down my cape and pile on the floor. I've never see such hair carnage. I can't bear to look in the mirror.

Vanessa doesn't say much as she cuts. She turns the chair to toward the door as she blows it dry, which only takes two minutes. She finishes it by applying some spray gel.

"Take a look."

I open my eyes and don't recognize the woman starring back at me. Vanessa has left a few inches of hair on top that fall to the right side of my face. The sides and back seem to taper off to nothing. It's a very sophisticated look if I had a graceful neck and high cheekbones.

"I can't believe you did this to me."

She grabs a broom and starts sweeping. "Things might be better this way."

Later that night I soak in the tub with Barb and a glass of merlot sitting to my side. It was another tough day and it's only my second glass.

"Why did I go to Vanessa?" I sink lower into the water, partially suicidal over a haircut.

I knew it was a bad idea.

"I didn't even find out how long she's been screwing Max." I totally emerge myself in the near scalding bath water. I'm only under for twelve seconds. I have limited lung capacity.

Your haircut is cute.

"What do you know about short hair? You're all about long blonde locks and hair play. Your bubble cut was short lived."

That gives me an idea. I stand up in the tub, wrap a towel around me and grab Barb.

Where are we going?

I leave a trail of wet footprints from the tub to my desk in the bedroom. I open the top drawer and see what I'm looking for.

I hold up the scissors for Barb to see.

I knew this was coming. She sighs.

With three quick moves of the scissors, Barb has a new

fashionable bob. Somehow it makes me feel better. That and a third glass of wine.

*Diamonds are nice, but sit-ups and shapewear
are a girl's best friend.*

Chapter 30

My realtor, Don, officially hands over the keys to my new home. "Congratulations, Paige O'Neal, you are a homeowner."

That's the nicest thing anyone has said to me in weeks.

After the closing, I take Erika out for a celebratory cheeseburger. We return to my parents' house, pick up a load of prepacked boxes, and head for our new home.

I sit in my driveway—in my mom's car—outside our new house on my little piece of property, and I feel I'm finally ready to make a life for myself and Erika. Either I'm incredibly brave or incredibly stupid for taking on this challenge. I can only afford the mortgage if I eat box macaroni and cheese and sell pints of my blood. Still, this almost-condemned, 1800-sq-ft Cape Cod is mine, all mine.

Barb sits atop the first box I carry from the car. A light snow has fallen overnight hiding some of the house's flaws. Still I notice the peeling paint and cloudy windows. The steps to the front door creak. The screen door is only attached by one hinge. I slip the key into the lock. It's not necessary—it isn't locked. The door swings open with a whine. I take a deep breath and look down at the threshold.

"No one is going to carry you over it," Erika says.

"I don't need anyone." I take a dramatic, independent step through the doorway proving to my daughter that this is a no-man-necessary household. My foot lands and causes a floorboard to snap.

"Dammit!"

I take a tour. It's horrible, but I'm in love. It's like when you fall head-over-heels for a man. You may notice his receding hairline or his ten-dollar-a-day smoking habit but his soul transcends the imperfections. When I make it to the master bedroom, all I can see is the soul of the house and the life we will have together. Lazy Sunday mornings in bed looking out the window at my oak tree. Private moments with a worthy man of my dreams. Erika wanting to talk to me at midnight after a great date.

A honk of a horn wakes me from my daydream. I run downstairs to greet the movers. While my home has a soul, I can't ask any of my family to see her just yet. They'd only judge her from the outside. I'll properly invite everyone over when the beauty from within shines through.

The movers take a few hours to unload the furniture. I desperately try to sweep and disinfect before they put each piece in place.

Erika works on her bedroom, hanging posters, setting up the dog kennel and unpacking her beloved computer. I convinced her to leave Beau at Mom's until the house was ready. I'm thinking that'll take thirteen years.

My work starts in the kitchen. Using rolls and rolls of paper towels and industrial-strength cleanser, I wipe the counter, cabinets, floor, and all other surfaces. Things seem to be looking up until a bug the size of a cell phone and as fast as lightning shoots out from beneath the fridge and runs under my table. My heart stops, and for a moment I just wanted it to find a hole and disappear. But it really won't disappear. I'll know it's there. It'll be living in my walls, eating my food, and making babies, hundreds of millions of bug babies. I need to stop this intruder now. Quietly, I tiptoe over to it, trying to stay in its blind spot, which is hard to do because I don't know which end is its head. When I'm within two feet, it takes off again, and I give chase, finally bringing my Nike down on it only inches from the baseboard. I don't know a lot about bugs, but judging by the crunching sound it made on impact, I'd guess it was some kind of killer-alien beetle.

As a necessary precaution, I start rebleaching the kitchen. I even find the courage—and strength—to move the twenty-year old fridge, probably its first move since its trip from the Sears warehouse judging by the collection of filth I find underneath. As I finish rinsing the sink, there's a knock at the front door.

"Who is it?" I yell, thinking the only person I'd like to see right now is Ed McMahon. But I think he's dead. Who hands out those giant checks from the clearing house now?

I see Trisha and Manny standing in the door as they answer, "It's us." And I know immediately that I was wrong. Best friends can beat out Ed any day.

"What are you guys doing here?" I hold the door open for my first guests. "I didn't want anyone to see the place until I've had a chance to clean and fix it up."

"We're not anyone," Trisha says. "Besides, we brought you a housewarming gift." She hands me a package wrapped in silver paper.

I step on a spider. "God, let it be a case of Raid." I put the present on the floor and tear into the paper, while Trisha and Manny smile and glance at each other. Lifting the lid and pushing aside the tissue paper, I pull out lengths and lengths of silky, bright-pink fabric embroidered with red hearts. Must be twenty yards of it.

I examine the fabric, when I find the loops on the end I realize that they're curtains. The ugliest, tackiest curtains I've ever seen in my life.

"Wow!" is all I'm able to choke out.

"We had these specially made," Manny says.

"They're based on the curtains from Barbie's original dream house. Do you like them?" Trisha asks.

"They're from you guys, of course I like them." I try to sound sincere.

"Let's hang them up," Trisha suggests.

"No. I'd rather wait until I've painted. I was thinking of doing the guest bedroom in a rose color." I wipe my hands on my jeans.

"Guest bedroom?" Trisha seems hurt. "These are for the living room, Paige."

I'm silent for a few moments. I guess they can go in the living room. Maybe if I tie them back with a cord they won't be so obvious.

"Enough already," Manny says and hands me a small envelope from his shirt pocket.

"What's this?"

"Your *real* house warming gift."

I open up the envelope. It's a $500 gift certificate to Home Depot. "Wow!" And this time I mean it.

"I found the curtains in a thrift store and couldn't resist playing with you. We'll use them as drop cloths." Trisha says.

"Thank you. How'd you know they were based on the dream house?"

"Hell, I've no idea. They look like they'd suit Barbie's taste."

"So," Manny says. "What do you need us to do? Clean? Paint? Move furniture?"

"Yes. Yes. And yes."

"Okay, here's the deal. We help you unpack and you carry our baby for nine months. That sound about right?" Trisha says.

I drop the gift card. "Are you serious?"

"Yes," Trisha says. "But we insist on paying for everything. Medical bills. Time off of work."

"Weird cravings like white chocolate and sardines," Manny says.

"Are you sure about this?" Trisha asks.

"Of course. Hell with unpacking. Let's go out and celebrate."

*If you're constantly worried about tucking
the back of your dress
in your underwear, just don't wear panties.*

Chapter 31

After gushing about my new fierce hairstyle, Father Nolan says a prayer over our meal.

"Amen."

"What's been going on?" He opens the sub sandwich I brought him and places it on a paper plate. I don't bother, barely removing the wrapper before biting into my turkey club.

With a full mouth I tell Father the good news. I'm going to be a surrogate. He nods and listens to all the details about my recent visit to Trisha's doctor at the fertility clinic.

"Of course, I think it is wonderful you want to help out your friend," Father Nolan says. "1 John 3:17 If anyone has material possessions and sees his brother in need but has no pity on him, how can the love of God be in him?"

"And the problem is?" I lean forward in my chair. I know the Catholic Church is not pro-surrogacy, but Father

Nolan usually supports me in every endeavor.

"Now may not be the right time for you. You have a new house and a new career. You're recently single. It's a lot to focus on." He gives up on his sandwich and clasps his hands together.

"I'm a strong woman," I say. "I can do anything. Like Barbie."

"You can't be a Catholic priest," he says with a smile.

Last July, I was the one millionth customer at the grocery store. I went in to buy margarita mix, Motrin, and a pint of Ben and Jerry's, and as I checked out, bells rang, music blared, and balloons came at me from all directions. I thought the store was under some kind of attack. Then the manager and a news crew appeared. They congratulated me, took a few dozen pictures, and gave me a plaque and an envelope of coupons. After all the excitement died down—a whole ten minutes later—I cornered the newspaper reporter and asked him not to disclose my purchases to the reading public. He agreed, and the next day the article said, "O'Neal-Russell refused to disclose her personal purchases and would not comment." I sounded like the bitchiest one millionth customer in the tri-city area.

I'll never have a millionth customer at Prrfect Connection. I did the math. If I got ten new clients a day and worked five days a week, forty-eight weeks a year, I'd be 447 when it happened. Therefore I decided to celebrate my smaller milestones.

After completing my interview with Tammy—a plain-looking, thirty-two-year old product support specialist who loves rhythmic gymnastics—I tell her she's my fiftieth client. She's none too impressed, so I say that means she gets fifty percent off. Then she has the nerve to ask if she were the fifty-first client, would she have gotten fifty-one percent off?

I walk Tammy to the door and she leaves without so much as a goodbye or a thank you. When I turn around to head back to my office, I notice two men waiting in the lobby. One is Isaac. I can't help smiling.

Hoping he didn't notice me noticing him, I hurry back to my office. I open the drawer to talk to Barb.

"You'll never guess who's here?" I sigh. "Again!"

Isaac Barber.

"How did you know?" I'm shocked.

I'd keep him waiting. She gives me her wicked smile. It's subtly different then her nice-to-meet-you smile, but I can tell the difference.

I call the receptionist using my desk phone. "Penelope, who's waiting?"

"Your next appointment—Robert Monroe. And Isaac Barber is also here."

"For me?" My voice cracks.

"He said he'd see anyone. He doesn't have an appointment, of course."

"Of course." I roll my eyes. Maybe I'm being a little too dramatic.

"Lisa's been available for the past twenty minutes. He said he didn't want to bother her. And he'd see anyone."

"Sure. Thanks." I walk out to the lobby. I give Isaac a nod.

He stands up. "Wow. You changed your hair."

I touch my practically bare scalp. "Mr. Monroe, would you care to join me in my office?"

Isaac sits back down.

"I'll be with you as soon as possible," I say to Isaac. Robert and I go to my office. Let's see if Isaac's good at waiting.

Robert and I settle in for the interview. We take ten minutes to do the preliminary, mundane stuff. All the while he's telling me his full name, address, occupation, I'm checking the window in my office door to see if Isaac has left. I can't tell from my vantage point.

"Excuse me, Robert." I need to take a quick break.

On my way to the bathroom, I confirm Isaac is still in the lobby. He's reading a paperback, looking comfortable and not fidgety. He's going to wait. In the bathroom, I check my makeup and play with my barely there hair before returning. As I pass, Isaac looks up and gives me a little wave. Dammit! He thinks I'm checking up on him. How vain.

Back to the interview. This time, I'm able to give Robert twelve minutes before I insist on beverages. The thirty-nine-year old widower is accommodating and doesn't fuss. I walk by the lobby on the way to the kitchenette. Isaac is still reading, lying down on the couch. Does he think this is his living room?

I grab a can of Diet Coke, a bottled water, and sneak back to Robert. I don't think Isaac saw me.

Robert graciously accepts the water and we talk more about his childhood. The poor guy was orphaned at age eight, lived with a dozen families, some of whom were abusive. He finally ran away to join the Marines at sixteen after faking his birth certificate. And all I can concentrate on is that damn man out in the lobby. Why is he here? Is he still here? I've got to know.

I pick up the phone. "Hello, Paige O'Neal." It didn't actually ring. "Uh-Hun." Pause. "Okay." Pause. "Sure. Thank you." I hang up.

"Sorry about that."

"I didn't even hear it ring."

"I have the ringer off, but I can see the blinking light. The receptionist knows to only put through emergency calls."

"Is there an emergency?" He looks genuinely concerned.

"No, not really. It's just my neighbor. She's older and needs help sometimes. You know, getting her cat out of the tree or opening a ketchup bottle."

"What's it this time?"

"A panic attack. She thought she saw someone snooping around outside her house. I'm sure it's her imagination. I'd better send someone to go check on her. Can you hang on a minute?"

"By all means." He motions to the door.

I'm going to have to give Robert a discount, too, because I'm sure not giving him any of my attention. After I'm safely outside my office, I sneak out the doorway to the lobby. It's empty. I circle around. No one's here—not in the doorway, not talking to the receptionist, not loitering in the hallway.

"Penelope, did Mr. Barber leave?" I ask.

She looks up from her magazine. "I don't know. He didn't say anything. Guess he's gone." Her gaze returns to her more pressing magazine.

Why didn't he wait? At least now I can give my all to Robert. I turn to head back to my office.

"Boo," Isaac whispers, inches from my face.

"Where did you come from?"

"Were you looking for me?"

"No. You shouldn't go around scaring people like that. It's not healthy."

"Oh, your heart could use a good jolt now and again."

"I mean, it's not healthy for *you*. You're going to get pepper spray in your face or a knife in your chest if you mess like that with the wrong person."

"Where are you from? South Compton?" He laughs, definitely not with me. At me.

I wish he'd just go away. "Excuse me, I have to get back to my client."

"Is that poor fellow still in there? You've been out here so much, I thought he'd left. Either that, or you have a bladder infection."

"You're being childish."

"You're being evasive."

"I'm leaving."

"And I'm waiting." He gives me a wide smile and wink that only makes me want to stab him in the eye with a pen. He actually seems to get a high out of annoying me. I'm his heroin.

"Then you'll be waiting for a long, long time." With that, I leave without giving him a chance for rebuttal. It's a small, yet noteworthy, victory.

"I'm sorry, Robert. I'm all yours." We'll see how long Isaac can wait. "Everything is taken care of. My neighbor's fine."

"Great," Robert says. And we dive into his twenties—his deceased wife, his child, his career. I ask question after question. You'd think I was writing a detailed biography. The longer I keep Robert talking, the longer Isaac is waiting. I could do this all day, even if it means hearing about every fly fishing trip to Lake Placid and every pitch thrown by his son in Little League.

A mere ninety-two minutes later, the cell phone in my purse rings.

"Hello."

"Hurry up," Trisha orders. "I'm double-parked in the fire lane."

"What time is it?"

"Dinner time. Almost six. I've got the results from the doctor." I can tell it's good news. Trisha and I went to her fertility specialist on Monday to see if I would be a suitable home to the newest Stevens.

"I'll be out in fifteen minutes."

"I'll circle the block twice. If you're not out by then, I'm unleashing a heard of ferrets on you. I'm a vet. I have connections."

"I'll be there as soon as I can." I close my phone and wrap up with Robert. I have enough information to make a match or deliver his eulogy.

Robert thanks me. He seems like a new man simply because I took the time to talk to him. Being widowed has to be even lonelier than being single.

"I'll be in touch shortly," I say as we walk out to the front doors.

"Great." He smiles. "Paige, thank you very much. May

I give you a hug?"

"Sure." We have a quick embrace, then he leaves. A month ago this may have sounded like a strange request. Now I'm use to it. However, not everyone asks, and I hug a lot more female clients than males—especially after a great first date.

"Can I have a hug, too?" Isaac asks from the couch.

"No. Now I have about thirty seconds, so get in my office now or wait until tomorrow."

"Yes, ma'am." He gets up and walks ahead without waiting for me. I follow and close the door. I plan to keep this short and sweet, so I lean against the door instead of taking a seat at my desk.

"How did it go with Nicole?" I ask, wanting to get the conversation immediately on a professional level.

"Good. She seems really nice. We haven't gone out yet. We haven't talked yet. Her message sounds sincere. Good tone. Nice pronunciation."

"You haven't even gone on a date and you're back already? This is the most extreme case of commitment phobia I've ever seen."

"No. I'm not ready for my next setup. I don't need another date. Unless you have someone you'd like to recommend."

What was that tone? Sarcasm? Flirting? Why can't I read him? "I recommended Nicole. Remember?" I cross my arms.

"I was hoping someone new had come on the market. Is there some kind of notification system like in real estate? If my perfect match comes on the market, you e-mail me."

"Isaac." I give him a motherly warning.

"Okay. Okay. You caught me. I'm not here for a date. I came by to see you. I've been worried. I know you're doing the Barbie Experiment for Erika but last time I was here you were talking to the doll. Maybe you're taking this a bit too far."

"Great material for your comic books. A psychotic woman who talks to dolls and dreams of strangling a certain client."

"You dream about me?"

"Everything's fine. Thanks for checking in." I open the door.

"Is she here now?" Isaac looks around the room like Barbie is a spirit not a living, breathing doll. Make that nonliving, nonbreathing, but she is a physical object.

"No." I over exaggerate a wrinkled brow.

"I don't believe you." He leaps up from his chair, and before I can stop him, he opens my drawer. I'm going to kill him.

"I knew it!" He holds Barbie high above his head like she's the torch and he's Lady Liberty.

"Out!" I point to the door. *And I may really kill you if you make fun of me one more time.*

"You can't get rid of me that easily." He takes a seat in my chair still holding Barb.

"Fine. Stay. I'm leaving." I grab my purse, slip on my jacket and pull Barb from his dirty, tight grip. I'll have to give her a Clorox bath tonight. I walk out of the office. Isaac follows.

It's raining outside. I left my umbrella in the office and Trisha's car is nowhere to be seen. I step back under the awning, semisheltered from the elements.

"Does she talk to you?" Isaac seems oblivious to the weather. "Give you fashion tips or advice on men?"

I give up. "She's just a reminder. Like a string around the finger. She reminds me what I'm trying to accomplish."

"Which is to prove she's a good role model?"

"No. I'm trying to improve my life and improve Erika's life."

"Tell me the truth, do you talk with the doll?"

"I may talk out loud. On occasion." I look up and down the street, still no Trisha.

Isaac is silent for a moment, and I begin to think he may actually understand. He may actually think I'm sane or at the very least not immediately in need of institutionalization.

"I don't get it," he says.

"What do you look for in a woman?" I ask. "And don't say personality, because everyone has a personality no matter if you think that personality is boring or shallow."

"She has to be interesting."

"Did you know Barbie has a middle name?"

"Most people have a middle name. That doesn't make them interesting."

"Okay. Did you know Barbie has her roots in German porn?"

"That's a bit more interesting."

"It's not really pornography. The Bild Lilli doll was a 3-D pinup for men based on a cartoon by the same name. And then there's—"

"No need to make excuses for her."

"Fine. What else do you look for in a woman?"

"She has to be attractive."

I give him credit for putting interesting above attractive. "Check. She's attractive."

"I don't think so. She looks fake."

"Uggghhhh. She's made of plastic. You don't get it." Screw the rain. I walk south just to get away from him.

"Where you going?" Again, he follows me.

Finally, Trisha's red Durango rounds the corner. I wave frantically, like a sole survivor on a deserted island and Trisha is the first boat I've seen in months.

"Paige. Wait." Isaac calls.

I don't. I reach Trisha's car and grab the door handle.

Isaac catches up to me and spins me around. Then— Boom!—he kisses me.

Fight him off, Paige. Stop him. My body seems to disagree with my highly functioning frontal lobes.

This kiss ends, and I have to order my eyes to open and my heart to slow down. Should I slap him? If this was a movie and I was the female lead, I'd slap him.

Isaac speaks before I can react. "How dare you kiss me like that," he jokes. "That's not very professional trying to steal the good looking clients for yourself."

"See how annoying he is." I turn to Trisha for confirmation. "Isn't he?"

"Annoying and cute. Must be Isaac. I'm Trisha." She extends a hand and they shake.

Then I notice Erika in the backseat. "I didn't know you were coming," I say.

"Hey, Erika," Isaac says.

Erika turns her head, giving both of us the silent treatment.

"Get in," Trisha says. "You're getting the leather all

wet. And what little hair you have is getting flat."

"One second," I turn back to Isaac. "This will never happen again." I put an authoritative finger in his face. Take that!

He kisses me again. This time I break away—after a good five seconds.

"What did I just say?" I ask him.

"I'm leaving," Trisha says and scribbles something on a piece of paper. "Here." She hands Isaac a piece of paper. "That's Paige's cell. Call her later."

"What?" I'm appalled at her betrayal.

"Bye." Isaac squeezes my hand in a friendly gesture and walks away.

I get into the car. "Why did you do that? What if he's some kind of maniac?"

"He's not. I have a sense about these things. Animal instinct." She smiles and throws the car into drive.

"Erika," I turn around. I'm probably not the best role model for my own daughter. "Is something wrong?"

"I don't know what you're thinking. Mr. Barber is not the right man for you."

"What are you talking about?"

"You're supposed to be looking for Ken. Mr. Barber is not it."

"Erika, it was just a kiss." *That will keep me up tonight.*

"Trisha," Erika says. "Can you bring me back home? I have a lot of homework to do and I'm suddenly not very hungry."

"Homework? It's a Friday." I turn to face Erika.

"I just want to go home." She stares out the window

avoiding eye contact.

"I'll take you home," Trisha says, "First I need to tell you something. The doctor thinks your mom will be a suitable surrogate for Manny and me."

"Suitable?" I ask. "I'll be a spectacular surrogate."

"Congratulations," Erika mumbles.

After a good-girl dinner of salad with chicken, oranges, and feta on a bed of greens accompanied by water with a lemon wedge, Trisha and I got naughty. We order a chocolate mousse cheesecake with two forks.

I play with a crinkled straw wrapper. "Do you think Erika is okay? She seemed really upset."

"She's got a little crush on her teacher and now that teacher is making out with her recently divorced mother."

"She has nothing to worry about. He probably won't ever call. Especially now that I'm going to be a big, hormonal pregnant woman."

"Sober and on daily hormone drugs. You're going to be a lot of fun to be around over the next few weeks."

"Just promise me you won't put a dozen embryos in my uterus. Two, okay. Three, max! I don't want to be a headline on *The Today Show. Woman in Albany Has a Litter of Nine.*"

"If you're having second thoughts..."

"Never." It's all I've thought about this week. Giving Trisha and Manny the family they've wanted. Doing something selfless for a friend. Eating anything I want. Becoming Aunt Paige. Where's the downside?

The cheesecake arrives and in the middle of enjoying my first bite, my cell phone rings.

"Do you think that's Isaac?" I ask, mousse oozing

from the corners of my mouth. I reach for the phone. The caller ID says unavailable. "Hello."

"Hello, Paige."

Ohmigod. I hold my hand over the mouthpiece. "It's Phillip."

Trisha lunges for the phone, but I avoid her. She gives me a warning look.

"Hello, Phillip," I say, keeping more than an arm's reach away from Trisha.

"I need to tell you something. My separation agreement is filed. I'm legally separated." A moment of silence ensues, probably waiting for my reply. "And I moved out."

I put my hand over the phone and tell Trisha he's getting divorced. She doesn't look impressed. She can be really hard to please sometimes.

"Where are you staying?"

"At my brother's house in Latham. He's set me up in a room in his basement. It's only temporary. I'm going to look for my own place this weekend."

As Phillip jabbers on about finally moving on with his life and all the lessons he's learned from being married, falling in love, falling out of love, building trust, the essence of passion, and the agony of heartache, I watch amusingly as Trisha rummages in her purse, looking for something. She shoves her hand in and gets frustrated. Then she dumps it on the table, not caring at all that tampons and fertility pills spill out into the open.

"Yep. Un-huh," I say over and over, so Phillip will know I'm listening to him.

Next, Trisha grabs my bag and rifles through it.

Thankfully, she doesn't dump it. After she gives up searching my bag, she scans the room for the elusive *whatever*. Her eyes light up when she spots a waiter taking an order. She gets up, walks over to the guy and takes his pen. I don't think she asked. The waiter, stunned, can only watch as Trisha returns, clears off the table with one sweep of her arm and proceeds to write on the table cloth "WWBD?" in letters large enough to be seen from the Space Shuttle.

"Phillip," I interrupt him. "I've got some news, too. I'm going to be a surrogate for a friend."

No reaction.

"I'm going to have a friend's baby."

Silence.

"Why don't you think on that one for a little while and call me back if you're still interested."

"Sure." He hangs up.

"I think I handled that fairly well," I say to Trisha.

"Sometimes you amaze me."

"Thank you."

"And what about your other Ken?"

"Who?"

"Isaac." She pounds her first against her forehead over and over.

"I know Isaac." I haven't forgotten about him. Phillip threw me for a loop. "Isaac won't call. And I'll probably never hear from Phillip again."

"Right." Neither of us really believes that.

Our debate is interrupted by the pen-less waiter and his manager. They stand over our table like a pair of mobster goons in a 1970s movie.

Trisha pipes up before they can speak. "What do you say if you buy dinner, and I'll pay for the table cloth?"

"Sounds good." We pay the bills and leave.

Through the years, even Ken has required a makeover.

Chapter 32

Bells wake me. I sit up in bed. What's that? It's the middle of the night. Another ring. Is it a fire? Where's Erika? Another ring. It's the damn phone.

I look at my clock. 1:30 a.m.

I grab my cell phone on the fourth ring. "Hello." I sound like an eighty-year old, chronic smoker.

"Hello, may I speak to Barbie Millicent Roberts."

"Who's this?" I imagine some kind of murderer on the loose outside my house.

"It's Isaac. I've been doing some research and you're right. Barbie is interesting. Did you know the original doll came as a brunette or a—"

"Do you know what time it is?"

"Ten-thirty."

"Huh?

"On the West Coast."

"Where are you?"

"Home." He pauses. "On the East Coast."

"Are you drunk? You wait almost a week to call me then do it in the middle of the night. You're nuts."

"I've been busy," he says. "Can I see you tomorrow?" he asks.

Now I'm awake. Thorough overanalyzing of a situation requires complete mental alertness. It's like a double shot of espresso. I pick up Barb off the pillow next to me. We don't snuggle. She just prefers to sleep in my bed.

"In what capacity would you like to see me?" I ask. "Do you need an appointment, because you should really call Penelope for that?" I put my hand over the receiver and say to Barb, "I hope it's more than an appointment."

It is.

"I'm thinking I'd like to see you in a full capacity. Yeah. I'd like to see all of you. If that's not possible, I'll take the head—I love your smile when you think you've outwitted me, one arm—either will do—and your right leg. You've got a really sexy right leg."

"And what's wrong with my left leg?"

"Nothing. I think it's a bit shorter. Maybe by a millimeter. Hardly noticeable to the untrained eye."

"Never mind. I'll be at the office from nine to six. Stop by." And I'll make you wait, only a little.

"No. I was hoping for outside the office."

"Fine. Five-thirty. The bike path near the town park in Scotia. And bring your running shoes."

"Awesome. I'll see you tomorrow night."

"Morning," I correct him. "Not night. Morning." If Barb was a full-sized woman we'd exchange high fives.

"Morning? I don't usually go to bed until three or four. Can't you make me dinner or something romantic?" I wonder if he's ever serious.

"Good night, Isaac. See you in a few hours."

When the alarm goes off at five, I curse myself for arranging an a.m. meeting—I'm not calling it a date. It was fun to punish Isaac. For some reason I didn't realize I'd have a hell of a time getting my own butt out of bed. I forego the full beauty ritual and throw on unmatched windpants, sweatshirt, and a Yankee ball cap. I do, however, go to the effort of brushing my teeth and applying deodorant. Only the best for Isaac.

I leave Erika a note on the kitchen table telling her I've gone for a run. Since Beau sleeps in her room, I don't want to tell her in person. And I don't tell her who I'm meeting.

I pull my car into the parking lot near the bike path five minutes early. I'm happy to see Isaac's already here. I half expected him to stand me up. I watch for a moment as he dances around trying to keep warm in the forty-degree weather.

I beep the horn and wave him over.

He jogs up to the passenger door.

I unroll the window. "What kind of nut would be out here on this kind of morning?"

"The kind who wants to impress a girl."

"Get in."

He smiles at my invitation and gets in the car. He didn't put much effort into his early morning attire, either. Sweats, sneakers, Budweiser sweatshirt. At least he smells good.

I hand him a cup of coffee I'd bought on the way.

"Your daily dose of cyanide."

"Thank you." He takes it.

"Do you care for some heart disease *a la* cholesterol? Just in case the cyanide doesn't do the trick?" I open the box of doughnuts.

Isaac selects a glazed doughnut and I take a cruller.

"Cheers." We touch pastries and down big bites. "I take it we aren't running."

"You're not up for a quick three miles?"

"Not after coffee and doughnuts."

"That's when I want to run the most. A guilt-jog."

"I hate running for running sake." He says. "Give me a ball and I'll chase it for hours, but just run, especially laps, don't see the point."

"Basketball? That's how you keep the gut off?" I poke him in the belly. Why am I initiating contact?

"I try to take the dog for a daily walk. He's lazy and about thirty pounds overweight. We average a twenty-minute mile."

I still can't believe Isaac has a dog. He doesn't smell like dog. I've never noticed any pet hair clinging to his T-shirts.

"Long walks with a disgruntled animal also help with writer's block. Not that it's something you'd ever try."

"No. Actually we have a pet now."

"Other than your Barbie doll." He gives me an evil smile, like he knows all about my deep, dark secret.

"Stop. Barbie is in my life because of you and your class."

"Is the Barbie lifestyle working out for you?"

"Don't make fun. That's like making fun of someone's

religion or political party."

"I'm serious. Is it working out?"

Feeling safe and beyond jokes, I take Barb out from under the seat. "Yes. I'm a happier person today than I was two months ago." Even if I lied to get a job and my daughter hates me, again.

"That's something." He polishes off the rest of his doughnut.

"And I'm more optimistic about my future than I've ever been in my life." This is not entirely true. I was really optimistic when I graduated from college and again on my wedding day, but I can't compare then to now. Those were special occasions where people expect you to be optimistic and happy.

"That's all that matters."

"Want another doughnut?" I ask.

He shakes his head. "Nah." Then takes one anyway.

Isaac finishes his second in a few bites while I'm still on my first. "I hate to cut this short...I have to go for a run then go home and get ready for work."

He looks at the clock. "You don't have to be to work for three hours."

"It takes me awhile to get ready."

"It must be hard to be naturally beautiful," he says. "And you have less hair than me. How long could it take to wash and dry?"

"Don't talk about the hair. That was an accident." On so many levels.

He reaches out and pushes a strand from my eye. "I like it."

"I really should go." I want to say *If you beg me to*

stay, I will.

"Okay. Just for that, no goodbye kiss." He opens the car door. "Plus, I don't want to expose you to my coffee breath." He gets out. "See ya."

"Bye." I say before he closes the door. I watch him walk away, feeling disappointed. I didn't expect a kiss. I don't think I even wanted one, but for him to say it like that is false advertising.

Just forget about it. I turn my attention to tidying up Mom's car by brushing doughnut crumbs off Isaac's seat and collecting napkins from the floor. I really need to get my own car. Then I won't have to worry about crumbs and spills.

As I'm leaning over the console trying to reach an old receipt, the passenger door swings open. I sit up.

"Problem solved. I found a mint." Isaac sits back down in the front seat and kisses me. Minutes, literally, go by before I can remember who I am or what I'm supposed to be doing. When we finally break, words elude me. It's like he sucked all rational thought out of my head through his lips.

Isaac gives me a smile. He seems to know he's had an effect. "Well that's one way to shut you up. I'll have to remember that." He gives me another quick kiss. "Come on let's get this running thing over."

My *date* with Isaac must have tapped into my hidden energy reserves. I was able to get ready this morning in under an hour. Granted, my new hair cut requires a dab of gel and thirty seconds with the hairdryer. I arrive at work early, and park my car a few blocks from the building. I feel like walking.

It's a quarter till nine. Late enough to call Trisha. I punch in her number and start my three-block walk to the office. If I were in a movie, they'd be playing *Walking on Sunshine* as I strut down the street.

Trisha picks up on the first ring. I tell her about my middle-of-the-night phone call and my early-morning rendezvous. She's excited but protective, like a mom with a teenage daughter.

Trisha/Mom: Did he ask you out again?

Me/Daughter: No.

Trisha/Mom: Do you even like him?

Me/Daughter: I don't know.

Trisha/Mom: Is he a nice boy?

Me: I guess so.

Trisha: What do his parents do for a living?

Me: I don't know.

Trisha: Well, don't let him break your heart. Remember what happened with Max and Phillip.

"He's not perfect. I mean he's a really poor dresser. He's sarcastic and maybe even a little rude. He doesn't care what others think. That's probably a plus. He's difficult, obnoxiously persistent, not good at following directions, and a bit childish."

"And what are his good characteristics?" she asks. "Other than being hot, under all those crappy clothes, of course."

"He's funny. And he's smart—at least he thinks he is. And...." I stop to think if I really have any basis for my next statement. Maybe it's just a sense; I don't have any hard proof.

"Yes," Trisha says impatiently.

"He's honest."

"That's a good quality to have."

"Yeah." There must be more than that. I have to add to the list. "And he's creative and smells really good. He always smells clean even if his clothes look like they've been at the bottom of the hamper. Then there's his smile, it's lopsided and—SHIT!" My knees hit the pavement, followed by my palms, the phone goes flying from my grasp.

"Are you okay?" asks a female jogger. "I'm so sorry."

"What happened?" I ask as I crawl toward my phone.

"You tripped over Chloe's leash. I'm so sorry."

Chloe? Who's Chloe? I turn to see a Weimaraner hovering above me. Yes, for someone deathly afraid of animals I can name and identify over twenty dog breeds. Know one's enemy.

The burning pain in my scraped knees suddenly disappears as fear tightens my chest. *Fight or flight* is B.S. I can't move.

"Come here, Chloe," the jogger says. "I'm sorry. She's really friendly."

Still unable to move. Can't take my eyes off Chloe. Hundred-pound, grey-coat, teeth-like-razors Chloe.

The woman moves toward my cell phone. Thankfully, she's holding the dog back. A frantic yelling comes from the phone. When I don't make a move to take it when she hands it to me, she tentatively puts it to her ear. "Hello?"

There's more indistinguishable chatter. The woman says, "Okay." Pause. "Okay." Pause. "Really?" Pause.

"Thank you." She puts my phone down and whispers, "I'm really sorry." She gives me a pathetic look before trotting away with Chloe in tow.

I'm finally able to pick up the phone.

"So, what was that about his smile?" Trisha asks.

I sob into the phone, more out of pain than anything else—my knees are on fire again. "Oh my God, Trisha. I was almost mauled by a dog."

"You were not. You fell."

"How? How did that happen? I can usually spot a field mouse a hundred yards away. How did I miss a hundred-pound Weimaraner?"

"Love makes you blind."

"Funny," I say, finally getting up and limping to the office.

The keyword to life is "limitless." This applies to everything—opportunities, careers, friendship, clothes.

Chapter 33

Daily Self-Assessment   *Wednesday, November 17*
Rate the degree to which you agree with the statement.
    5–completely agree 1–completely disagree
1. I accomplished something today. *5*
2. I felt connected with my friends and family today. *5*
3. I was interested in sex today. *0*
4. I laughed today. *5*
5. I am looking forward to tomorrow. *5*
Notes: *I haven't had a drink in two weeks.*
One of my "matches" at work got engaged. (Personally, I think it's a bit fast.)

***

People make millions of dollars on simple little ideas all the time. There's the sticky note, disposable sock-slash-hose that they give you in shoe stores, salad in a bag. Okay, I really don't know who invented these things or how much money they made from the sale of the idea. It must be millions. Now, I need to find a small, simple, can't-live-without-it idea to get me out of debt and out of that litter box that Lisa calls an office. Actually, the office doesn't really smell, but the Weimaraner almost-mauling this morning has put me back in code red animal alert.

On my drive to St. Mary's, I make a mental list of all the wonderful, fabulous products I could invent, then retire on the earnings. The list is incredibly short and incredibly ludicrous. There's *Get A Grip*, my own line of children's clothing with cloth handles sewn into them, so parents can grab their children and keep a grip. Unfortunately, this might aid kidnappers in snatching children, or a kid could snag the handle on a jungle gym or something. Next is a new line of Barbies called Trisha. A curvy, ethnic doll with an attitude, a career, and a wonderful husband. I struggle with her accessories—fecal kit, rabies shots. My other ideas are even less thought out—a board game that involves riddles and doing shots of tequila, a bookmark that's also a dictionary, and a shower timer that automatically starts the hot water in the morning. The old pipes in my dream house take more than two minutes to deliver hot water to my bathroom.

How am I ever going to get out of debt? I have exterminator bills, a mortgage, and growing credit card debt because I have to charge everything from toilet paper to fast food. And I've already sold anything of value on eBay.

Father Nolan lets it slide that I'm a few minutes late because he's impressed with my attire. A cream cashmere sweater, flared jeans in the darkest blue, brown suede boots with a chunky heel, and a knit, gray cap. I never wear hats—thought I'd try a new accessory.

"You're radiant," he holds my arms out for a good look. Why are all the good men married, gay, or dedicated to a higher calling?

"I'm not radiant. It's the hormone pills. They make my skin pink and shiny."

For a moment I forget about my financial problems and settle back into the cozy office chair to tell Father Nolan all about my early morning date with Isaac. Wish I had more than an hour for my lunch break, I could go on and on.

"I take it you will be seeing him again."

"I intend to."

"Have you told him about your upcoming pregnancy?"

"I intend to do that, too." Since the fertilized eggs won't be implanted for another two weeks and there's a chance I won't become pregnant, I haven't brought it up.

"I like Isaac," he says. "I had a feeling about you two."

"You did?"

"Who do you think gave him the gift certificate?" It is very unbecoming for a priest to look so smug.

"And what if I found him a girlfriend? He could have hit off with anyone."

"No, not Isaac."

"Well, Erika doesn't think I should be seeing Isaac."

"Why?"

"I haven't asked her. Think she might have a crush on him."

"Erika is with Dylan. They're very involved. I don't

think she feels—"

"Very involved?" I sit up straight. "What does that mean?"

"She's very happy with Dylan. And we at St. Mary's frown at teacher-student dating." He pours on the sarcasm.

"That's reassuring."

"Erika is a good girl. Talk to her."

I never get around to telling Father Nolan about my poverty issues. It was nice talking only about the good stuff. And with my improved attitude I feel I can conquer these little obstacles. I had it all wrong. Instead of trying to invent a million-dollar product, I should focus my attention on my current job. A job I like. A job I'm good at. (I've even matched Thelma with a man. They've been out three times.) Lisa said I get a percentage, beyond my salary, of all new business I bring in. Maybe I can drum up so much new business, I'll need to hire an assistant.

During my lunch break on Friday, I try to place advertisements at a few coffee shops and bookstores. The managers all say no solicitation. Next, I head to Wal-Mart and place fliers on car windshields.

Brilliant, Paige.

Problem one—a twenty-mile-an-hour wind steals half of my fliers. (Maybe that's where the word *flier* comes from.) Problem two—the client pool. After thirty minutes of setting off car alarms, I realize most Wal-Mart patrons on Friday afternoons are moms with little kids in tow and older couples who spend more time driving around looking for a parking spot close to the entrance than they do shopping.

Forget it. I'll go to the mall this afternoon. At least it's heated and I can window-shop. I call Penelope and tell her I won't be back in the office until two.

The mall requires a permit to solicit its patrons. Luckily, all I need to do is pay a fifty-dollar fee and let the General Manager check my material for vulgarity. When I take fifty out of my bank account, I'm left with six dollars until next payday. Hopefully, Lisa will reimburse the expense.

I work the food court, handing out fliers to anyone not wearing a wedding ring. Sometimes it's hard to tell if my prospective clients are old enough. Prrfect Connection only handles people over eighteen. Some of these girls at the mall could be twelve or twenty. They have baby faces, zero body fat, tiny sexy clothes, and perfect makeup and hair. (Could this have been a subliminal, Barbie-inspired message from their younger days?) I give these ageless girls my advertisement, anyway. It may lead to a few angry calls from parents, or worse, a six o'clock action news exclusive about an underground teen prostitution ring. I'll take my chances.

You'd think I was handing out smallpox samples the way people go out of their way to avoid me. At least that's better than the person who takes my flier, then a few steps later, uses it to dispose of his gum.

Next time, I'll print the information on one-dollar bills.

I look down at my pile. I started with 200 fliers. I still have more than 150 left. God, I'll be happy to get rid of even half. I make a deal with myself. If I hand out half, I'll splurge and buy myself a ninety-nine-cent hot fudge sundae.

As I try to chase down a woman on a cell phone, someone taps my shoulder.

"Can I have one of those?" a man asks.

I recognize the voice and turn to see Isaac. "Hi." There's an instant flood of emotions. I'm glad to see him, but I have to wonder if he's stalking me.

"Hey, your office told me where to find you," he says, as if he could read my mind.

"Isaac, this really isn't a good time. I'm working. This may seem like nothing to you, but it's part of my job."

"I brought you something." He completely ignores my brush-off.

"What?" I completely ignore my brush-off, too.

He holds out two closed fists. It's something small. Jewelry, maybe. Maybe it's nothing. He does have a weird sense of humor. I slap his left hand, and he opens it. In his palm is a small, Barbie-sized, plastic bouquet of flowers. Then he opens his other hand. It's a small, Barbie-sized, plastic box of chocolates.

"Thanks."

"They're for the girl who's happier today than she was two months ago."

"Thanks. That's sweet." These silly trinkets are the corniest and cutest gifts I ever remember receiving. I kiss him on the cheek.

"Do you want to get something to eat?" He reaches into his pocket and pulls out a crumpled dollar bill. "I can afford a small fry if we share."

"Isaac, I really am working. And don't you ever work? For someone who has three or four jobs, you never seem to be working."

"The one class I teach isn't for an hour. I'm coaching at four. I don't have any illustration jobs at the moment. I write when inspiration strikes. It's all very taxing."

"Sounds it."

"Hey, that girl Nicole called me yesterday."

"Yeah?" I plaster on a smile. More games.

"Should I call her?"

I shrug. I don't want to play these games.

"I'm not going to," he says.

"Do whatever you want to do." This is me playing uninterested. "Now, really. I have to pass these out." I hold up my stack.

"I'll help." Before I can protest, Isaac grabs a handful and starts harassing two twenty-somethings who are busily chatting away as they walk.

"Excuse me," he starts, "have you been swept off your feet recently?"

I hide my eyes, but not before I see the girls change pace from leisurely stroll to Olympic speed walking. I can't blame them. I'd be panicked if a guy started following me in a mall. Leave it to Isaac not to give in. The more challenging a task, the more game he is.

"I know it's hard being single," he shouts to the girls as they get on the escalator. He also gets on; at least he's two steps behind them. I follow, in case there's a scene. "You're sick of bars or blind dates set up by your mothers. You've probably even considered taking Rick from finance up on his offer of drinks and *who knows*. There is a better way."

The girls actually giggle, like they're twelve instead of

twenty-four-ish.

"There is a better way to find that special someone!" Isaac announces, not only to the girls but to everyone in the vicinity. To his credit, he's gained an audience. "Check out Prrfect Connections." He holds the fliers up, leans to me and whispers, "That's an awful name."

I shrug.

"Prrfect Connection is not your ordinary, Internet-driven dating service," he preaches to his followers. "A qualified dating counselor will work with you personally, one-on-one, to help you find a match. A cold computer doesn't pick your mate. An actual human being takes the time to understand your needs and wants, and matches you with someone who has similar values, tastes, and lifestyle."

The two women, still giggling, take fliers. One even hands Isaac a business card and mouths, "Call me."

"I'll take that." I grab the card. "I just want to run a background check, first."

Isaac laughs. That doesn't stop him from handing out sheet after sheet. Even people from the first level get up from their burgers and fries, and ride the escalator up to get a flier. The man's attractive and a good salesman. And I think he knows he's done a good job.

That is, until a large woman with a shopping bag gets up off the bench next to us and makes no move toward taking a flier.

"Wait! You haven't heard my testimonial yet." Isaac addresses the woman but speaks loud enough for this entire wing of the mall to hear. He jumps up on the bench where she previously sat. "I was—am—was a client. I got a gift certificate from my priest of all people."

"He told me," I whisper.

Isaac continues. "I'd rather have had a gift certificate to a nail salon in Istanbul—I'd probably get more use out of that, right? I finally gave it a try. I went through the interview process and the background check, and I met a fantastic girl that same week."

Great job, Isaac. Lay it on.

"It didn't work out."

There's an audible sitcom-like sigh from the small crowd.

"I didn't give up. And neither did Prrfect Connection. I went back, and this time I met the most unique and wonderful woman I've ever known."

Who's he talking about?

"She's beautiful and intelligent and just as lost in this world as anyone with half a brain and a huge heart would be. I'm crazy about her."

Is he telling the truth? Or is he trying to drum up business?

He gives me a wink as he hands out fliers as if they were free Super Bowl tickets. The wink clears up nothing, but, God, I hope he's talking about me.

"Sir, get off the bench." A security guard appears from another corridor.

"Sure." Isaac hops down immediately, still handing out fliers.

"Do you have a permit to solicit on the premises?"

"I do." I hand over my papers. The guard checks them out like the Border Patrol.

"This looks good. Keep him off the fixtures."

"Yes, sir."

As the guard walks away, Isaac starts humming "Matchmaker" from *Fiddler on the Roof*. He's distributed more fliers in fifteen minutes than I could have in a week.

When all the papers are gone, I treat Isaac to a soda and an oversized cookie. It's five dollars well spent.

"Thank you," I say.

"For?"

"Helping me reach new clients."

"My motivations were purely selfish. I only wanted this cookie." His smile is innocent, but his eyes say otherwise.

I want to slug him and rip off his clothes at the same time. I settle for a playful punch to his arm.

"My real motivation is only to spend some time with you. I think you're my muse."

"You mean, I'm amusing, easy to laugh at?"

"That, too."

"Well, for all your hard work, I'm only yours for another three minutes." I look at my watch.

"Whatever I can get. I have a class to teach anyway." We waste the next minute slurping sodas and sharing a chocolate chip cookie. Somehow, it's not awkward at all.

"So, you're not going to call Nicole?" I ask, bringing awkward right back into the mix. I just can't let well enough alone.

"No."

"Oh." More soda guzzling, awkward.

Break the silence, Paige.

"I think I'm going to come clean to my boss." I say.

"About Kenneth?"

"Yes."

"Does that mean you'll be getting out there? Jumping back into the dating pool?" He takes a napkin and wipes my lower lip. I haven't had a rush like that all week.

"In a while. I may need some time."

"So how much time does a girl need to get over a pretend marriage to her brother? Would it help if I told you we are long-lost second cousins?"

I laugh.

"How much? A day? A week? A month?"

"No. Hopefully by next weekend?"

"I'll make a note."

"Isaac, can we be serious for a minute?"

"Yes." His eye contact is intense. I'm tempted to look away.

"I don't know whether Lisa's going to be keen on me dating a client. After Kenneth and all, I don't think I should push it. Honestly, we have a shortage of attractive, male clients."

"Okay. No dating. Dating involves nice dinners, movies and things that cost money. We can do walks, phone calls, and Sunday mornings in bed. No receipt means there was no date."

"There's a more important issue. Erika. I think she has an issue with...us."

"What did she say?"

"That you aren't Ken material."

"Ouch! That's a major insult."

"And there's one more thing," I take a breath. "I'm almost pregnant."

"Not sure what that means? Is that like almost famous?"

"I'm going to be a surrogate for my best friend. With any luck I'll be pregnant the week after Thanksgiving." I study his face.

He stares off toward the merry-go-round. "And this means…"

"I'm giving up the dating game until next fall. So maybe you should give Nicole a call."

"I'd rather call you."

"Really?"

"Yeah. I always found dating nonpregnant, non-married-to-my-brother, non-Barbie-following women to be too simple."

"Well…I'll give you phone calls for now. We'll see about the rest. Deal?"

We shake on it.

"I'll walk you to your car," he says.

"You haven't been approved for walks yet."

"But when I am, I know Sunday mornings in bed aren't too far off."

"Goodbye, Isaac."

"Goodbye." He walks off, denying me the kiss I'd planned on denying him. I watch him head down the south side of the mall. I don't move until he disappears through the exit.

***

Daily Self-Assessment   *Saturday, November 20*
Rate the degree to which you agree with the statement.
    5–completely agree 1–completely disagree
1. I accomplished something today. *5*
2. I felt connected with my friends and family today. *5*
3. I was interested in sex today. *1*
4. I laughed today. *4*
5. I am looking forward to tomorrow. *4*
Notes: *Ran in the Turkey Trot! Forty minutes to run a 5K—at least I finished. Fed Beau a dog biscuit—threw it to him from my moving car.*

***

The Monday before Thanksgiving is not prime matchmaking season. All day I've had two phone calls and no visitors. At four o'clock I tell Penelope to go home and I'll cover for her. It's just me and the two cats left.

When the front door to Prrfect Connection opens I jump up to find Erika walking in. She's in her school uniform and carrying a messenger bag full of homework.

"Hey, how did you get here?" I ask.

"Father Nolan dropped me off."

"And basketball practice?"

"I'm skipping."

"That's not acceptable. You're first game is this weekend and you've made a commitment to—"

"Mom, stop. I came so we could talk. Father Nolan thought we needed to clear some things up."

The worst thoughts come to mind. Pregnancy. Drug addiction. Expulsion.

"Let's go to my office," I say. Barb may need to hear this, too.

We both take a seat in the chairs across from my desk. I don't know what she needs to talk to me about. I have a guess. The vibe is definitely negative.

I only speak up after I've given her adequate pause to begin. "Are you in some sort of trouble?"

"No." Erika chews on her lower lip.

"Then…"

She takes a deep breath.

"Does this have anything to do with Mr. Barber?"

"Yes."

"Erika, do you have feelings for him?"

She straightens up. "Like do I love him? No. That's gross. He's so old."

"He's a year younger than me!"

"Still."

"Then why isn't he my Ken?"

"I don't know. Maybe he is. I just want you to be careful. He kinda knows a lot about you."

"What do you mean?"

"I've been telling him stuff. Like background information on the subject for the experiment."

"What kind of stuff?" My fists are clenched driving my fingernails into my palms.

She hangs her head. "He could probably write your biography."

I give her the Mom-look.

"Well, he knows you stabbed Max. That you were arrested. That you were hospitalized for stress."

"I thought I was having a heart attack."

"Told him you gave me up for adoption. That you bicker with your mom. That you eat chocolate for breakfast when you have your period."

"Ugghh."

"Want me to stop?"

I shake my head.

"Kinda told him you didn't sleep with Phillip."

I rub my eyes with my palms. "How would you know that?"

"Well, I know he didn't spend the night and you didn't spend the night at his place. So unless you had a quickie…"

"We didn't."

"I didn't think so."

"Why didn't you tell him about the surrogacy?"

She shrugs.

"Any other big revelations?" I can't really think of anything else she could have told him. I haven't murdered anyone. Never took anyone hostage. Never took nude photos—at least I think they've all been destroyed.

"I said that I think you're in love with Father Nolan."

I throw my head back. "Erikaaa."

When Isaac calls me on Monday night, I don't answer it. Same on Wednesday afternoon. Erika's confession has made me feel vulnerable. Like being asked out by your gynecologist. That happened to Trisha once. It was after the pelvic exam, once she changed out of the paper robe. But still…

"It's not the same thing," Trisha snaps after I explain the gynecology similarity. "Not at all." She's on my living room floor rubbing Beau's belly which is full of Thanksgiving leftovers.

"He's seen my private stuff and he wants a date. It's the same." I sit at the kitchen table eating another piece of pumpkin pie. A wooden baby gate separates me from Beau and Trisha. I know he could easily jump the barrier.

"Everything she told him he probably could've found out on the Internet."

"She told him I was in love with Father Nolan."

"Are you?"

"Would it matter? He's a priest." Maybe Father Nolan has made a cameo appearance in a few of my dreams. What woman hasn't fantasized about being the mesmerizing heroine who makes a man question all he's ever known?

"Listen, if Isaac knows all your flaws and still wants you, that's not a bad thing. Maybe all relationships should start like that. It could be a new angle for you as a dating consultant."

"Sure, but I don't know any of his crap. And maybe he's just amused by all this. The experiment. The crazy subject."

"How much longer are you under the Barbie regimen?"

"The experiment is over a week from tomorrow. Erika gives her presentation on the seventh. But I'm not giving it all up. No more leaving the house looking like I'm going to work out unless I'm going to work out."

"You're going to keep running?" Trisha gets off the floor.

"No. Especially once I'm pregnant. And sorry, Beau, you'll need a new home." Some things will never change.

No need to look your age. No need to deny it either.

Chapter 34

Trisha's infertility doctor is a pretty blonde who seems too young to be a specialist. She has to be in her twenties. It's easy to picture her in a club dancing and doing body shots. The white lab coat looks like dress up.

"And we're done." Doctor Curtis pulls the flexible tube out of my vagina. Her nurse, who's a good decade older, turns off the ultrasound machine.

"How many of these have you done?" I ask.

"In vitro? I've lost count. I've performed all of Trisha and Manny's procedures. In vitro with a gestational carrier? Only a handful." She moves my feet out of the stirrups and puts a pillow under my knees. "I'd like you to lay here for a few hours. Then you're good to go. Keep taking your prenatals and folic acid."

"Give me your honest opinion," I say. "What are the odds I'm pregnant?"

"IVF with a gestational carrier run an average of—"

325

"Thirty to thirty-five percent. I know the averages, but how do you feel about this specific situation?"

"It may take a few tries." She throws her gloves into the trash. "I'll send Trisha and Manny in now."

"Wait!" I hold up Barb. She's been by my side under the paper sheet. "Can you put her in my purse, please?"

Trisha is smiling when she walks into the room. Manny's behind her carrying flowers, a bottle of orange juice and three plastic champagne glasses. I wish they'd save the celebrating. We won't know if I'm pregnant for fourteen days and even then, so many things could go wrong.

"How are you feeling?" Trisha asks.

"Three embryos heavier."

Trisha has experienced IVF two times. Because of her medical history, her odds of becoming pregnant after the embryos were transferred into her uterus were around ten percent. Luckily the eggs they harvested from Trisha and the sperm donated by Manny had produced enough viable embryos that the doctor was able to freeze them. That's what I got—the previously frozen.

"I want you to know, that if this doesn't work, we can try again." I say.

"No, we can't," Trisha says. "We've put all our eggs in your basket. There are no more embryos in storage."

The pressure settles on my chest. "You could make more, right?"

"Technically," Manny says. "Let's not worry about that now."

There's a light snow falling when Trisha and Manny drive me home two hours later. They stop and pick up a pizza—ham, olives, pineapple and jalapenos.

"Don't tell me cravings are kicking in already?" Erika says when she inspects the pizza.

The four of us sit around the kitchen table, Beau safely resting on the other side of the baby gate. I tried telling everyone that a pregnant woman shouldn't be around a dog. No one believed my Internet-based medical study.

"How was school?" I ask Erika.

"Fine." She gets up from the table and gets a sheet of paper from her messenger bag. "Mr. Barber has requested a conference with you."

"Why?"

"I've a feeling it has little to do with Erika," Trisha says.

The snow that began as flurries yesterday dumped eight inches overnight. St. Mary's cancelled school and I called Prrfect Connection, telling them I was stuck at home. I'm in no condition to shovel the driveway. Instead, Erika and I make a day of it, watching a *Law and Order* marathon on cable, eating popcorn, and drinking cocoa.

"Aren't you going to call Mr. Barber?" Erika asks after we watch a riveting episode that involves a teacher seducing her students.

"Do you think I should?"

"It's the one open item on your Barbie list—Find your own Ken."

"Maybe I did find him, I just didn't reel him in." I rub my belly. "Plus, I have other things on my mind."

Daily Self-Assessment   *Friday, December –Last One*
Rate the degree to which you agree with the statement.
     5–completely agree 1–completely disagree
1. I accomplished something today. *4*
2. I felt connected with my friends and family today. *4*
3. I was interested in sex today. *1*
4. I laughed today. *4*
5. I am looking forward to tomorrow. *4*
Notes: *Got a new career. Got a house. Got a dog. Tried golf. Tried modeling. Ran a 5k. Helped a friend. Looked the part. Overall, I feel good!*

***

I continue to avoid Isaac's phone calls and notes home for the rest of the week. But on the following Monday I'm forced to give in.

"Someone got a present." Penelope is standing in my office door with a small bouquet of lilies. "They just arrived."

"Who are they from?" I ask.

"I'd assume your husband." She looks confused and hands over the envelope that is no longer sealed.

I won't give up. Meet me tomorrow for dinner at Café 42. 7PM

I look up. "Of course, they're from Kenneth. We've been fighting."

Penelope returns to her desk and leaves me alone with my flowers and Barb. The experiment may be over, but our relationship is still going strong.

"What do you think?" I show Barb the card. "I told

him no dates."

It would be rude not to go.

I call Isaac on my cell and get his voicemail.

"Hello. It's Paige. You certainly are persistent. I will see you tomorrow night at Café 42, but this isn't a date. It's too soon to date. I'm only going on one condition. You have to wear a real shirt. No T-shirts. No sweatshirts. It's not my rule. It's you-know-who's. See you in…" I glance at the clock, "thirteen hours."

Good manners are a seldom used superpower.

Chapter 35

Since Isaac Barber only teaches the one class, he does not have his own classroom. Social Science is held in the same room as American History, taught by Mr. Nelson—the teacher I had sixteen years ago. And the only change to the room is a few new presidential portraits on the wall.

I sit behind the class listening to a painfully thin boy explain the results of his project. It has something to do with birth order and grade point average.

When Erika steps to the front I get butterflies in my stomach. The same thing happens when she's announced at a soccer game or when she's at the free-throw line. I'm more nervous for my daughter than I ever was for myself. I can only imagine what it'll be like on her wedding day.

She connects her laptop to the projector and opens her presentation. Long gone are the days of simple transparencies. Her first screen reads "Barbie Doll: Ultimate role model or anti-feminist icon? Erika O'Neal"

All in shades of pink.

Isaac is sitting at a desk in the front row. Before she begins he turns and gives me the slightest head nod.

Erika clears her throat. "The Barbie Doll was introduced to the world in 1959. Originally, she was a teenage fashion model from Wisconsin. In her first commercials, Mattel never refers to Barbie as a doll. From the beginning she was marketed to be a cultural icon. But is she the perfect role model for middle class America or does her focus on body image and material possessions weigh negatively on impressionable, young girls?"

Erika is doing great. She's making eye contact and only referring to her note cards occasionally. She touches the laptop and the screen changes to a silhouette of Barbie surrounded by basic facts and history. Erika talks on about the factual Barbie.

I'm shocked when she clicks to the next page of the presentation. It's a silhouette of me. Maybe I should have asked for a private presentation first. My weight, my height, my measurements—how did she get that—my age, my college major, my hometown and more are all on the screen for twenty teenagers—and Isaac—to analyze.

"For this experiment, my thirty-four year old subject agreed to live life according to the Barbie standard."

The screen changes to the list of requirements and Erika explains each—how it was derived and its level of importance.

"The subject was required to complete a survey at the end of each day." The screen switches to a copy of the survey. A few kids snicker over the *interested in sex* question. For a teenage boy, they're probably wondering if there is ever a time that wouldn't be a five.

"Using these five statements I was able to conclude the overall happiness and success of the subject throughout the experiment." The next page has a graph with time along the horizontal axis and the numbers one through five on the vertical axis. According to Erika, my happiness—the pink line—increased overall but not without a few peaks and valleys along the way. Success also improved, not as dramatically, and without all the erratic shifts.

"Let's take a closer look." Click to more graphs. "The three days with the highest happiness rating, the subject followed the guidelines closely. Specifically adhering to the dress-code, the exercise regimen, avoiding alcohol, and accomplishing items on the to-do list."

"Hmm?" I say, causing a few kids in the back row to turn.

Erika continues explaining correlations in her data. With only one subject and a limited timeline the experiment is not scientifically sound, but it is interesting. She goes through four or five more graphs—all very favorable to Barbie and to the subject.

"So the question remains," Erika continues, "was Barbie designed by women to teach the next generation of women how to set and achieve goals and be successful? Or was she designed to teach girls they must act and dress in her image to be a *woman*? And why can't she do both?"

I smile proudly until...

The screen flashes to bold words. "The Barbie Syndrome. When the Subject Makes a Major Connection."

"A surprise that resulted from this experiment was the subject's heavy reliance on Barbie for support and decision making."

Oh, boy.

"The subject not only had a physical connection with the Barbie doll—constantly carrying a Barbie with her like a toddler would cling to a favorite teddy bear—she was also observed speaking with the doll. Mostly asking Barbie questions. It is not clear whether the subject could hear an answer coming from the doll."

Isaac slowly turns around. I barely catch sight of his huge smile before I am out the classroom door.

"This is worse than when I got my skirt caught in my locker," I say, clutching my purse. "Stop, Paige. Who do you think you are talking to?"

Maybe I am going insane.

I lean against the wall not having the self confidence to walk back in. I can't leave either. I have two things to tell Erika. As her mother, "You did a great job." As the subject, "You got it all wrong."

Then there's Isaac. My life may be easier if I never see the man again. There has to be a limit to my quirkiness that he can endure.

The door to the classroom opens and Isaac steps out. "Erika is taking questions. Don't you want to come back in?"

"That depends. Do you think all the students know I'm the subject of the experiment?"

"They're fifteen, not five."

"In that case, I'll get the recap at home. Tell Erika goodbye for me?"

"Sure thing." He winks and retreats into the room before I can ask him if we're still on for dinner. I'm afraid his answer may be no. Almost more afraid because the answer could be yes.

Café 42 is the kind of establishment Father Nolan loves. (He refuses to go to chain restaurants.) The food is served on square plates with ornate, inedible decorations around the edges. The wine list is extensive. The service is attentive. It's a place where I'd dress up even if I wasn't a Barbie-follower.

Barb helped me select a plain, short black dress for this non-date. Classic and not over the top. Since my notorious haircut, my prep time is down to twenty minutes for both hair and makeup. My only fashion faux pas is my oversized brown leather purse. Barb insisted on coming and I knew Isaac would not object.

I arrive ten minutes early and debate whether I should wait in the car or go inside and ask for our table. I don't see Isaac's Toyota in the parking lot—it would stand out. So I head inside and find a place at the bar.

The waiter brings me my second seltzer and lime before my *date* arrives.

It's not Isaac.

When Phillip walks through the door I think for a moment that it is only a coincidence. Until he walks over and kisses me on the cheek. Then I'm only wishing for a coincidence. I'm speechless and unable to move.

"I almost didn't recognize you with the new haircut," he says. "Thanks for meeting me. I was afraid I'd be dining alone."

"That would be rude," is all I can think to say.

"Do you want to finish your drink or should we get our table?" he asks.

"Thanks. I have to use the ladies room. Why don't you get our table? I'll catch up in a minute." I hop down, smooth my dress and walk to the restroom. Soon as we're safe inside, I open my purse.

"It's Phillip." I hold Barb inches from my face.

What about Isaac?

"I should have known he wouldn't have asked me to come here. The food isn't served on Styrofoam."

You asked Isaac here.

"You're right. When I called him. Did I mention the time? Did I really mention the place? What if he shows up, too?" I would splash cold water on my face, but I don't want to mess my makeup.

When I calm down, I leave the sanctuary of the bathroom. Phillip is sitting at a table looking at a wine list. He looks good—like he always does—in a suit and tie that obviously aren't from Sears. In Phillip's case, it's true that the clothes make the man. He wouldn't be nearly as handsome in jeans and an old sweatshirt. So if Isaac looks so good in whatever he pulls from the hamper, I'd melt at the sight of him in something ironed.

"I'm back," I say from behind him.

He stands and gives me a hug. It's more like a slow-dance-between-lovers hug than a brother-sister hug. His arms are around my waist and his hands are dangerously close to my butt. I can feel every muscle in his body from his neck to his knees.

Reluctantly, I wrap my arms around his shoulders. He squeezes even tighter. And I'm happy to report his full body hug does nothing for me. No spark. No desire. No real attraction.

He pulls out my chair. "Are you in the mood for red or white?"

"Phillip, I can't—"

"The baby?"

"No, that's not what I mean. I can't stay." I take a seat anyway because I want to explain.

"What's wrong? I'm not bothered by the surrogate pregnancy. It's really nice what you're doing."

"Let me be honest. I thought you were someone else."

"I told you I'm getting divorced. I'm legally separated." He lays some legal looking documents on the table. His own Exhibit A.

"It doesn't matter." I take a deep breath. "I don't like how this all started. Dishonest."

"Because I had an ex-wife."

"She wasn't your ex-wife when we met. And it's not that. Well, it's not just that. It's because of what I did. I orchestrated our second meeting. I claimed to be dating you before that just to get Max upset. And I did it because you used to live in Kenmore apartments."

"I never lived in Kenmore."

"Yes, you did." As if I'd know better. "In college."

"I lived at home. From the day I came home from the hospital to the day I left for law school, I lived on Cherry Ave. My parents still live there. The two-story, gray farm house with the—"

"Wraparound front porch. Then who lived in Kenmore? It doesn't matter. There are other reasons."

"I don't mind that you came searching for me. I like to

be pursued." Phillip puts his hands on mine.

A waiter approaches our table. "Have you selected a wine?" he asks.

"Can we have another minute," I say.

I hold my purse for strength. "Phillip, this isn't going to work." I stand up to leave. I don't want to give Phillip a chance for closing arguments.

Instead of an argument, Phillip grabs my hand as I walk by. He kisses the back of it. "Goodbye, Paige."

"Goodbye." I free my hand and walk to the entrance. I continually scan the room for Isaac. Thankfully he's not here. I check the parking lot again and his Toyota is nowhere in sight. My relief tapers off.

Why isn't Isaac here? He stood me up.

During the drive home I convince myself Isaac never got my message about Café 42. He seems like the kind of guy who only checks his messages occasionally. Like on Columbus Day or during a lunar eclipse.

When I pull up to my house, I stop obsessing about Isaac and allow a surge of pride to rise within me. This is my house, and though it's still in need of work, it's no longer the haunted house it first appeared to be. I walk up the front steps without fear of falling through and into the front door without worrying about the hinges coming off.

As a housewarming gift, Ryan gave me an antique telephone table. It's truly an uncharacteristically nice gift from my brother, who prefers to give gift certificates when he has a job and candy bars when he doesn't. He said I should put the table near the door, so it'll be the first thing people see when they enter the house. He also said maybe the table would distract guests from the *hole* that is the rest of my house. Insult or not, I love his gift.

I put my keys on the table next to the tiny bouquet and box of chocolate Isaac gave me—or Barbie—at the mall. That's it. I'm going to call him.

Erika is in the hall bathroom.

I knock on the door. "I'm home."

"Short date?" She comes out in her pajamas.

I give her a kiss on the top of her head. "Wrong date."

Alone in my bedroom I dial Isaac's number on my cell without having to look it up. When did I memorize his number? Did I do it subconsciously?

After several rings, his machine picks up.

"Hi, this is Paige. Maybe I was being too strict earlier. Phone calls are good, so are walks or dinner at my place. Please call me. Bye." I hope I didn't sound too pushy.

I could use a bubble bath. The best therapy known to women. I take the phone with me into the bathroom, hoping Isaac calls back soon. From under the sink, I grab my favorite bath gel—Mango—and turn on the water. It trickles out—then nothing.

"Huh?"

I try the sink. Nothing. The shower. Nothing. I run downstairs to the kitchen and find the same problems. Armed with a flashlight and a steak knife, I open the door to the basement. I'm thirty-four years old and still afraid of the basement. I point the beam of light to the bottom of the stairs.

A few feet of water cover the last couple of steps. Water starts pouring out, not from the pipes, but from my eyes. Instead of calling a plumber, I call Father Nolan.

Onward and upward, but don't forget your pink parachute.

Chapter 36

Three days or five days? Some guys have a waiting period before calling a girl. On the other side of the equation, a girl is never supposed to accept a date without forty-eight hours notice, and if it's a date for a Friday or Saturday night, seventy-two hours is better. I don't know who makes these rules or who enforces them. They're suburban myths.

I implemented the forty-eight-hour rule once. A friend of a friend asked me to a party at the last minute. I said I was busy, even though I had nothing planned but watching *Must See TV*. So, the guy asked someone else and that someone else ended up being his future wife. For awhile, I thought it all made sense because that night I met Max at a drug store. I was buying antacids, hidden under a pile of other items. He was buying laxatives, hidden under a pile of other items. It seemed like fate. Now I wish I could glimpse into what my life would have been like if I'd accepted the short-notice date.

Isaac doesn't seem like a guy who'd follow any kind of dating rules. He barely follows any rules. But he never bothered to call back. Not Tuesday. Not Wednesday. Not Thursday. Like a desperate fool, I called him five more times, hanging up two of those times.

Maybe it's better that he didn't call. I wouldn't have had any time for him, anyhow. I spent two days mopping up a moldy basement after my Uncle Charley fixed my broken pipe. Thank God for family. He only charged me for parts and I had to get him one of Mom's lasagnas.

I get to the office at nine on Friday, and the phone is flashing with messages. I have seven calls from prospective new clients who picked up my flier. No calls from Isaac.

Lisa warned me that Christmas is a busy time for Prrfect Connection. No one wants to spend the holidays alone. A last-minute attempt to find love before New Year's.

"It's time to get real," I tell Barb as I pull her out of my bag and settle her into her plush drawer-home. I take the wedding ring off my finger and throw it away.

I walk out to the reception area. "Is Lisa in?"

"Yes, she's meeting with someone."

"Let me know when she's available." I turn back toward my office.

"Paige, you have a visitor," the receptionist calls after me.

I spin around expecting Isaac dressed in stained jeans and a faded shirt carrying cups of coffee. "Who?" I ask, craning to peer around the corner to the waiting area.

She shrugs.

I walk to the lobby to find a woman holding my flier.

"I'll be right with you," I tell her and run to my office. I call Isaac, again.

And again, I get his machine. "Paige, again." I attempt to sound playful. "You're probably not up yet. When you are, call me. I'm at work. Or stop by. I'd love to talk to you. Okay?" I don't hang up for a few more seconds as I imagine him scrambling out of bed to answer the phone.

Nope.

I straighten my skinny brown skirt and yellow sweater. I wore this ensemble hoping to *bump into* Isaac today. Father Nolan says I need one outfit that makes me feel sexy and confident, no matter what the cost. "Great things will happen when you wear your uniform of confidence." I'm dressed for destiny.

Trying to adopt a sunny attitude, I go back to the woman and invite her into my office. We begin the interview. By the time we're finished, forty-five minutes later, I have two other clients in the waiting area and another three messages on my voice mail. I take client after client for the rest of the day, skipping lunch and only thinking about Isaac every ten seconds.

When there's a knock at my door at five-thirty, I'm ready to jump out of my sealed window. I cannot listen to one more person tell me they're looking for someone kind with a sense of humor. I half wish a client would say "I'm looking for a mean-spirited witch who'll promise everything and give me nothing because I've grown rather fond of this pathetic lifestyle and I'm only here because my mother has kicked me out of the house."

"Come in," I yell, too lazy to get up.

Lisa walks in. "Wow! We did a good bit of business

today. How many?"

"Twelve."

"A dozen. That's a new individual record. I should give you a raise." She takes a seat across from me. "I heard you were looking for me."

Lisa's in a great mood. This is my opportunity to come clean. Fix my errant ways. "Yes. I need to tell you something."

"Shoot."

"First, I really appreciate you giving me this job. I know I was inexperienced, and you took a risk. I think things are really working out."

"Me, too." She examines her nails. Her acrylics are more interesting than my blabbering.

"I need to clear the air. I'm afraid I may have given you the wrong impression."

"How so?" She makes eye contact.

"Well, first, I don't like cats. Or any animal for that matter. There's nothing wrong with them. I just don't like to be around them."

"Paige, honey, I know. I've known since the first day you spent forty minutes in the bathroom waiting for Pumpkin to finish his nap in the hallway."

"You've known?" Maybe I'm not as good an actress as I've given myself credit for.

"Yes. And you may have noticed I've been trying to keep them confined to my office ever since then." She gives me a rapid-fire set of head nods.

"I thought I'd just been lucky in avoiding them."

"Is that all?" Lisa asks.

"No." Deep breath. "I—uh—I'm afraid I gave you the

impression that I'm—um—married." Hold breath. Wait for a response.

"The impression?" she asks.

"Yeah."

"Are you married?"

"No."

"Were you married?"

"Yes. But not to Kenneth. And I was separated before I ever started working here." Maybe if I keep talking I can throw her off track. "His name's Max and we were married for nine years. He's dating my hairdresser now. I did learn a lot from the experience of being married. I think it makes me a qualified dating—"

"Paige! Shut up! Who's Kenneth?" She reminds me of my mom's flustered line of questioning when she'd catch me in a lie.

"My brother. His name is actually Ryan."

"And what about the pictures?" She picks up the frame on my desk.

"Fabricated. I wanted this job. I needed this job. I've felt horrible deceiving you."

"Lying."

"Yes, lying. I feel so bad, Lisa. I'm going to make it up to you." Don't know how, though.

"No need." She sits up. She's taking this so much better than I imagined.

"Thank you. Thank you so much. Nothing like this will ever happen again."

"Good. Please take all your things when you leave today." She gets up, like I've already wasted too much of her time.

"What? Are you letting me go?"

She turns around when she hits my doorway. "I don't want to give you the wrong *impression*, so I'll be blunt. You are fired!" Lisa storms out, not giving me a second for a rebuttal.

"Lisa, wait." I give chase. This job means everything to me. Not only do I need it to live, I may actually be good at it.

I hit the hallway just as Lisa reaches her office. Something catches my eye. It's Isaac walking out of the lobby. Hesitation. Lisa or Isaac? Isaac or Lisa? What's my priority?

"Hey, Isaac. Hey!" I yell. He doesn't stop.

He's halfway down the block by the time I catch up to him. "I'm so glad to see you." I give him a hug. He's as warm as a flag pole in January. "Did you come to see me?"

"Actually, I just dropped off a note for you."

"Poem or prose?" I ask playfully.

"A thank you note. I spent yesterday with that woman, Nicole, you set me up with. We really hit it off. She's fabulous!"

Fabulous? When did he start using *fabulous*?

"So, I don't think I'll be coming in any more." He offers me a handshake. I can't move.

"Is this because of the mix-up at Café 42? I thought I was meeting you and then Phillip showed up. It was nothing but a misunderstanding. See, I got a bunch of flowers and the card wasn't signed and—"

"I never went to the restaurant."

"But... then... why? I thought you and I were...."

"No. We're not." He runs a hand through his hair. I

can tell he has more to say. "I've got go. I'm meeting Nicole for dinner. Good luck with the baby and everything."

Is it possible? Was I just dumped and fired within two-minute time frame? This could only happen to me.

I'm burning this outfit when I get home.

*When life comes crashing down and no one
is around to hear it,
it doesn't have to make a sound*

Chapter 37

After being *let go* by both Lisa and Isaac, I try to stay positive. I can find another job. I've done it before. I can find another man. I've done that before, too. When I take a pregnancy test on Monday morning I can't fight off the tears any more.

"I'm not pregnant," I call Trisha. "I've taken three tests."

"We knew the odds weren't in our favor."

"I'll take another test tomorrow," I say, trying to make it all better. I'll keep taking tests until I can give my friend what she wants.

I get my period before I get a chance to take the fourth pregnancy test. I tell Trisha with a text message. I don't want to say the words. Then I crawl into bed and stay there for more than two weeks.

Today is the day to start over. Let's get out of bed. Barb says the same thing every day, several times a day. I learn to tone her out.

I only get out of bed when it is absolutely necessary—to go to the bathroom, kill a bug on the wall, to fulfill my motherly duties, Christmas day. On occasion, I take a bath (five occasions to be exact). I only leave the house when Erika needs a ride and on Christmas day. This Christmas will forever be known as the one where Paige knocked over the tree, dropped the ham, and gave everyone the same gift—e-gift certificates sent out on December twenty-sixth. I haven't washed my sheets. I don't answer the phone, which doesn't ring that often. I lie in bed with my remote, my box of sustenance—Ritz crackers—and my Barbie. Our relationship right now could best be described as love-hate.

Sometime during the middle of my eighteenth day of bed rest, I'm startled by a banging at my front door. Three weeks ago I would have been worried that it was a rapist or a serial killer, but not now.

"Paige O'Neal! Let me in!" screams a woman. It's Trisha. I told her I was taking some time off from my life, and once I assured her I wasn't suicidal, she agreed to give me my solitude. This is the first time she's come around.

"Paige?" asks a softer voice. "Doll, you okay?" It's Father Nolan.

Boom! Boom! It sounds like they're kicking the door in.

"Let me in!"

"Not by the hair of my chinny-chin-chin," I say, doubting she can actually hear me. Then again, maybe she can because the banging stops.

A minute later, the front door creaks open.

"We're coming in." She stomps through the hallway and up the stairs. I take cover under my comforter. If I hold my breath, maybe she won't realize I'm here.

"God, what's that smell?" she asks when she reaches my doorway. "You'd better be a rotting corpse to justify smelling that bad." She tugs at my covers, but I've made myself an impenetrable cocoon.

"How did you get in?" I ask.

"Found the key in the plant box," Father Nolan says.

"I never put a key in the plant box."

"Then the previous owner did." Trisha walks around my bed, canvassing my cocoon looking for a weak point. "It's been three weeks. You need to get out of that bed!"

Needing air, I flip the comforter back. Trisha jumps in horror.

"Why?" I ask. "My dream house is flooded. I lost my job. I lost my Ken. I lost my dog."

"You didn't want the dog. And he went to a good home." Trisha says.

I retreat back under my comforter. "And I couldn't give you a baby."

"That's life. Now, get up." Trisha yanks all the blankets off my bed, and a bottle falls to the floor. "What's this?" She holds up the empty bottle of Smirnoff. Vodka has been the other half of my sustenance—Ritz crackers and vodka. "Come on. You're going to your parents' New Year's Eve party."

"Is that today?"

"Yes. Starts in less than an hour." Father Nolan taps his watch. "Time for a makeover." He sounds excited.

Mom's New Year's Eve party is an O'Neal family

tradition. My parents invite every relative and person they've ever befriend over for a six-hour celebration. Mom usually spends more on alcohol than on food. It's drinking for celebration's sake without the pretence of giving thanks or exchanging gifts.

"I can't go. My shower isn't working."

Trisha grabs a plastic bottle of spring water from my night stand and gives me a shower.

"Hey. Bitch!" I yell.

She laughs. I'm probably more amusing and challenging than a cat with a splinter. I've always thought Trisha's choice of occupation went deeper than wanting to help animals.

"You can shower at my place," Trisha says.

"I have nothing to wear and no date."

Father Nolan opens up my closet and selects the ridiculous pink dress from the wedding.

"I hate pink."

"Let's not be nasty," Father Nolan gives me a tsk-tsk with his fingers.

"And I still don't have a date."

"Why do you need a date to visit with your parents and relatives?" Father Nolan asks.

"Because Ryan is bringing a date, and I'm his pathetic, older, spinster sister. What will everyone say?"

"You're not older. More mature doesn't make you older. And you don't need a date." Trisha says.

"Can I take her?" I pull Barb out from under my pillow. She's the only one who understands me. We need each other.

Trisha sighs. "Sure, bring a doll. That'll make

everything better."

I'll smuggle Barb into Mom's house in a bag of potato chips if I have to. I need her to be with me tonight even if she smells of salt and vinegar.

After hiding Barb behind an overgrown peace lily, I mingle with the guests—kissing cheeks, smiling brightly, chatting endlessly about the weather, which is outrageously cold. Erika has disappeared with her second cousins. I wonder if they're sneaking sips of champagne like Ryan and I did at her age.

Apparently, a significant portion of my extended family hasn't heard about my divorce. Fair enough. I can handle Cousin Margaret asking, "Where's Max?" Or Uncle Frank extending an invitation, "You and Max should come out to the beach house this year. You'd love it." I finally have enough when my own maternal grandmother asks, "When are you and Max going to have a baby? A little bouncing boy?" Gram knows we're not together any more. I told her when it happened, then again over Thanksgiving dinner, and again on her birthday when we went on a shopping spree at the Gap. I've got the only grandmother who lives for khakis and trendy knits.

"You're not as young as you use to be," Gram points out. "Women today wait too long to have children. I was twenty when your uncle was born."

"I was nineteen when Erika was born. I'm probably done having children."

"Doesn't Max want more children? I think he's a great father."

"He doesn't want more kids, Gram. And he doesn't want me."

"That's nonsense. You've always been so dramatic. I told your father you'd do great in theater, but he insisted on pushing you into soccer." She stops talking long enough to take a swig of her Manhattan. "Is that Max over there?" She points to the dining room.

"No." I don't even look, assuming it's a Manhattan-induced hallucination. She once swore she saw Bill Clinton at JC Penney.

"Yes, it is." She waves. "Max, honey, over here."

"Gram, stop." I rub my temples. How long do I have to stay? I'd leave right now if I weren't certain Trisha was guarding the front door and Father Nolan's got the back. They also swiped my keys when we first arrived.

"Hello, Grandma Carter," says the voice that once made my heart flutter, but now causes palpitations.

"Max." I look up to see my ex-husband hugging my beloved Grandmother. "What are you doing here?" I both scream and whisper.

"I received an invitation, I had to come. You look great. Your hair is sexy and this dress…wow!" He leans in for a hug; I push him back into an end table littered with drinks and knickknacks.

The crash stops everything. Everyone stares. Blood rushes to my face.

"What was that?" Mom hurries into the room. "Paige, did you knock over my Christmas tree, again?"

"Sorry, Nancy. I bumped into your table and broke this." He picks up a piece of a ceramic cherub statue.

"That silly thing. No harm."

"I gave you that for Mother's Day when I was like ten."

She shrugs.

"Never mind." I pull Mom aside. "Why is my ex-husband here?"

"He's been a part of this family for the past nine years. I couldn't *not* invite him. That would have been rude."

"I've been a member of this family for over thirty-four years. Shouldn't my feelings count?"

"Of course." She pulls me forward for a kiss on the forehead. "You can handle him, sweetie. He wouldn't be here if I didn't believe that." Then she saunters off to entertain. With open arms she directs everyone into the other parts of the house—away from the broken knickknacks and spilled drinks. She closes the French doors. I'm left alone with the mess—and Max.

He puts an arm around my waist. "I've missed you, Paige."

"You're the one who wanted the divorce." I remove his hairy arm.

"My mistake. I should have tried harder, but I couldn't understand why you always put me last."

"Maybe I'm not wife material." I don't want to argue. I move toward the door, hoping the conversation is over.

"I fell in love in with you because you give yourself completely to one thing. And when that one thing was me, we were really happy. Maybe we could have that again."

I stop cold. Do I respond? Do I go on? I stand frozen with my back to him for two minutes.

"Paige?"

I turn around, still not sure what to say. I speak

anyway. "What did you say?"

"I think we could have that again." He gives me a smile. "If your focus was on our marriage and on me, not everything else."

"Is that why you left me for Vanessa? She made you a priority?"

"First point, we weren't serious until I moved out. Second point, I am important to her. She makes time for me. She tries to make me happy."

I sink into the couch. "You were my Ken." I whisper. The unobtainable item on my list. The one area I screw up over and over. And it turns out I'd had Ken for nine years previously and had no clue.

"Who's Ken?" Max sits down next to me and takes my hand. "Are you seeing someone?"

"No." I shake my head. "Ken is Barbie's boyfriend. You know. The doll?"

He nods. "What does that have to do with—"

"I thought Ken was everything to Barbie. Boyfriend. Best friend. An equal partner. But he's not."

I get a blank look from Max.

"He's really just an accessory. Her life goes on with or without him. Sure, It's nice when he's there but when he's not… who misses him?"

"And you think I'm just an accessory?"

"Pretty much. So I guess I owe you an apology, huh? Not because I burned a few dinners and not because I spent weekends going to Erika's soccer games. I'm sorry I didn't give you all I had and I'm sorry I didn't need you."

"Apology accepted." He rubs his thumb on my cheek.

"Whoooo. Don't get me wrong. You're still the two-timing jerk and the needy, jealous-for-my-time-husband. I'd recommend therapy before you get into another relationship."

"I'd go to marriage counseling."

"We're not married." I hold up my ring finger. "And I can't commit to an accessory. Come spring, you'll be out of style. Again." Accountant husbands were so last season. This fall is all about carpenter as lovers and oversized handbags.

"Paige," Trisha pokes her head inside the French doors. "What are you doing?" She looks concerned because Max has his head in my lap and he's sobbing.

"Cleaning out my closet." I push Max off of me. "Goodbye, Maxwell. It's all over—for certain."

Barbie would be proud. I can feel my self-esteem rising as forcefully as a burp after chugging a beer. Maybe that's not the best analogy.

Trisha has to leave the party early to pick Manny up from the airport. Before she goes, she makes me promise not to leave until at least half the guests do, not to drive drunk and to stay away from the wobbly Christmas tree. But I don't agree to more mingling.

I grab a Diet Coke, Dad's winter coat, and go sit on the deck. It snowed two inches earlier. Now it is clear and cold. The party is still going strong inside. Dad is playing the piano and Mom is singing a collection of show tunes. She actually has a nice voice.

As Mom belts out a tune from *Guys and Dolls* a pickup pulls up in the driveway. It's Ryan and a girl. Why didn't he have to be here two hours ago? The date looks familiar, but I can't tell because of the distance, the darkness and the fact that my brother is attached to her lips.

"Enough already," I shout.

"Hey, Paige," Ryan says. "What are you doing?" They walk up the steps to the deck.

"Getting some air."

Ryan's date steps into the light. It's—

"Paige, you know Nicole." Ryan introduces.

Nicole is *The Nicole*. The Nicole from Prrfect Connection. The Nicole who's dating Isaac.

She offers her hand. "Hello, again. Thank you for setting us up." She squeezes Ryan around the waist. "At first, I had my doubts, but you definitely know people." They kiss again like teenagers. At the very least there's a sexual attraction. How the hell did this happen?

"We better go say hello to the parents," Ryan says.

"Ryan, can I talk to you alone?" I drag him off without waiting for an answer. We stand by Mom's frozen 3000-gallon koi pond.

"What do they do with the fish in the winter?" Ryan says.

"Haven't a clue. How did you meet Nicole?"

"Um…"

"Ryan, answer me."

"I took a sheet from her file."

"From my office?"

"Yeah. I didn't think you'd mind. Look at her." He waves. "She's hot. I really had no choice."

"What if I set her up with someone else?" Like Isaac.

"So? She's only interested in me. I'm not worried."

"Well, she is seeing someone else." I try to burst his cocky bubble. While we shared a uterus, he must have absorbed most of the self confidence.

"Who? When?" He doesn't seem to believe me.

"She went out with someone a few weeks ago."

"When?" he asks.

"I think it was the weekend of the tenth. They went out a couple of times."

"No she didn't. We were in Boston. Scored tickets to a Patriots game."

"Ryan, stop. Stop and think. Are you sure it was the tenth? When you don't have a job or any responsibilities sometimes the weeks run together. You can't tell a Wednesday from a Sunday."

Frustrated, he drops his shoulders. "Hey, Nic," he shouts. "When did we go to Boston? The tenth right?"

"No," she yells back.

For a moment I deflate.

"We were in Atlantic City for the fight on the tenth."

"That's right," Ryan says to me. "Her uncle works for a casino. He really hooked us up. I didn't pay for a thing."

Isaac claimed to be with Nicole…

"It's freezing," Ryan says and we all go inside.

I wait back in the corner of the living room while Ryan goes over to Mom and Dad. They all hug and Mom gushes over Nicole. I don't need to hear the conversation to know Mom is thrilled Ryan is dating someone over twenty-one and without any visible tattoos.

After Ryan and Nicole talk to the parents they move on to other relatives—talking, eating, laughing, drinking. After fifteen minutes of watching them I begin to feel like a stalker.

When Ryan goes for a second helping of Swedish meatballs, I make my move, cozying up to Nicole.

"Having a good time?" I take a seat next to her on the couch.

"Yes. Your parents are great. They're so in love. Mine divorced when I was five. They can't even live in the same town."

"It must be hard." I tilt my head sympathetically. "Can I ask you a question?" There's no time to beat around the bush. "Are you seeing Isaac Barber?"

She looks at me. "Are you one of those overprotective siblings who is going to threaten to kill me if I ever break Ryan's heart?"

"What? God, no. Break away. I'm just doing a follow up. I gave you his voice number three or four weeks ago. I want to know how it went."

"I called him twice. He never called back. Then I started dating Ryan."

"So you didn't go to dinner?"

"Never met the guy."

Sometimes I wish I hadn't either.

"Excuse me." Promise to Trisha or not. It's time for me to go.

Only carry what can fit in a purse.
Worries and fears are far too large.

Chapter 38

I kiss my parents goodbye and wish them a Happy New Year. They try to cajole me into staying two more hours until midnight. But I have business that needs to be finished this year, not next.

Twenty minutes later, I'm knocking on the door of Isaac Barber's ranch-style home. You can smell the adrenaline pumping through my pores. Maybe he's not home. It is a popular date night. Then I have a worse thought. What if he is home and has a date?

The door opens and he appears to be alone. Isaac doesn't say a thing. Dressed only in flannel pajama pants—no shirt—he stares me down. I'll admit, it's hard to maintain eye contact.

"Hi," I say, trying to sound cute and sweet.

Without responding, he walks back into his house and lies down on the couch. He grabs a small ball and throws it, then catches it, then throws it again. Since he didn't close the door in my face, I assume I've been invited in.

I step over the threshold onto the wood floor of the foyer and see the gray mass of a dog sacked out on the easy chair.

Isaac notices my stare. "He won't hurt you."

I take another step. The dog doesn't really seem to care.

Isaac's living room is simple, but stylish. He has a leather coach and chairs. An oversized ottoman that doubles as a coffee table. Of course, a flat screen television. And an entire wall of bookshelves, all filled with books—not a vase or picture frame mixed in.

"I just came from a party. Guess who I just saw?"

He doesn't take a guess.

"Nicole. She said she never went on a date with you. In fact, she said she's never even met you. What's going on, Isaac?"

Ball up. Ball down. Ball up. Ball down.

Dammit! I wonder if the dog would move if I attacked its owner.

"Tell me what's going on," I demand.

"Nothing." He sits up.

"Why did you tell me you were going out with someone else? Why did you say you went out with Nicole? I don't understand."

"I thought it was a good way to end it. If you thought I was in a relationship, maybe you'd leave me alone." He stretches his back like he's about to get up.

"Me leave *you* alone? You were the one calling me in the middle of the night, showing up at the mall, coming by my office. Even after I told you about the surrogate pregnancy."

"Sorry to hear that didn't work out."

"Thanks." I say, relieved he's finally being civil. "So what now?"

"I think my gift certificate has expired. I won't be bothering you anymore."

"That's it?"

He nods.

"Fine." My face is burning with rage. I show myself out, slamming doors and stomping the whole way.

I'm half way up the driveway when his door opens. I pause.

"Paige," Isaac shouts and jogs out to my car in the freezing weather. "Okay. Here it is. I lied about Nicole for your own good."

"Really?"

"I realized something during Erika's Barbie report. You've never been independent."

"Excuse me?"

"This project is the closest you've ever come to being independent and I think it's working for you. Look at your past; you went from living with your parents to living with your husband to living with your parents, again. It's time to fly solo."

"I wasn't dependent on Max."

"Call it codependent."

"Listen Isaac," It takes everything I have to keep from yelling. "I don't need you to save me from myself." I get into the car and start the engine.

Isaac knocks on the window. Instead of unrolling it, I back out of the driveway. I should run over his foot. *I'm independent. Always have been.*

When I get to the end of the street I look in my purse for Barb. She's not there.

"Help," I call out quietly.

It's after midnight when I get back to Mom and Dad's. The party is winding down. Father Nolan and Erika have already left. Mom is collecting empty glasses.

"I didn't think you were coming back," she says.

"I forgot something." I go right for the plant. Barb isn't there.

"She's in your old room. Uncle Pat found her when he was about to use my peace lily as a urinal."

"Thanks." I pause. "Mom, do you think I'm independent?"

"Enough so."

"What does that mean?" I follow her into the kitchen.

"You're independent *enough* that I don't have to worry about you constantly. I know you can read a map and balance a checkbook."

"Yes, I *did* graduate high school."

"But," she looks at me as she seems to search for the right words. "You prefer that others make decisions for you."

"That's not true."

"It was until recently. No one would have suggested you buy that house." She shudders.

Having enough of the pep talk, I run upstairs to reunite with Barb. In the car, I fill her in on everything that's happened with Max, Nicole and Isaac. She only smiles.

The next few nights I sleep on the couch. I fear if I get back into my bed I may be tempted to take another extended stay. I'm folding my sheets and blankets when Erika comes bounding down the steps. I double check the clock. It's only eight-thirty on a Sunday. Weekends usually mean bed at two a.m. and up sometime after noon.

"Erika." I startle her. "Where are you going?"

"Nowhere."

She's dressed in khakis, a navy and cream sweater from Lands End and brown boots. It may not be formal attire, but it's a little preppy for my daughter.

"What's going on?"

"Mom, don't freak out. I invited someone over. I thought, maybe, you didn't need to be here."

Oh God, she's sneaking boys in the house. "Erika, we have rules. No boys in the house when I'm not home."

"Since when did that become a rule?"

"It's an assumed rule like don't throw spaghetti on the ceiling and no raising a family of penguins in the refrigerator."

She sighs.

"It basically falls under the general ask-before-you-breathe rule."

"Calm down. I know enough not to invite a guy over when you aren't home. It's not worth the trouble, especially when we can make out in his car. College guys have the best rides."

"Stop it." Now I know she's kidding. "Is someone coming over or not?"

My question is answered by the ringing of the door bell. I rush toward the front door.

"Mom, wait."

I open the door without hesitation.

"Hello, Paige."

"Mr. Swanson?" I step aside. "Erika, it's Mr. Swanson. It's Mr. Swanson at my doorstep. Your grandfather. And I don't know what to say. Not that it keeps me from talking." I laugh. "Do you want to come in?"

"Yes, and please call me Ron." He steps inside and Erika immediately gives him a hug.

"Sorry if I'm being rude…What are you doing here?"

"Erika wrote me a letter and asked me to come."

"Don't you live in Virginia?"

"Yep. I was in town for the holidays. My sister still lives in Troy."

"Let's go into the kitchen." I feel the need to put on a pot of tea, which I guess means boil water. I don't have a kettle so I fill a small saucepan and put it on the stove. I also don't have tea cups, just jumbo-sized coffee mugs. I do have a few tea bags. Do these things go bad?

We take seats around my kitchen table. Erika sits between us. She looks happy and fidgety. She doesn't seem to know where to put her hands.

"I'm very glad you wrote me, Erika. I've thought about you every day. I still think about Michael every day."

"I never meant for you not to be part of our lives," I say. The guilt weighs down on me like the lead blankets they use during dental x-rays.

"Paige, don't you go takin' all the blame. I…well, Helen and I… pulled away from you." Ron turns to Erika. "When your father died, our world ended. I couldn't continue…"

"You were like my parents for seven weeks. How could you just go away? Unless you were forced to."

Is that what she thinks?

"I was never your father," Ron says. "I loved you and we would have loved raising you. Paige was always your mother. She needed a little time to grow up. Nine months and an additional forty-five days."

The pot of water boils and I pour the three cups of tea. I set them on the table with fat-free half and half, a plastic lemon of juice, and plastic bear of honey.

I sip my English breakfast tea—I'm definitely a coffee person—feeling like the third wheel. Erika asks Ron endless questions about Michael. Most I've already answered over the years. What sports did he play? What was his best subject? Was he allergic to anything? Hearing the answer from his father must give Erika comfort. Ron looks so happy talking about his son.

"Why don't you two go get some breakfast? All I have in the house is Pop-Tarts." I say.

"I could go for some breakfast. You should join us." Ron says.

"No. I have things I need to do."

"I'll be right back," Erika says. "Gotta get my phone."

"Paige," Ron says, after Erika is out of the room. "She's a wonderful girl. You've done a great job."

"Thanks. I'm still sorry about what I put you and Helen through."

"Honestly, Helen hated you for years. But it was the right thing for you and it was the right thing for Erika. Let the guilt go."

"Ready?" Erika reappears in the kitchen with her

handbag.

"Let's go get some eggs. How do you like yours?" Ron asks.

"Scrambled and covered with ketchup."

"That's how Michael ate them as a kid. When he was a teen he switched to Tabasco sauce. Thought it would put hair on his chest."

Erika walks over and gives me a kiss on the cheek. "Bye, Mom. Love you." That's the first time she's kissed me in weeks.

You can tar your own roof. You can play in the WNBA.
You can travel to space. But don't ever cut your own bangs.

Chapter 39

Today's parents don't want their kids to lose. They don't keep score at soccer games. Everyone gets a trophy at the end of the season. No one is MVP, and no one is the loser.

Not so for my childhood. Mrs. MacDoodle, my eighth grade physical education teacher, made sure I knew what it was like to strike out, miss the game-winning shot, and be a total loser. Sometimes I half feel like writing Mrs. MacDoodle a thank you letter. All that embarrassment and shame gave me a baseline to measure my future failures against.

I'm thirty-four, divorced, unemployed, broke, without my own transportation, maybe infertile, and only a month away from being homeless. Unlike eighth grade gym class, this one won't be over in forty minutes. God only knows if it'll ever be over.

While eating cereal for lunch—it's all I can afford—I circle job ads in the paper. The prospects aren't any better than they were four months ago, but somehow, my situation is even more desperate.

"All right, Mrs. O'Neal," the plumber says as he ascends the basement steps. "The problem is solved. "You should have hot water and good water pressure in all of your faucets."

"Thanks." The job my uncle did fixing my pipes turned out to be temporary—as most things fixed with duct tape are. In the end, I was forced to hire a professional from the yellow pages.

"Here." Wheezing, he hands me the bill.

I look at the wrinkled, damp sheet. "This is twice the quote."

"It was twice the work."

I write him a check post-dated for two weeks from today. Luckily, he doesn't inspect the check when I hand it over. He accepts it and leaves.

My next move is a desperate one. I grab my cordless phone and call Dad.

"Hey, Honey," he says.

"Hi, Daddy. I need a favor."

"Anything." I half expect him to call me *Princess* like he used to. My father would have given me a pony when I was five (maybe then I wouldn't have been deathly afraid of animals), let me get my ears pierced when I was ten, and bought me a Corvette at sixteen if Mom hadn't always been there saying, "You're spoiling her."

"Does your department still have an opening for a data clerk?"

"Yes."

"Can I apply for one of the positions?"

"I think you could find something better," he says.

It takes me twenty minutes to get Dad to agree to the deal. He'd rather have just given me money than have his daughter working as a lowly clerk. He thinks I'm above the position. I had to remind him that in the past nine years I've only had one job and that ended with my forceful termination. It's either the clerk job or something in the fast-food industry. I could try McDonald's. Barbie has always had a connection with them.

I look over at my little friend who's lying on the table smiling brightly as always. I pick her up. We both know...this isn't working out as I planned.

"Maybe it's time."

An hour later, I'm wandering around the pink, Barbie section of my local toy store. If possible, she has even more accessories and merchandise than she did when I was here a few months ago. I pat Barb, hidden now in my purse, trying to comfort her.

As I peruse a collection of tiny shoes that would make any woman jealous, two girls rush into the aisle. They're probably six years old. Young enough to see Barbie as the ultimate, cool, beautiful woman.

"Madison, look. Look!" The blonde shouts. "This is the house I want." They gather around a dream house.

"My mom said I could get it for my birthday. And I'm getting this," Madison points to a Princess Barbie. "And this." She chooses a car. "And all these." She motions to the entire wardrobe section.

"Me, too," says the blonde.

"Girls," a woman pushing a cart snaps. "Don't wander off. We're here to get Jake a birthday present." The Barbie fans, looking disappointed, follow the woman toward the less glamorous toys.

Alone again, I pull Barbie from my purse. She has a weathered look, compared to her clones still in boxes. I try to clean her up—smoothing her short hair with my fingers, wiping her face with a tissue and some Purell.

"Beautiful," I tell her in a whisper. I set her down alongside the dream house. "This is where you belong."

Her smile fades a degree.

"I tried," I say. "You know I really tried to be like you. I was optimistic and nice, yet assertive. My clothes were always ironed, my purse matched my shoes. I even bought a house on my own. And no man was involved. Then I found a job I loved. That didn't work out. Let's just say it was good while it lasted."

I stand back up. "So, this is goodbye." I wait a second. More needs to be said. She knows it. I know it. "Okay. I know where it all went wrong. I wasn't honest. I lied. And I lost Isaac. I tried to come clean. And look where it got me. No job. No Isaac, not even as a friend. I'd love to have Isaac even as a friend."

It's your bed, Sister. Barb says to me in a new tone that I don't like. Reminds me of when Erika turned twelve and started saying *whatever* as an answer to everything.

"This isn't fair. It's not. I followed most of your rules. No one's perfect. Not even you. A lot of people think you're too skinny."

Insults don't make me feel any better. "I'm sorry. Who cares what others think. You're still a great role model. Why couldn't you be great for me?" Tears begin to well. When I grab another tissue from my purse, I see the list from Erika's experiment.

"Look at this." I show it to Barbie. "I was a good follower. I exercised. I used good manners. I cut back on the alcohol. I even got a dog. So, tell me why can't I be like you? It has to be something more than a few white lies?" I lean my head against a display of ethnic Barbies and close my eyes. Every day seems to bring me a new low. When will I hit bottom? What will tomorrow bring? Petty larceny and preaching on street corners?

"Excuse me, ma'am." The sweet voice brings me back. It's the blonde shopper.

"Yes, sweetie?"

"Why are you yelling at Barbie?"

"It's nothing." I can't explain the situation to a child. Hell—I can't explain it to myself.

"Don't you know the difference between real and make believe? She's just a doll. She'll be whatever you want." She raises her nose, apparently pleased that she's smarter than this confused adult, and swaggers off.

She'll be whatever you want? These words repeat over and over in my head.

Having still not learned my lesson, I say one last thing to Barbie. "Goodbye. It's time we went our separate ways."

I leave the toy store without my friend. I feel both unsteady on my feet and free—all at the same time. As I walk to my car, resisting the urge to go back for her – who knew Barbie could be addictive—a pigeon waddles out in front of me. I jump back and dump my still-open purse all over the frozen parking lot. I bend down and start cramming stuff back in before the pigeon can come back with his friends. After I throw in my wallet, checkbook and phone, I gather up the less important stuff like receipts and papers. The last piece I pick up is a napkin that appears dirty. Instead of putting it back in, I walk over to the trashcan. Before I throw it in, I take a closer look. On the folded side of the napkin is my original doodle of *Over Coffee*. My dating-service-slash-coffee shop.

"Useless," I mumble as I recall the idea that Lisa dismissed so quickly. Then I notice it. A small, empty store in the mini-mall across the parking lot. That's it!

I run across the asphalt, scaring a group of birds that were in my way. "Sorry!" I shout as they scatter and fly away.

The store is for lease. I press my face to the glass. It's perfect. It used to be a juice bar, so the set up is ideal— counter space, sinks, refrigeration equipment. Not that it doesn't need work. The place isn't exactly what I originally envisioned Over Coffee to be, but it has potential.

I call the real estate agent on my cell phone. We make an appointment for that evening. Next I call Trisha.

"Trisha," I say when she answers. "I have a great idea, and I'm looking for investors." I leave the site twenty minutes later, my hands numb from the cold, thrilled at the prospect of finally taking control of my own life.

When I reach the car, I instinctively open my purse looking for you-know-who. She'd be so proud of my initiative and drive. I'd forgotten I'd returned her to her natural habitat. This must be what those environmentalists who raise bear cubs as their own must feel.

I could always run back to the store to get her. What if she's gone? I guess I could buy another.

Paige, stop it! You're just going through Barbie

withdrawal. For a moment, I wonder whether opening a coffee shop near her is going to be a problem. It's like a recovered drug addict moving into an apartment on the corner where her dealer does business.

Maybe I can find a support group.

*Live life so when others think of intelligence,
beauty, and honesty, they think of you.*

Chapter 40

My mom has told me that it took me thirty-seven weeks and two days to enter this world—conception to birth. Thanks for that tidbit, Mom. She keeps a very detailed journal. It took me *thirteen* months to plan my wedding. Should I have noticed that omen? And it's taken me five months and two weeks to open my coffee shop. Assuming all goes well, I'm supposed to have my grand opening next Friday night.

So far, everything seems to be on schedule. My 1400-sq-ft store is painted, decorated, and set up—with everything but the tables. There's been a snafu with my two-person, bar-high tables. They're lost. The supplier shipped them. The trucking company says it delivered them, just not to me. I've been told not to worry. They have ten days to figure it all out.

In the meantime, the electrician is almost finished. He's hanging a large *Over Coffee* sign in the front window.

The neon sign cost more than my first two month's rent, but it's worth it. It tells the world, "Here we are."

It's been an obstacle course getting to this point. The first month I spent planning, doing paperwork, and securing money. In the end, Mom and Dad lent me more money. It was enough to incorporate and obtain a small business loan.

In the second month, I lost eight pounds because I was working around the clock and I forgot to eat. To save on cash, I didn't want to start the lease until April, so I worked from home, doing research on restaurants, business practices, and reading the latest relationship books to make me a better consultant.

In April, I moved the business into the store and all monies started moving out—fast! I spent so much more time at the store than at my house, I could have rented it out. Erika came by after basketball practice to pitch in. I did as much of the remodeling as I could myself—mostly cleaning and painting. Ryan helped a lot, which worked out great because we agreed I didn't have to pay him until I opened.

At first, between my investors and my loan, I figured I had plenty of dough. Not the case. I ended up applying for a business credit card, too. That gave me an extra thirty days to pay off new purchases.

The final few months have been a roller coaster of emotions. One minute, I think this is the best idea I've ever had. The next, I'm ready to quit or sell the place. I probably would have, too, if I had any other options. I have no husband to take care of me and no fall-back job—Dad gave the clerk position to some nineteen-year old who was eager to please.

The number of decisions I had to make was also daunting. Technically, Mom, Dad, Trisha, and Manny were investors, though they didn't want to make any decisions. If I was going to succeed, I had to do it on my own. And likewise, if I was going to fail, I would have to do that on my own. Every day brought a new bunch of decisions—What color coffee mugs? What size? Ceramic or all paper cups? What about food? Décor colors? Operating hours? Number of employees? Fees, rates, prices? Advertising? Amount of insurance? How much do I pay employees, including myself? It was fun picking the napkin colors. That seemed trivial compared to setting up health care benefits. Then I read that painting the walls the wrong color in a restaurant could lower the number of clients and profits by twenty-five percent. Suddenly, every question seemed important and required research. I was happier mopping the floor than I was selecting the tile color for that same floor.

During this latter part of my business initiation, I lost another five pounds—down a total of thirteen. I've been eating muffins from my supplier—a small mom-and-pop bakery—trying to gain back a pound. Call me superstitious. I've also sworn off dating. I have no time and I certainly have no energy. I almost ran off to the bowling alley, looking for a fling when I heard Max had eloped in March. His marriage didn't last much longer than my fling would have.

I don't think I could find a date now if I wore a *free milk* sign around my neck. I haven't even been able to find time to get my hair done. It now covers my ears again. I've worn the same three pairs of jeans week in and week out.

And I have this rash on my arms that is related to either stress or scraping paint.

It's all been worth it.

"Thank you," I say to the electrician as he hands me his bill. I don't bother to look. I know it'll be more than his quote. Why should he be any different? The plumber was more, the general contractor was more. Everything is more than initially quoted.

The place is empty of people (and tables), but it's almost ready. The walls, now a golden color that creates both warmth and a sense of belonging, are decorated with charcoal sketches of historical and literary couples—Romeo and Juliet, Napoleon and Josephine, Archie and Betty. There aren't any of Barbie and Ken. I'm not sure their relationship fits here. While the tables are AWOL, I do have several two-seater couches placed around the edges—a space for cuddling and intimate conversation. The granite bar extends the length of the room. Behind it are thousands of dollars in espresso machines. My place isn't huge. The Fire Marshal says our maximum capacity is sixty. That's enough. In the back of the café are restrooms, a supply closet, and my office where I will hold private interviews. While I don't have a window overlooking a park, it is my own office and I do have a two-way mirror so I can keep an eye on the shop.

Everything has been purchased on credit. The mini egg roll appetizers I've ordered won't be paid for for months. The DJ agreed to a swap—he'll turn tunes for free, and I'll set him up for free.

In my best handwriting, I address envelopes at the bar. They're invitations to my opening night celebration. I invite almost everyone I know. Word of mouth is the best advertising. It doesn't matter if they're single, married, young, old, gay, straight, or a priest—I'm determined to drum up business right from the start. The guest list is nearing one-fifty. The Fire Marshal would have a fit if he knew. But not everyone will show up, and not everyone will be here at the same time.

My hand amazingly hasn't cramped yet, but I'm still unable to write out the last invitation. It's to a Mr. Isaac Barber. Do I invite him? Do I want him to come? Then what if he does? What do I do? What if he doesn't?

Screw it!

I write out his name and address. It's only an invitation. Easy enough.

Then I go back through the pile, sealing and stamping all the envelopes. Again, I come to the last invitation. I put a postage stamp in the corner. Do I really want to send this? He was so rude last time I saw him.

I pick up the invitation and tap it in my hand. I need a sign. I could flip a coin. Or better yet, I could flip the invitation. If it lands address up, I'll send it. I throw it into the air. It spirals quickly to the ground and lands address down.

Fine. I put Isaac's invitation to the side and put the rest in a box, ready for a trip to the post office. I can't leave it. It's silly to waste a stamp.

I pick up the damn thing, again. It's still not sealed. Maybe I should put a little note in it. After all, we haven't spoken in months. What would I say? Isn't sending the invitation gesture enough?

Just a quick note. Using my calligraphy pen and a

scrap of paper I jot something down, trying not to give it too much thought.

>Isaac,
>I know you like coffee.
>Paige.

Well, that's stupid. The note gets crumpled. Maybe I shouldn't write anything. What can it hurt? This time, instead of using a second sheet of paper, I scribble on the invitation itself.

>Isaac,
>Hope you can come. I miss you.
>Paige

No, no. I sound pathetic. What's wrong with me? I sound needy and lonely. Sad and unworthy, and I also sound—

Honest.

I decide to send *all* the invitations.

A little lipstick can only make your smile brighter.

Chapter 41

The biggest parties of my life: my first sleepover when I was ten; my sixteenth birthday party where all my friends—six of us—shared two beers; Erika's first birthday; my wedding reception; and tonight—the grand opening of Over Coffee.

Sixty minutes into the three-hour shindig, I dare to say it—everything is perfect. The tables arrived yesterday, so the place is exactly as I envisioned. The caterer came through. Everyone is raving about the food. The DJ, while maybe high, is playing a nice selection at a comfortable volume. The crowd has hovered around fifty, and I know of at least a dozen people who want to become clients.

I take a moment and study the crowd and my place. I've really accomplished something here. Even if I'm forced to close the doors in a few weeks, tonight I'm a success.

Trisha squeezes through the crowd and walks over to

me.

"Congratulations," she says.

"Thanks."

"I'm sorry he's not here." She rests her hand on my shoulder.

"What? Who?"

"You're straining your neck, checking the crowd for one particular single man." She does her best giraffe imitation.

"I'm not. And he's not coming." I pull my neck back in. "He never responded to my invitation."

"I'm sorry."

"That's okay. It's no big deal."

"Of course, it's not a big deal. You're a beautiful, intelligent businesswoman, who will soon have the biggest database of eligible people in the capital district." She raises her cup of coffee to me.

"I can't date a client. That's unethical. We have rules here at Over Coffee."

Trisha laughs. "For now."

"And I want you to know, I still have a womb for rent if you're interested." I say. Trisha and Manny have begun the adoption process. They've been approved, now they're waiting for a birth mother to select them as parents.

"I know. If we ever need a home for our unborn children, we know who to call." She pushes me away from the wall. "Now go mingle and enjoy all the compliments. This is your moment."

With that, I'm forced back into the mix of friends and relatives who are here to show their support and drink free cappuccinos. Each "congratulations" and pat on the back hits me like a shot of vodka. I feel warm and fuzzy and a little like I can fly. I know, later on, a crash of reality will settle back in. I try not to think about that tonight.

I'm talking with the daughter of my mother's friend from the library committee when Ryan shouts my name.

"Paige, over here." He waves a hand above my guests. The crowd has swelled to over seventy—a little too crowded.

"Excuse me," I say. We agree to continue the conversation next week. She's eager to be a client and even more eager to have a baby and get married. The order of events doesn't seem to concern her.

Ryan gives me a bear hug. "Congratulations, sis."

"Thanks. Hi, Nicole." She's standing next to him smiling.

"The place looks great. But I won't be coming here." Ryan finally releases me and I can breathe again.

"Why? Because I won't let you run a tab?"

"No, because I'm now a kept man." He holds up Nicole's left hand, and I see the diamond ring before he can say, "We're getting married."

"Ohmigod," I scream, like I'm thirteen. "I'm finally getting a sister!" I give Nicole a hug. "This is great. When's the wedding? Who have you told? Are you pregnant?"

"No, we're not pregnant." Ryan says, then looks at Nicole. "Are we?"

"No. And we don't have a date yet. You're only the third person we've told. Don't worry about that. Tonight's your night. We'll talk about all this—"

Blaring sirens cut off Nicole's words. I look around wildly. Is there a fire?

Everyone grabs their ears.

It takes me a second to realize it's the security alarm. I push through the crowd to the touch panel and turn off the noise. The now-quiet crowd looks to me for an answer.

"False alarm," I assure them breezily, having no idea what happened. It can't be a robbery. I don't have any money.

Murmurs run through the crowd as my guests turn their attention back to each other. They seem satisfied.

I let out a relieved breath as the phone rings. It's on its fifth ring before I locate it behind the counter.

"Hello, Over Coffee."

"This is Reliance Security," a woman says. "Your security alarm has been activated."

"Yes. Sorry. Just a false alarm."

"Please verify the pass code."

I look to see if anyone is listening and then whisper into the receiver. "Bye-bye, Barbie."

"Thank you." The woman disconnects.

But before I can put the phone back in its cradle the alarm sounds again. Pushing through the crowd. Back to the key pad. Try to punch in the code. Nothing. Try again. It's off—finally.

The phone—still in my hand—rings.

"This is Reliance Security. Your security alarm has been activated. Again. Would you like me to call the police?"

"God, no." I could imagine the parking lot filled with police cars, fire trucks, and SWAT vans. There really is such a thing as bad publicity.

"Pass code." The woman didn't try to hide her impatience.

"Wait. Can you tell me what's setting off the alarm?" If it's poor instillation I'm going to demand a refund.

"One moment." She sighs into the phone. "It's zone three."

"Zone three?"

"Probably a back door or secondary entrance. Pass code."

"Bye-bye, Barbie." I make sure to hang up first this time.

Mom taps me on the shoulder. Her head is still shaking, probably from hearing the name Barbie. "Is everything alright?"

"Watch the store for me. I need to check something out." I put the phone down on the counter, grab a plastic knife, and head to the back door.

"What's with the knife?" Erika asks as I walk by.

"Stay here. Stay with Uncle Ryan. Don't worry." I smile. "Everything's fine."

There's nothing to be afraid of. Just a windowless door marked *Emergency Exit Only* that might have a killer or monster or a kitten hiding on the other side. Please don't let it be a kitten.

I walk down the hall, past my office, a supply closet, and the restrooms. If I screamed, my guests might not hear over their jovial conversations. I make a note to scream really loudly, if need be.

I slip the plastic knife in my back pocket. Then, in a quick motion, I put my hands on the push-bar and force the door open. If there was a kitten on the other side, my momentum would have sent it flying across the pavement.

There's no kitten. It's Isaac.

"Hey. Watch it." He's rubbing his shoulder. "You almost knocked me out."

"Isaac, what are you doing here?"

"I was trying to bring you a gift." He motions to the crumbled gift bag I ran over with the back door.

"Why not go through the front?"

"I didn't want to disturb the party."

"Paige," a voice calls behind me. "Why are you hiding?" Father Nolan joins us. "Hello, Isaac. Glad you could make it."

Did Father Nolan just wink at him?

"What's in the package?" I feel like I'm the only one who doesn't know.

"Here." Isaac scoops it up and hands me the small pink bag with matching tissue paper. "It was three dimensional before you charged through the door."

Carefully, I pull the tissue out of the bag without touching the bag itself. I feel like I'm playing the game Operation. Once the tissue paper is gone and nothing has exploded, I peer inside.

It's a Ken doll, still in its box—though it's now a flatter, torn box.

"What's this?" I ask, putting Ken two inches from his face, in case he forgot what he'd put in the bag.

"He's for you." As if it was obvious. "There's something else in the bag."

I look again and find an envelope. It contains a single sheet of paper. Father Nolan bobs over my shoulder trying to read the typed page.

I turn to Father Nolan. "How about I read it out loud?"

Isaac shrugs his agreement.

"W.W.K.D? What would Ken do?" I give Isaac a you're-crazy look. "Number One—Ken would be willing to start over. Two—Ken would stick around when times get tough. Three—Ken would fight for Barbie even if she were dating another guy."

"She's not dating anyone," Father Nolan says.

"Well that makes the fighting easy," Isaac says. "Keep reading."

"Number Four—Ken is always a friend and never more than a phone call away. Five—Ken would follow Barbie to the ends of the earth."

"What do you say?" He winks. "A Barbie without a Ken is like a tree without leaves. A hot dog without a bun."

I raise an eyebrow. I would have thought he'd have come more prepared.

"A reality series without a homosexual."

"They're getting worse," I say.

"A football game without beer."

"Enough."

"So what do you say?" Isaac asks.

"You can keep your doll." I press Ken to his chest. Then I press my lips to his.

That same night at my house, Isaac sits on my couch watching the local eleven o'clock news. I return from the kitchen with two bottles of beer and take a seat next to him.

"To your new business venture," he raises his bottle for a toast.

"To all new ventures." I take a drink.

"I don't think I ever apologized for interrupting your big opening night. I'm sorry."

"You owe me one."

"I have many talents." He moves across the couch and kisses my neck. "I can take out the trash." His lips move to my ear. "I can open jars of pickles."

My eyes close and a sound escapes my lips without permission. The beer in my left hand tilts. The cold liquid hits my skin and wakes me from my dream. It's not a dream. He's still here.

"Here, let me help." Isaac takes the bottle and puts it

on the coffee table. He moves his hands to the first button of my shirt and undoes it. Then the next and the next, all the way down. Somehow, he manages to never touch my skin.

He waits for me to make the next move. I grab his collar and pull him in for a hard kiss. Five seconds or five minutes pass. I don't know.

"Upstairs." I push him back after I collect my thoughts. "Erika could be home any minute."

Ken and Barbie never had it so good!

Ken never would have been without Barbie.
Not vise versa. But she loves him just the same.

Chapter 42

Ruth Handler may have created Barbie in 1959. Mattel may reinvent her every holiday season. Only Barbie's owner can bring her to life. That's the greatest thing about this adult-like doll made for little girls—she comes with free will. Each girl can make Barbie her own. Whether she's an astronaut, a stripper, or a mommy, no one can dictate how each girl perceives and makes believe. And not every girl wants to be Barbie. Barbie can role-play the scary next door neighbor or a friendly teacher or the little girl twenty years in the future. Barbie is free will personified.

From behind the two-way mirror in my office, I watch people drinking coffee in my shop. Half-dozen patrons are here. Only one couple that I set up. I matched them a week ago, and this is the second time I've seen them in here talking. I swell with pride. Two of the other customers—both women—are dating service clients, too.

They're enjoying their beverages alone. By the window, a man reads the paper while sipping a drink. He isn't a client, and I doubt he ever will be. Over Coffee is probably just closer to his home or work than any other coffee bar. While I've only been open six months, I'm happy with the direction of the business. I make money selling coffee, especially during the morning rush, but I love running the dating service.

The sixth person in the place is a good-looking man at the corner table. He's busy drawing in a notebook. He doesn't have a drink. Damn freeloader. This isn't a library. I'm going to have to take care of him.

I leave my office and go behind the bar. I help myself to a cup of coffee before heading over to confront the man. I usually hate being the bad guy, but this will be fun.

"Excuse me, sir," I say with a smile.

He looks up from his notebook and gives me a smile that makes my knees weak. Only for a moment.

"The tables are for customers only," I say. "So here." I put the cup down in front of him. "Here's your poison."

Isaac laughs. "Thanks."

I lean down and give him a kiss that's appropriate for public display. Now, if we were in my office, it'd be different story. Actually, last Friday things got out of hand in my office. The two-way mirror made it strange and exciting. If the dozen people in the coffee shop only knew what was going on behind that mirror!

Maybe I should invite him back to my office. "How's it going?" I ask.

"I'm ready for a break." He takes my hand and leads me back to my office. Maybe he had the same idea I did. Unfortunately I have an appointment with a potential client at ten.

Isaac closes the door. He seems uncharacteristically nervous as he wipes his hands on his jeans.

"What's up?" Now I'm getting nervous.

"I need to ask you something." He motions to the chair. "Maybe you should sit down."

I take a seat on one of the chairs across from my desk. "You better not be proposing Isaac Barber. I'm warning you." We've talked about this before.

"Nice, Paige." Isaac drops to his knee.

I'm going to kill him!

He takes my left hand. "Paige, you drive me nuts. In both a good way and a bang-my-head-against-a-brick-wall way. You know I love you. I love your family. You're beautiful, smart and crazy."

What girl doesn't want to hear the words *crazy* and *you drive me nuts* in a marriage proposal?

"What I'm trying to say is…" He reaches into his pocket. "Will you water my plants because I have to go outta town next—"

"Isaac!" I grab a file off my desk and start beating him over the head with it. "What's wrong with you?"

"Stop. I'm kidding." He shows me the content of his hand. It's a single key. "I just wanted to give you this. Let you know you are welcome into my life anytime."

I take the key. "Thanks."

"Do you think Barbie and Ken would ever consider moving in together?" he asks.

"Probably not." I don't bother explain to Isaac, again, that Ken is only an accessory.

"It would be too hard getting a tiny plastic pink key duplicated. Don't ya think?" He's all smiles. "And his stuff might not coordinate with all her pink."

"I think she's beginning to outgrow pink."

"And is there room in her garage for his—"

"Isaac, enough. Now you're driving me nuts." I give him a kiss that must remind him of what we have. I love him, too, and want him around. For a moment I wonder what Barbie would do. Move in together? Get married? I now know it doesn't matter. My inner Barbie thinks— *knows*—this is right. Paige and Isaac are meant to be together, maybe for eternity, certainly for right now.

And I'm the only one who can make this decision.

ABOUT THE AUTHOR

in no particular order...Stacy is a wife, daughter, mother, sister, owner/mother of a crazy German shepherd, author, mechanical engineer (retired), wine connoisseur, coach, complainer, cook, chauffeur, storyteller, dark chocolate aficionado, avid reader, klutz, disgruntled Walmart shopper, rebound dieter, internet addict, friend, Packers fan, traveler, writer, and concerned citizen